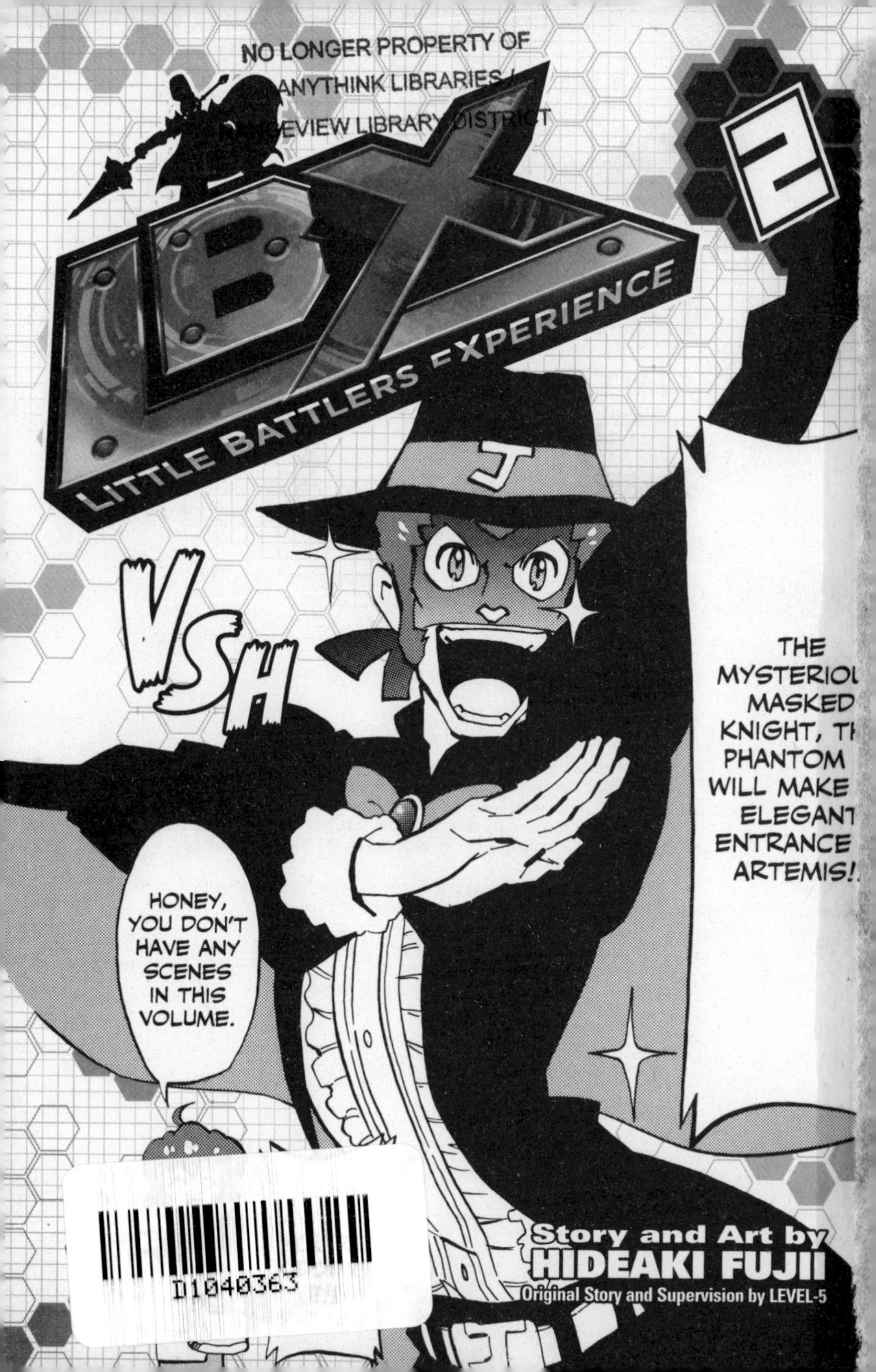
LBX
LITTLE BATTLERS EXPERIENCE
2
THE MYSTERIOU MASKED KNIGHT, T PHANTOM WILL MAKE ELEGANT ENTRANCE ARTEMIS!!
VSH
HONEY, YOU DON'T HAVE ANY SCENES IN THIS VOLUME.
Story and Art by
HIDEAKI FUJII
Original Story and Supervision by LEVEL-5

LBX Volume 2
Artemis Begins
Perfect Square Edition

Story and Art by Hideaki FUJII
Original Story and Supervision by LEVEL-5

Translation/Tetsuichiro Miyaki
English Adaptation/Aubrey Sitterson
Lettering/Annaliese Christman
Design/Izumi Evers
Editor/Joel Enos

DANBALL SENKI Vol.2
by Hideaki FUJII
© 2011 Hideaki FUJII
© LEVEL-5 Inc.
All rights reserved.
Original Japanese edition published by SHOGAKUKAN.
English translation rights in the United States of
America, Canada, the United Kingdom, Ireland, Australia
and New Zealand arranged with SHOGAKUKAN.

Printed in Canada

Published by VIZ Media, LLC
P.O. Box 77010
San Francisco, CA 94107

10 9 8 7 6 5 4 3 2 1
First printing, November 2014

www.perfectsquare.com

www.viz.com

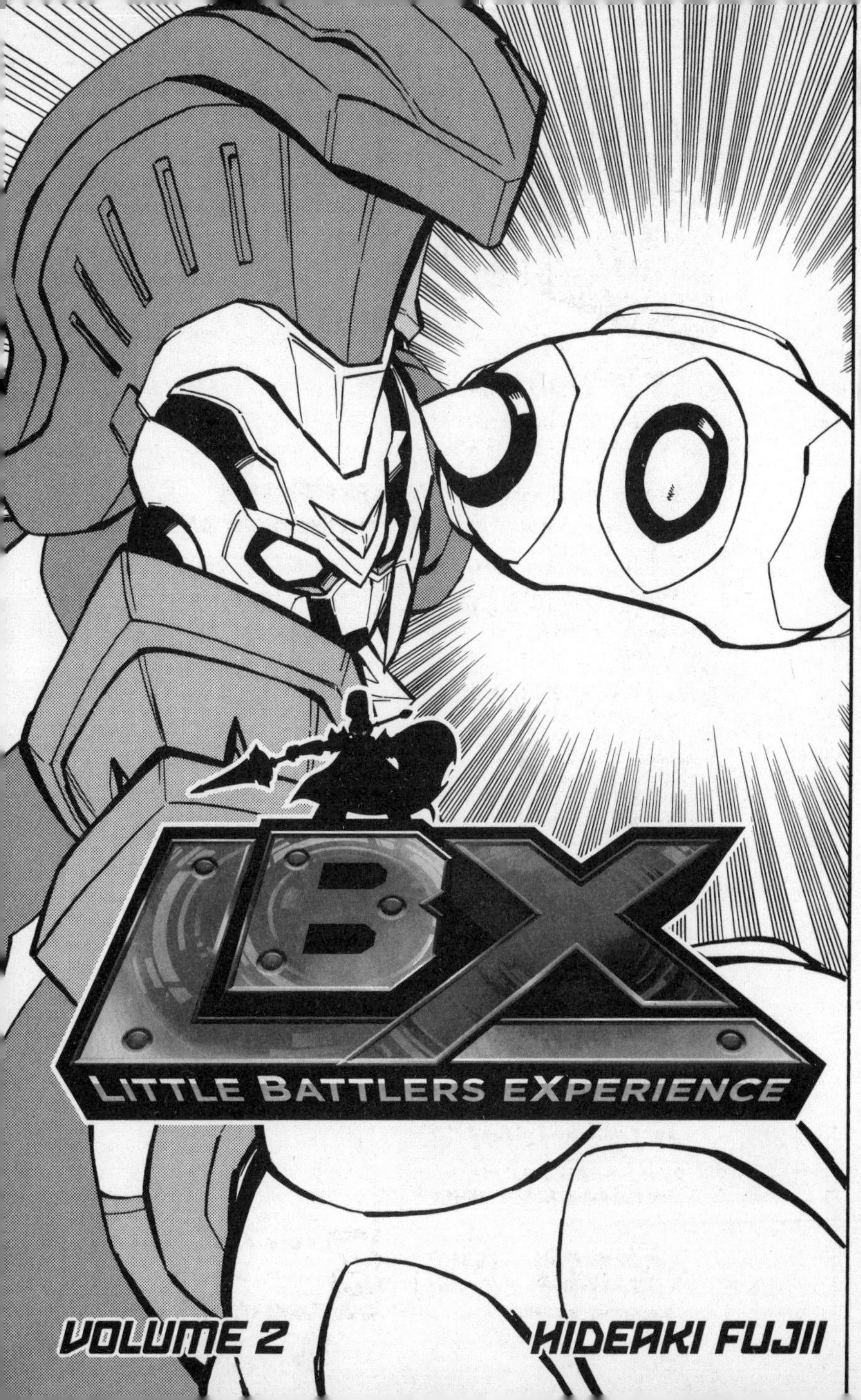
LBX
LITTLE BATTLERS EXPERIENCE
VOLUME 2
HIDEAKI FUJII

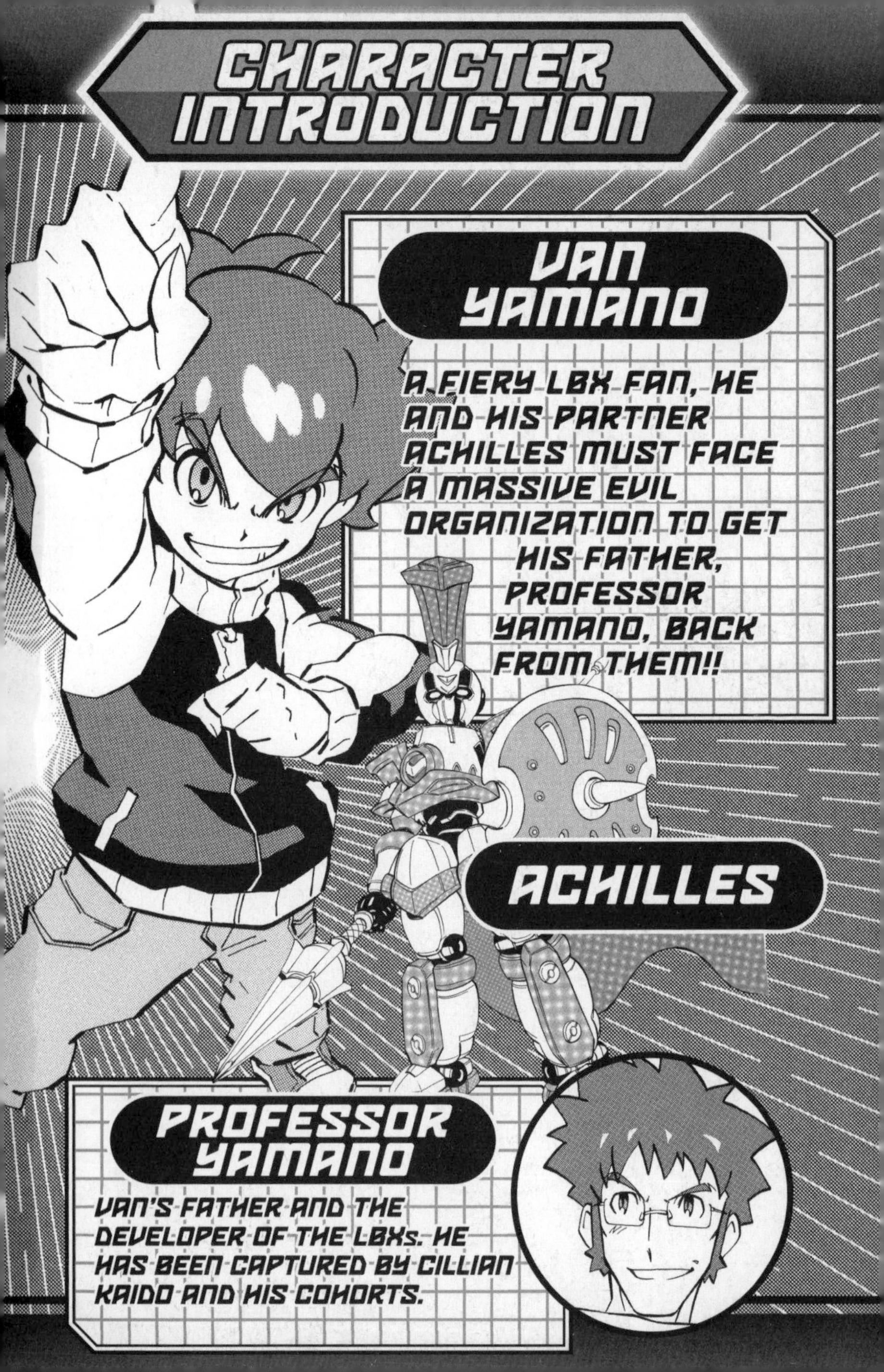
CHARACTER INTRODUCTION
VAN YAMANO
A FIERY LBX FAN, HE AND HIS PARTNER ACHILLES MUST FACE A MASSIVE EVIL ORGANIZATION TO GET HIS FATHER, PROFESSOR YAMANO, BACK FROM THEM!!
ACHILLES
PROFESSOR YAMANO
VAN'S FATHER AND THE DEVELOPER OF THE LBXs. HE HAS BEEN CAPTURED BY CILLIAN KAIDO AND HIS COHORTS.

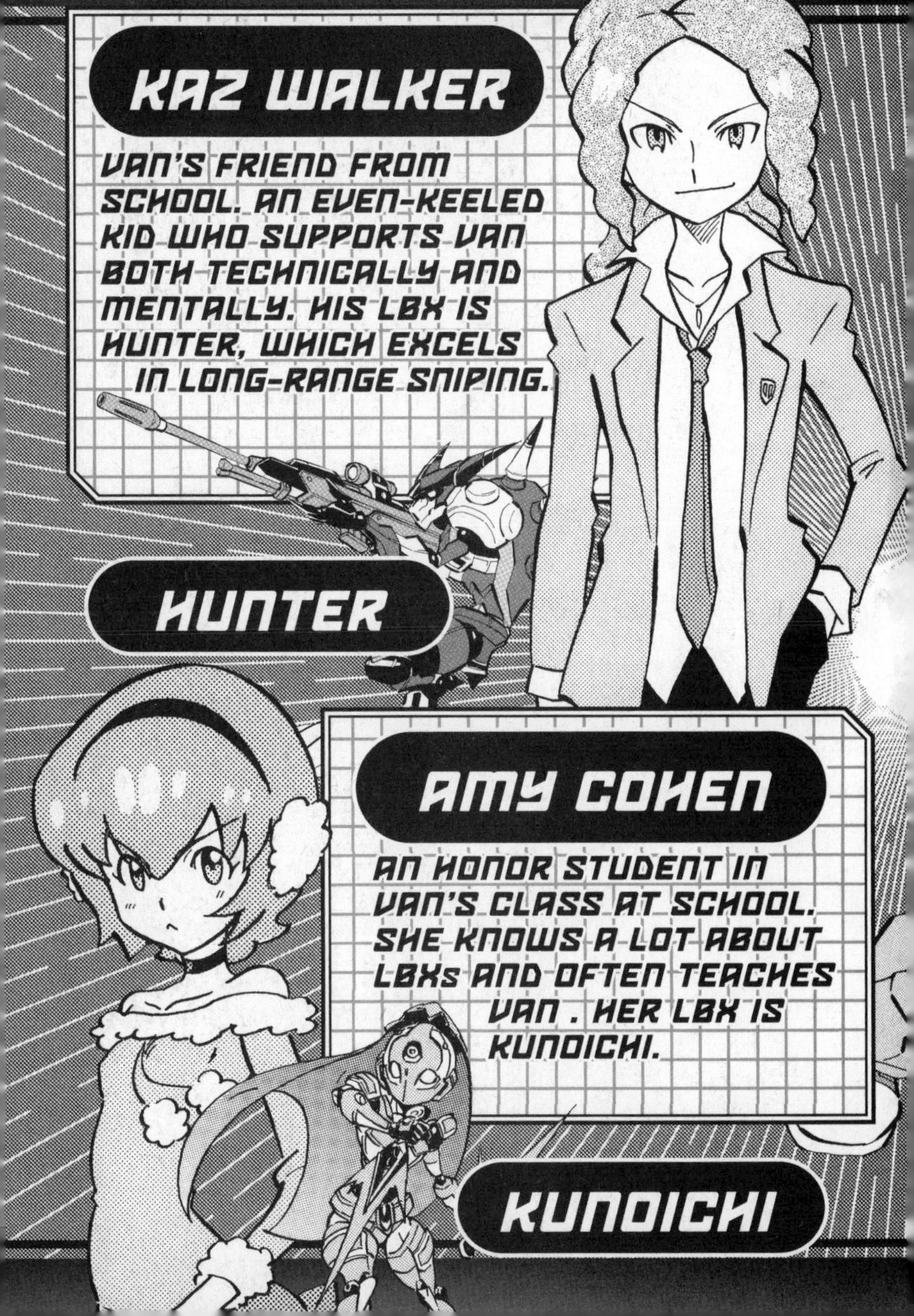
KAZ WALKER
VAN'S FRIEND FROM SCHOOL. AN EVEN-KEELED KID WHO SUPPORTS VAN BOTH TECHNICALLY AND MENTALLY. HIS LBX IS HUNTER, WHICH EXCELS IN LONG-RANGE SNIPING.
HUNTER
AMY COHEN
AN HONOR STUDENT IN VAN'S CLASS AT SCHOOL. SHE KNOWS A LOT ABOUT LBXs AND OFTEN TEACHES VAN . HER LBX IS KUNOICHI.
KUNOICHI

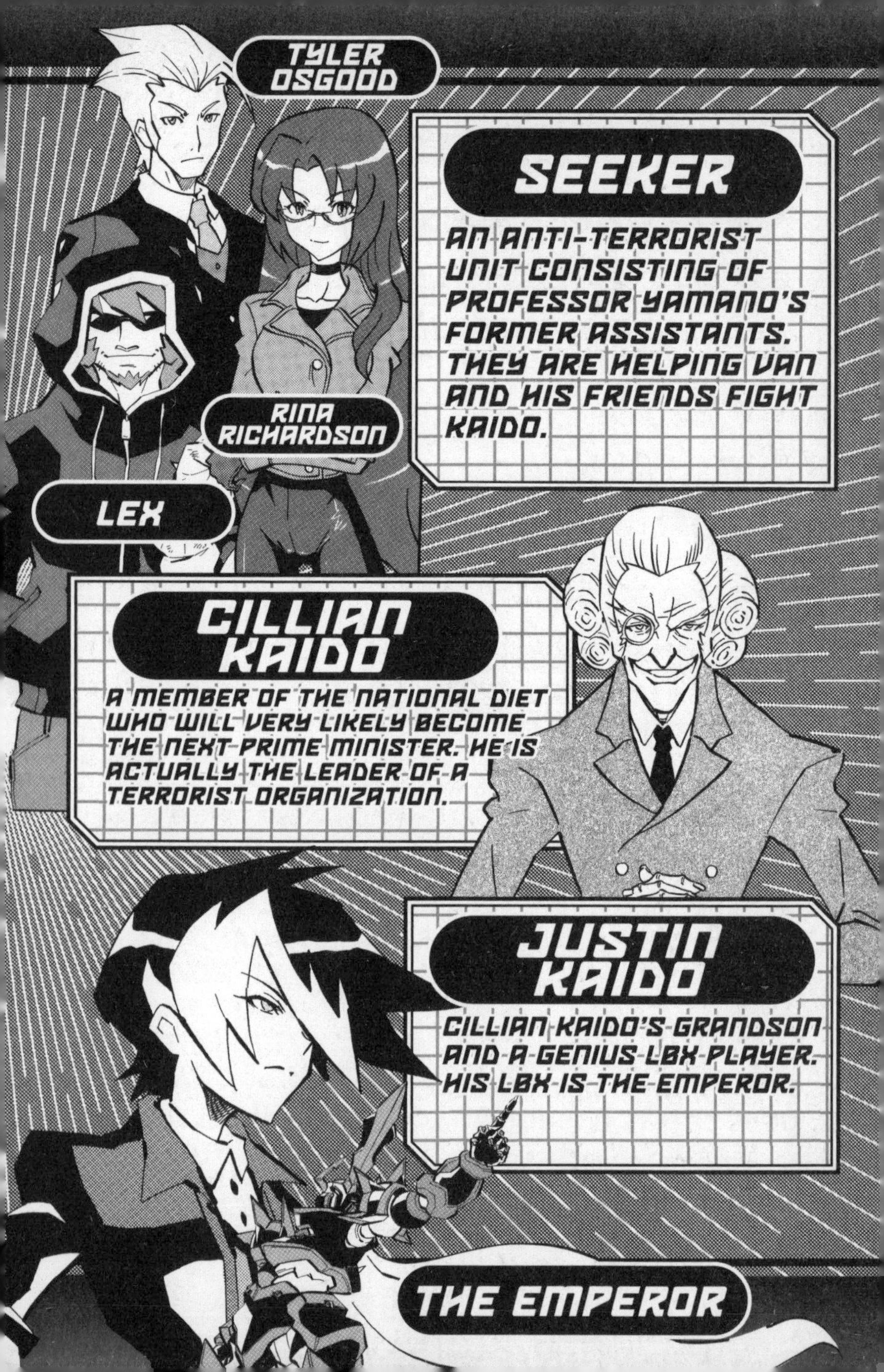
TYLER OSGOOD
SEEKER
AN ANTI-TERRORIST UNIT CONSISTING OF PROFESSOR YAMANO'S FORMER ASSISTANTS. THEY ARE HELPING VAN AND HIS FRIENDS FIGHT KAIDO.
RINA RICHARDSON
LEX
CILLIAN KAIDO
A MEMBER OF THE NATIONAL DIET WHO WILL VERY LIKELY BECOME THE NEXT PRIME MINISTER. HE IS ACTUALLY THE LEADER OF A TERRORIST ORGANIZATION.
JUSTIN KAIDO
CILLIAN KAIDO'S GRANDSON AND A GENIUS LBX PLAYER. HIS LBX IS THE EMPEROR.
THE EMPEROR

TABLE OF CONTENTS

STORY SO FAR

CILLIAN KAIDO TELLS VAN THAT HE WILL RELEASE HIS CAPTIVE FATHER, THE RENOWNED PROFESSOR YAMANO, IN EXCHANGE FOR THE METANOIA GX, THE PRIZE THAT GOES TO THE WINNER OF THE LBX WORLD TOURNAMENT, ARTEMIS. BUT IN THE FIRST BATTLE, VAN SUFFERS A CRUSHING DEFEAT AGAINST POWERFUL LBX PLAYER JUSTIN KAIDO. NOW VAN IS MORE DETERMINED THAN EVER. TO SAVE HIS FATHER, HE MUST WIN THE ARTEMIS TOURNAMENT!

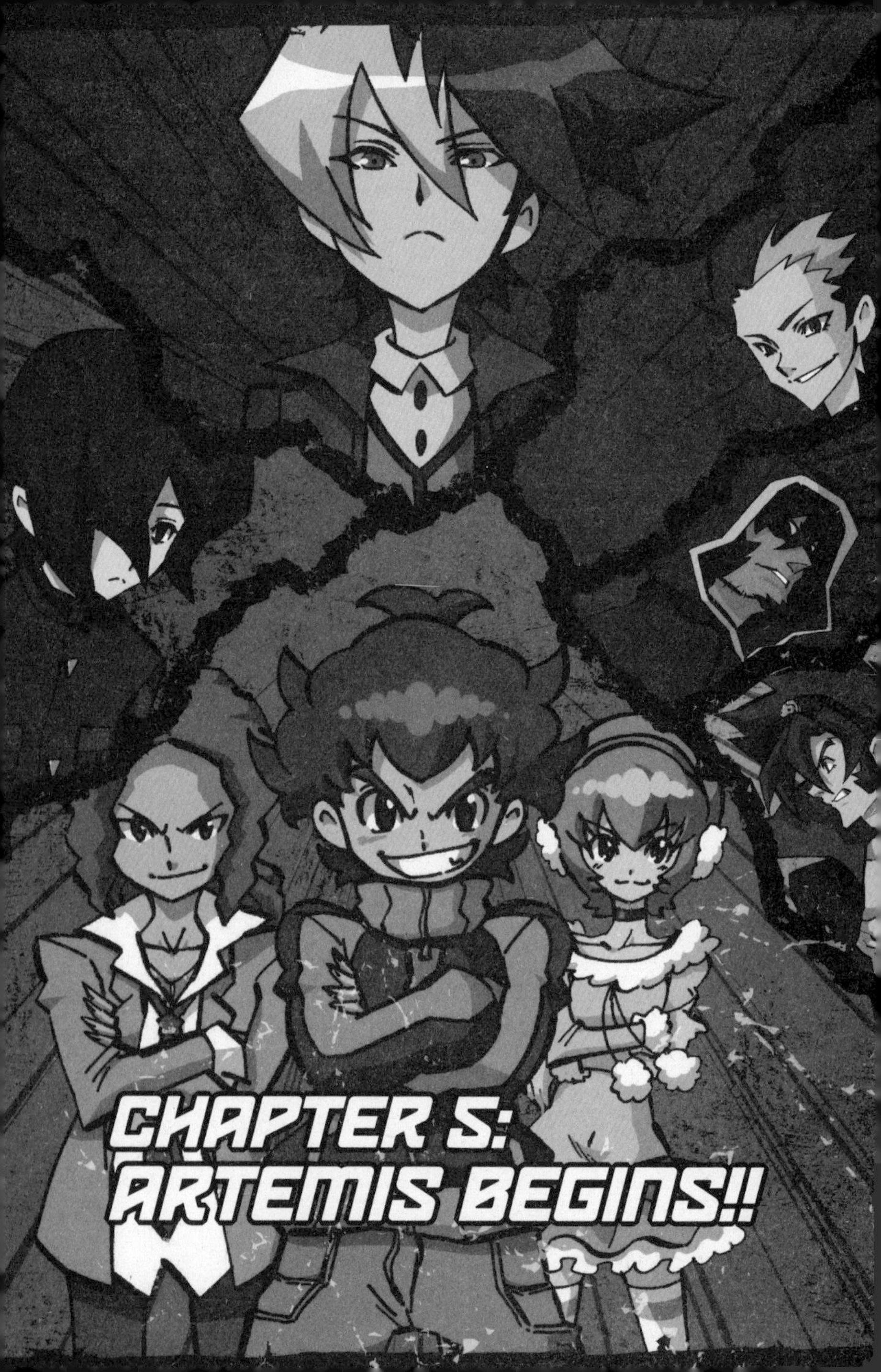
CHAPTER 5:
ARTEMIS BEGINS!!

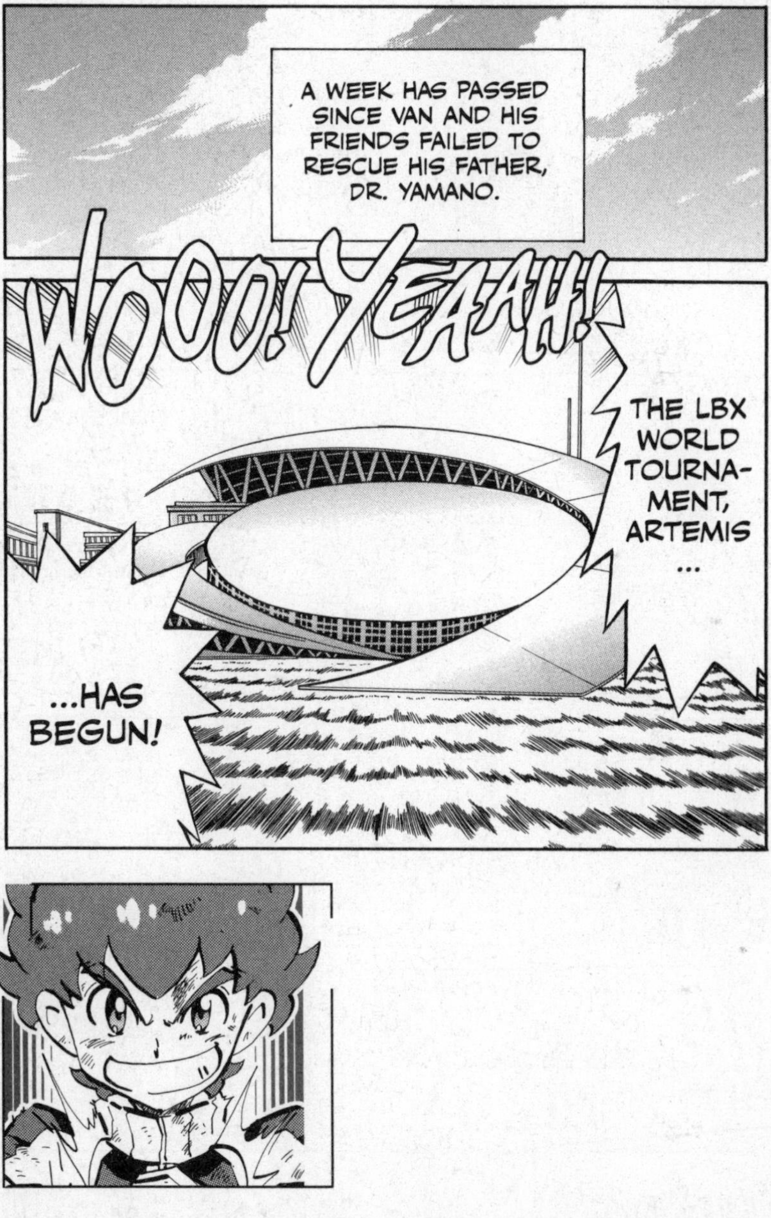
A WEEK HAS PASSED SINCE VAN AND HIS FRIENDS FAILED TO RESCUE HIS FATHER, DR. YAMANO.
WOOO! YEAAH!
THE LBX WORLD TOURNAMENT, ARTEMIS ...
...HAS BEGUN!

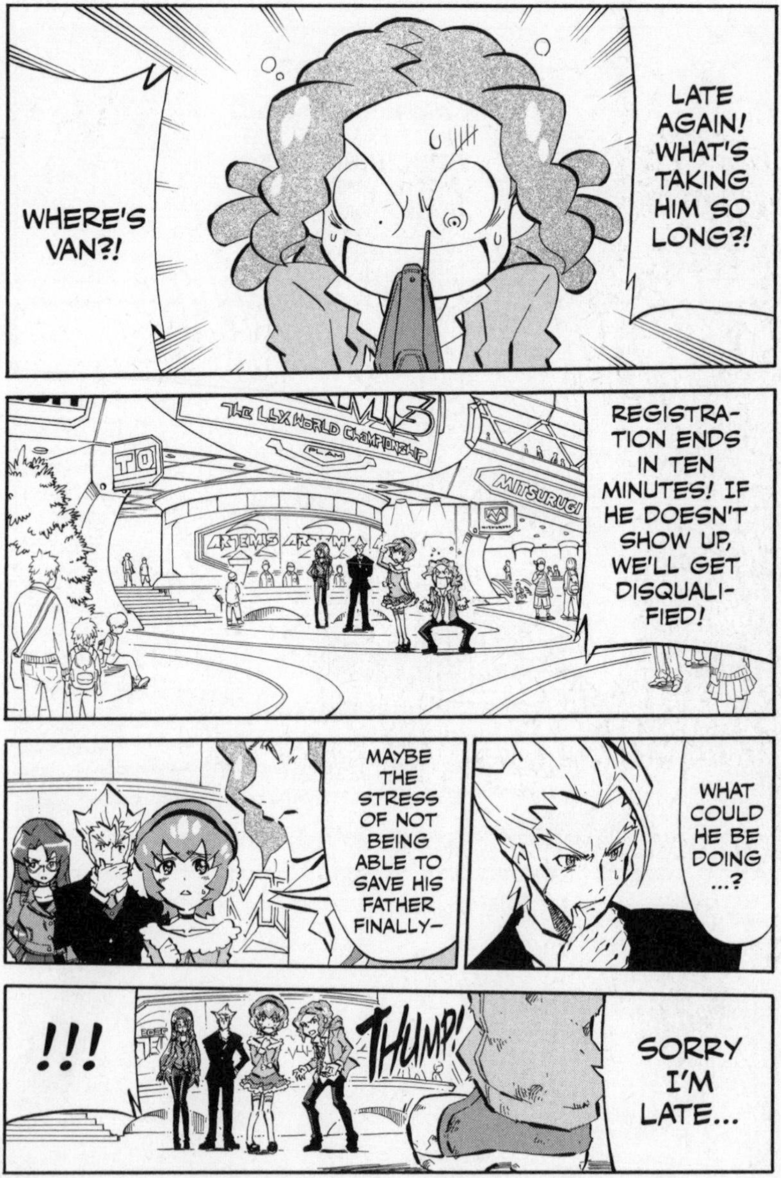
LATE AGAIN! WHAT'S TAKING HIM SO LONG?!
WHERE'S VAN?!
REGISTRATION ENDS IN TEN MINUTES! IF HE DOESN'T SHOW UP, WE'LL GET DISQUALIFIED!
The LBX WORLD Championship
MITSURUGI
ARTEMIS
TO
WHAT COULD HE BE DOING ...?
MAYBE THE STRESS OF NOT BEING ABLE TO SAVE HIS FATHER FINALLY—
SORRY I'M LATE...
THUMP!
!!!

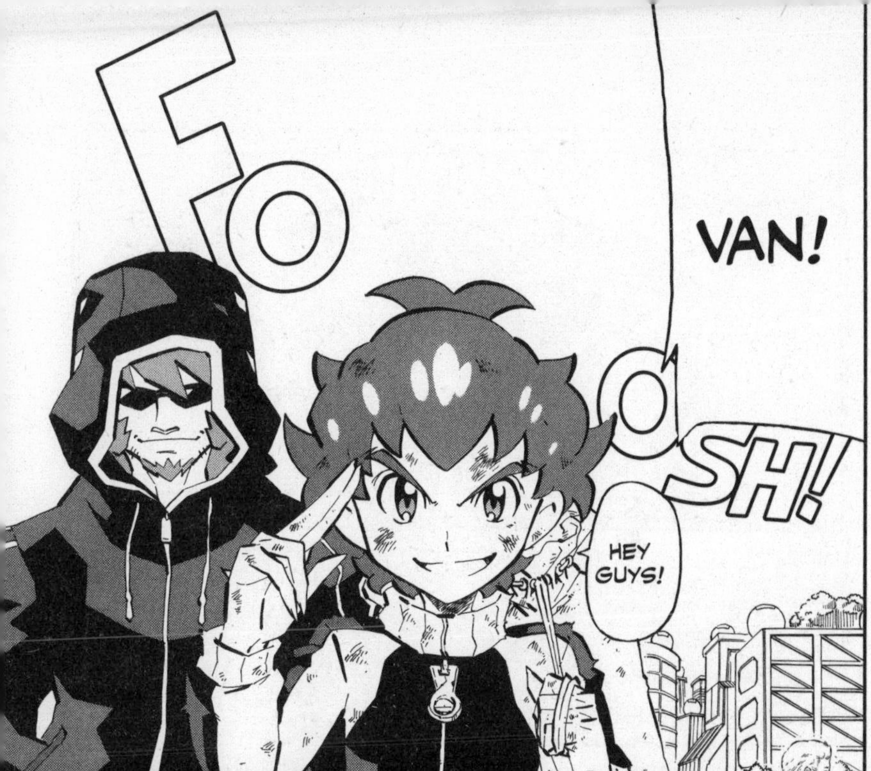
VAN!
FOOSH!
HEY GUYS!

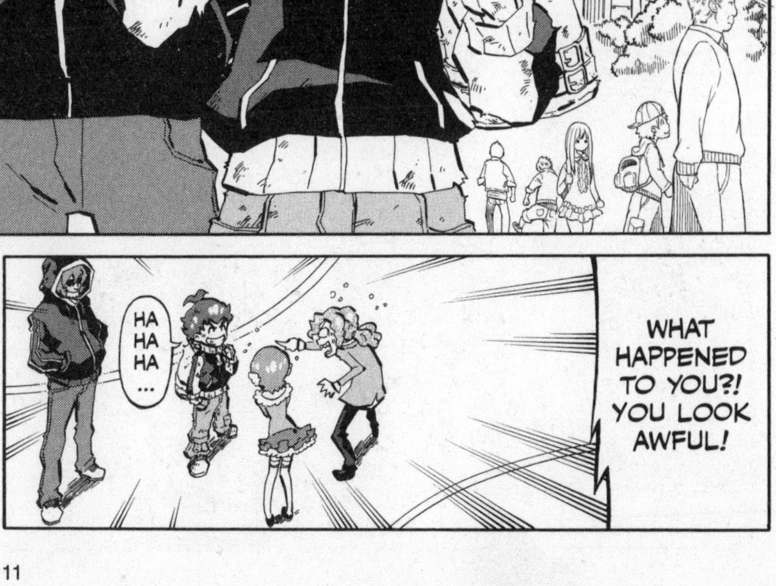
WHAT HAPPENED TO YOU?! YOU LOOK AWFUL!
HA HA HA ...

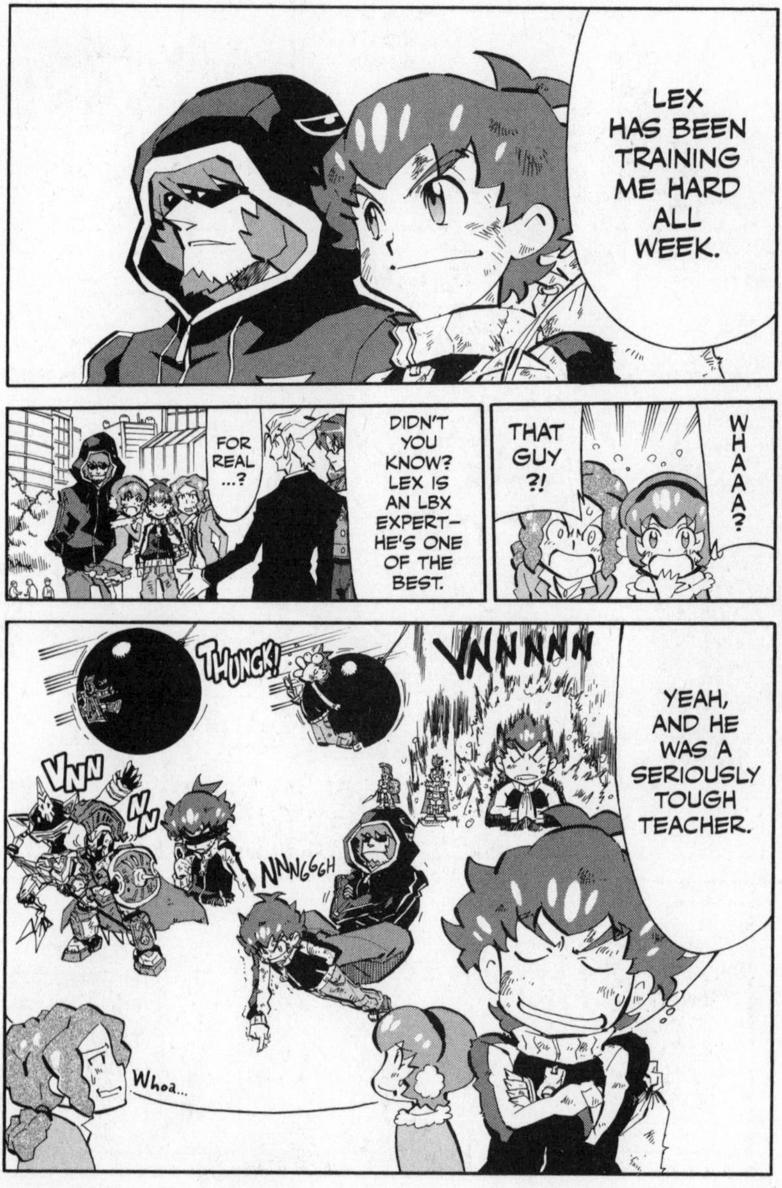
LEX HAS BEEN TRAINING ME HARD ALL WEEK.
WHAAAA?
THAT GUY ?!
DIDN'T YOU KNOW? LEX IS AN LBX EXPERT—HE'S ONE OF THE BEST.
FOR REAL ...?
YEAH, AND HE WAS A SERIOUSLY TOUGH TEACHER.
VNNNNN
THUNCK!
VNN
NN
NNNGGGH
Whoa...

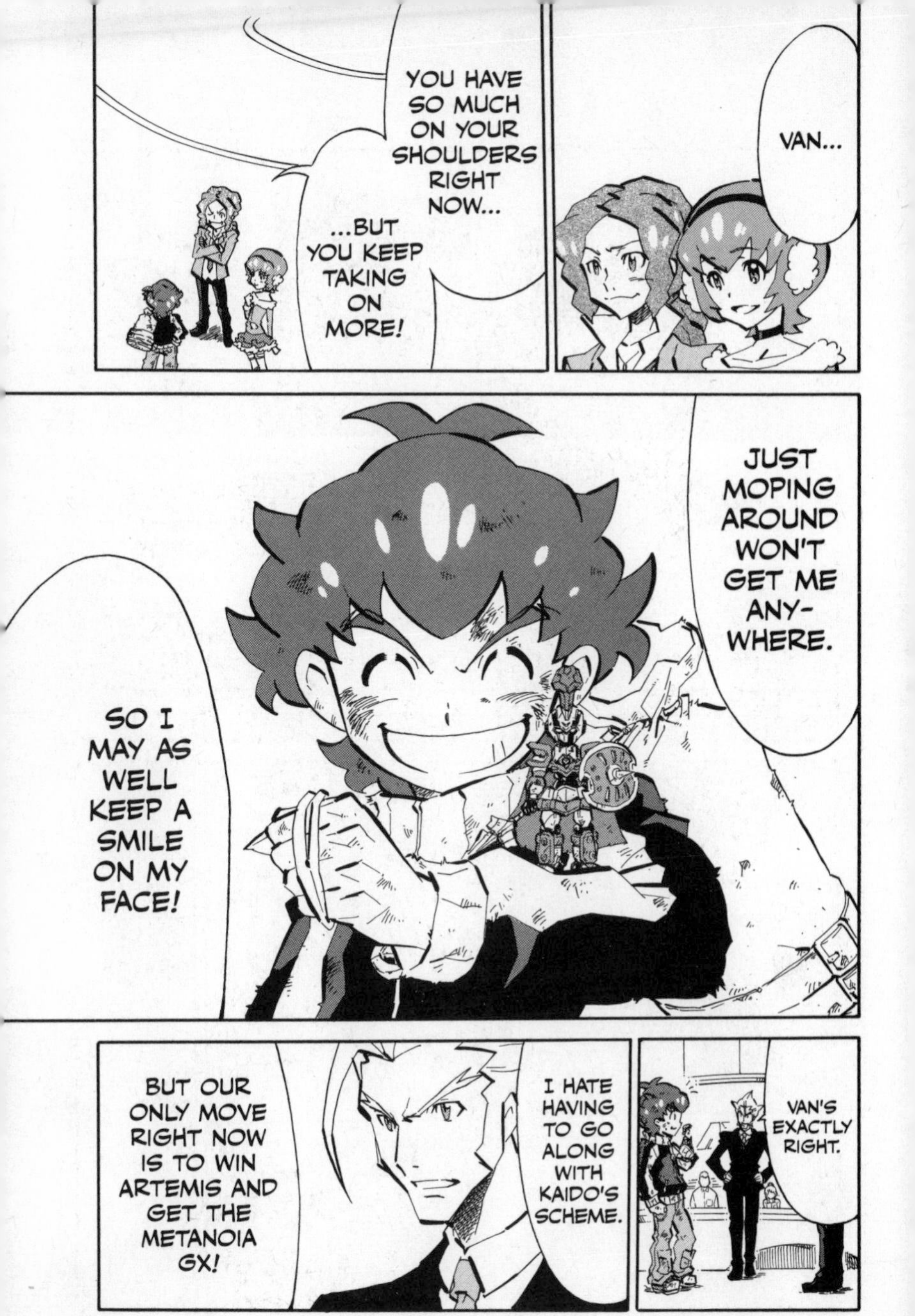
VAN...
YOU HAVE SO MUCH ON YOUR SHOULDERS RIGHT NOW...
...BUT YOU KEEP TAKING ON MORE!
JUST MOPING AROUND WON'T GET ME ANY-WHERE.
SO I MAY AS WELL KEEP A SMILE ON MY FACE!
VAN'S EXACTLY RIGHT.
I HATE HAVING TO GO ALONG WITH KAIDO'S SCHEME.
BUT OUR ONLY MOVE RIGHT NOW IS TO WIN ARTEMIS AND GET THE METANOIA GX!

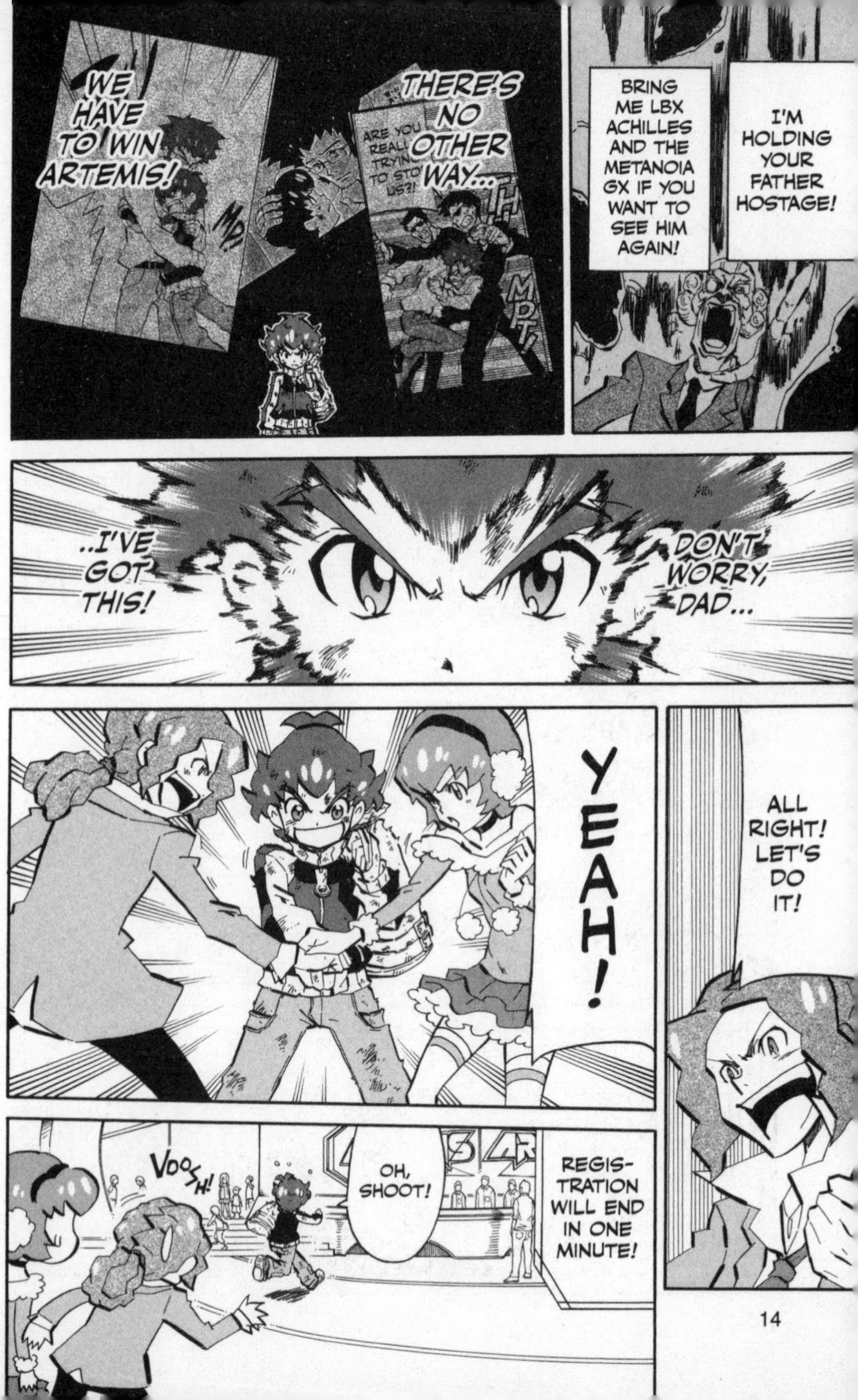
I'M HOLDING YOUR FATHER HOSTAGE!
BRING ME LBX ACHILLES AND THE METANOIA GX IF YOU WANT TO SEE HIM AGAIN!
THERE'S NO OTHER WAY...
ARE YOU REALL TRYIN TO STO US?!
THMPT!
WE HAVE TO WIN ARTEMIS!
MP!
DON'T WORRY, DAD...
..I'VE GOT THIS!
ALL RIGHT! LET'S DO IT!
YEAH!
REGIS-TRATION WILL END IN ONE MINUTE!
OH, SHOOT!
VOOSH!

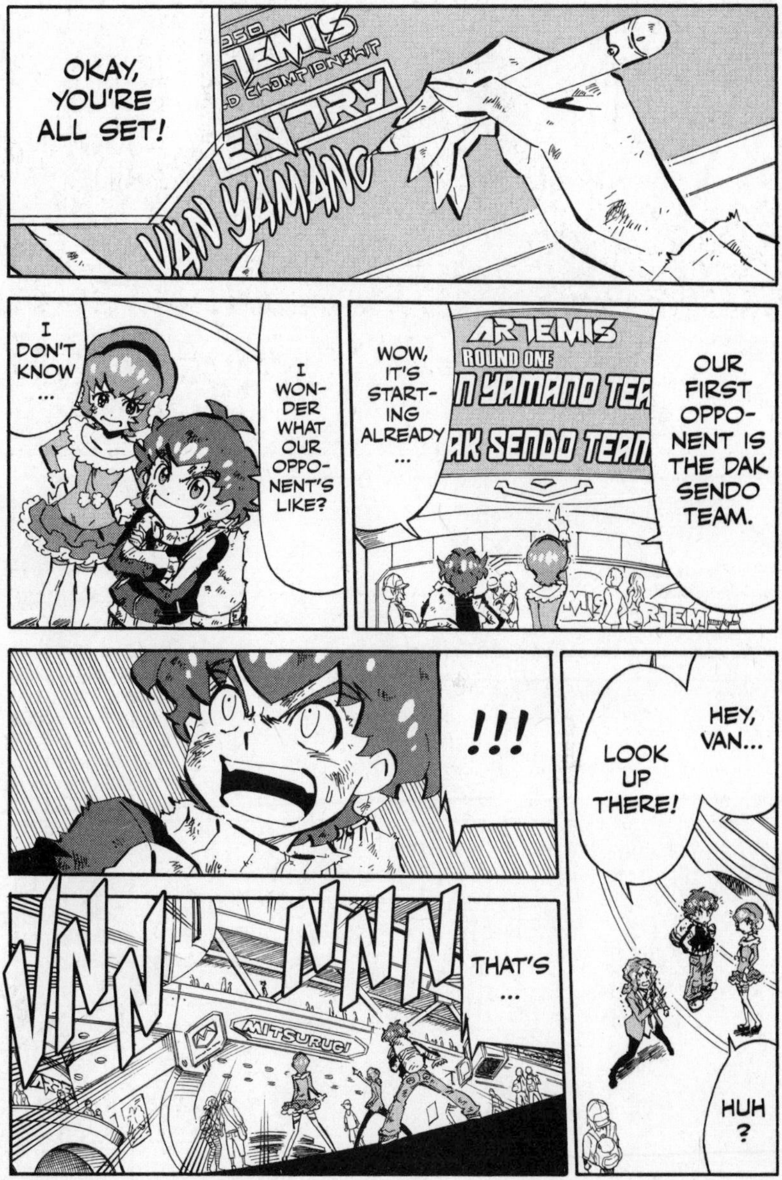
ARTEMIS
CHAMPIONSHIP
ENTRY
VAN YAMANO
OKAY, YOU'RE ALL SET!
ARTEMIS
ROUND ONE
OUR FIRST OPPO-NENT IS THE DAK SENDO TEAM.
WOW, IT'S START-ING ALREADY...
I WON-DER WHAT OUR OPPO-NENT'S LIKE?
I DON'T KNOW...
HEY, VAN...
LOOK UP THERE!
HUH?
!!!
VNNNNNN
THAT'S...
MITSURUGI

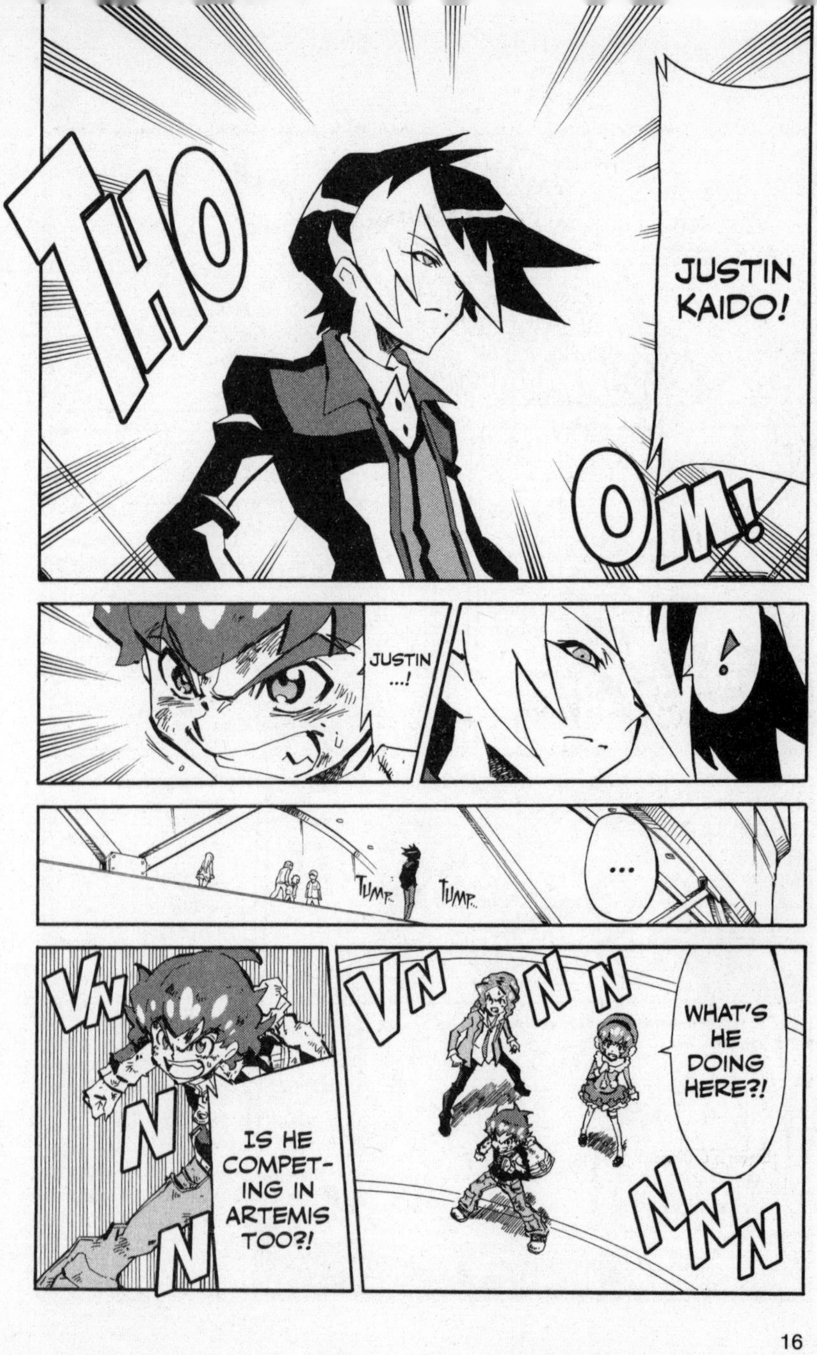
JUSTIN KAIDO!
THO
OM!
!
JUSTIN ...!
...
TUMP..
TUMP..
WHAT'S HE DOING HERE?!
VN
N N
NNN
VN
N
N
IS HE COMPET-ING IN ARTEMIS TOO?!

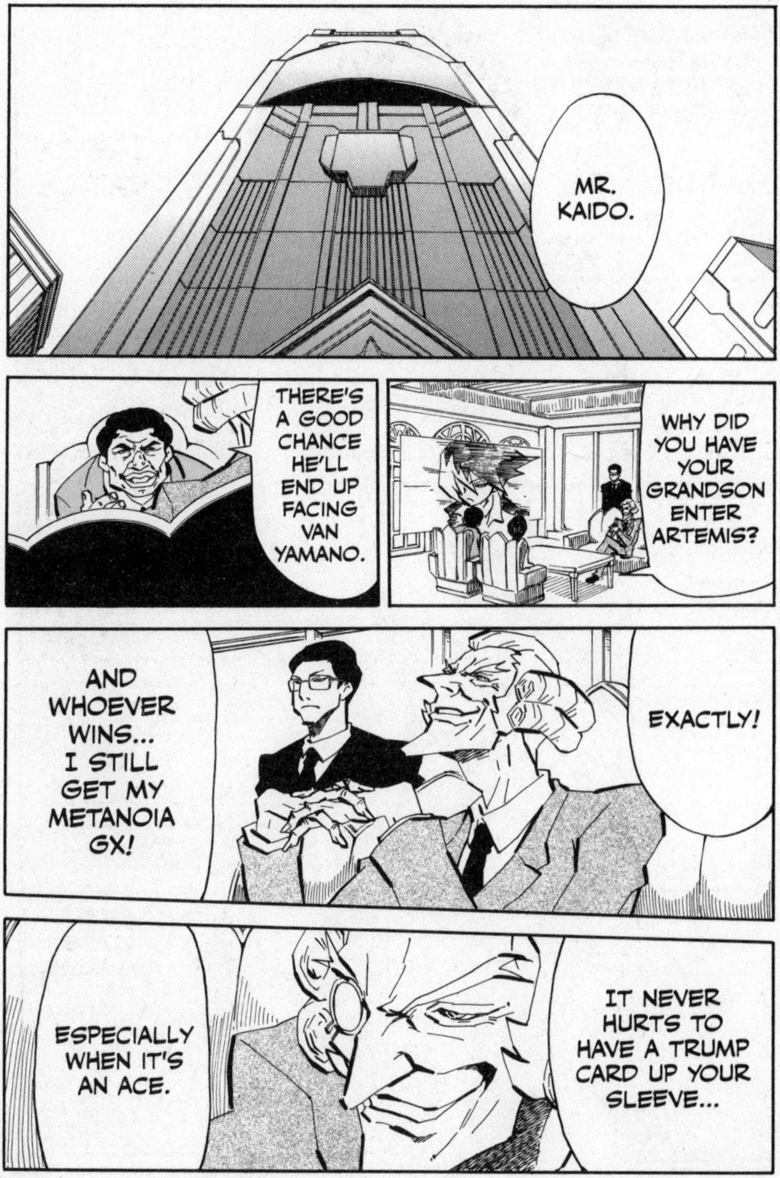
MR. KAIDO.
WHY DID YOU HAVE YOUR GRANDSON ENTER ARTEMIS?
THERE'S A GOOD CHANCE HE'LL END UP FACING VAN YAMANO.
EXACTLY!
AND WHOEVER WINS... I STILL GET MY METANOIA GX!
IT NEVER HURTS TO HAVE A TRUMP CARD UP YOUR SLEEVE...
ESPECIALLY WHEN IT'S AN ACE.

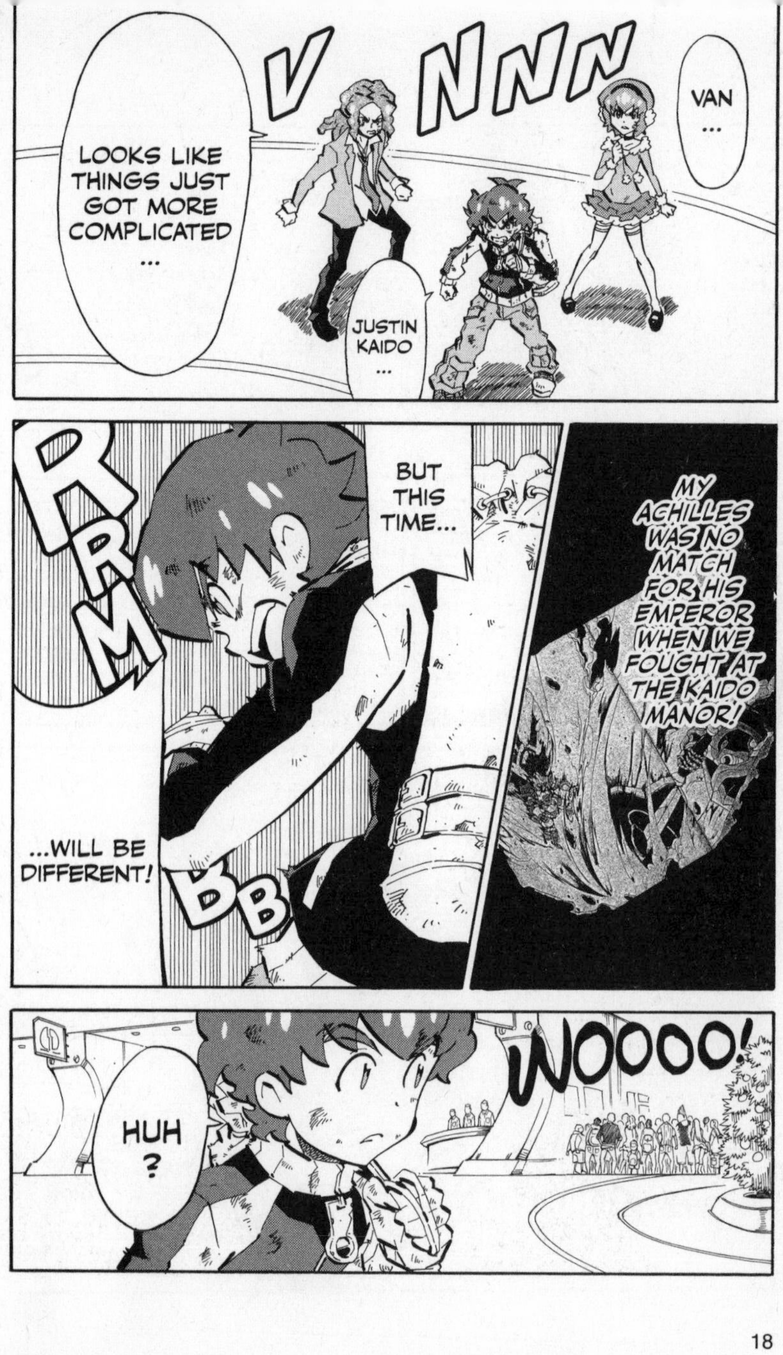
VAN ...
VNNN
LOOKS LIKE THINGS JUST GOT MORE COMPLICATED ...
JUSTIN KAIDO ...
MY ACHILLES WAS NO MATCH FOR HIS EMPEROR WHEN WE FOUGHT AT THE KAIDO MANOR!
BUT THIS TIME...
RRM
...WILL BE DIFFERENT!
BB
WOOOO!
HUH ?

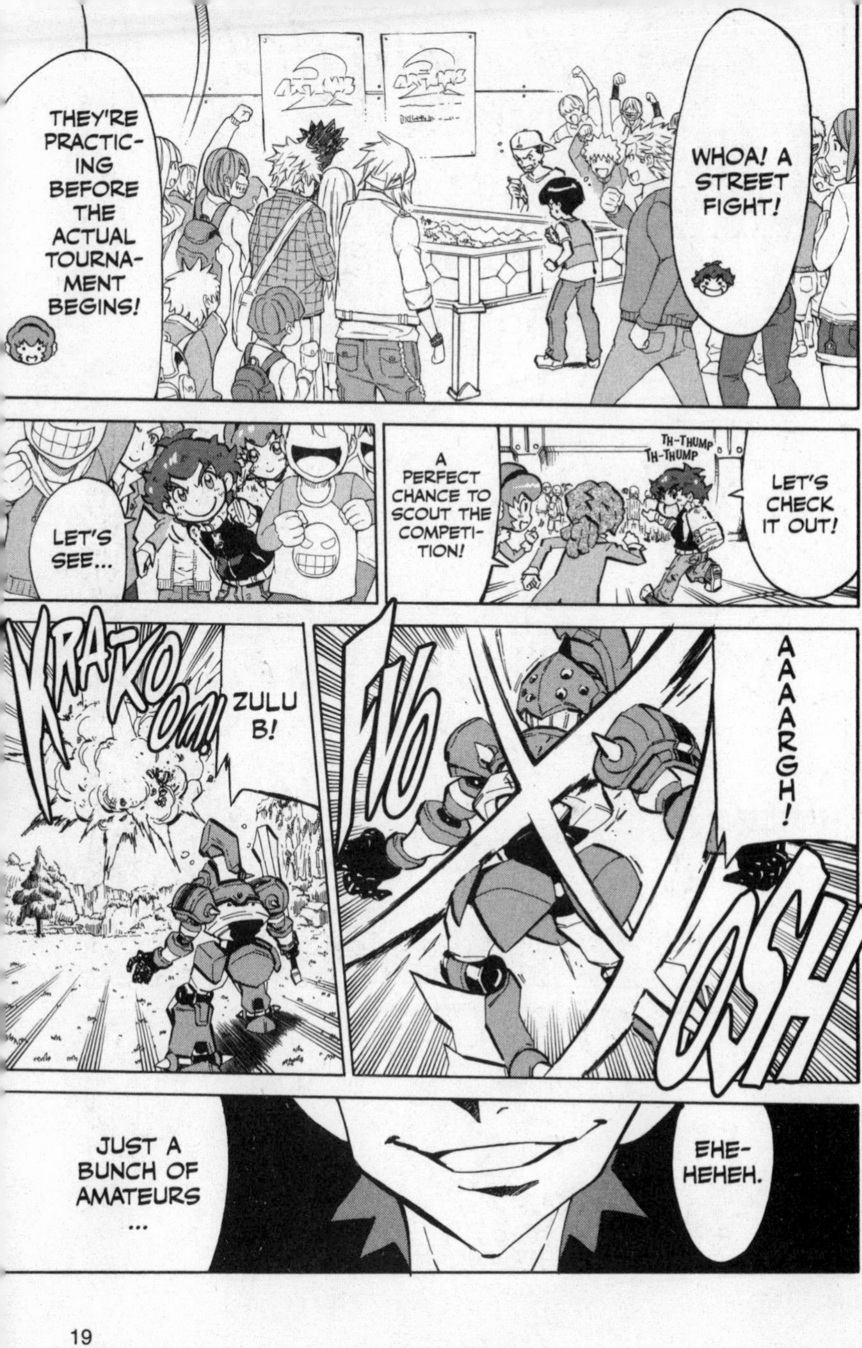
WHOA! A STREET FIGHT!
THEY'RE PRACTIC-ING BEFORE THE ACTUAL TOURNA-MENT BEGINS!
LET'S CHECK IT OUT!
TH-THUMP TH-THUMP
A PERFECT CHANCE TO SCOUT THE COMPETI-TION!
LET'S SEE...
AAAARGH!
NO
XOSH
KRA-KOOM!
ZULU B!
EHE-HEHEH.
JUST A BUNCH OF AMATEURS ...

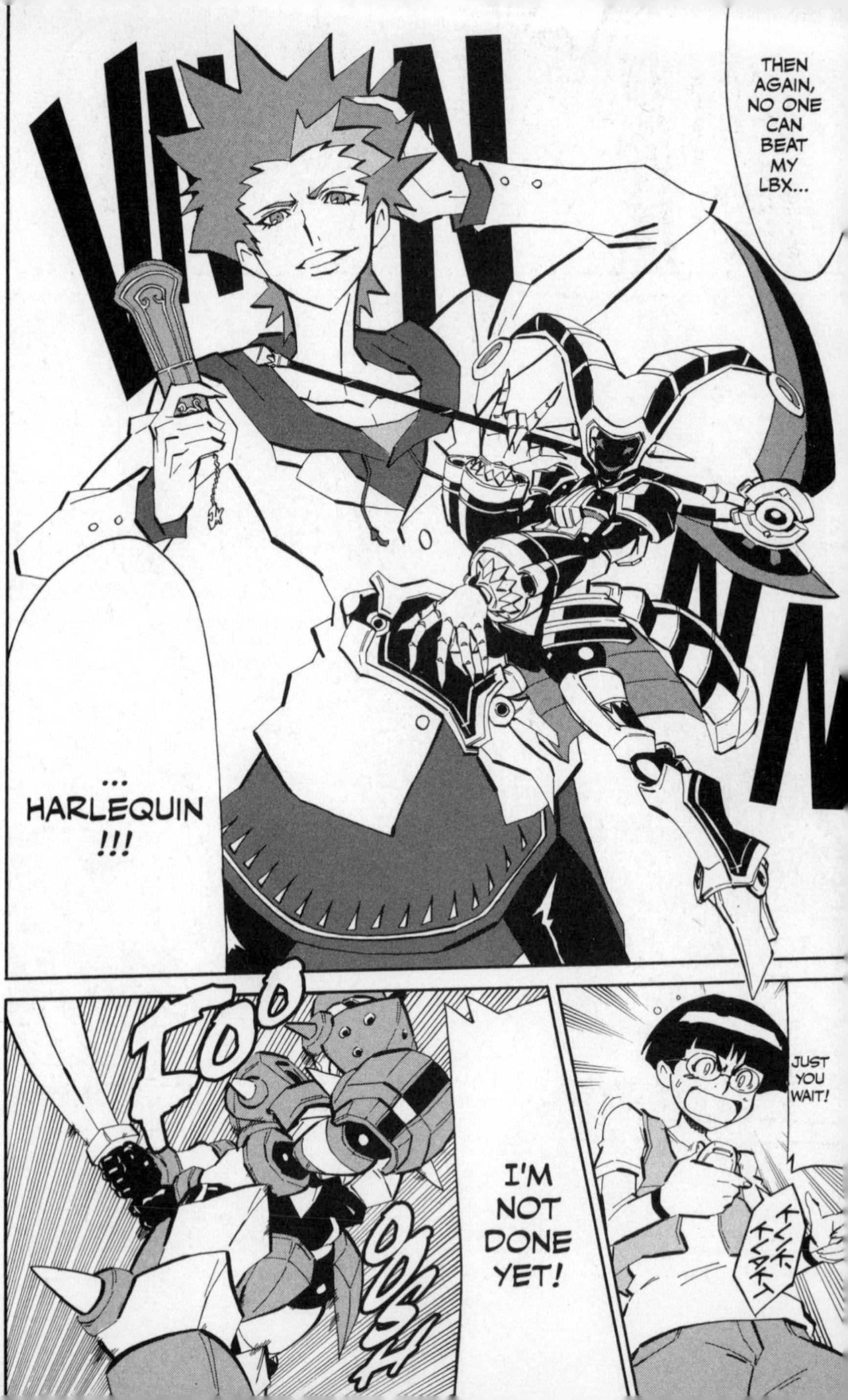
THEN AGAIN, NO ONE CAN BEAT MY LBX...
... HARLEQUIN !!!
JUST YOU WAIT!
I'M NOT DONE YET!

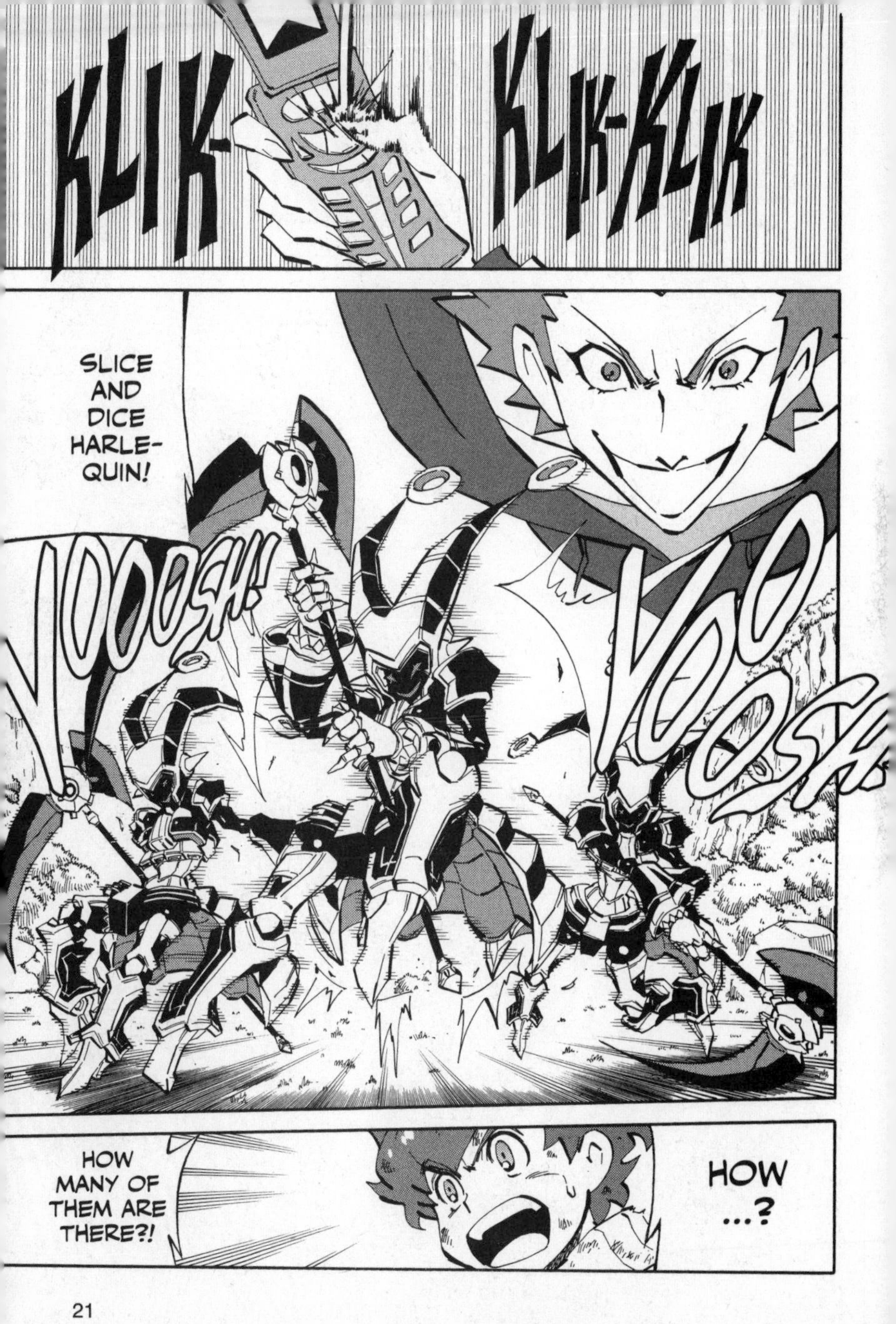
KLIK-
KLIK-KLIK
SLICE AND DICE HARLEQUIN!
VOOOSH
VOOOSH!
HOW ...?
HOW MANY OF THEM ARE THERE?!

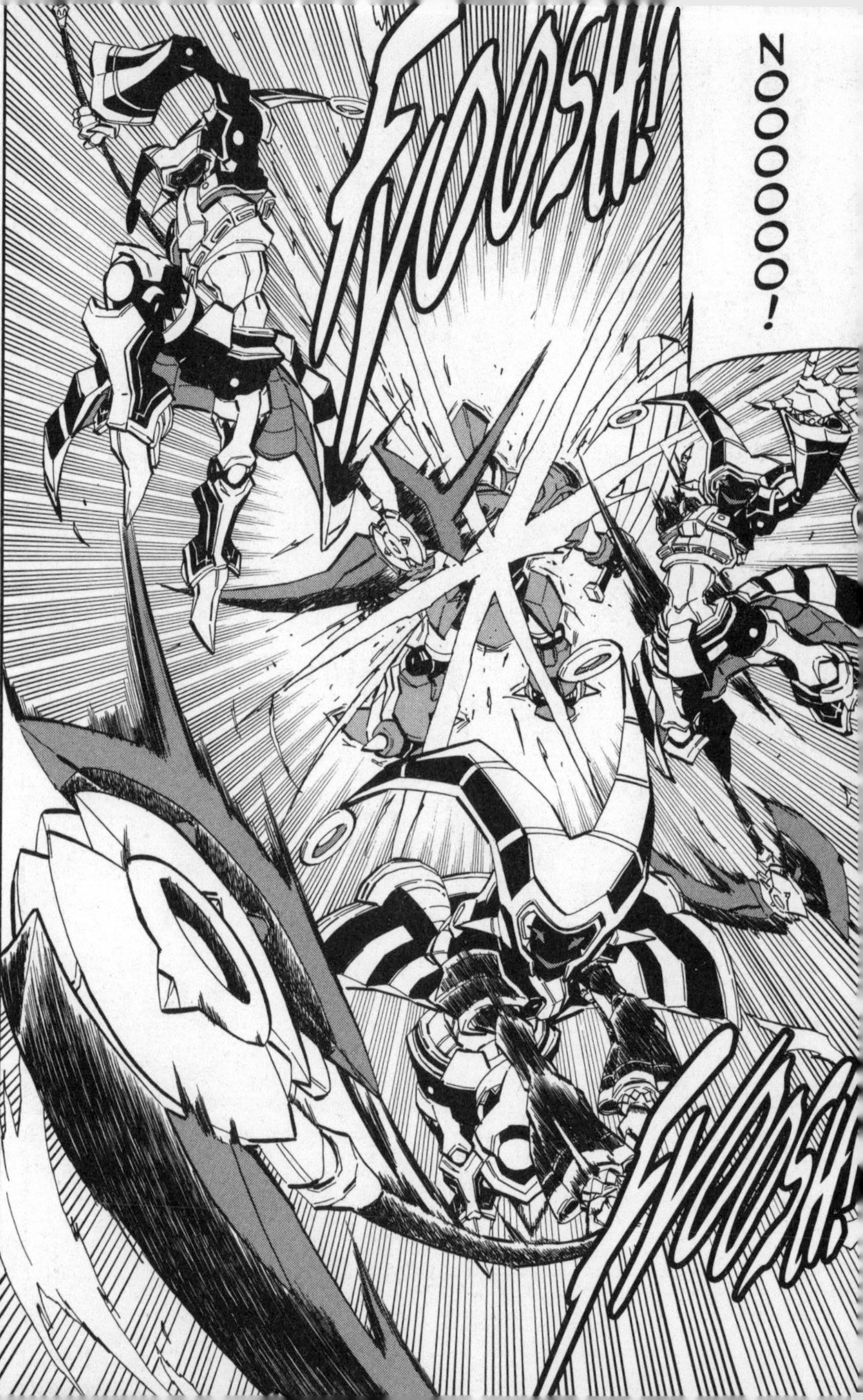
NOOOOOO!
FOOSH!
FWOOSH!

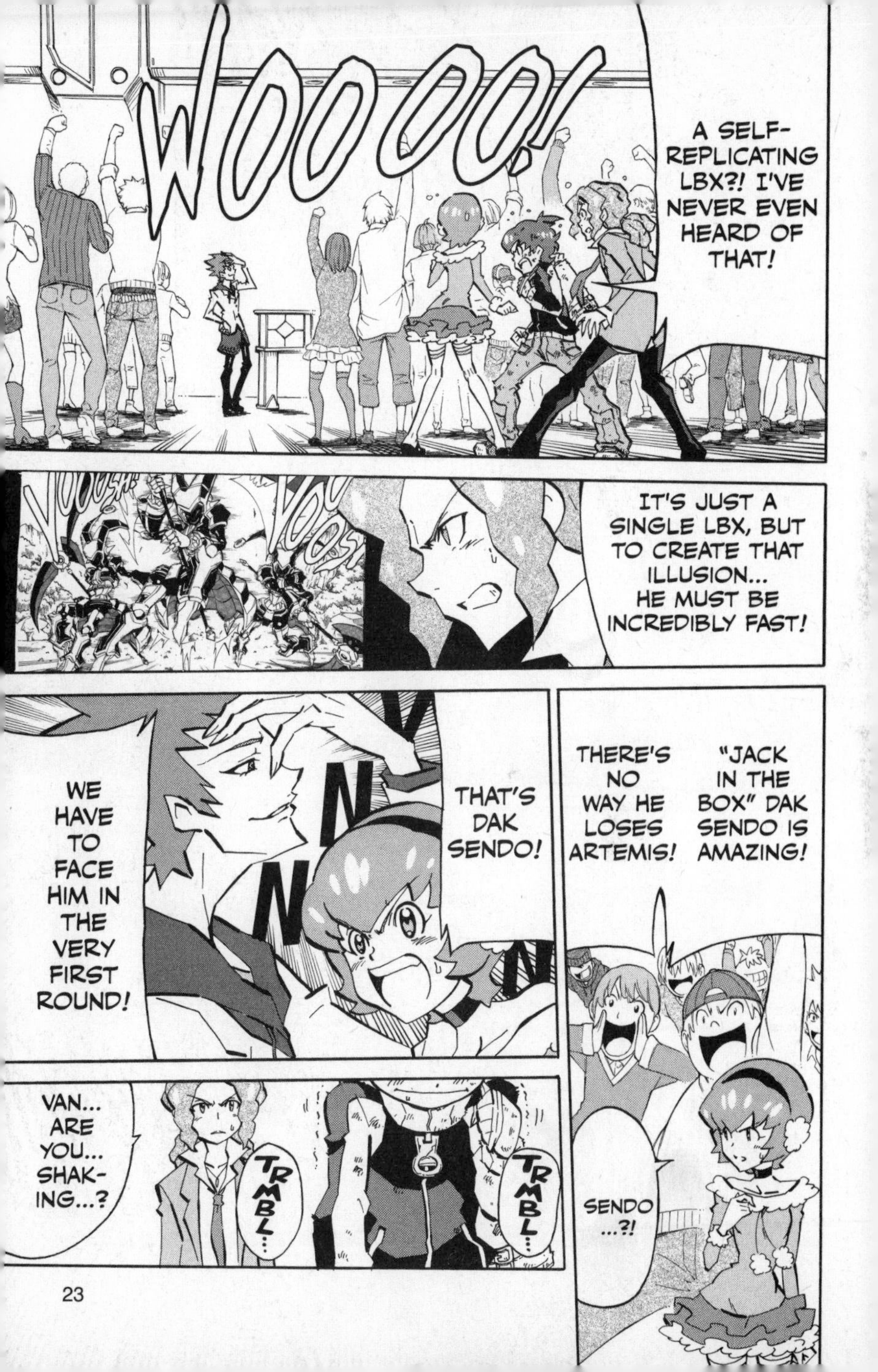
WOOOO!
A SELF-REPLICATING LBX?! I'VE NEVER EVEN HEARD OF THAT!
IT'S JUST A SINGLE LBX, BUT TO CREATE THAT ILLUSION... HE MUST BE INCREDIBLY FAST!
"JACK IN THE BOX" DAK SENDO IS AMAZING!
THERE'S NO WAY HE LOSES ARTEMIS!
THAT'S DAK SENDO!
NNN
WE HAVE TO FACE HIM IN THE VERY FIRST ROUND!
SENDO...?!
TRMBL...
TRMBL...
VAN... ARE YOU... SHAK-ING...?

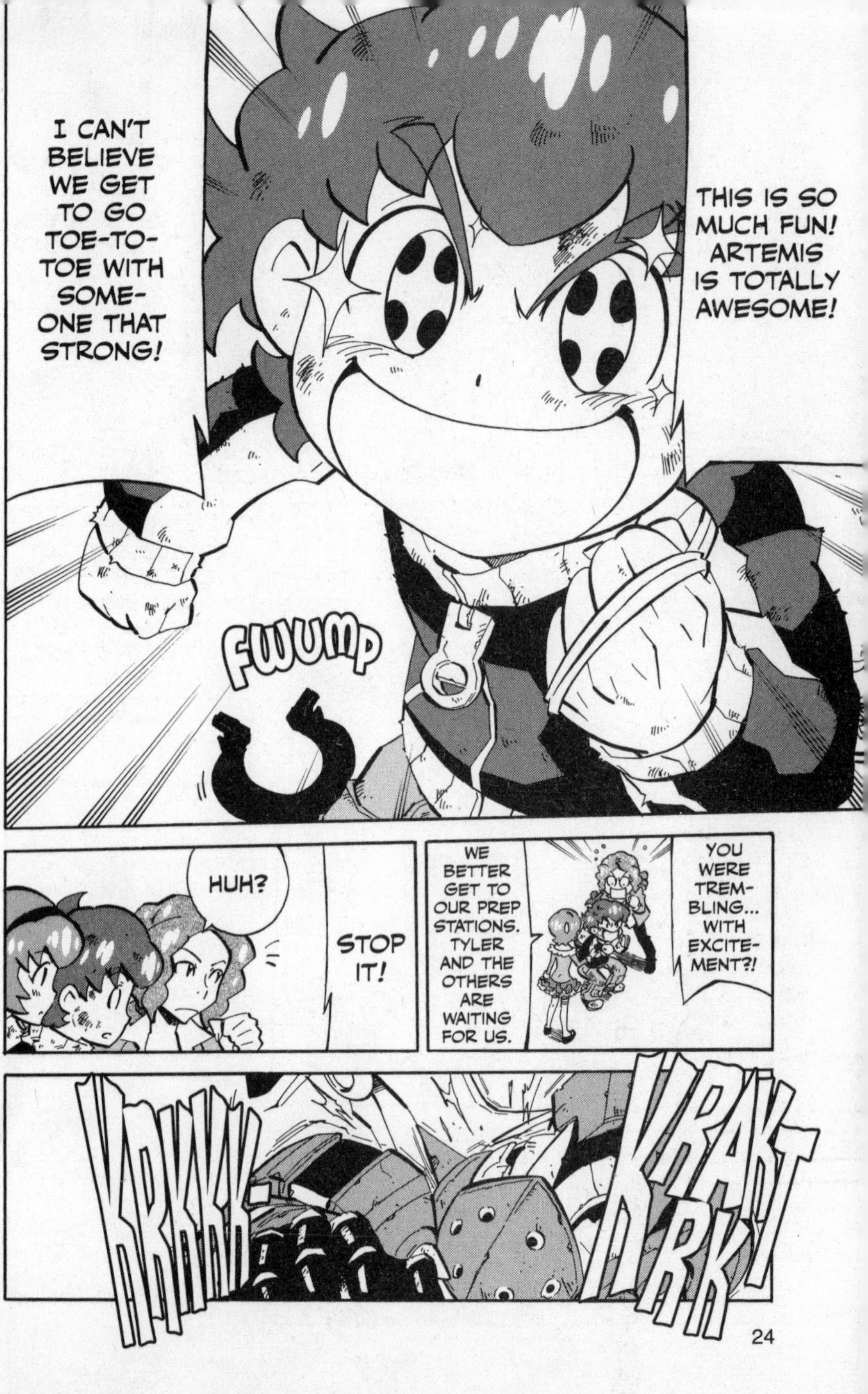
THIS IS SO MUCH FUN! ARTEMIS IS TOTALLY AWESOME!
I CAN'T BELIEVE WE GET TO GO TOE-TO-TOE WITH SOMEONE THAT STRONG!
FWUMP
YOU WERE TREMBLING... WITH EXCITEMENT?!
WE BETTER GET TO OUR PREP STATIONS. TYLER AND THE OTHERS ARE WAITING FOR US.
STOP IT!
HUH?
KRAKT
KRK

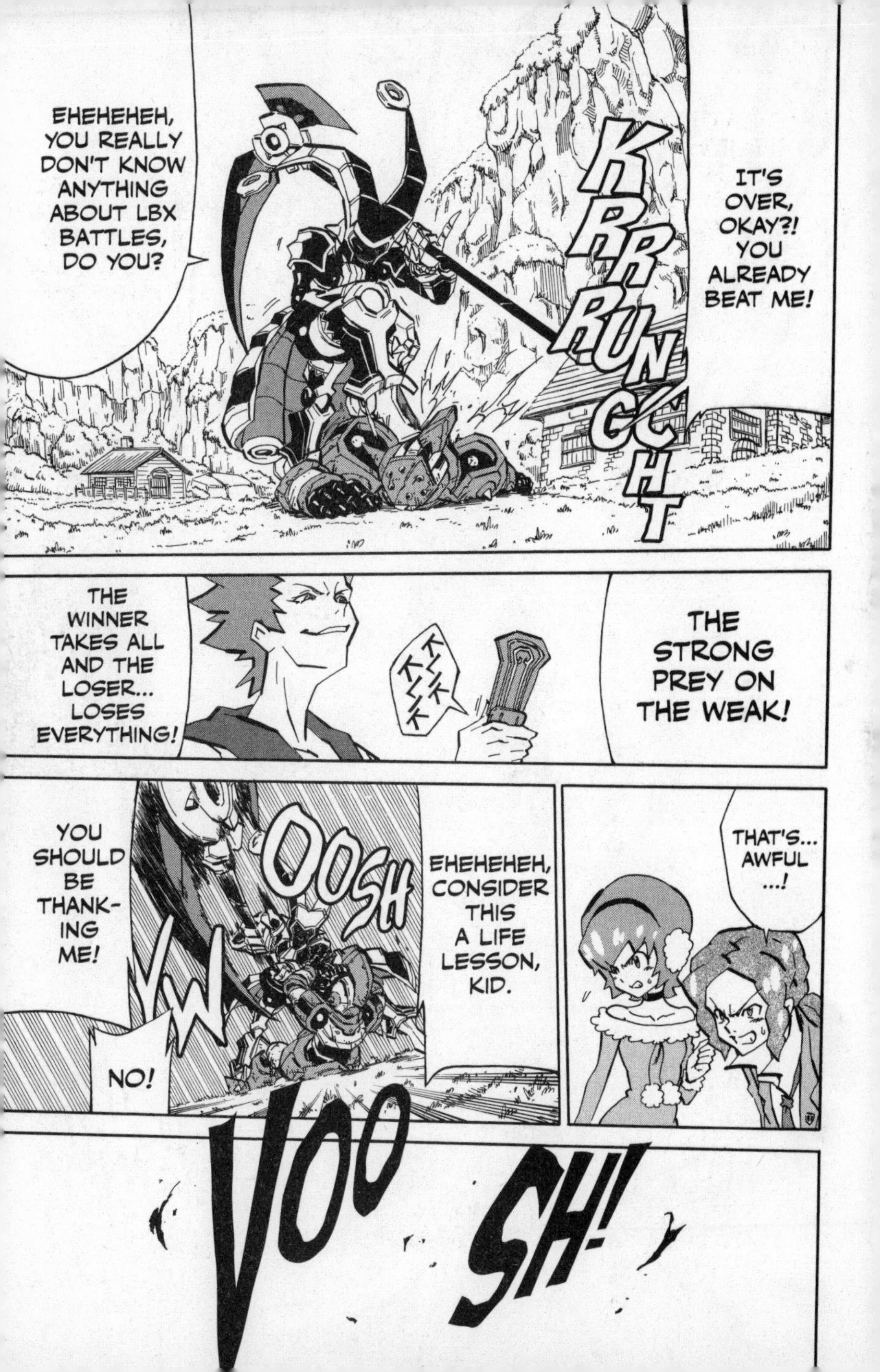
IT'S OVER, OKAY?! YOU ALREADY BEAT ME!
KRRRUNCCHT
EHEHEHEH, YOU REALLY DON'T KNOW ANYTHING ABOUT LBX BATTLES, DO YOU?
THE STRONG PREY ON THE WEAK!
KLIK KLIK
THE WINNER TAKES ALL AND THE LOSER... LOSES EVERYTHING!
THAT'S... AWFUL ...!
EHEHEHEH, CONSIDER THIS A LIFE LESSON, KID.
VOOSH
YOU SHOULD BE THANK-ING ME!
NO!
VOOSH!

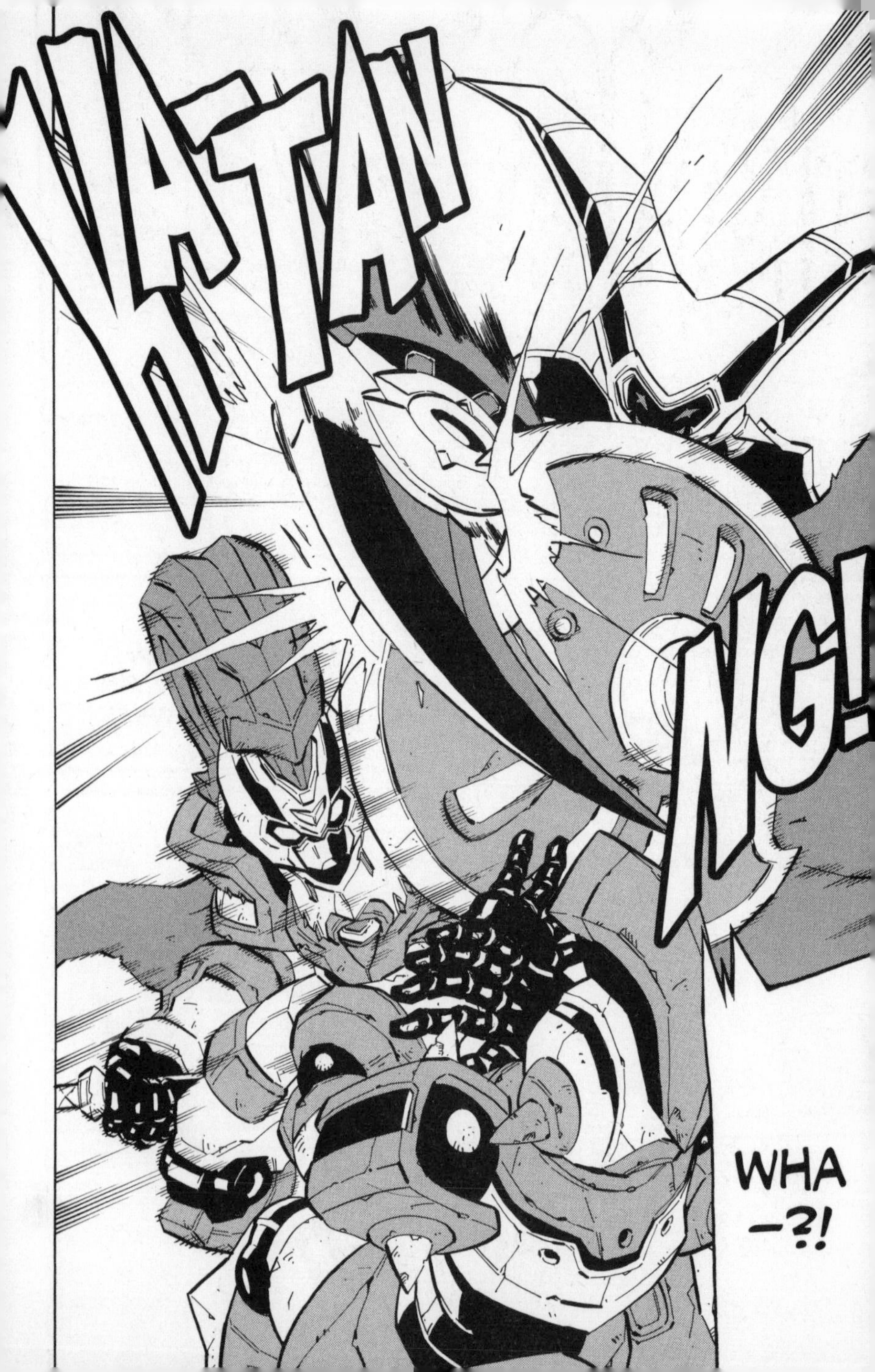
VATAN
NG!
WHA
—?!

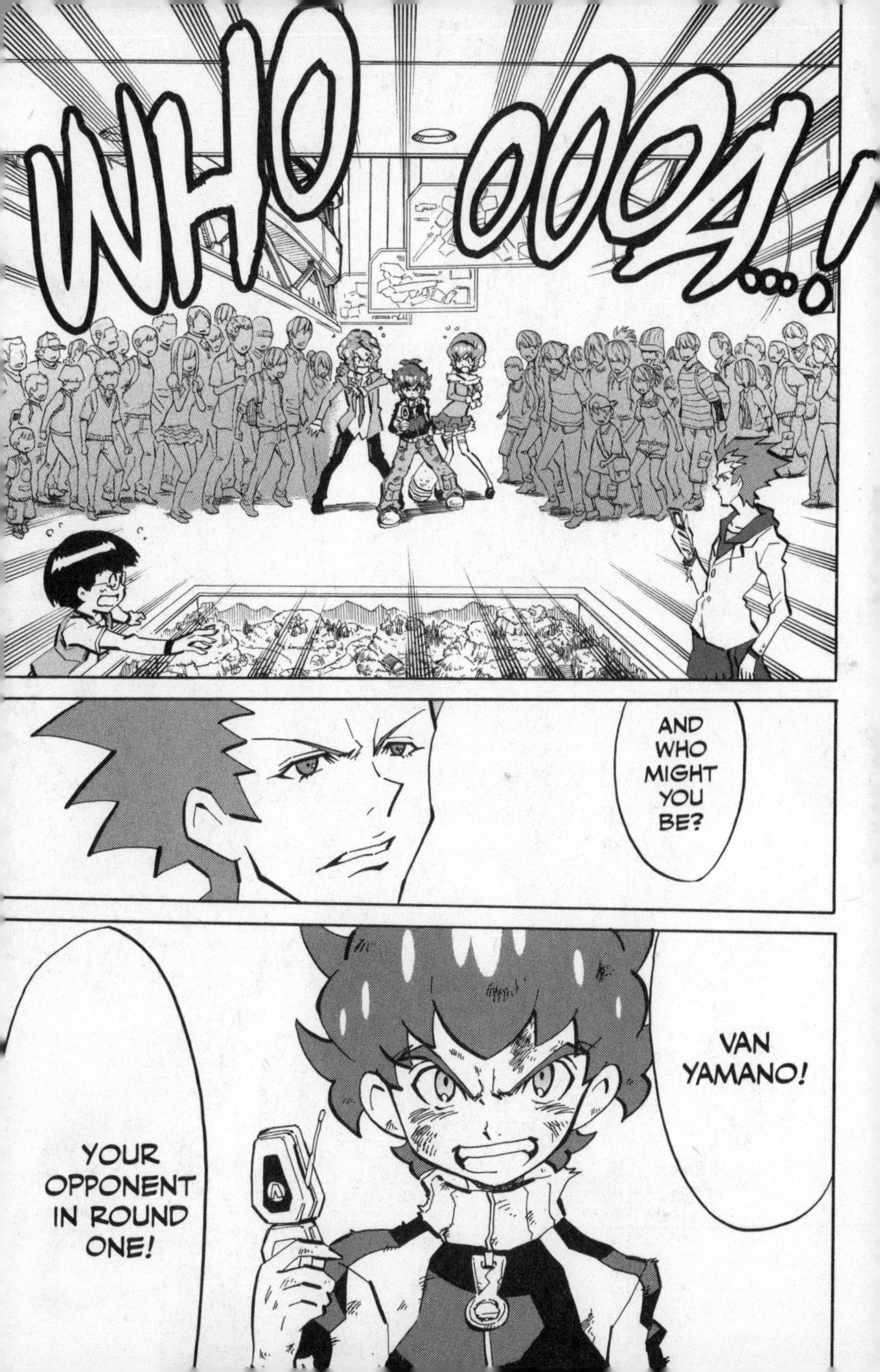
WHO-OOOA...!
AND WHO MIGHT YOU BE?
VAN YAMANO!
YOUR OPPONENT IN ROUND ONE!

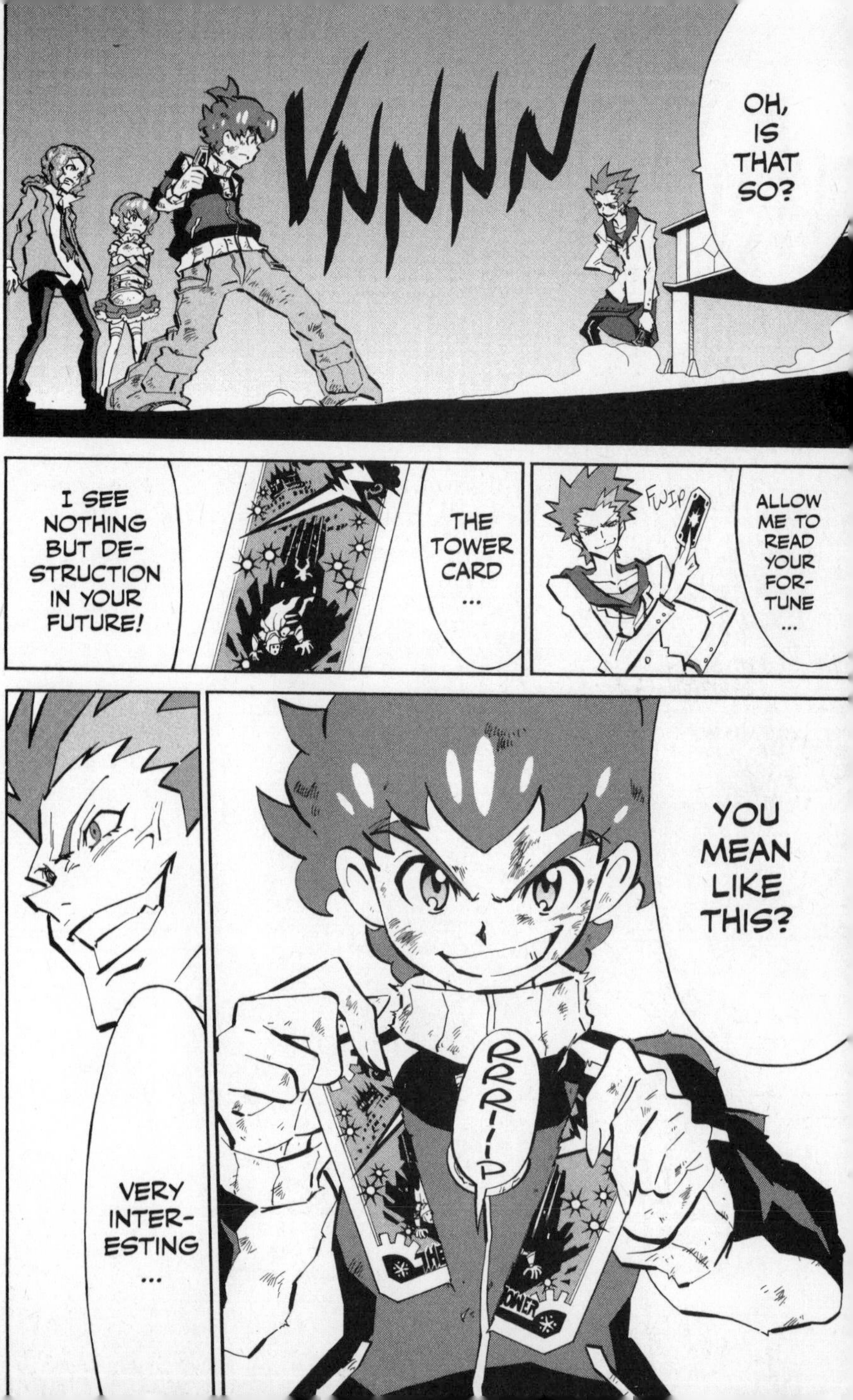
OH, IS THAT SO?
VNNNN
ALLOW ME TO READ YOUR FOR-TUNE ...
FWIP
THE TOWER CARD ...
I SEE NOTHING BUT DE-STRUCTION IN YOUR FUTURE!
YOU MEAN LIKE THIS?
RRRIIP
VERY INTER-ESTING ...

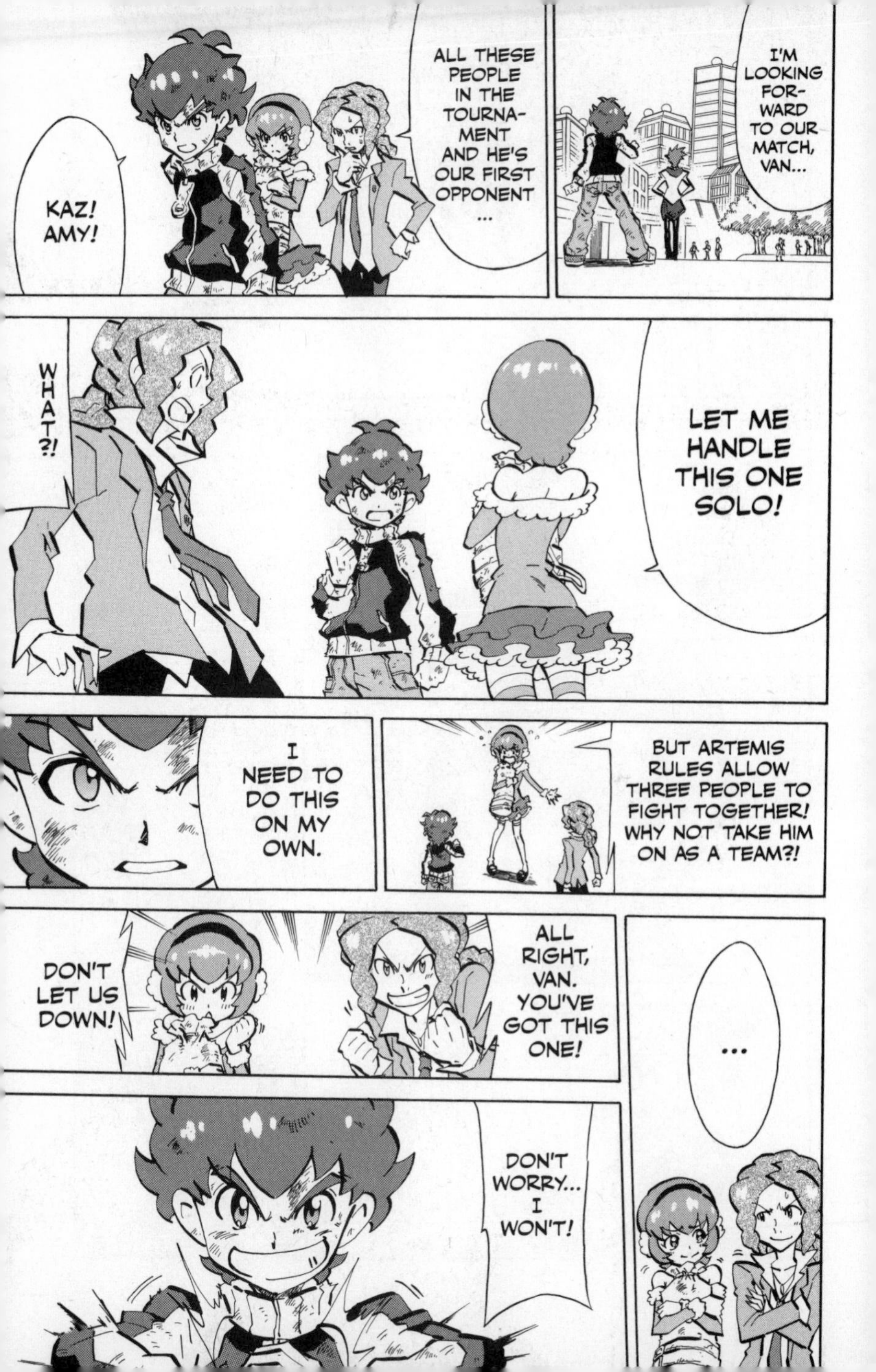
I'M LOOKING FOR-WARD TO OUR MATCH, VAN...
ALL THESE PEOPLE IN THE TOURNA-MENT AND HE'S OUR FIRST OPPONENT ...
KAZ! AMY!
LET ME HANDLE THIS ONE SOLO!
WHAT?!
BUT ARTEMIS RULES ALLOW THREE PEOPLE TO FIGHT TOGETHER! WHY NOT TAKE HIM ON AS A TEAM?!
I NEED TO DO THIS ON MY OWN.
...
ALL RIGHT, VAN. YOU'VE GOT THIS ONE!
DON'T LET US DOWN!
DON'T WORRY... I WON'T!

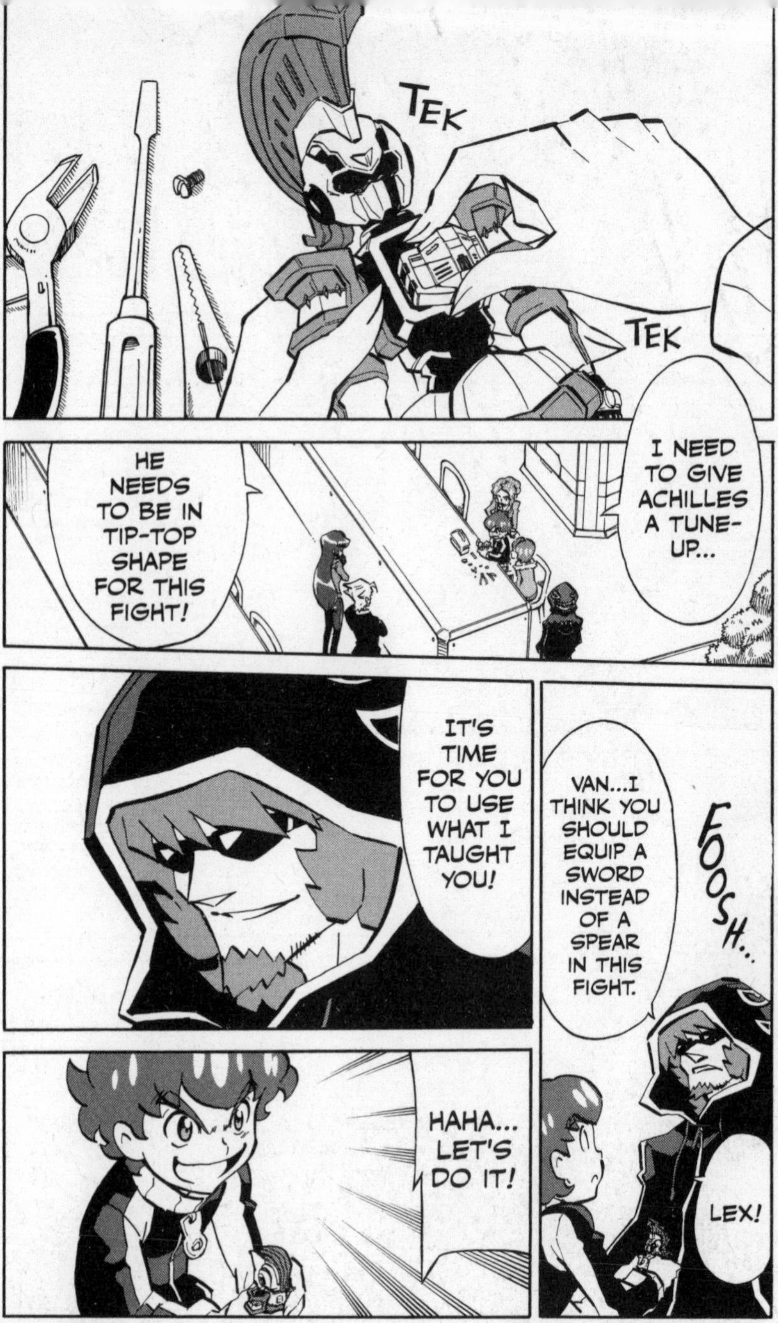
TEK
TEK
I NEED TO GIVE ACHILLES A TUNE-UP...
HE NEEDS TO BE IN TIP-TOP SHAPE FOR THIS FIGHT!
VAN...I THINK YOU SHOULD EQUIP A SWORD INSTEAD OF A SPEAR IN THIS FIGHT.
FOOSH...
LEX!
IT'S TIME FOR YOU TO USE WHAT I TAUGHT YOU!
HAHA... LET'S DO IT!

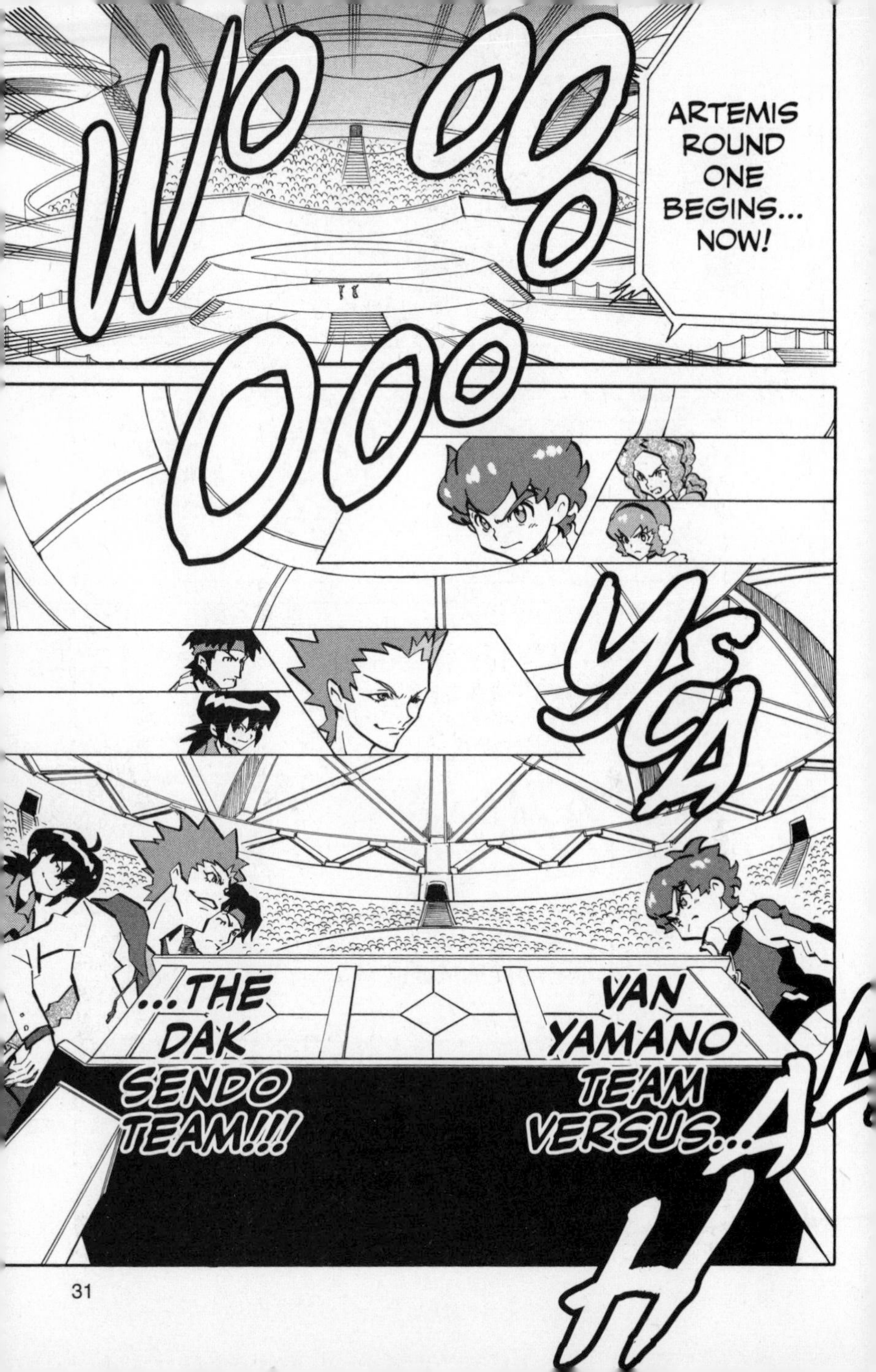
ARTEMIS ROUND ONE BEGINS... NOW!
WOOOOOOO
YEAAAH
VAN YAMANO TEAM VERSUS...
...THE DAK SENDO TEAM!!!

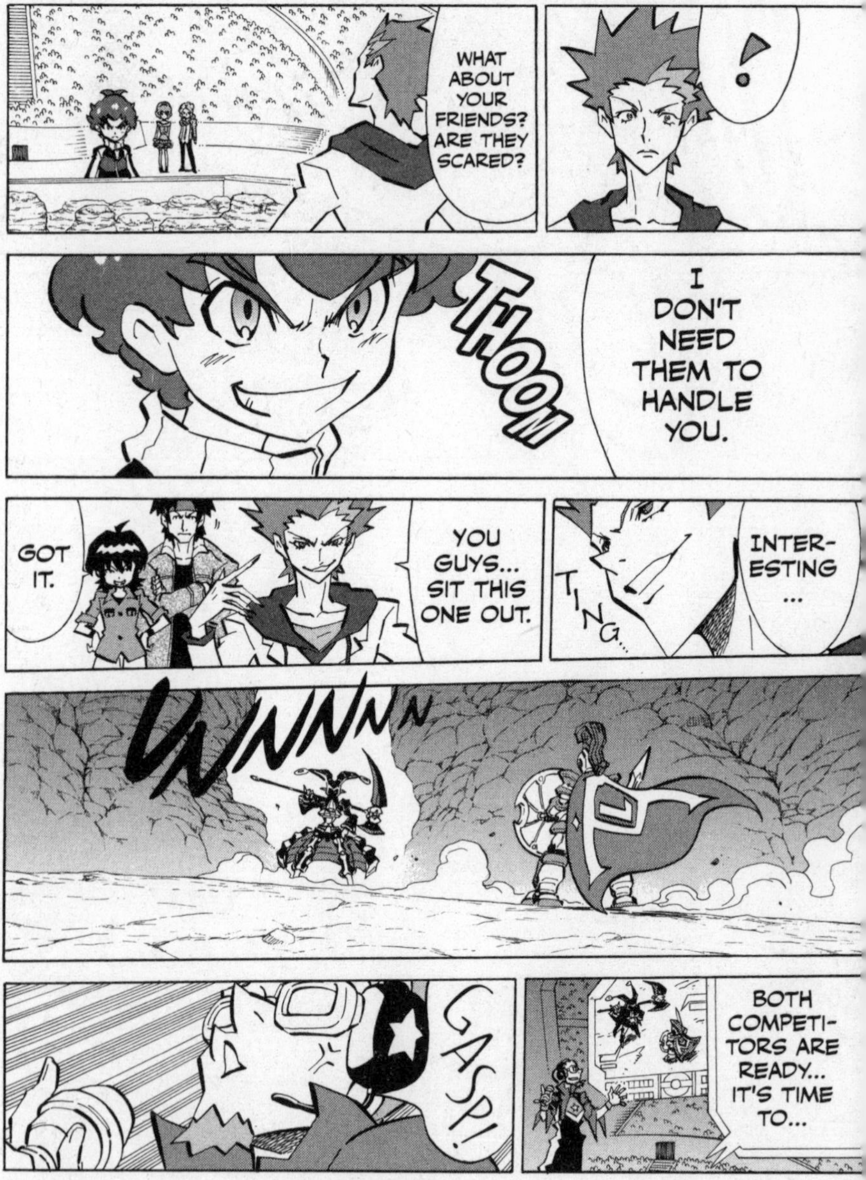
!
WHAT ABOUT YOUR FRIENDS? ARE THEY SCARED?
I DON'T NEED THEM TO HANDLE YOU.
THOOM
INTER-ESTING ...
TING...
YOU GUYS... SIT THIS ONE OUT.
GOT IT.
WINNNNN
BOTH COMPETI-TORS ARE READY... IT'S TIME TO...
GASP!

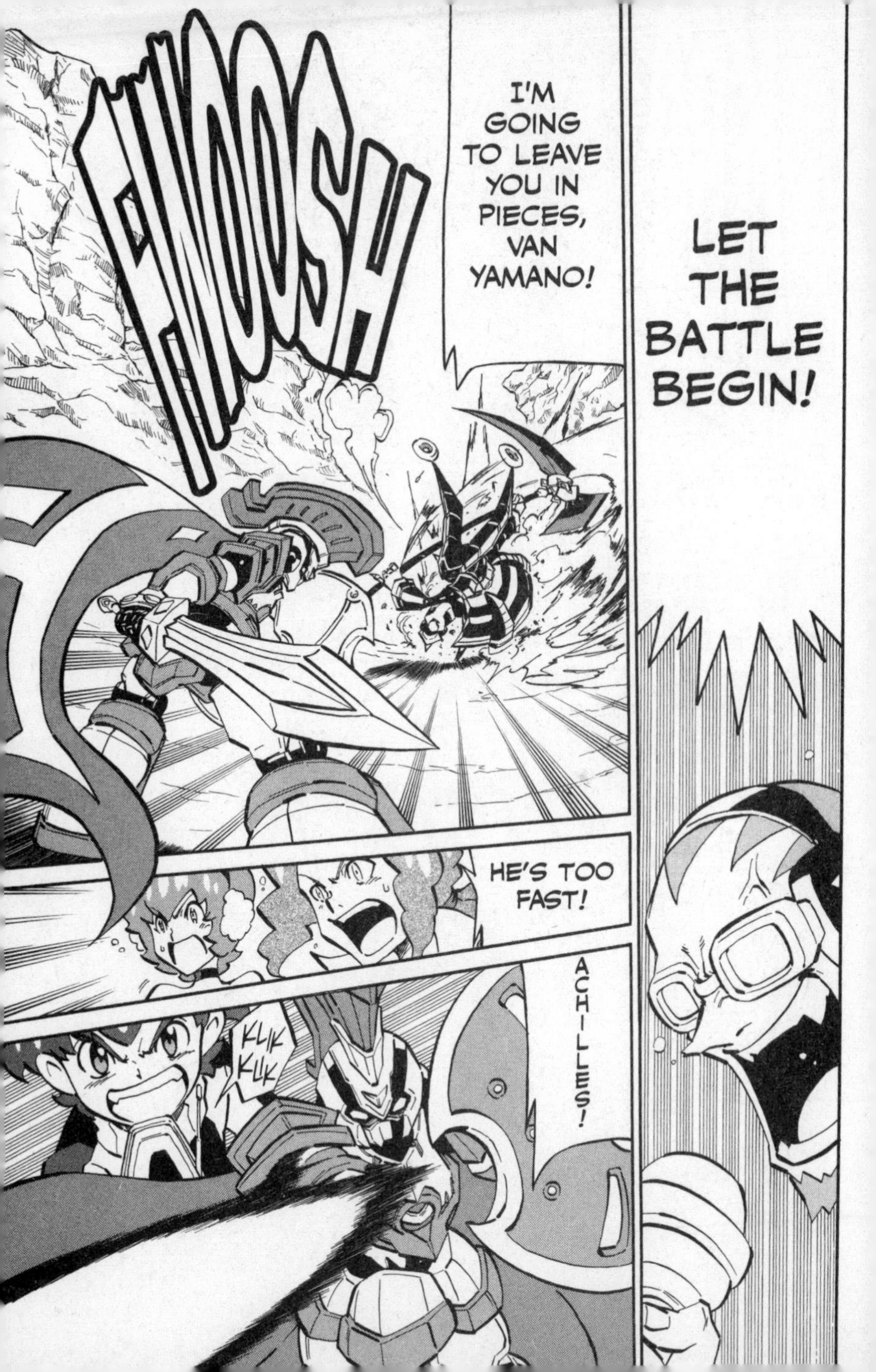
LET THE BATTLE BEGIN!
WHOOSH
I'M GOING TO LEAVE YOU IN PIECES, VAN YAMANO!
HE'S TOO FAST!
ACHILLES!
KLIK KLIK

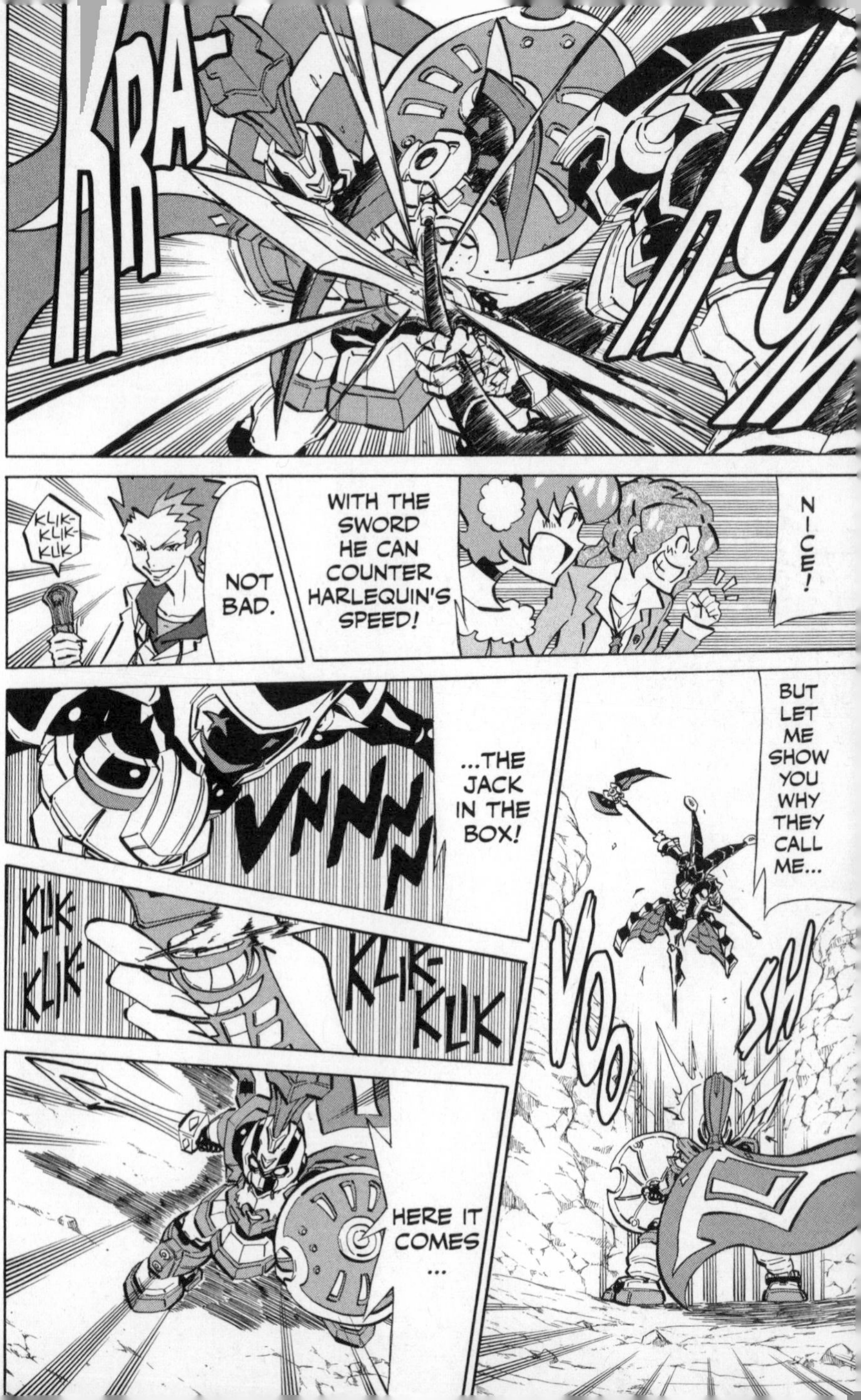
KRA-
KO
NICE!
WITH THE SWORD HE CAN COUNTER HARLEQUIN'S SPEED!
KLIK-KLIK-KLIK
NOT BAD.
BUT LET ME SHOW YOU WHY THEY CALL ME...
VOOSH
...THE JACK IN THE BOX!
VNNN
KLIK-KLIK-
KLIK-KLIK
HERE IT COMES...

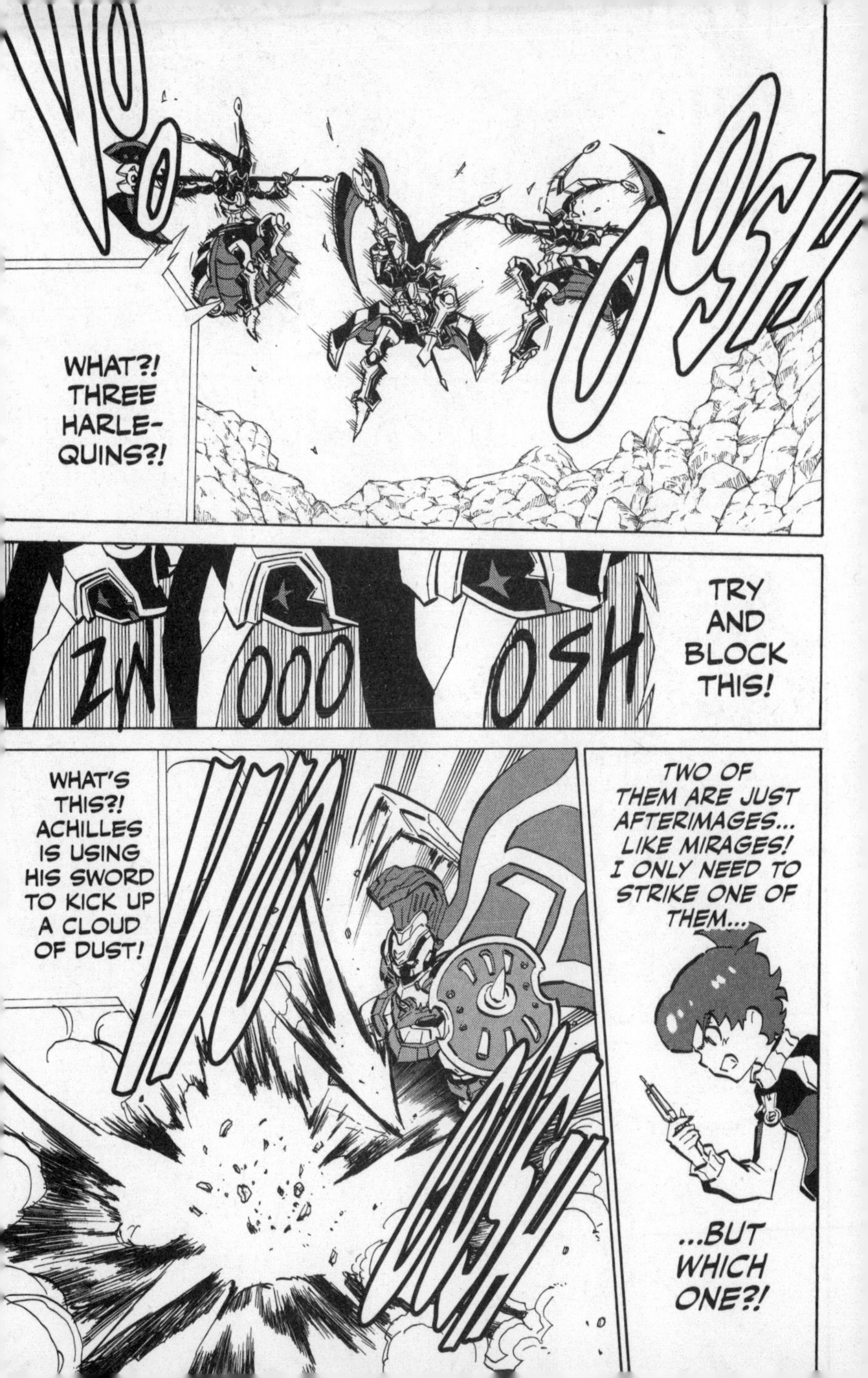
WHAT?! THREE HARLE-QUINS?!
TRY AND BLOCK THIS!
ZWOOOOSH
TWO OF THEM ARE JUST AFTERIMAGES... LIKE MIRAGES! I ONLY NEED TO STRIKE ONE OF THEM...
...BUT WHICH ONE?!
WHAT'S THIS?! ACHILLES IS USING HIS SWORD TO KICK UP A CLOUD OF DUST!

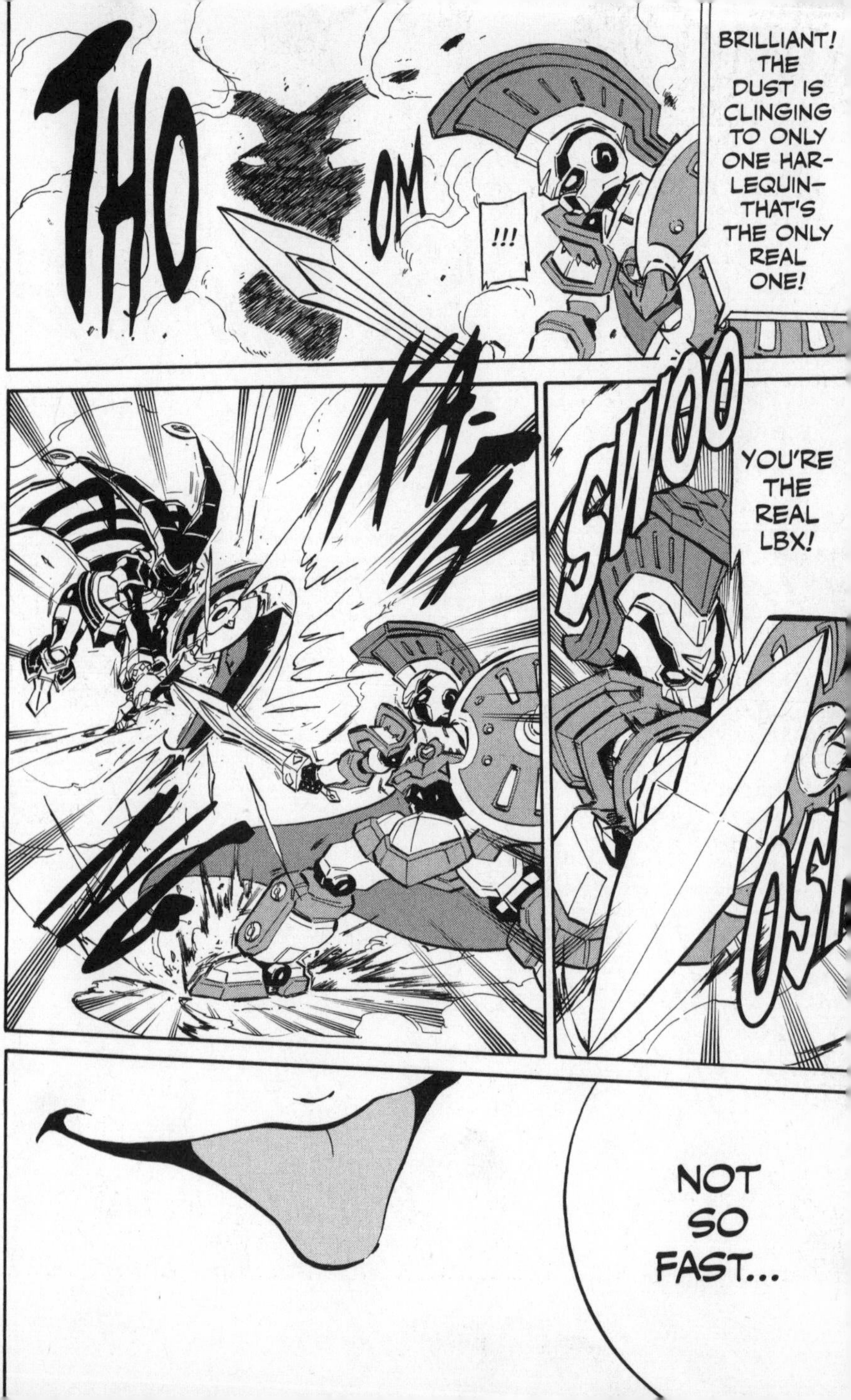
BRILLIANT! THE DUST IS CLINGING TO ONLY ONE HAR-LEQUIN—THAT'S THE ONLY REAL ONE!
!!!
THO OM
SWOO
YOU'RE THE REAL LBX!
KA-
NOT SO FAST...

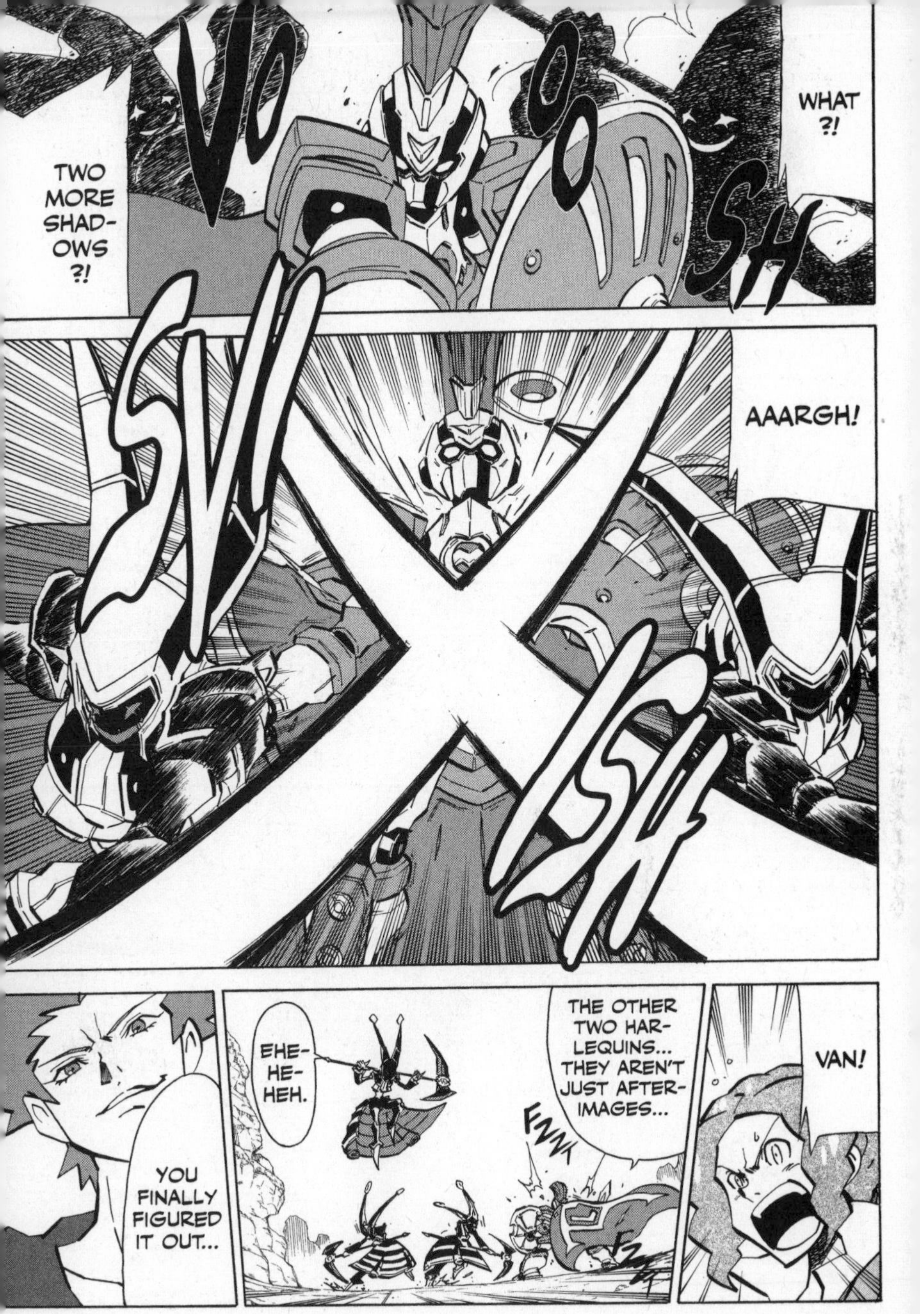
WHAT ?!
VOOOSH
TWO MORE SHADOWS ?!
AAARGH!
SWISH
VAN!
THE OTHER TWO HARLEQUINS... THEY AREN'T JUST AFTERIMAGES...
EHEHEHEH.
YOU FINALLY FIGURED IT OUT...

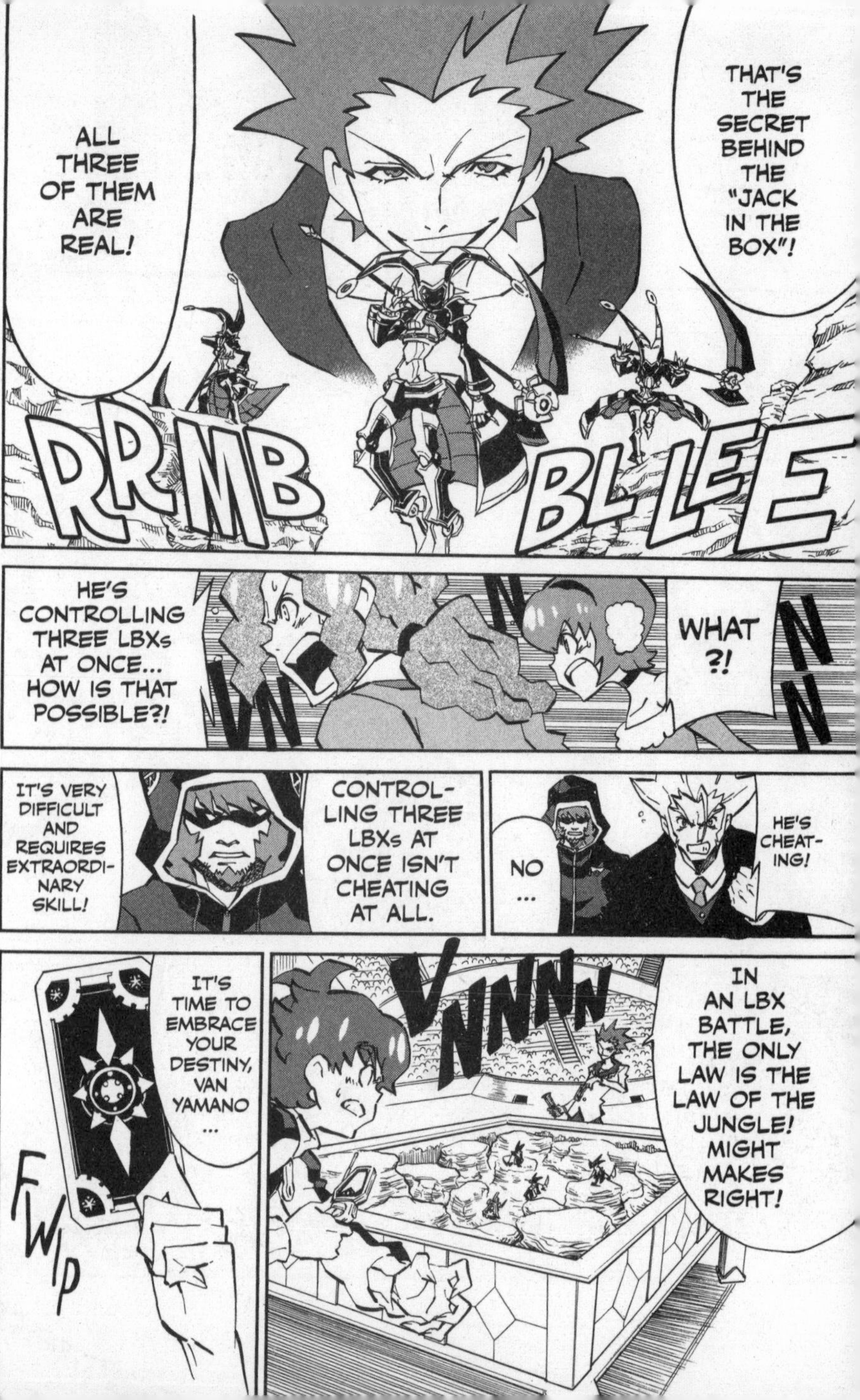
THAT'S THE SECRET BEHIND THE "JACK IN THE BOX"!
ALL THREE OF THEM ARE REAL!
RRMB BLLEE
WHAT?!
HE'S CONTROLLING THREE LBXs AT ONCE... HOW IS THAT POSSIBLE?!
HE'S CHEATING!
NO ...
CONTROLLING THREE LBXs AT ONCE ISN'T CHEATING AT ALL.
IT'S VERY DIFFICULT AND REQUIRES EXTRAORDINARY SKILL!
VNNNN
IN AN LBX BATTLE, THE ONLY LAW IS THE LAW OF THE JUNGLE! MIGHT MAKES RIGHT!
IT'S TIME TO EMBRACE YOUR DESTINY, VAN YAMANO ...
FWIP

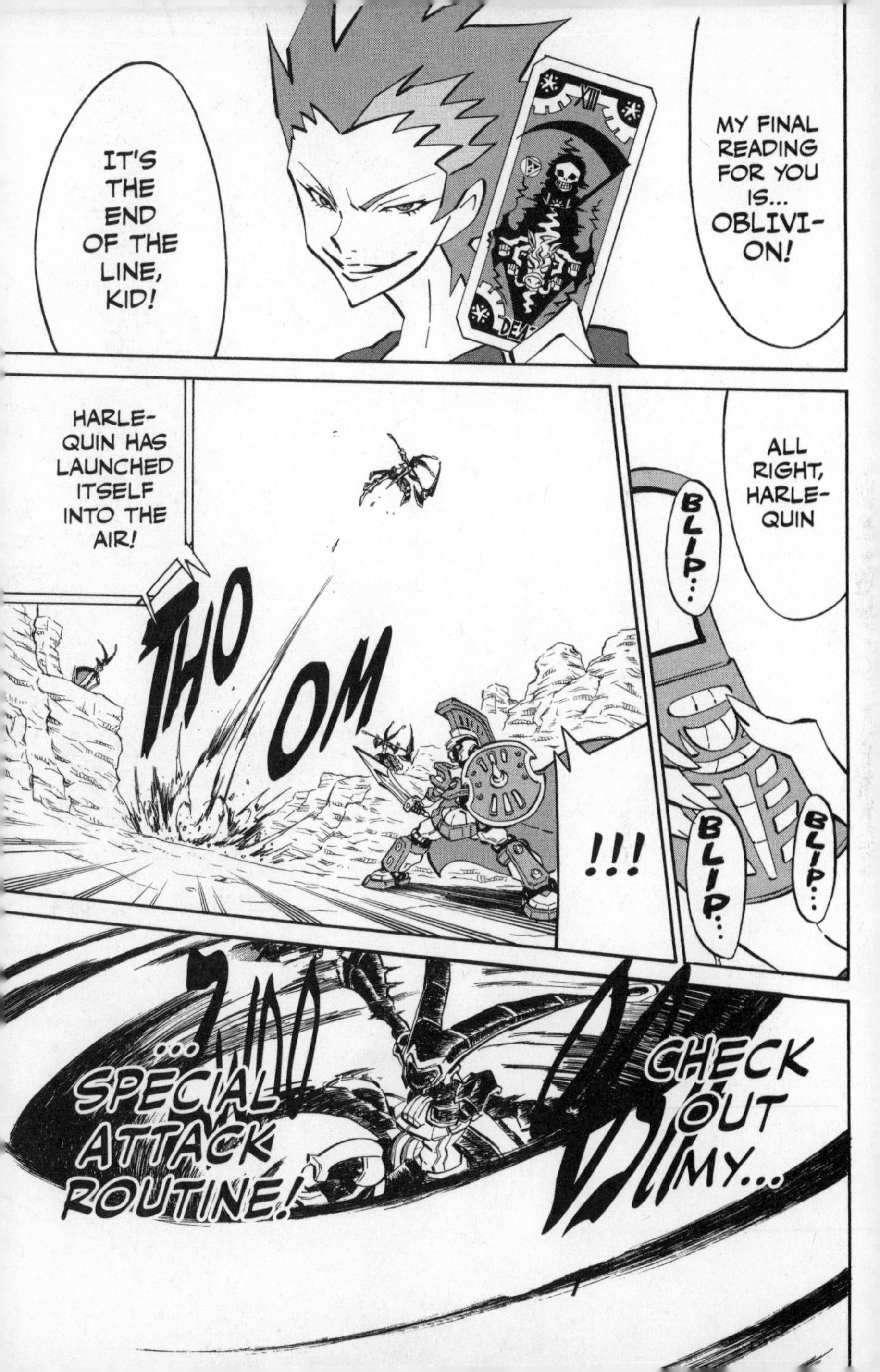
MY FINAL READING FOR YOU IS... OBLIVI-ON!
IT'S THE END OF THE LINE, KID!
ALL RIGHT, HARLE-QUIN
BLIP...
BLIP...
BLIP...
HARLE-QUIN HAS LAUNCHED ITSELF INTO THE AIR!
THOOM
!!!
CHECK OUT MY...
...SPECIAL ATTACK ROUTINE!

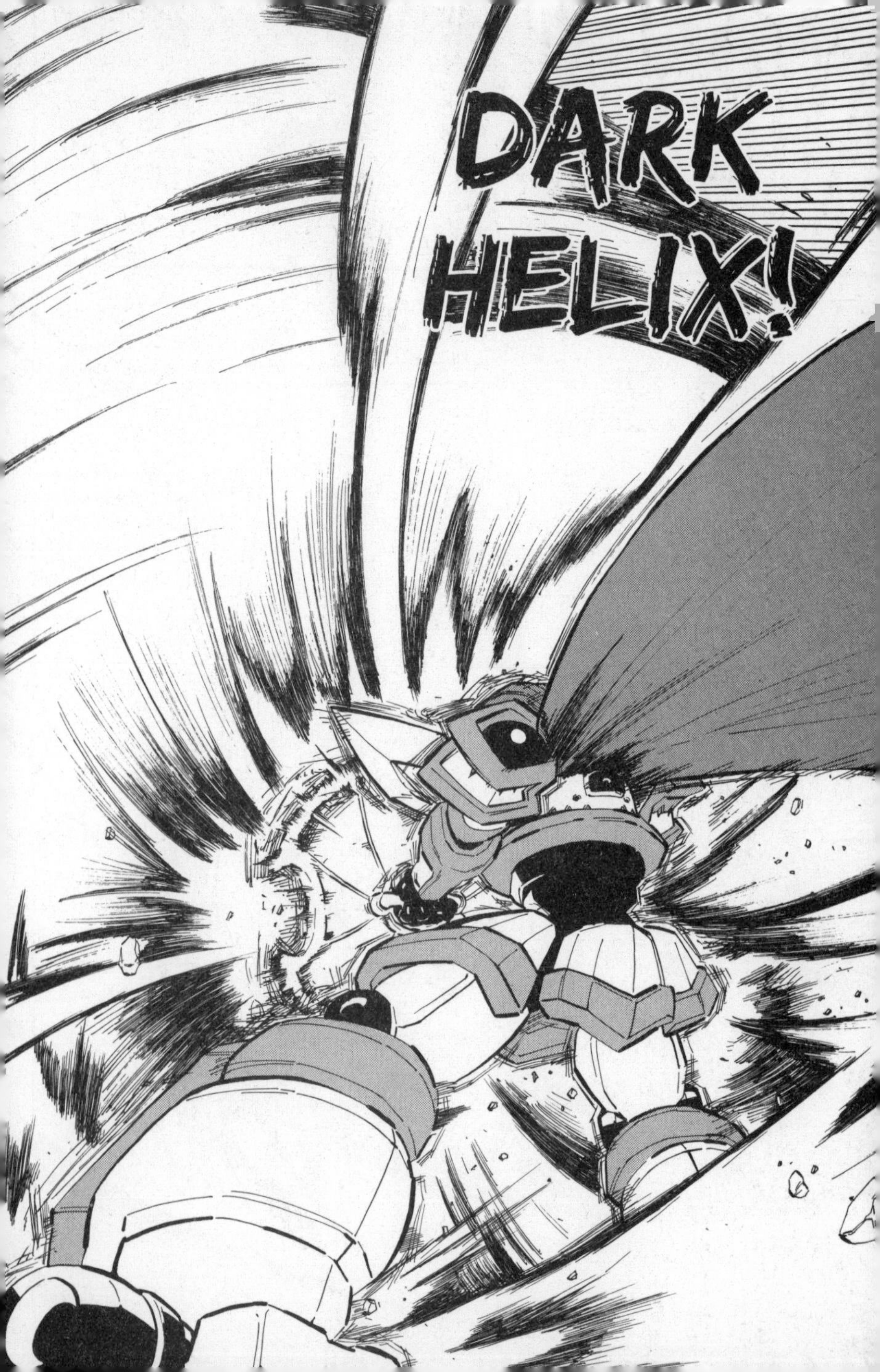
DARK HELIX!

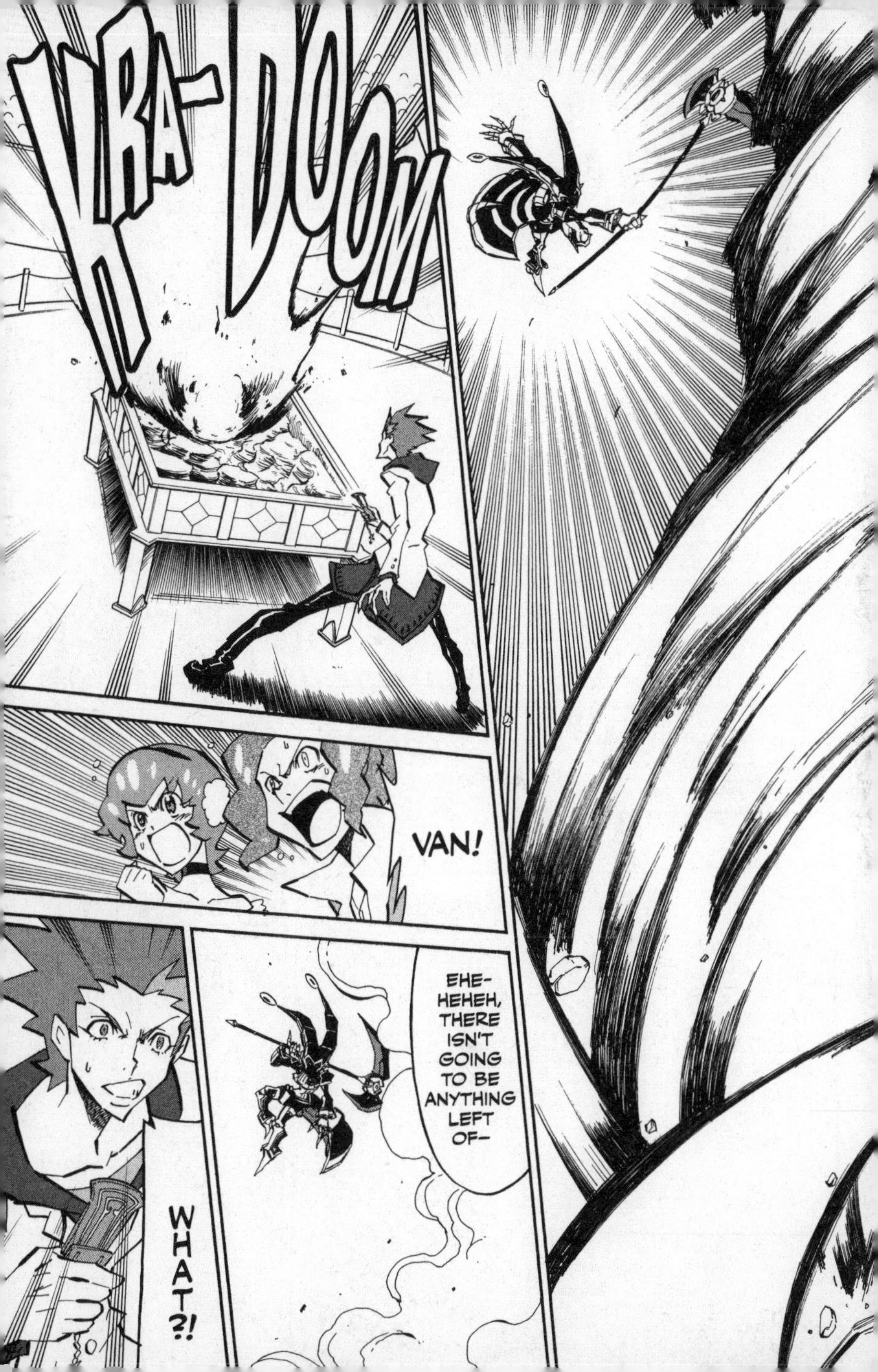
KRA-DOOM
VAN!
EHE-HEHEH, THERE ISN'T GOING TO BE ANYTHING LEFT OF-
WHAT?!

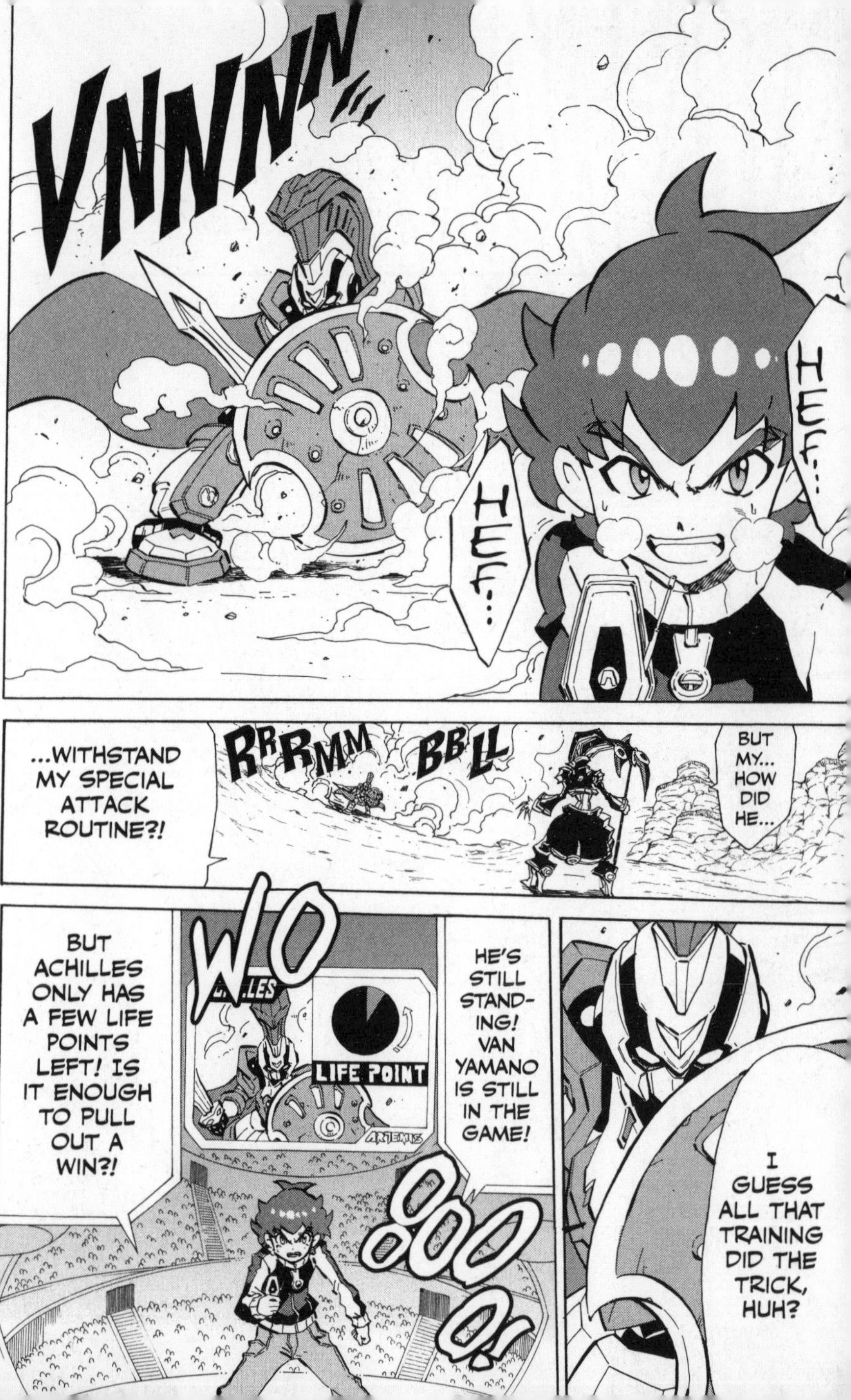
VNNNN
HEF...
HEF...
BUT MY... HOW DID HE...
RRRMM
BBLL
...WITHSTAND MY SPECIAL ATTACK ROUTINE?!
I GUESS ALL THAT TRAINING DID THE TRICK, HUH?
WOOOO!
HE'S STILL STAND-ING! VAN YAMANO IS STILL IN THE GAME!
LIFE POINT
ARTEMIS
BUT ACHILLES ONLY HAS A FEW LIFE POINTS LEFT! IS IT ENOUGH TO PULL OUT A WIN?!

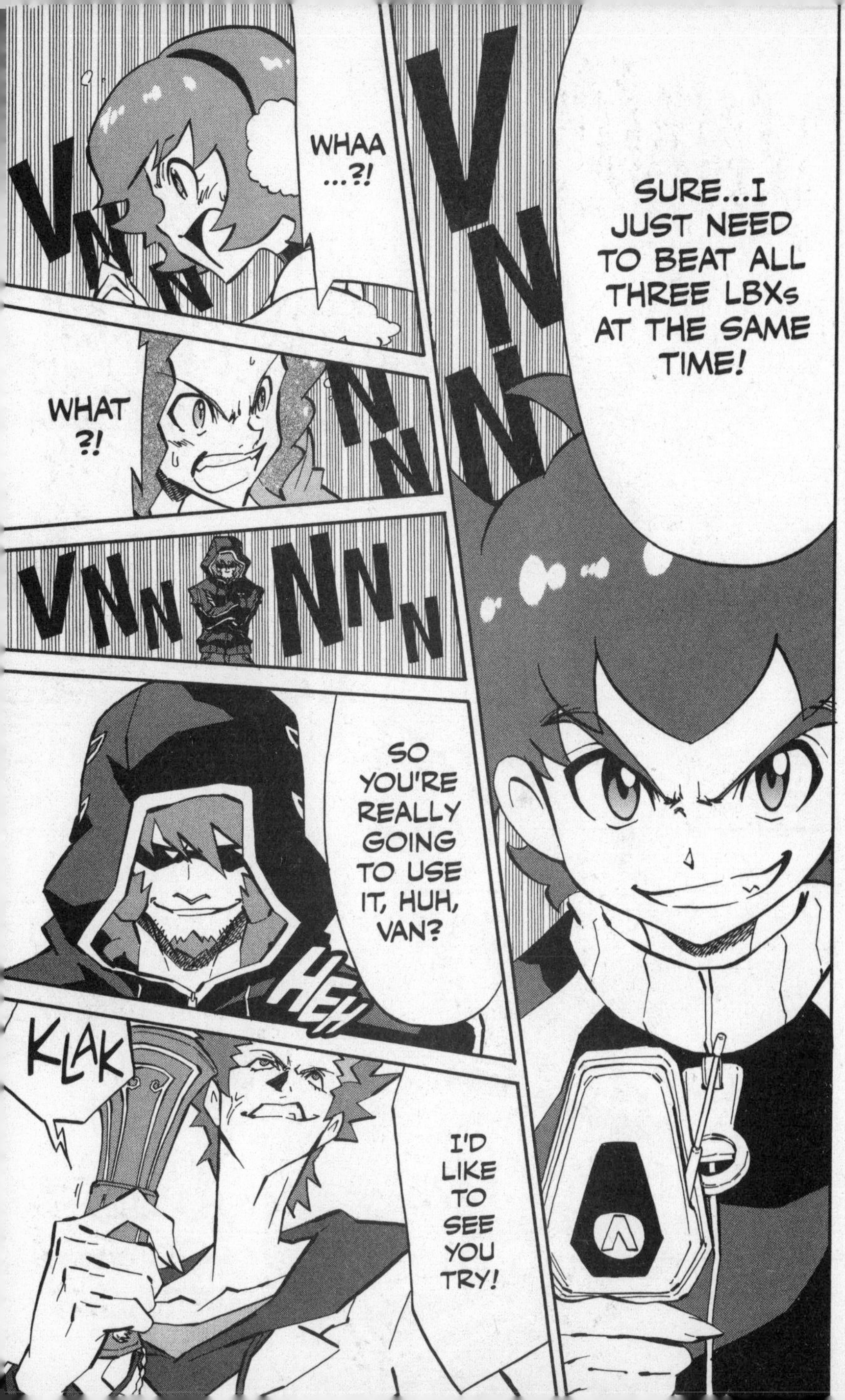
VNNN
SURE...I JUST NEED TO BEAT ALL THREE LBXs AT THE SAME TIME!
VNN
WHAA ...?!
WHAT ?!
VNN NNNN
SO YOU'RE REALLY GOING TO USE IT, HUH, VAN?
HEH
KLAK
I'D LIKE TO SEE YOU TRY!

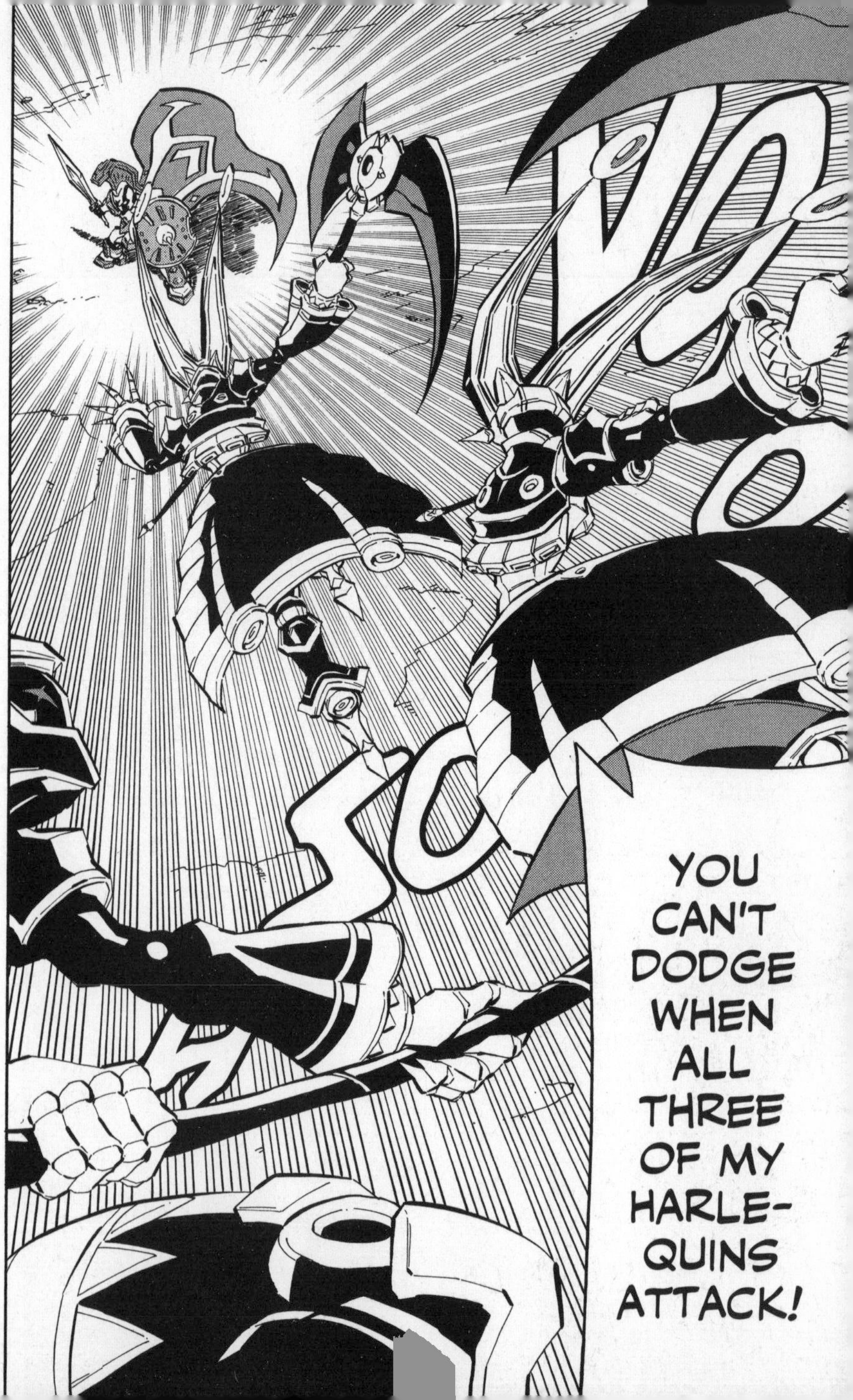
YOU CAN'T DODGE WHEN ALL THREE OF MY HARLE-QUINS ATTACK!

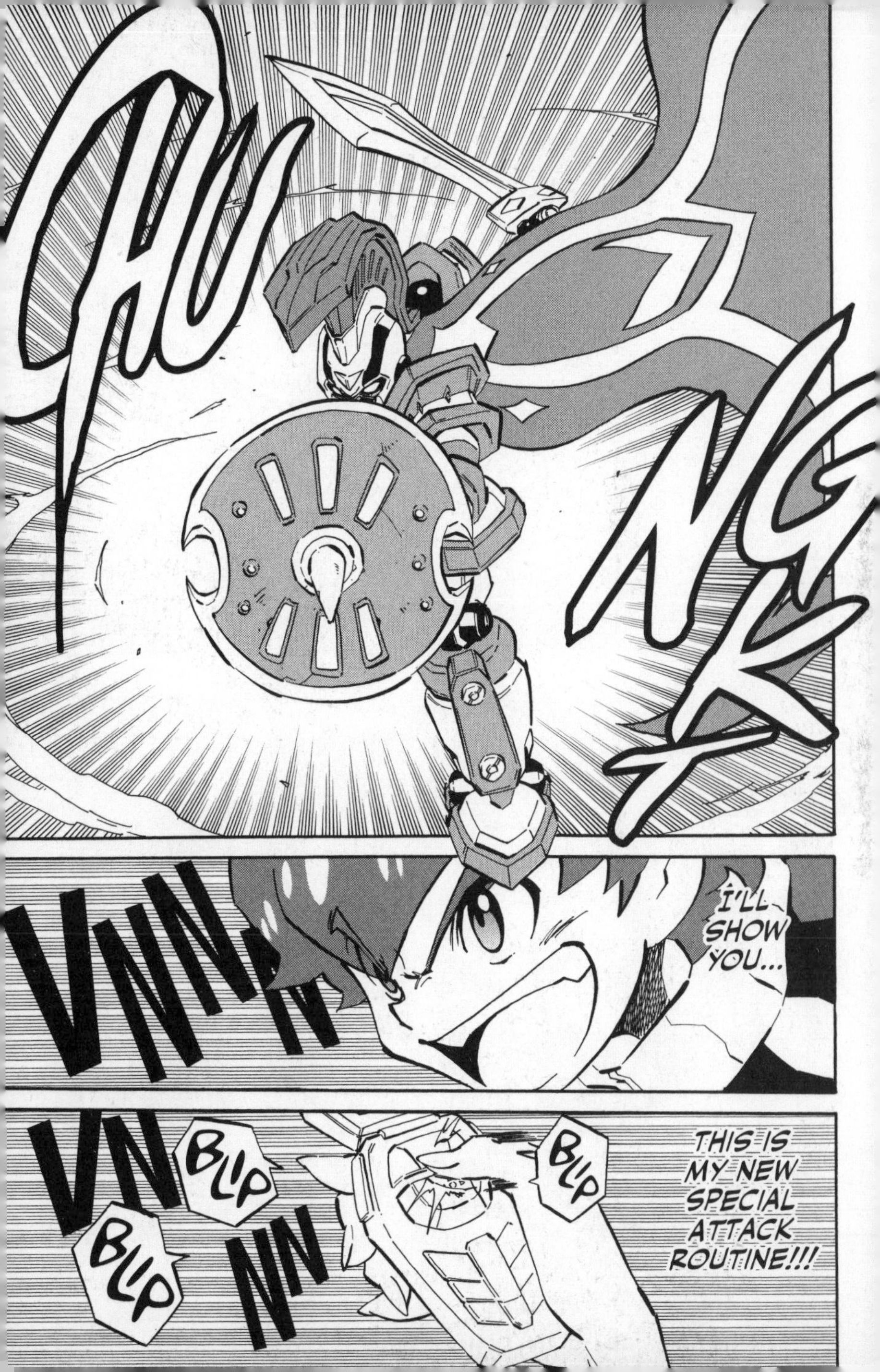
I'LL SHOW YOU...
THIS IS MY NEW SPECIAL ATTACK ROUTINE!!!
BLIP
BLIP
BLIP

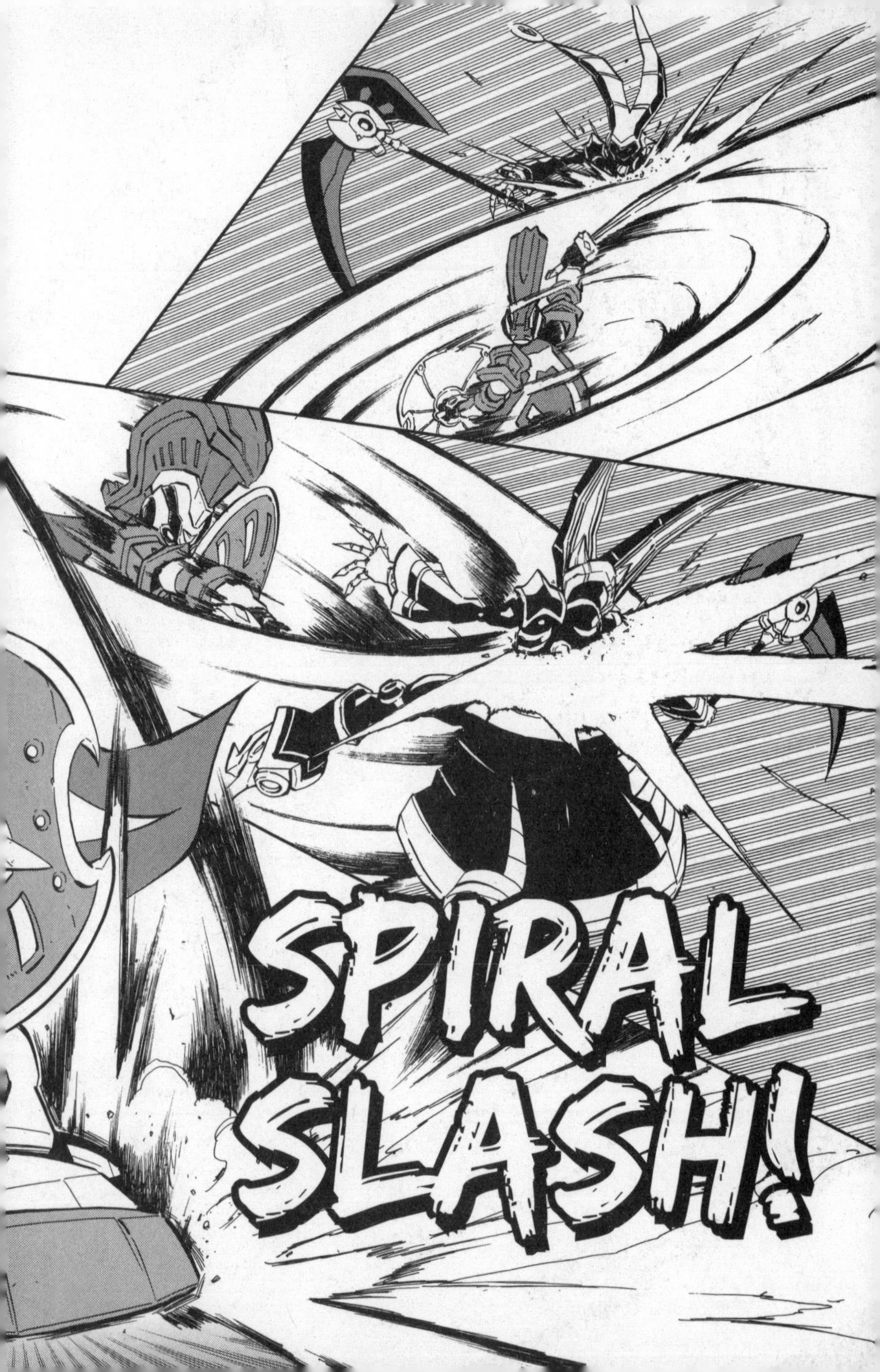
SPIRAL SLASH!

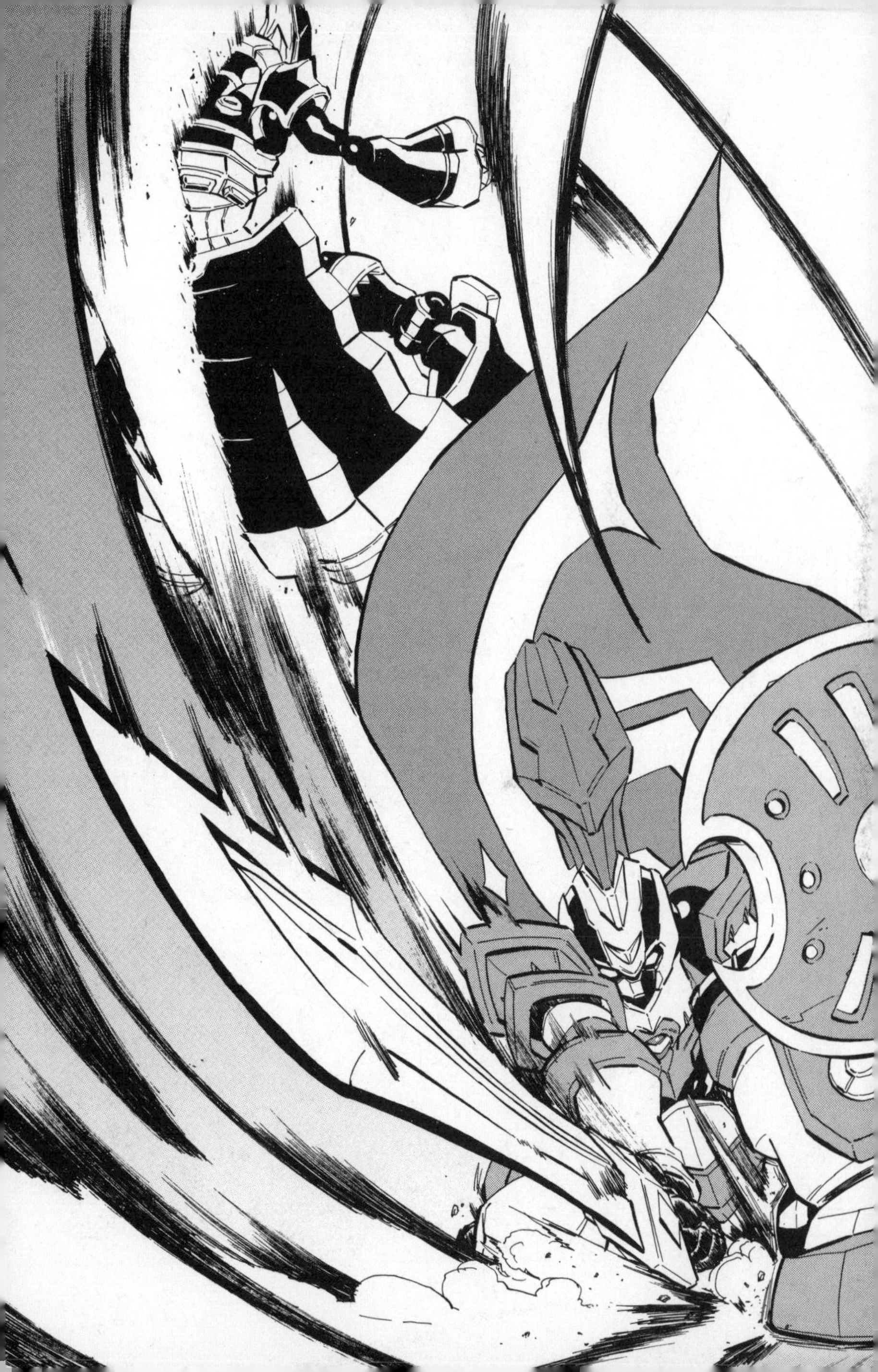

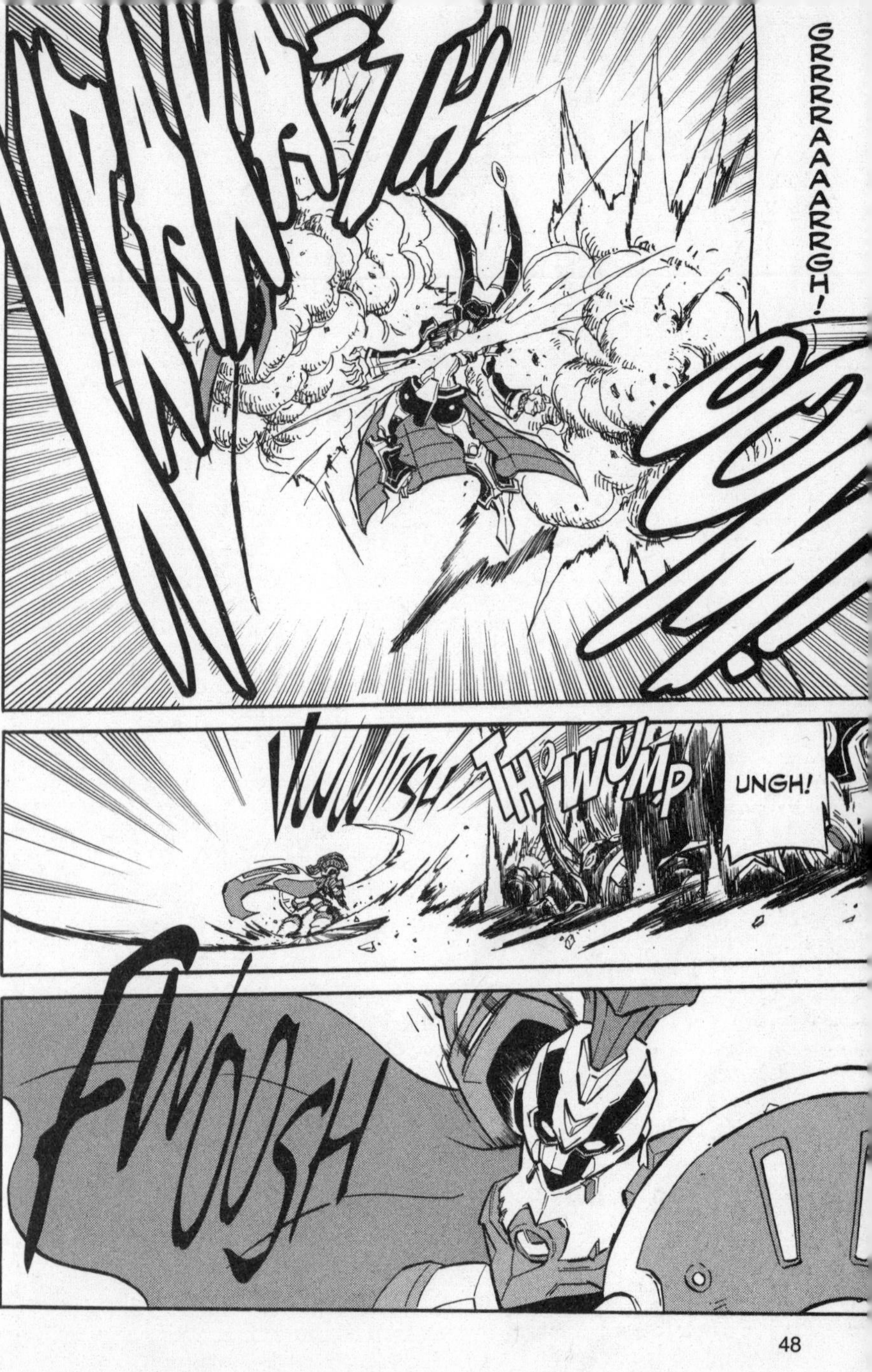
GRRRRAAAARRGH!
UNGH!
THWUMP
FWOOSH

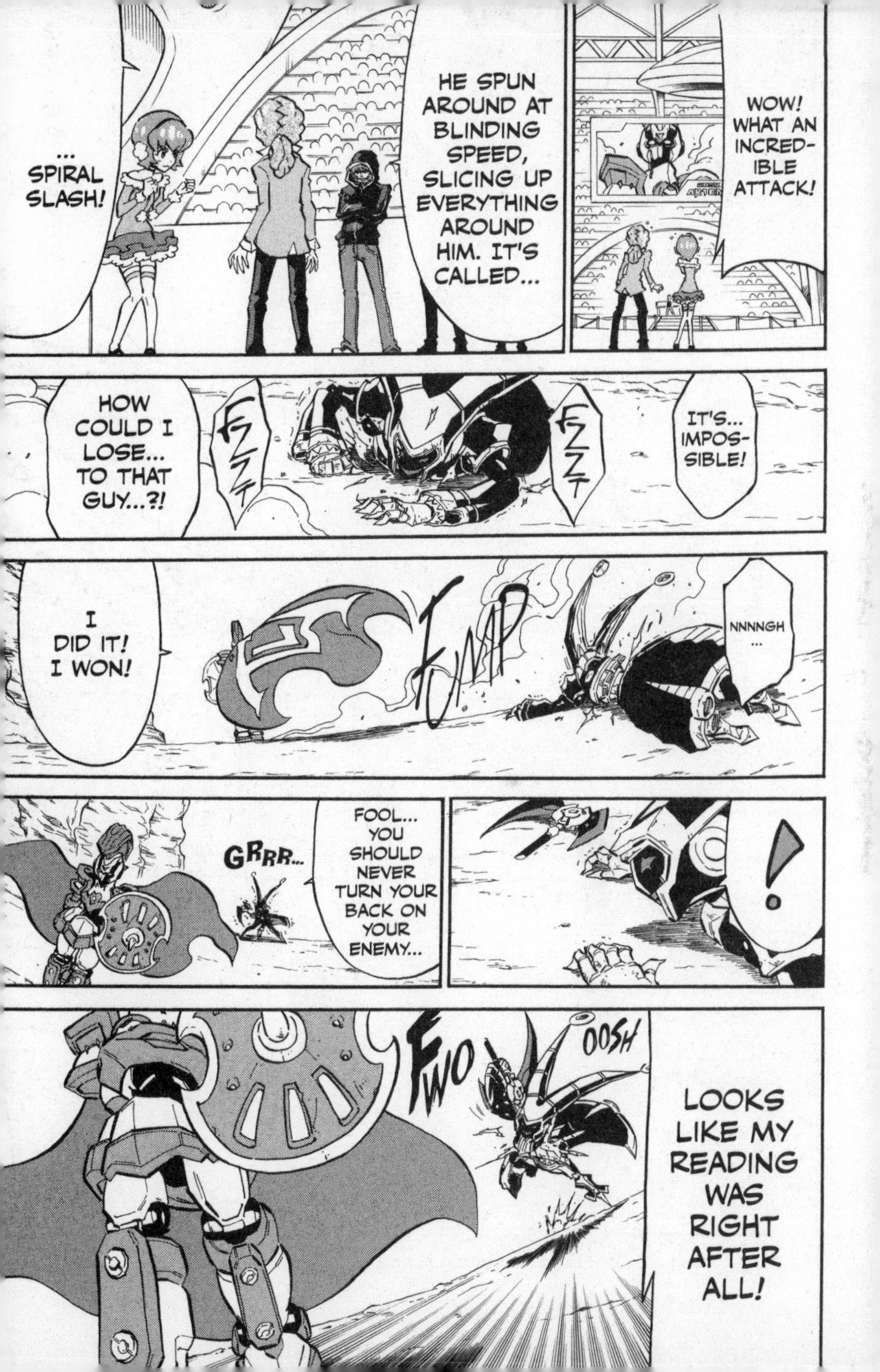
WOW! WHAT AN INCRED-IBLE ATTACK!
HE SPUN AROUND AT BLINDING SPEED, SLICING UP EVERYTHING AROUND HIM. IT'S CALLED...
... SPIRAL SLASH!
IT'S... IMPOS-SIBLE!
FZZT
FZZT
HOW COULD I LOSE... TO THAT GUY...?!
NNNNGH...
FUMP
I DID IT! I WON!
!
FOOL... YOU SHOULD NEVER TURN YOUR BACK ON YOUR ENEMY...
GRRR...
LOOKS LIKE MY READING WAS RIGHT AFTER ALL!
FWOOOSH

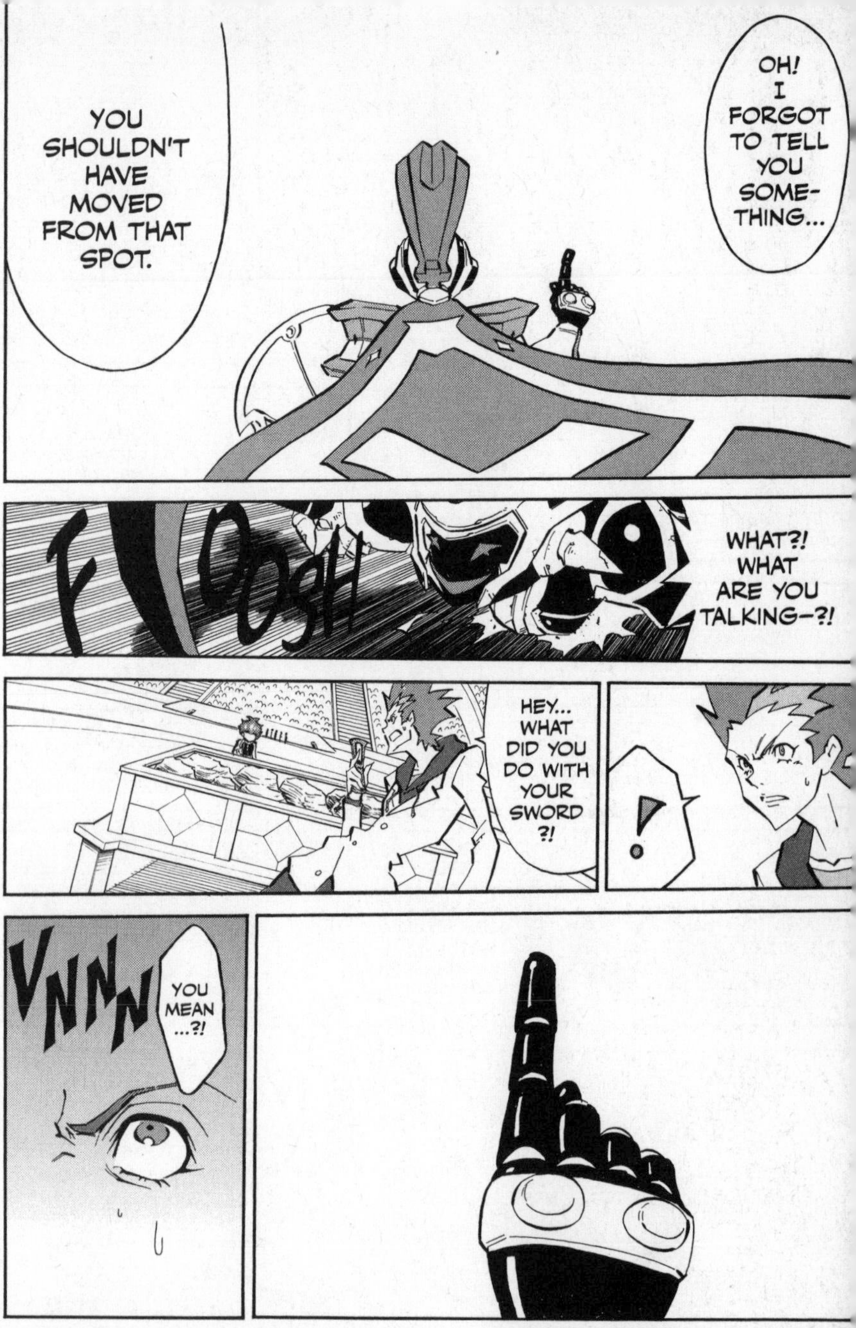
OH! I FORGOT TO TELL YOU SOME-THING...
YOU SHOULDN'T HAVE MOVED FROM THAT SPOT.
WHAT?! WHAT ARE YOU TALKING-?!
FOOSH
!
HEY... WHAT DID YOU DO WITH YOUR SWORD ?!
YOU MEAN ...?!
VNNN

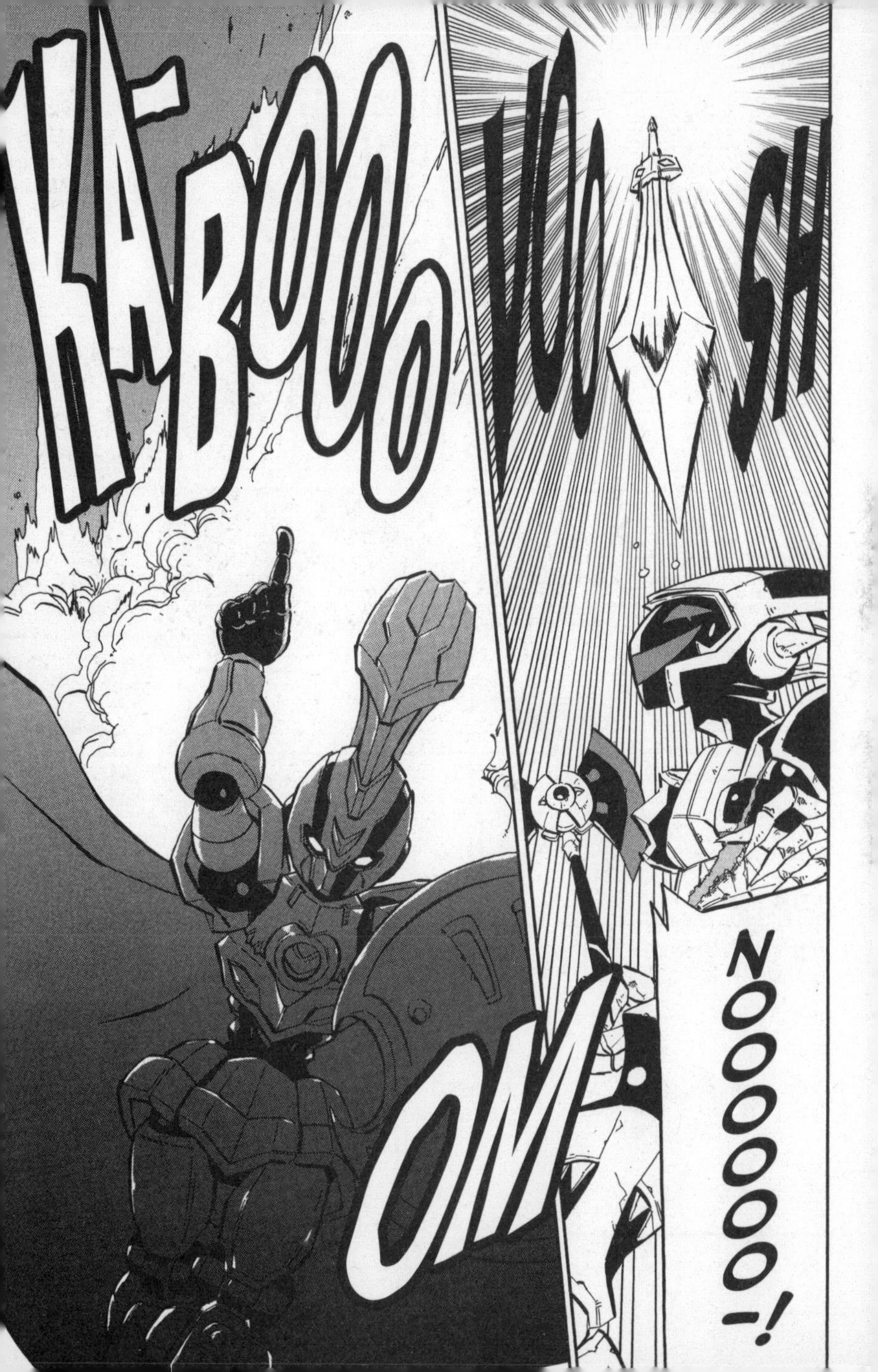
VOOSH
NOOOOOO-!
KA-BOOOOOM

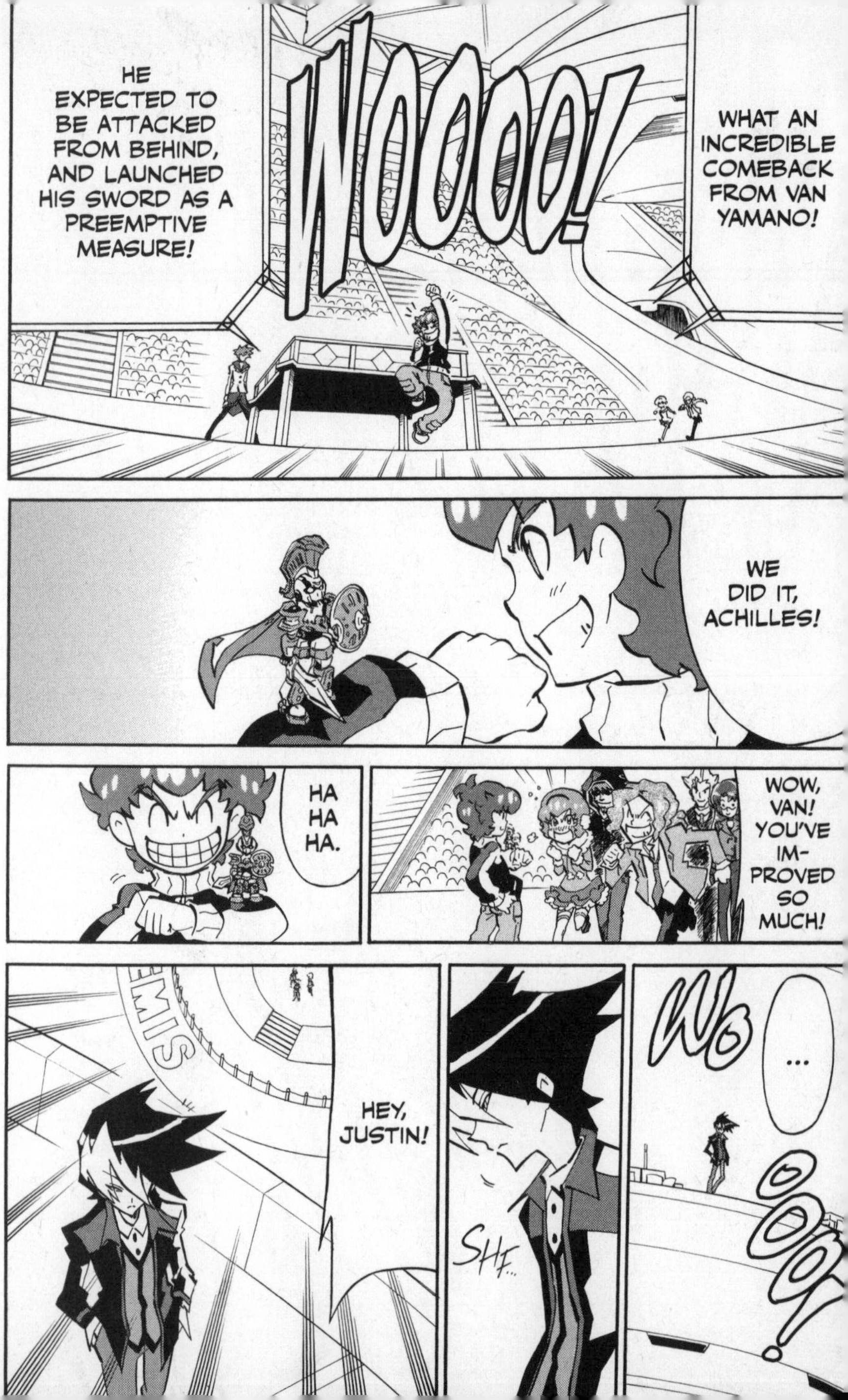
WHAT AN INCREDIBLE COMEBACK FROM VAN YAMANO!
WOOOO!
HE EXPECTED TO BE ATTACKED FROM BEHIND, AND LAUNCHED HIS SWORD AS A PREEMPTIVE MEASURE!
WE DID IT, ACHILLES!
WOW, VAN! YOU'VE IM-PROVED SO MUCH!
HA HA HA.
WO
...
OOO!
SHF...
HEY, JUSTIN!
EMIS

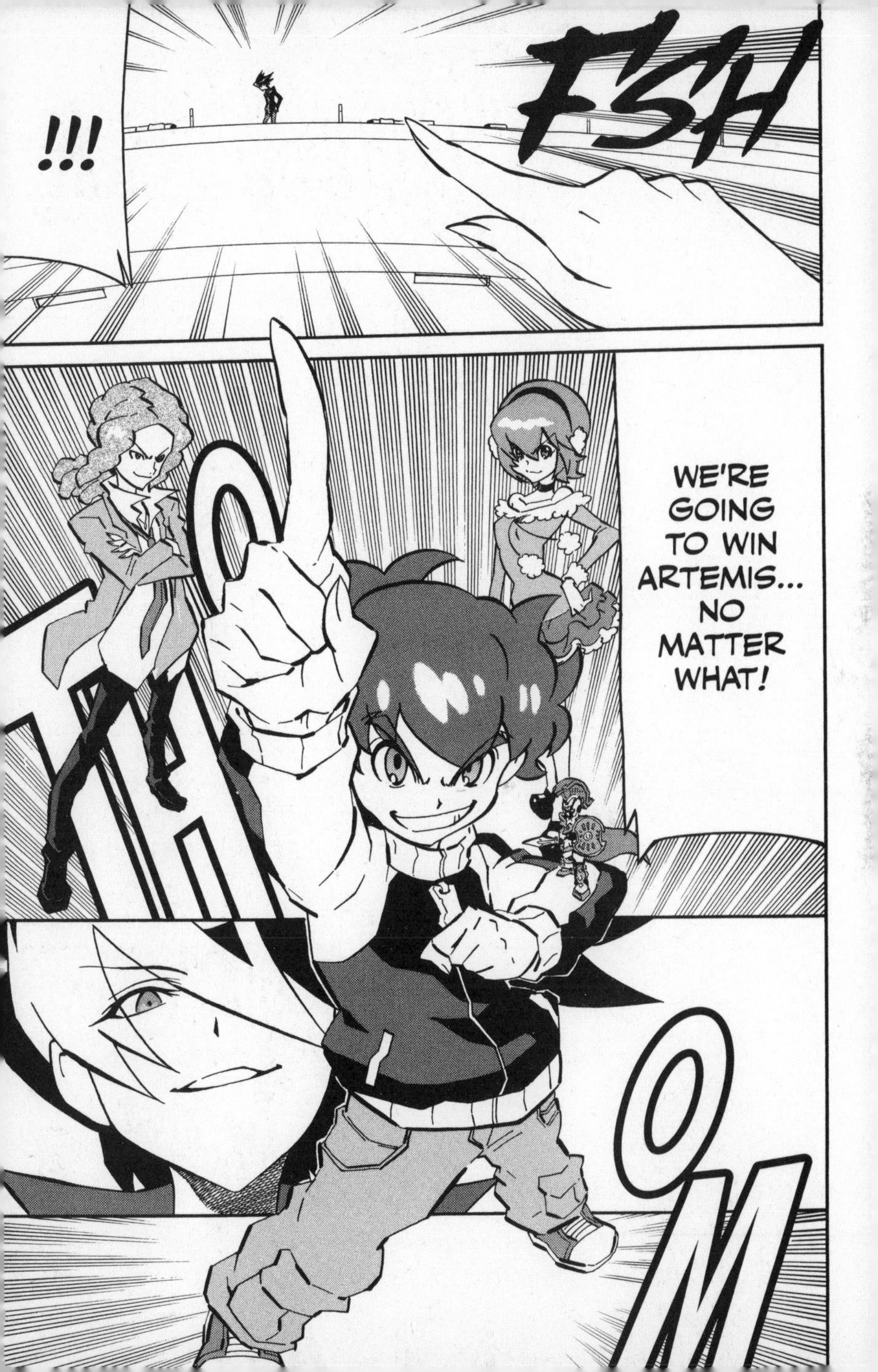
FSH
!!!
WE'RE GOING TO WIN ARTEMIS... NO MATTER WHAT!
OM

CHAPTER 6: THE MYSTERIOUS NILS RICHTER

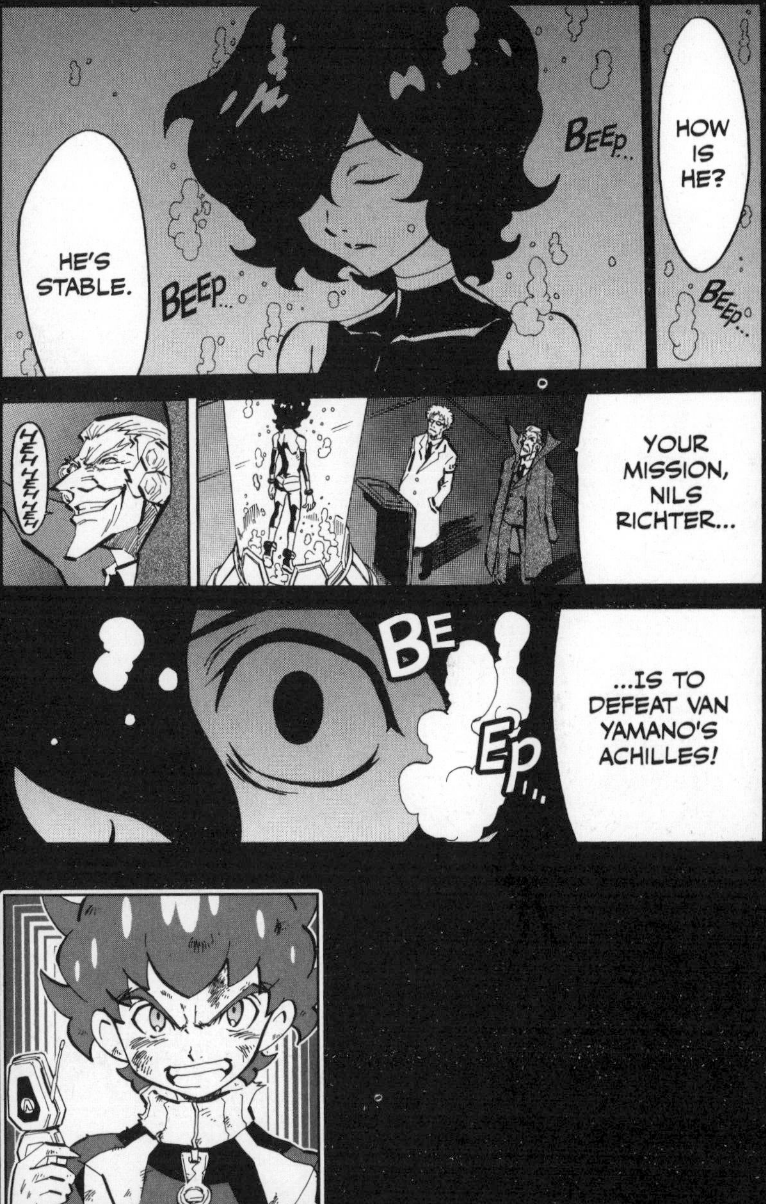
HOW IS HE?
BEEP...
BEEP...
HE'S STABLE.
BEEP...
YOUR MISSION, NILS RICHTER...
HEHHEHHEH
...IS TO DEFEAT VAN YAMANO'S ACHILLES!
BEEEP...

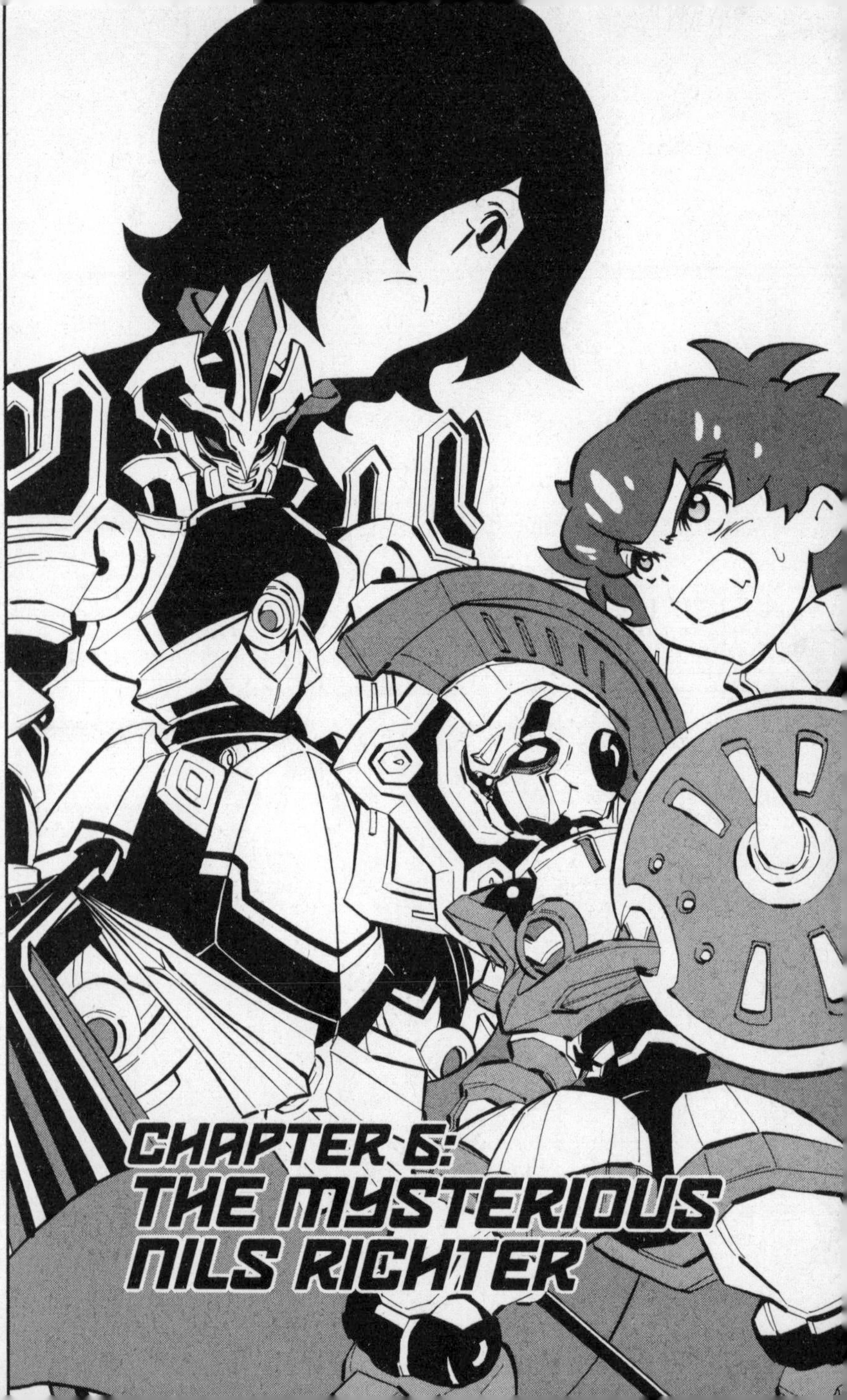
CHAPTER 6:
THE MYSTERIOUS
NILS RICHTER

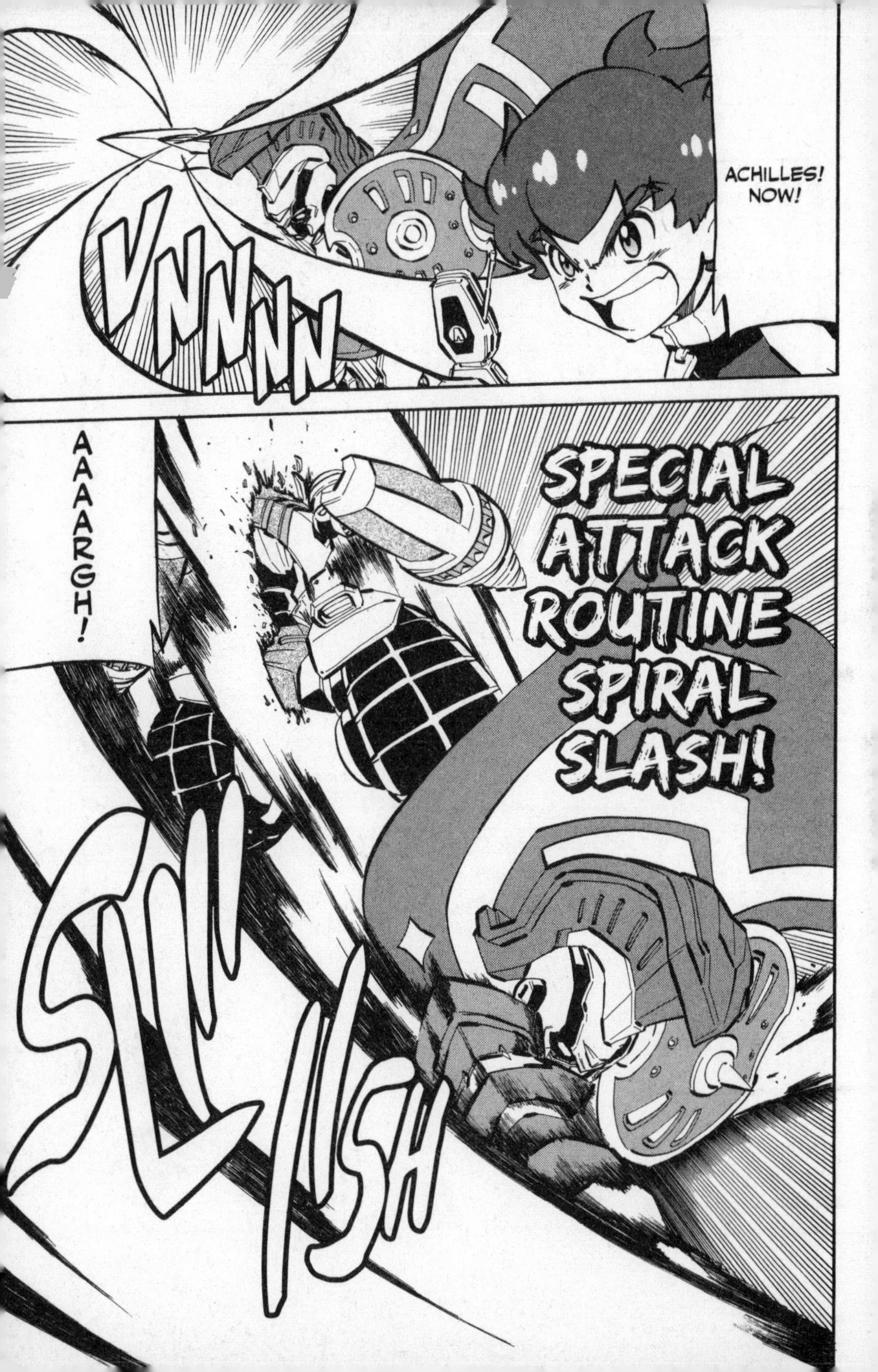
ACHILLES! NOW!
VNNNNN
SPECIAL ATTACK ROUTINE SPIRAL SLASH!
AAAARGH!
SLASH

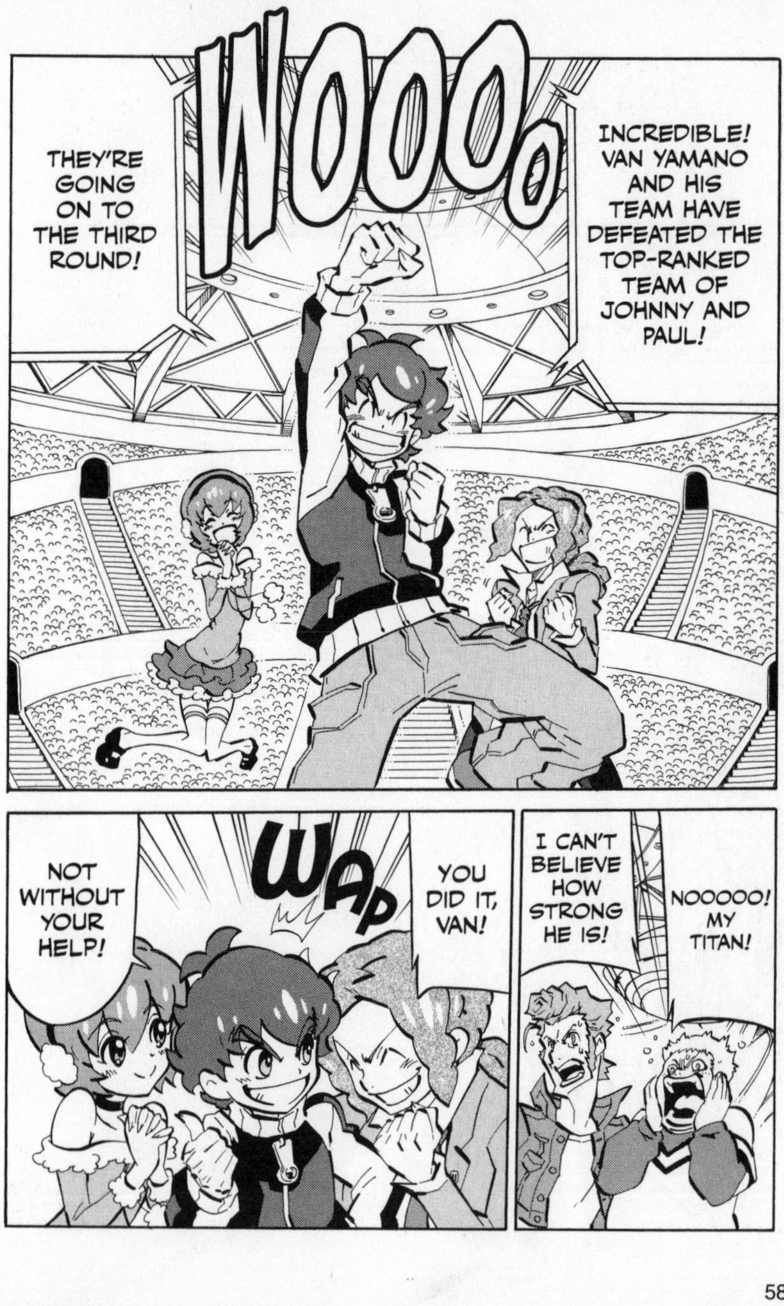
WOOOO
INCREDIBLE! VAN YAMANO AND HIS TEAM HAVE DEFEATED THE TOP-RANKED TEAM OF JOHNNY AND PAUL!
THEY'RE GOING ON TO THE THIRD ROUND!
NOOOOO! MY TITAN!
I CAN'T BELIEVE HOW STRONG HE IS!
YOU DID IT, VAN!
WAP
NOT WITHOUT YOUR HELP!

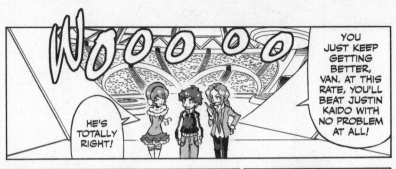

YOU JUST KEEP GETTING BETTER, VAN. AT THIS RATE, YOU'LL BEAT JUSTIN KAIDO WITH NO PROBLEM AT ALL!
WOOOOOO
HE'S TOTALLY RIGHT!
NO...
I'M STILL NOT GOOD ENOUGH. NOT YET AT LEAST.
WHAT?!
IT'S TRUE.
EVEN AFTER ALL MY TRAINING, I COULDN'T MASTER THE MOST POWERFUL SPECIAL ATTACK ROUTINE!
WHAT SPECIAL ATTACK ROUTINE IS THAT?!

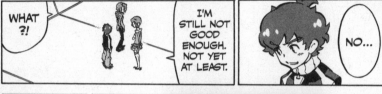

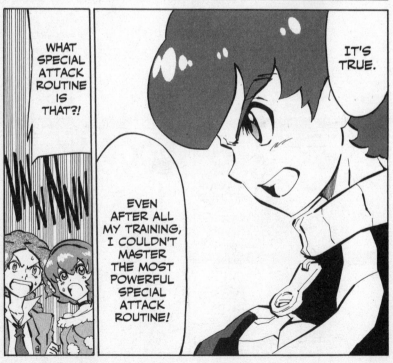

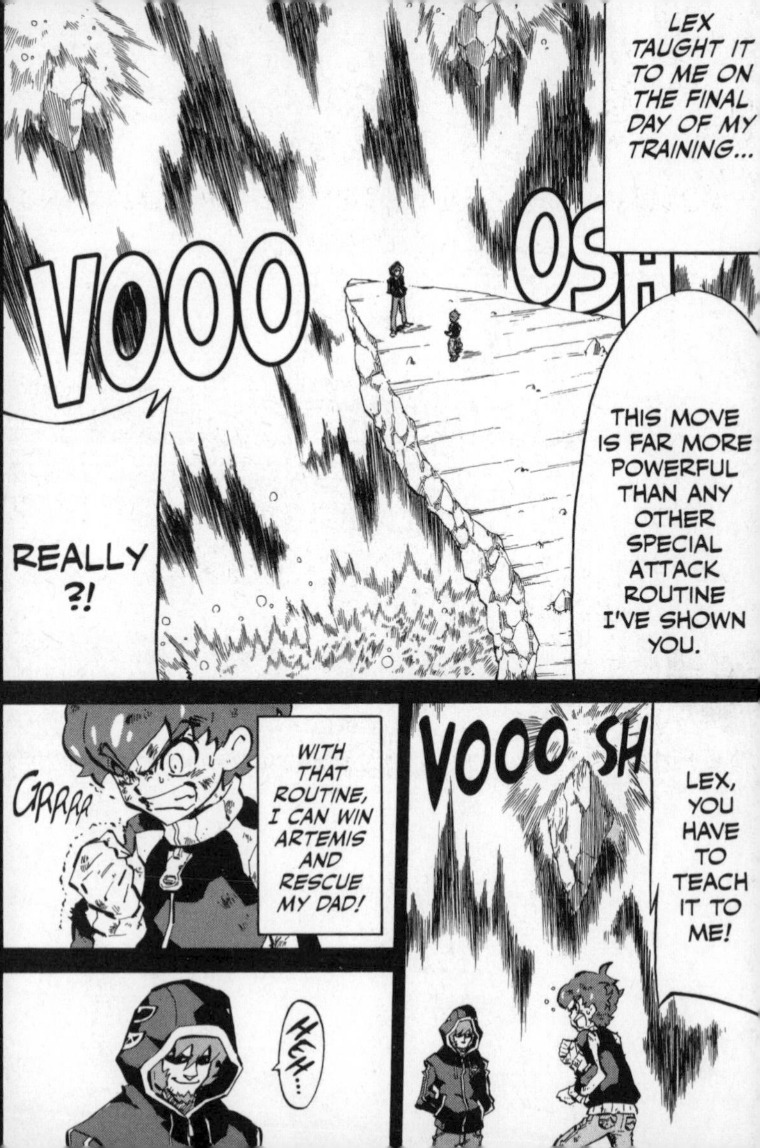
LEX TAUGHT IT TO ME ON THE FINAL DAY OF MY TRAINING...
VOOOOSH
THIS MOVE IS FAR MORE POWERFUL THAN ANY OTHER SPECIAL ATTACK ROUTINE I'VE SHOWN YOU.
REALLY ?!
VOOOSH
LEX, YOU HAVE TO TEACH IT TO ME!
WITH THAT ROUTINE, I CAN WIN ARTEMIS AND RESCUE MY DAD!
GRRRR
HEH...

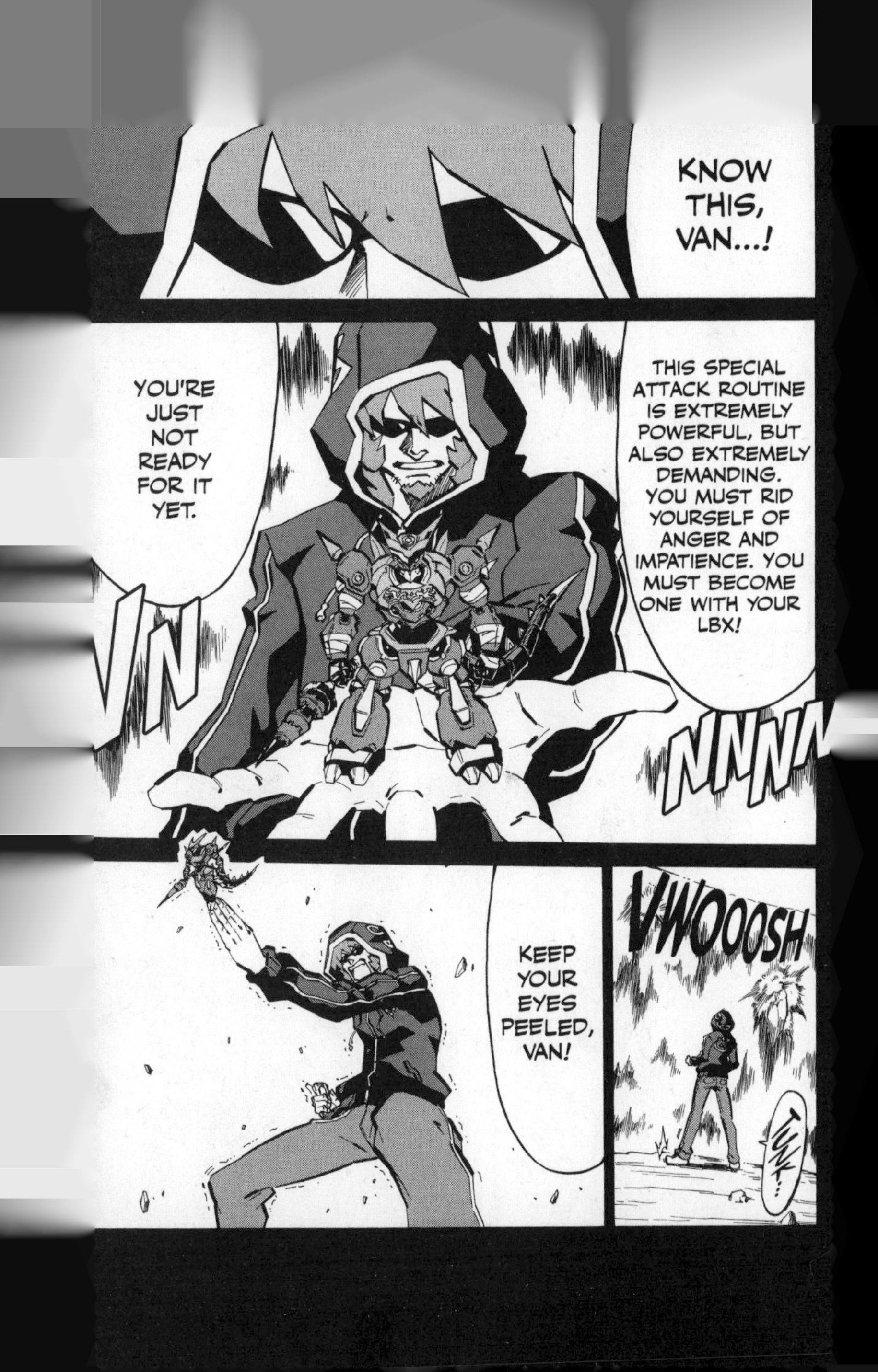
KNOW THIS, VAN...!
THIS SPECIAL ATTACK ROUTINE IS EXTREMELY POWERFUL, BUT ALSO EXTREMELY DEMANDING. YOU MUST RID YOURSELF OF ANGER AND IMPATIENCE. YOU MUST BECOME ONE WITH YOUR LBX!
YOU'RE JUST NOT READY FOR IT YET.
NNNN
VN
VWOOOSH
TUNK...
KEEP YOUR EYES PEELED, VAN!

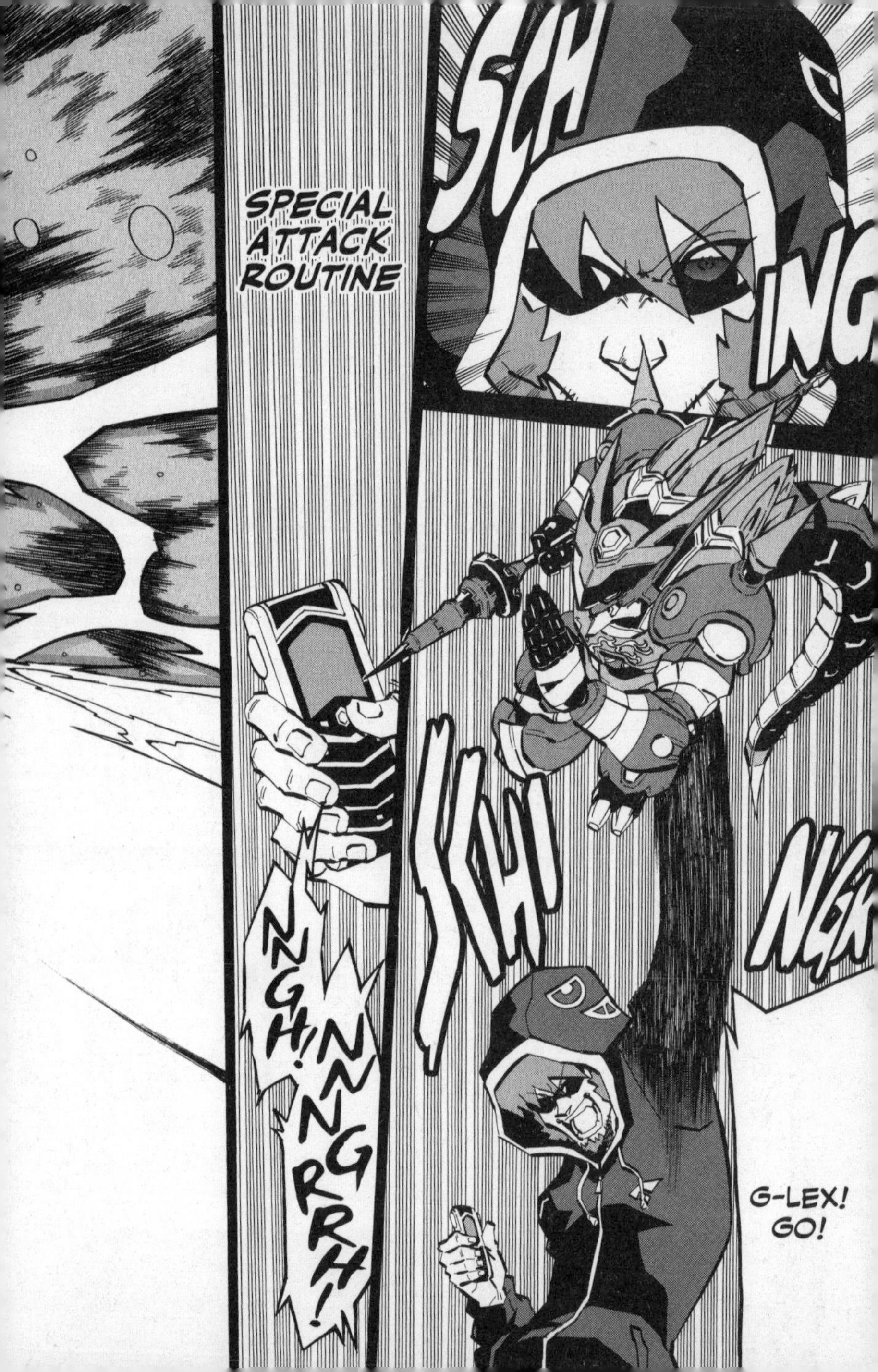
SCHING
G-LEX! GO!
SHH
SPECIAL ATTACK ROUTINE
NNGH!
NNNNGRRH!

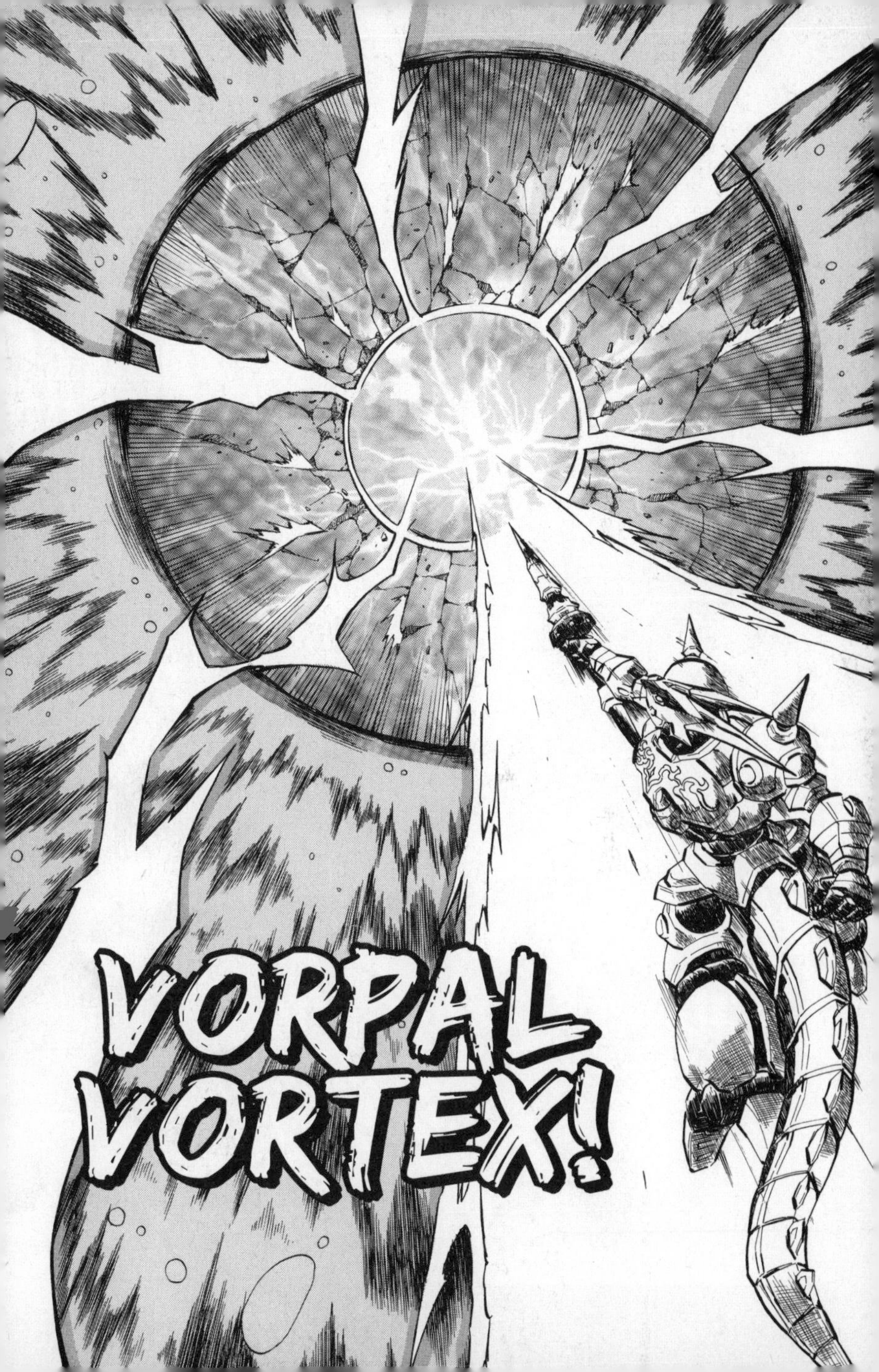
VORPAL VORTEX!

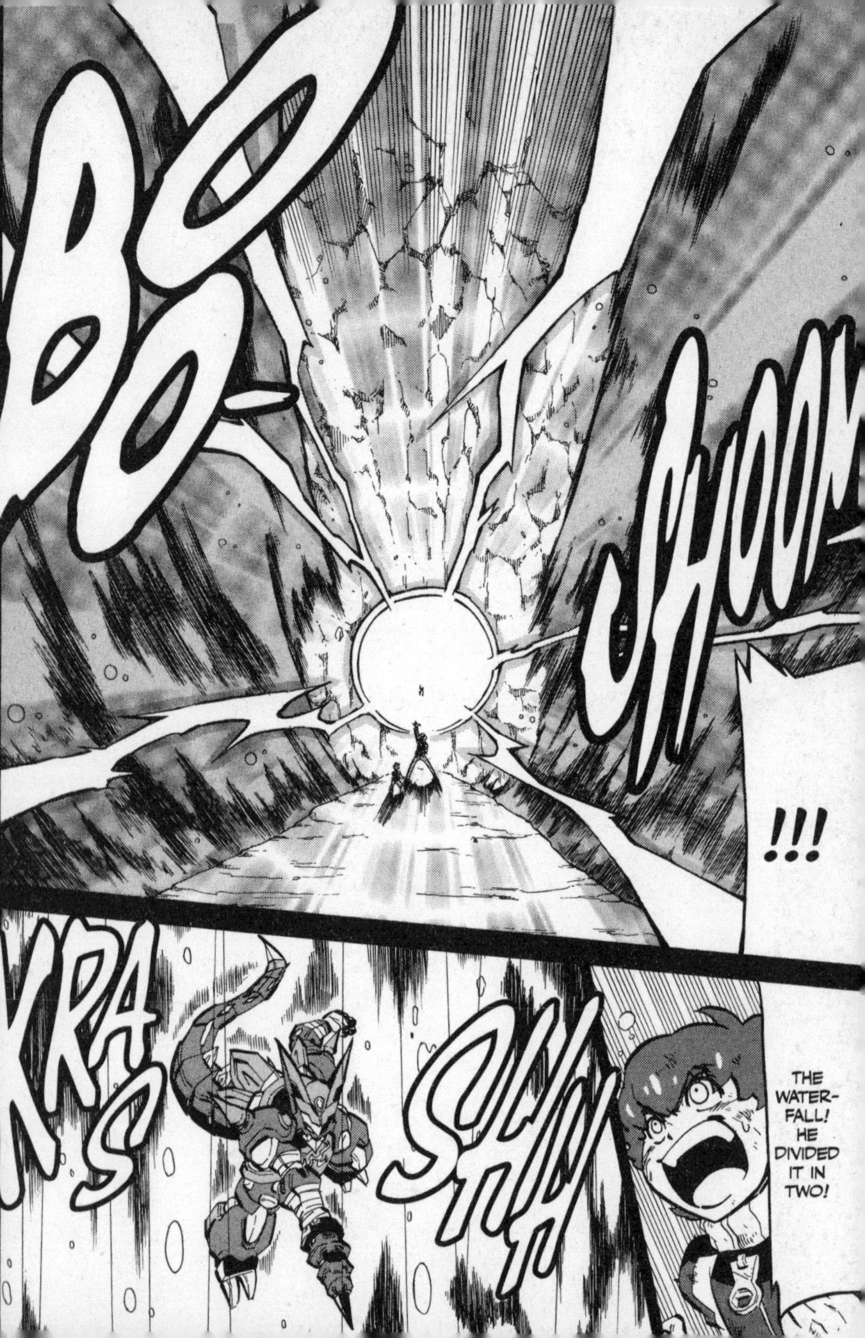
!!!
THE WATER-FALL! HE DIVIDED IT IN TWO!
KRASH

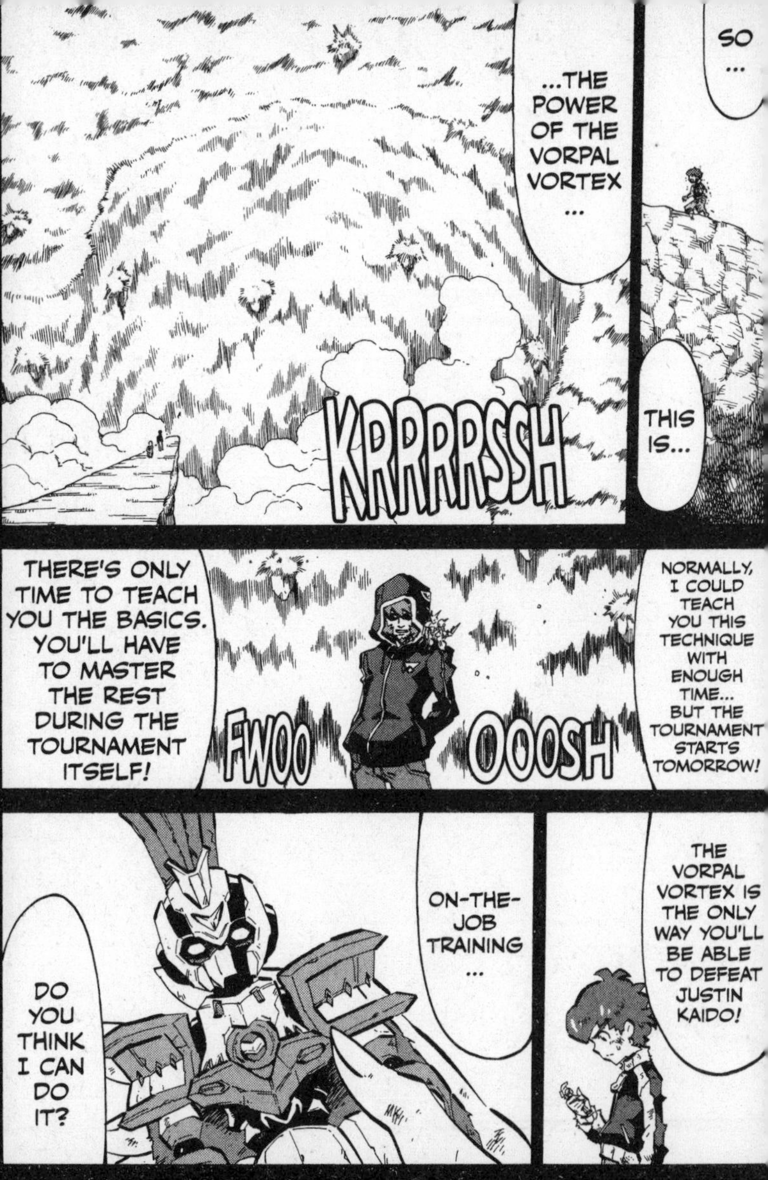
SO ...
THIS IS...
...THE POWER OF THE VORPAL VORTEX ...
KRRRRSSH
NORMALLY, I COULD TEACH YOU THIS TECHNIQUE WITH ENOUGH TIME... BUT THE TOURNAMENT STARTS TOMORROW!
FWOO OOOSH
THERE'S ONLY TIME TO TEACH YOU THE BASICS. YOU'LL HAVE TO MASTER THE REST DURING THE TOURNAMENT ITSELF!
THE VORPAL VORTEX IS THE ONLY WAY YOU'LL BE ABLE TO DEFEAT JUSTIN KAIDO!
ON-THE-JOB TRAINING ...
DO YOU THINK I CAN DO IT?

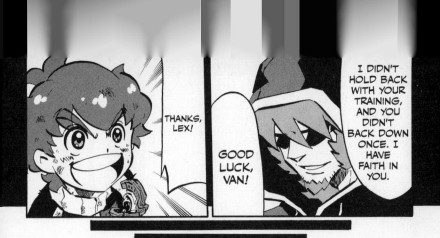

I DIDN'T HOLD BACK WITH YOUR TRAINING, AND YOU DIDN'T BACK DOWN ONCE. I HAVE FAITH IN YOU.
GOOD LUCK, VAN!
THANKS, LEX!
SO YOU'RE STILL WORKING ON YOUR FINAL MOVE?! I DON'T KNOW, VAN...
DON'T WORRY, I KNOW WHAT I NEED TO DO.
WHAT?
I JUST NEED TO FIGHT MORE SKILLED LBX PLAYERS!
C'MON! THE NEXT MATCH IS STARTING!
WOOOO

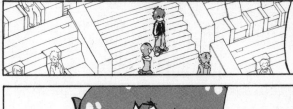

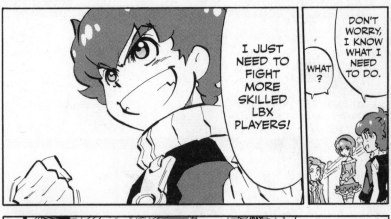

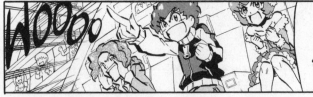

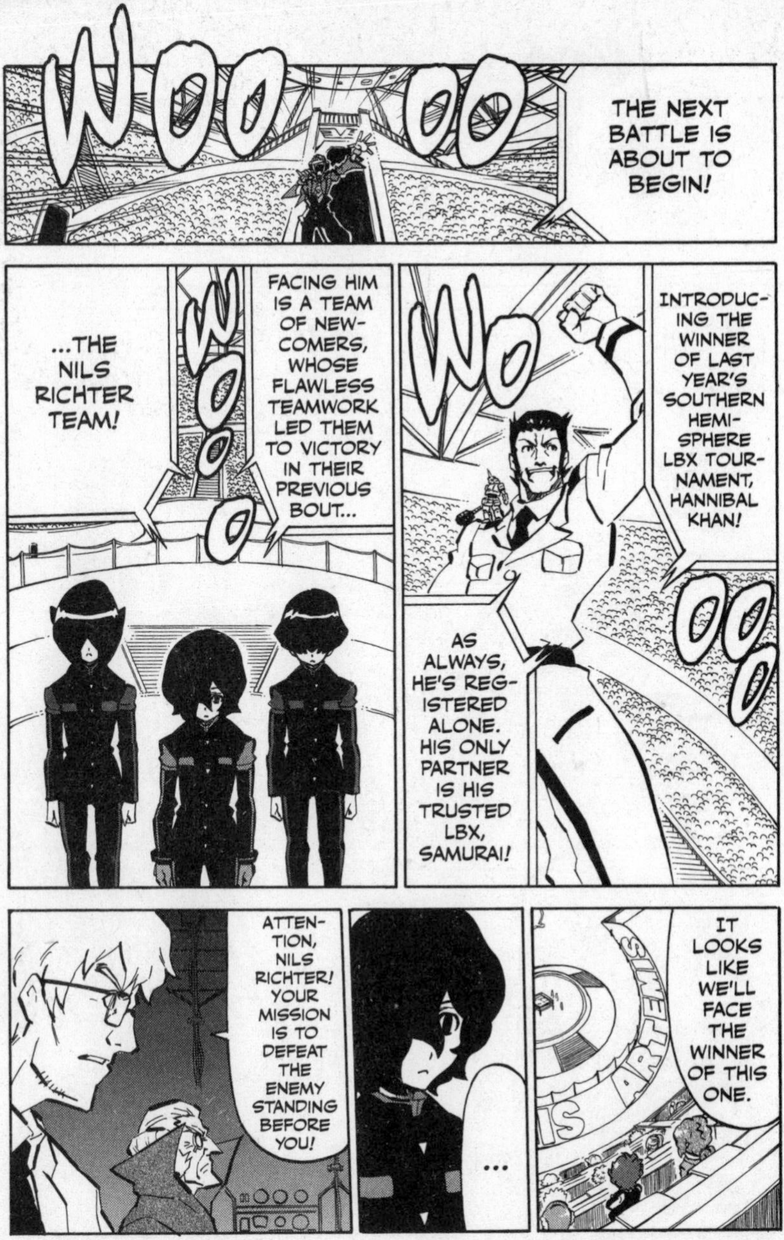
WOOOO
THE NEXT BATTLE IS ABOUT TO BEGIN!
WO
INTRODUCING THE WINNER OF LAST YEAR'S SOUTHERN HEMISPHERE LBX TOURNAMENT, HANNIBAL KHAN!
OOOO
AS ALWAYS, HE'S REGISTERED ALONE. HIS ONLY PARTNER IS HIS TRUSTED LBX, SAMURAI!
WOOOO
FACING HIM IS A TEAM OF NEWCOMERS, WHOSE FLAWLESS TEAMWORK LED THEM TO VICTORY IN THEIR PREVIOUS BOUT...
...THE NILS RICHTER TEAM!
ARTEMIS
IT LOOKS LIKE WE'LL FACE THE WINNER OF THIS ONE.
...
ATTENTION, NILS RICHTER! YOUR MISSION IS TO DEFEAT THE ENEMY STANDING BEFORE YOU!

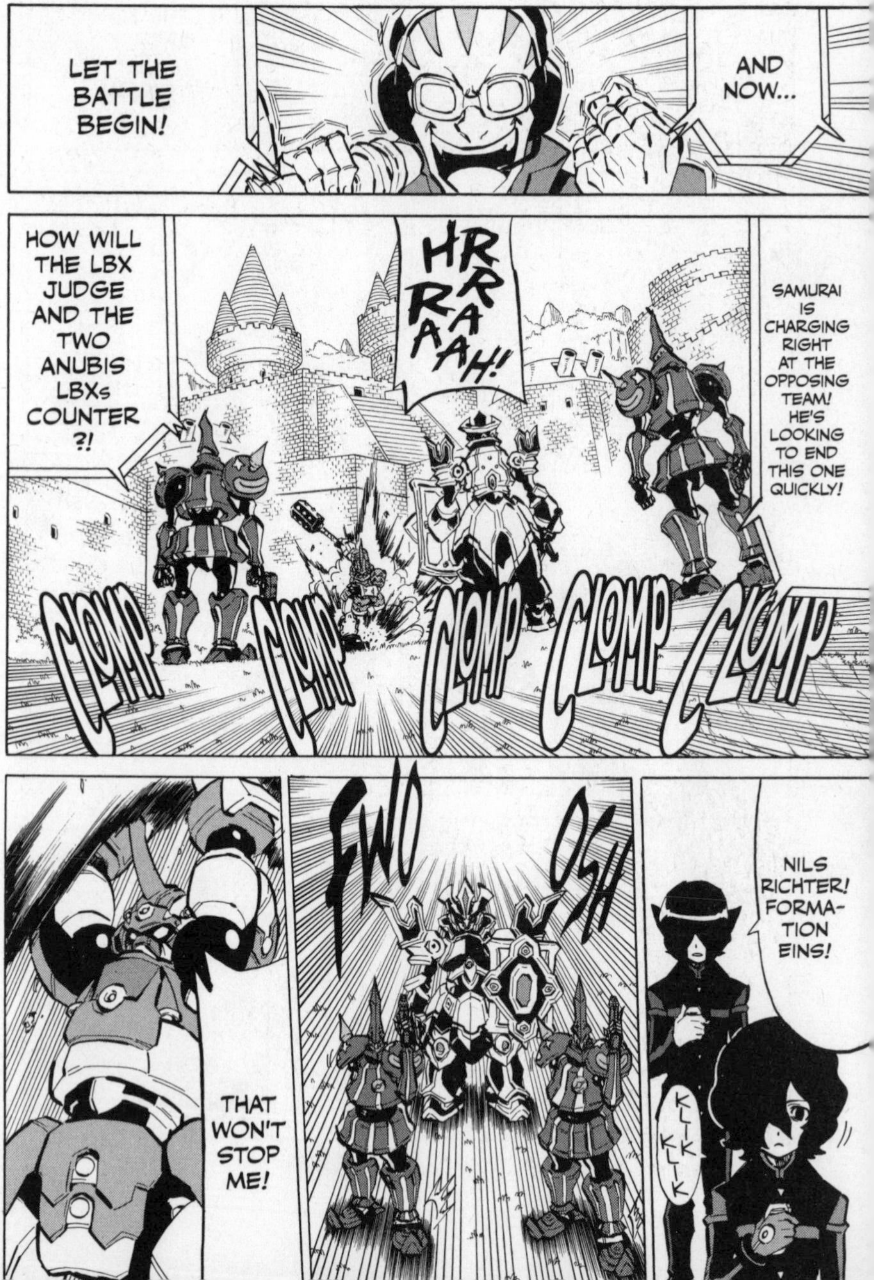
AND NOW...
LET THE BATTLE BEGIN!
SAMURAI IS CHARGING RIGHT AT THE OPPOSING TEAM! HE'S LOOKING TO END THIS ONE QUICKLY!
HRRRAAAH!
HOW WILL THE LBX JUDGE AND THE TWO ANUBIS LBXs COUNTER ?!
CLOMP CLOMP CLOMP CLOMP CLOMP
NILS RICHTER! FORMATION EINS!
KLIK KLIK
FWOOSH
THAT WON'T STOP ME!

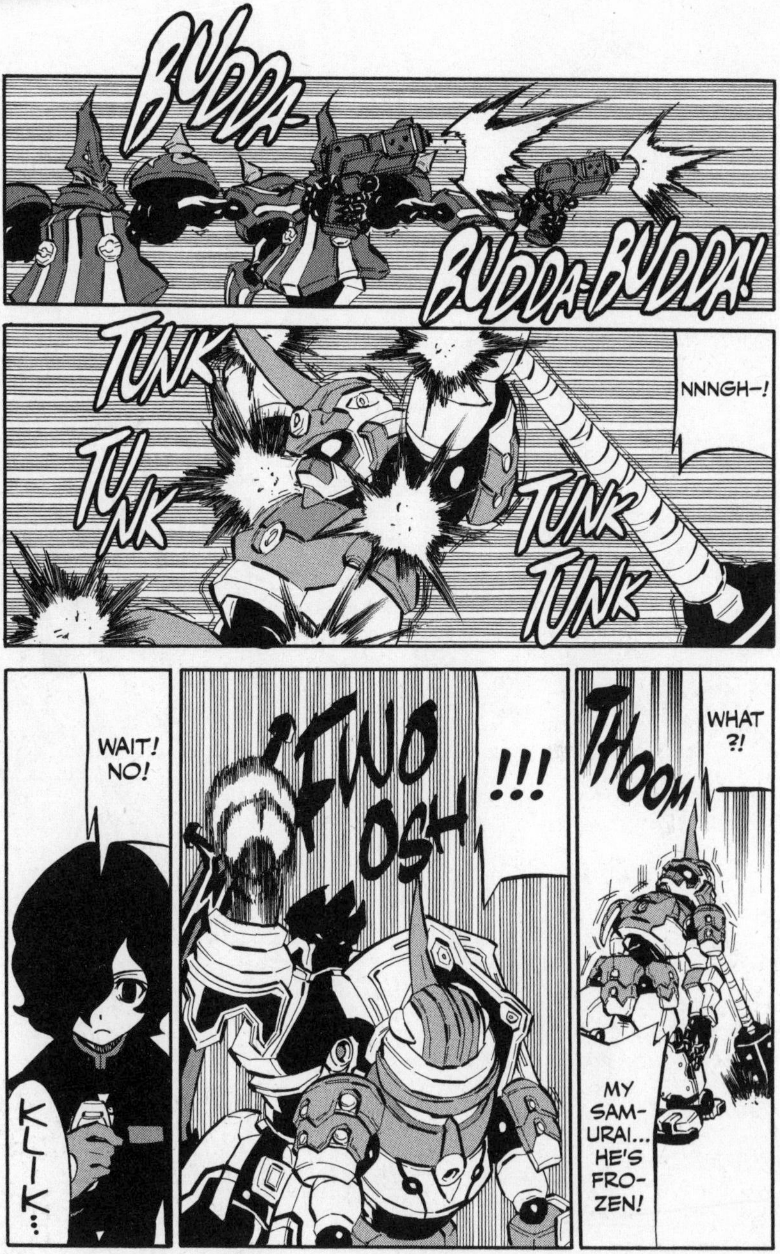
BUDDA-
BUDDA-BUDDA!
NNNGH-!
TUNK
TUNK
TUNK
TUNK
WHAT?!
THOOM
MY SAMURAI... HE'S FROZEN!
FWOOSH
!!!
WAIT! NO!
KLIK...

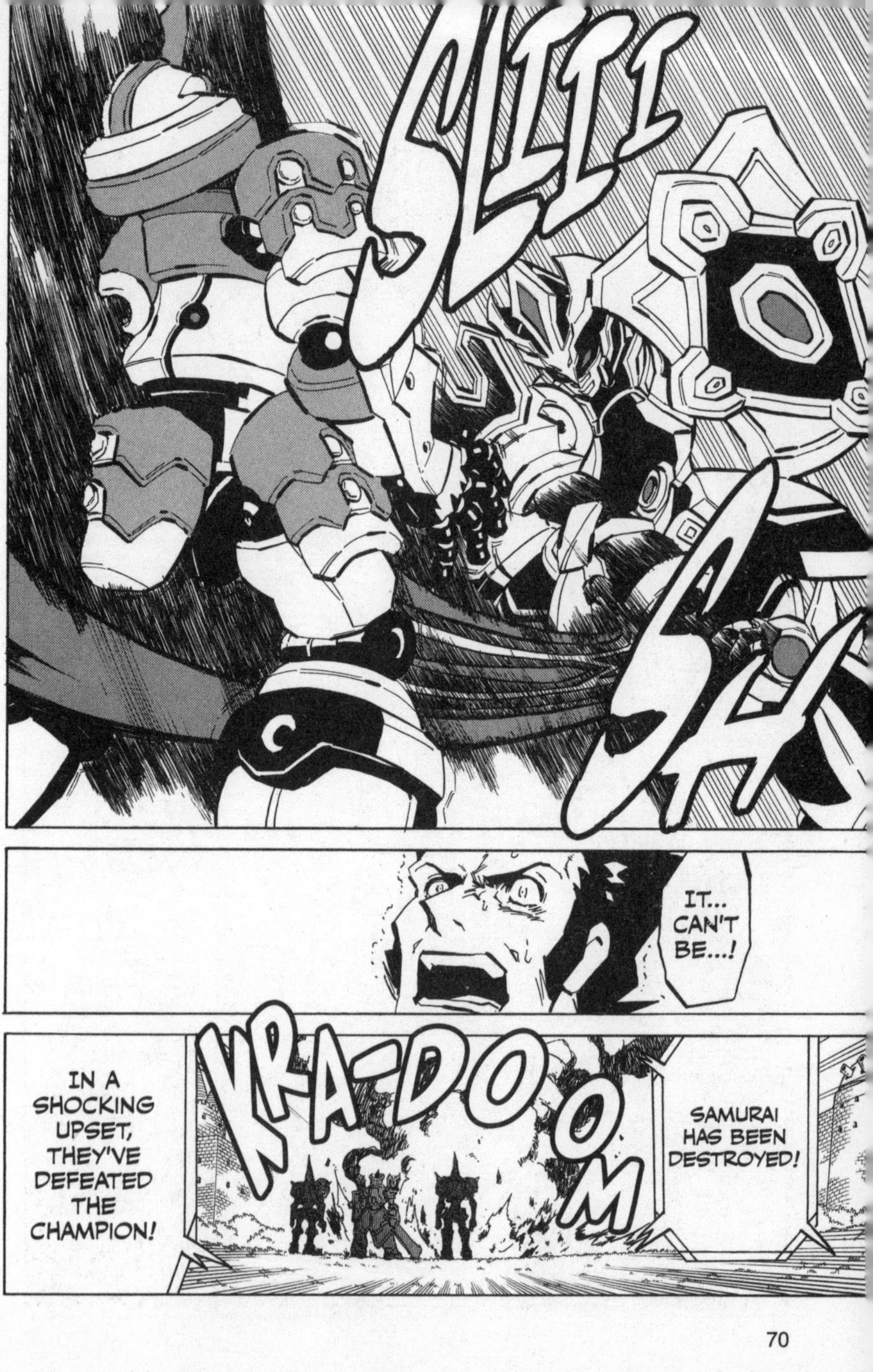
IT... CAN'T BE...!
SAMURAI HAS BEEN DESTROYED!
KRA-DO-O-OM
IN A SHOCKING UPSET, THEY'VE DEFEATED THE CHAMPION!

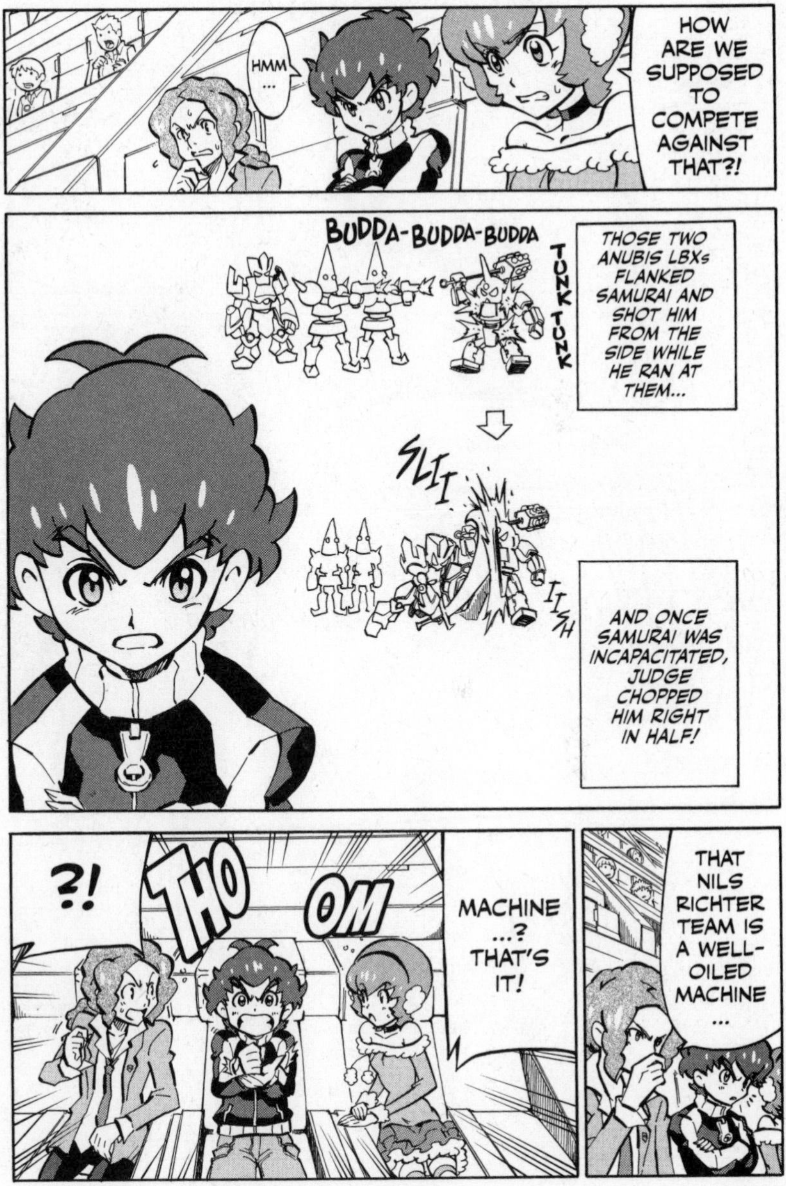
HOW ARE WE SUPPOSED TO COMPETE AGAINST THAT?!
HMM ...
BUDDA-BUDDA-BUDDA
TUNK TUNK
THOSE TWO ANUBIS LBXs FLANKED SAMURAI AND SHOT HIM FROM THE SIDE WHILE HE RAN AT THEM...
SLIIIISH
AND ONCE SAMURAI WAS INCAPACITATED, JUDGE CHOPPED HIM RIGHT IN HALF!
THAT NILS RICHTER TEAM IS A WELL-OILED MACHINE ...
MACHINE ...? THAT'S IT!
THOOM
?!

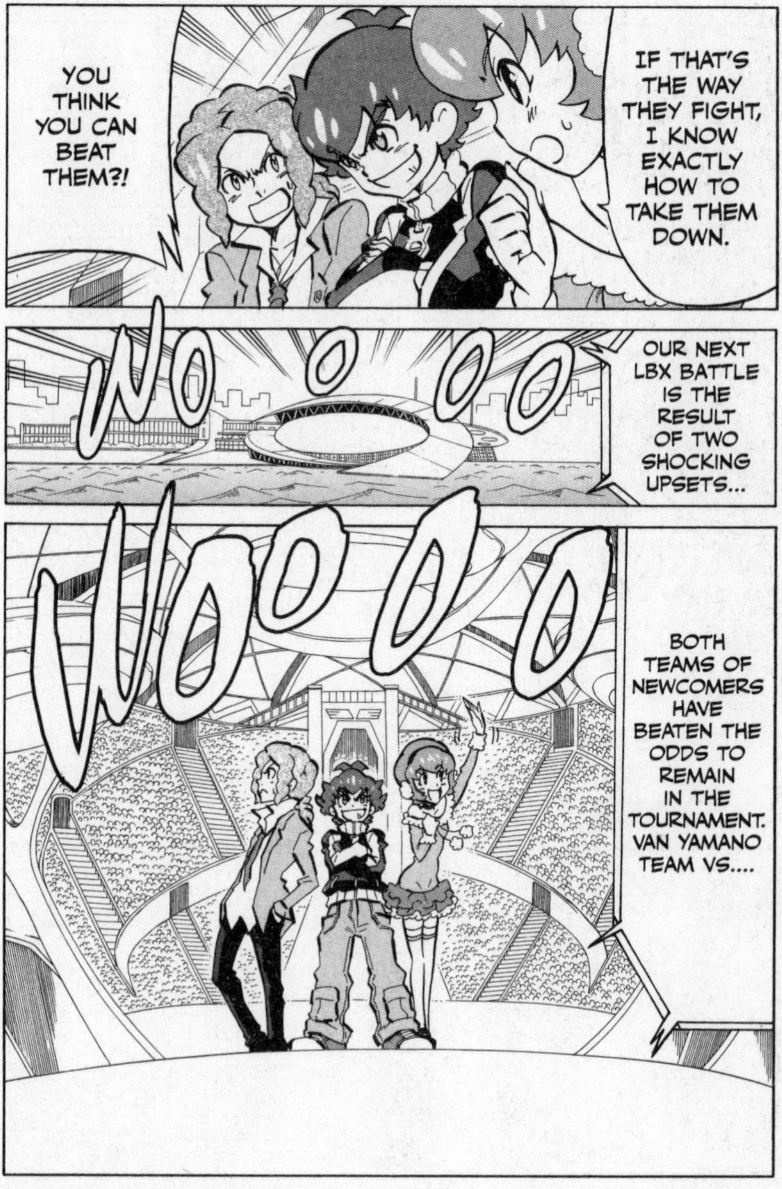
IF THAT'S THE WAY THEY FIGHT, I KNOW EXACTLY HOW TO TAKE THEM DOWN.
YOU THINK YOU CAN BEAT THEM?!
OUR NEXT LBX BATTLE IS THE RESULT OF TWO SHOCKING UPSETS...
WOOOO
BOTH TEAMS OF NEWCOMERS HAVE BEATEN THE ODDS TO REMAIN IN THE TOURNAMENT. VAN YAMANO TEAM VS....
WOOOOO

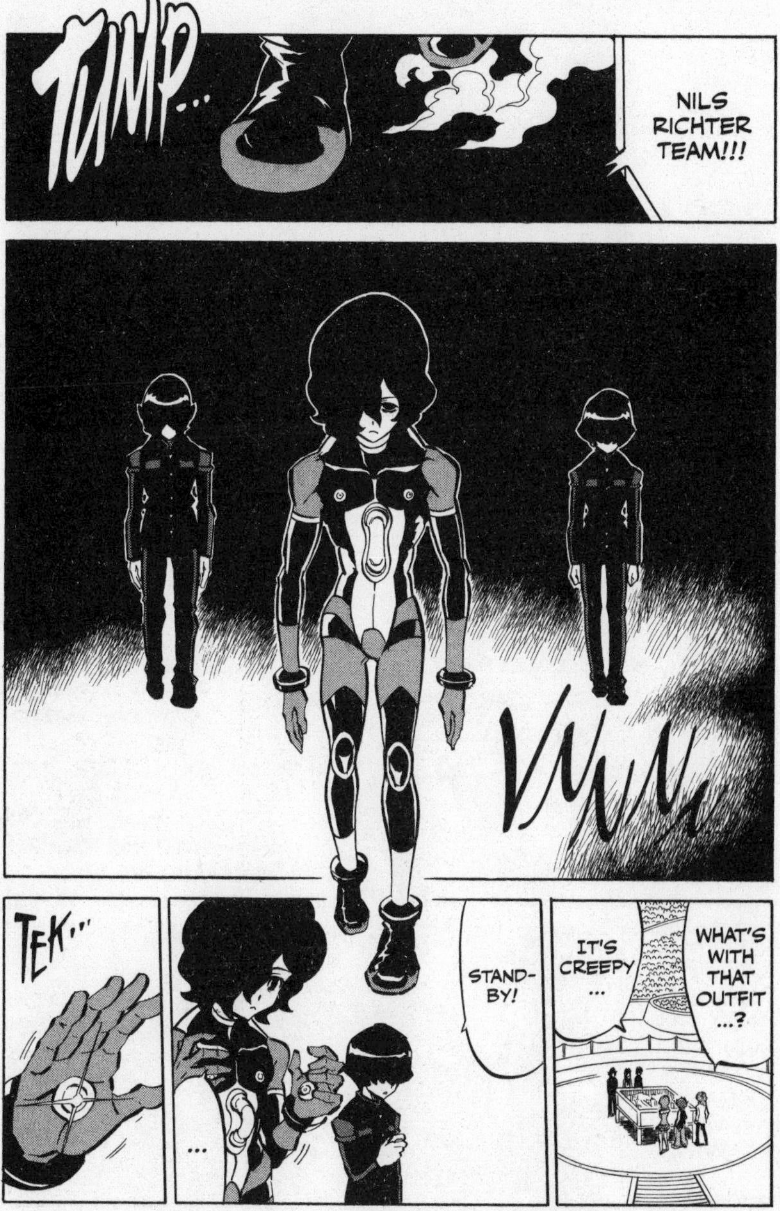
NILS RICHTER TEAM!!!
TUMP...
VMMM
WHAT'S WITH THAT OUTFIT ...?
IT'S CREEPY ...
STAND-BY!
...
TEK...

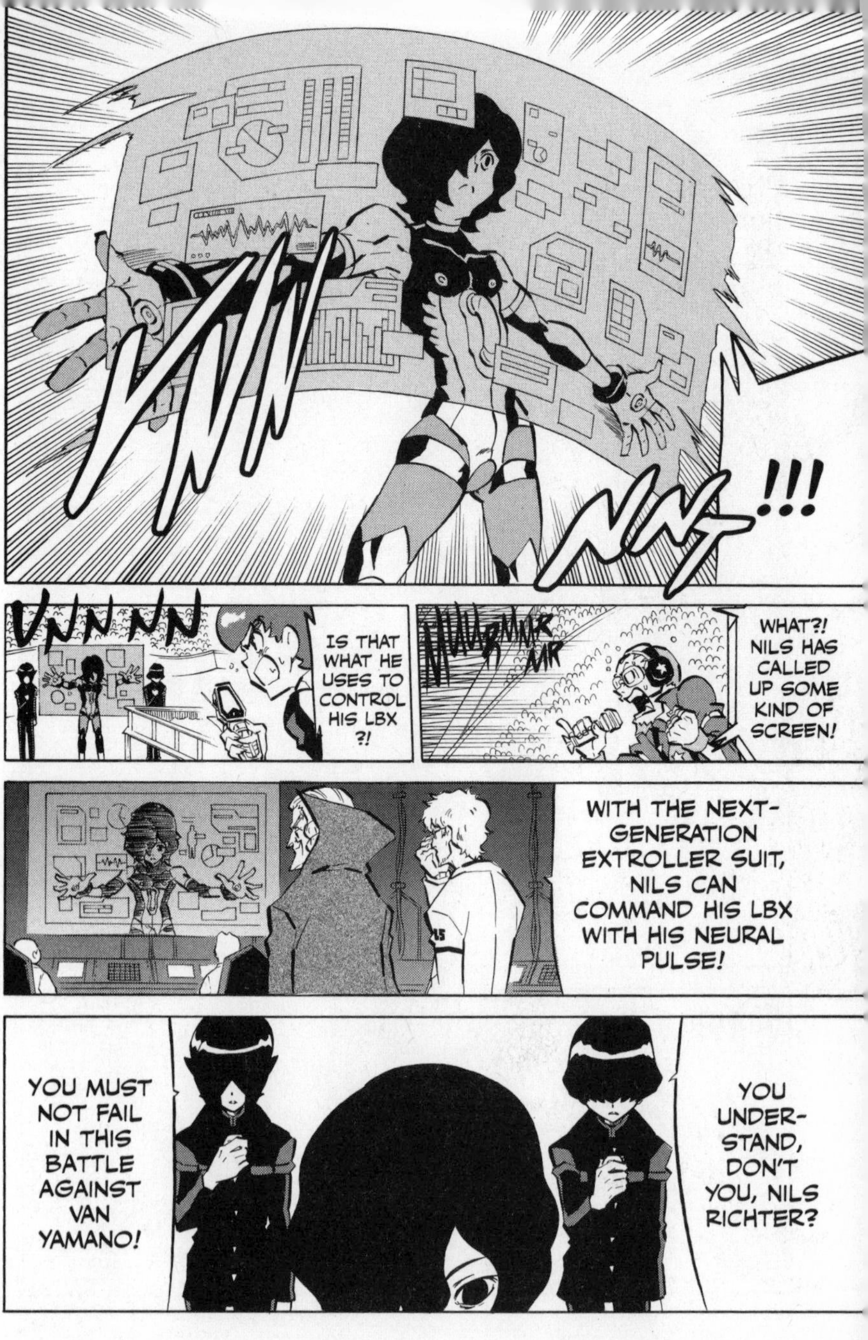
VNN
NNT!!!
WHAT?! NILS HAS CALLED UP SOME KIND OF SCREEN!
VNNNN
IS THAT WHAT HE USES TO CONTROL HIS LBX ?!
WITH THE NEXT-GENERATION EXTROLLER SUIT, NILS CAN COMMAND HIS LBX WITH HIS NEURAL PULSE!
YOU UNDER-STAND, DON'T YOU, NILS RICHTER?
YOU MUST NOT FAIL IN THIS BATTLE AGAINST VAN YAMANO!

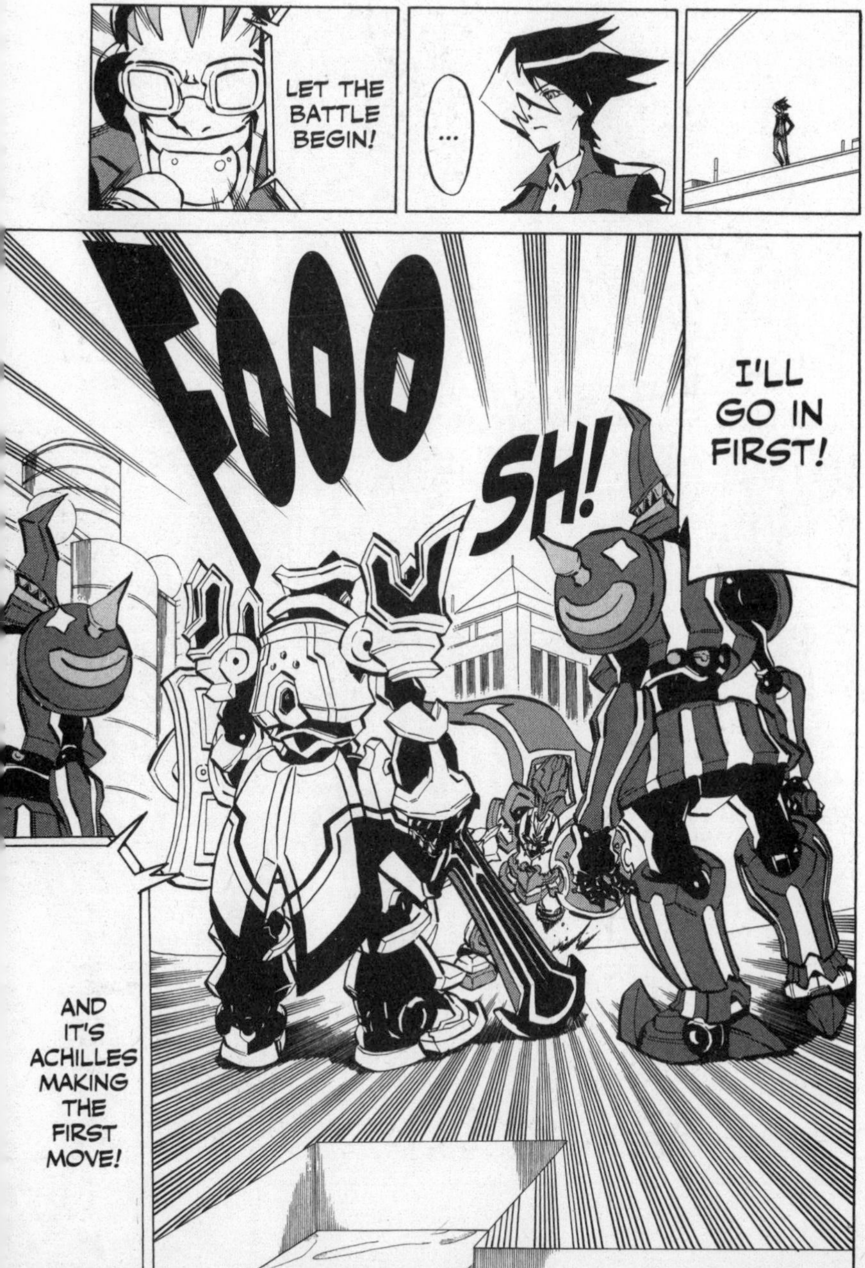
...
LET THE BATTLE BEGIN!
I'LL GO IN FIRST!
FOOOSH!
AND IT'S ACHILLES MAKING THE FIRST MOVE!

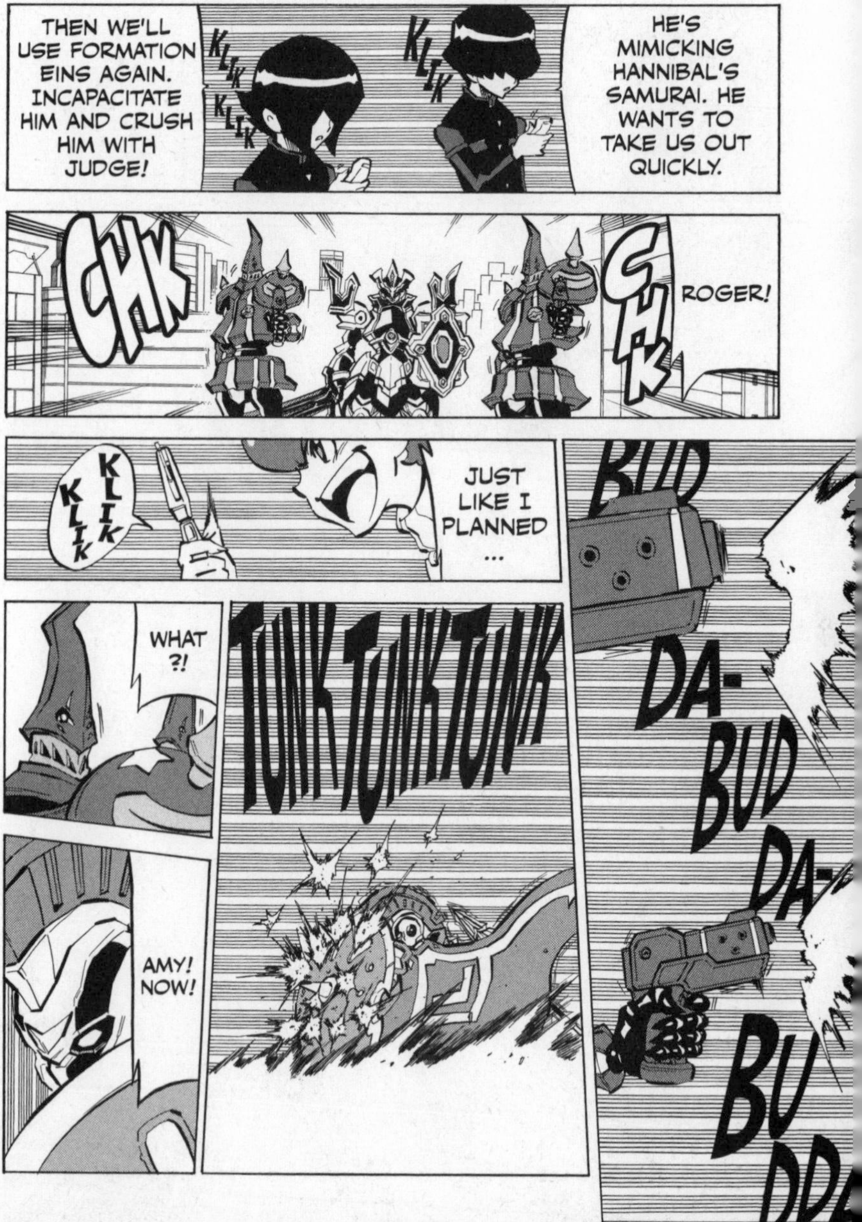
HE'S MIMICKING HANNIBAL'S SAMURAI. HE WANTS TO TAKE US OUT QUICKLY.
KLIK
KLIK KLIK
THEN WE'LL USE FORMATION EINS AGAIN. INCAPACITATE HIM AND CRUSH HIM WITH JUDGE!
ROGER!
CHK
CHK
BUD
DA-BUD
BUD
DA-
BU
DDA
JUST LIKE I PLANNED...
KLIK KLIK
TUNK TUNK TUNK
WHAT?!
AMY! NOW!

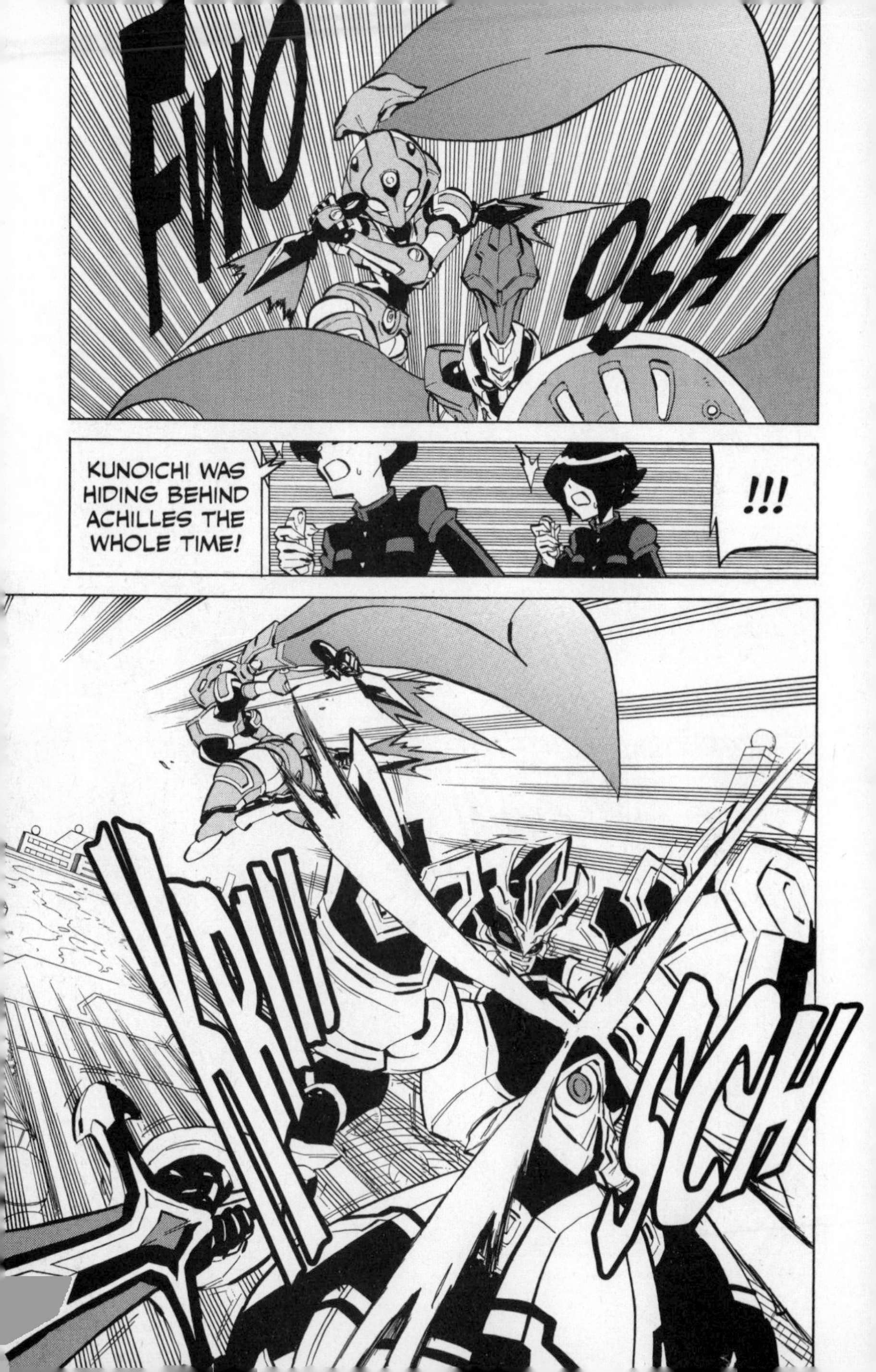
FWO
OSH
!!!
KUNOICHI WAS HIDING BEHIND ACHILLES THE WHOLE TIME!

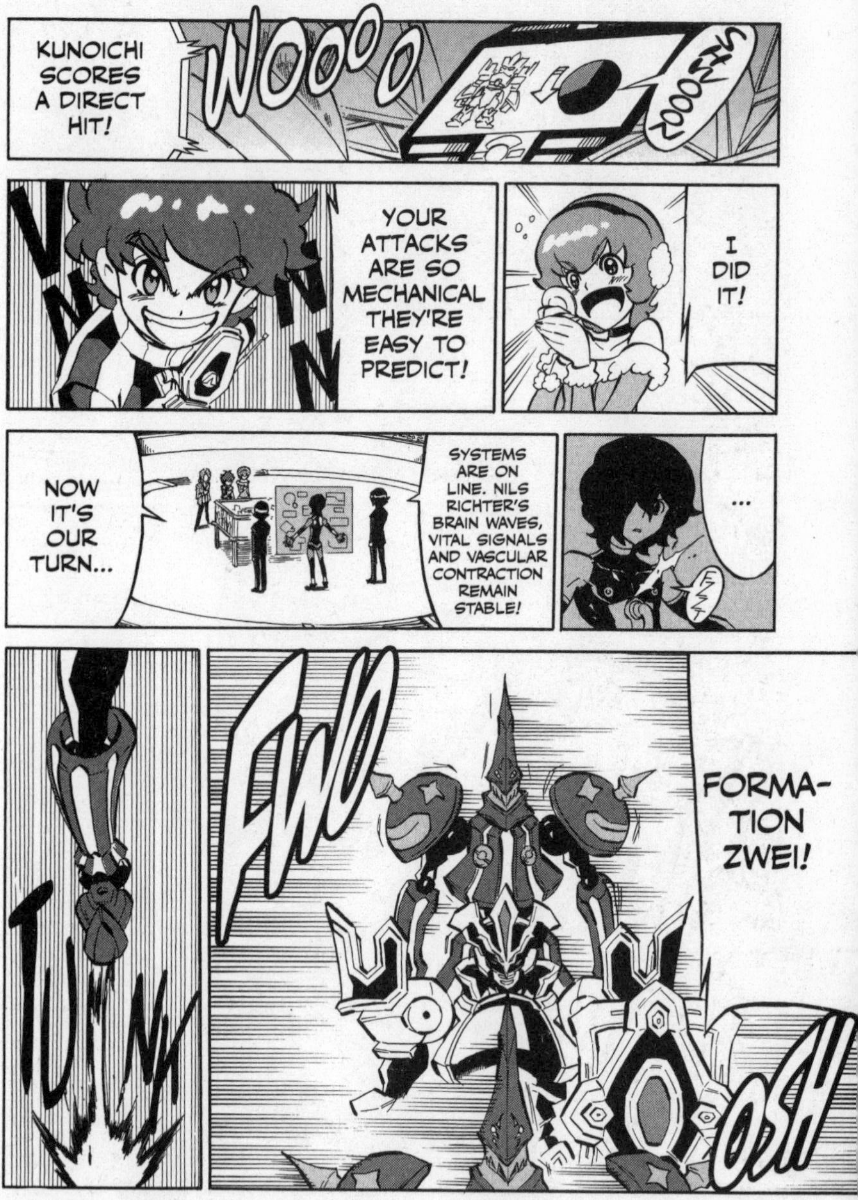
KUNOICHI SCORES A DIRECT HIT!
I DID IT!
YOUR ATTACKS ARE SO MECHANICAL THEY'RE EASY TO PREDICT!
...
SYSTEMS ARE ON LINE. NILS RICHTER'S BRAIN WAVES, VITAL SIGNALS AND VASCULAR CONTRACTION REMAIN STABLE!
NOW IT'S OUR TURN...
FORMATION ZWEI!

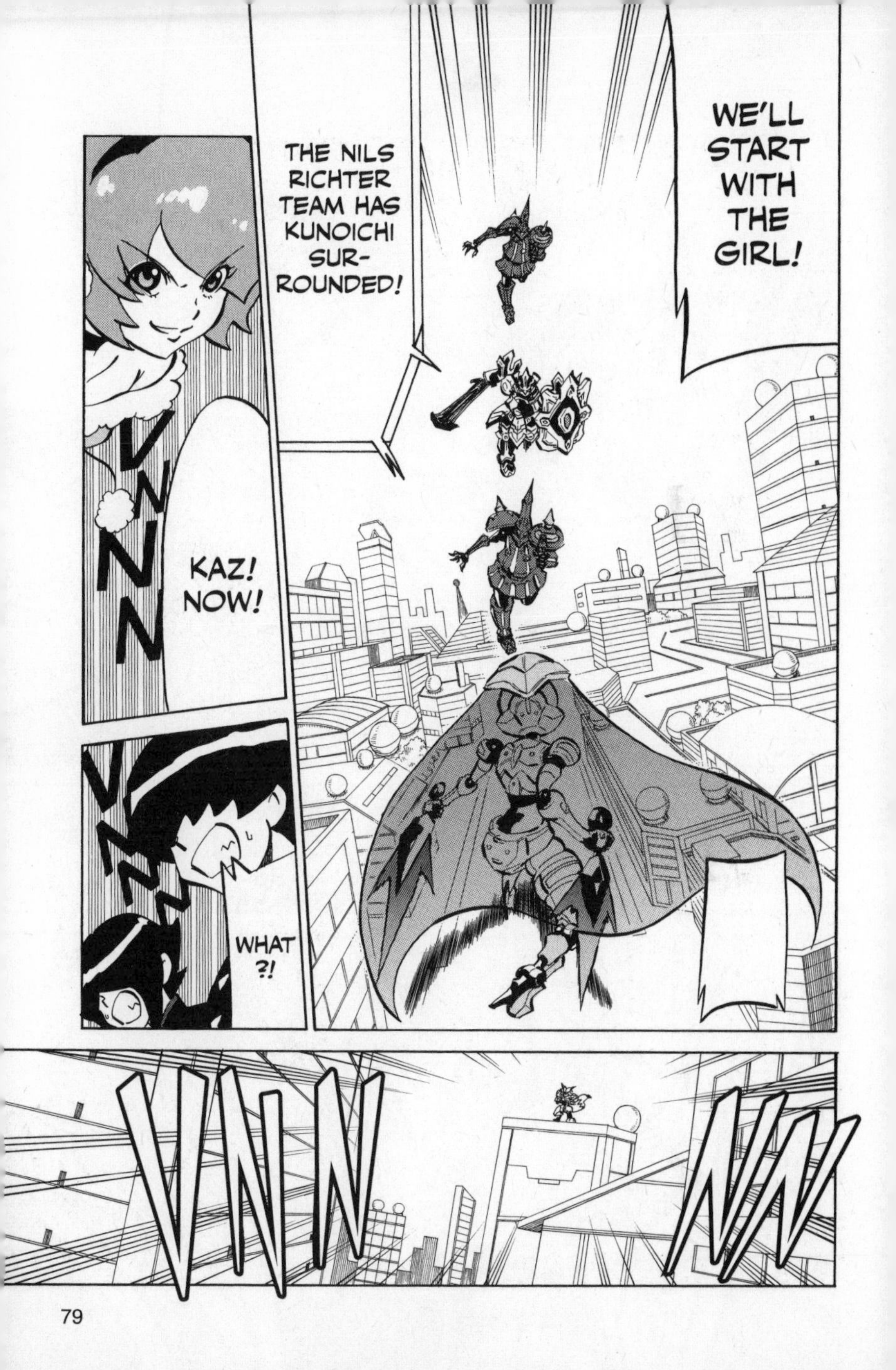
WE'LL START WITH THE GIRL!
THE NILS RICHTER TEAM HAS KUNOICHI SUR-ROUNDED!
KAZ! NOW!
VNNN
WHAT ?!
VNN
VNNN
NNN

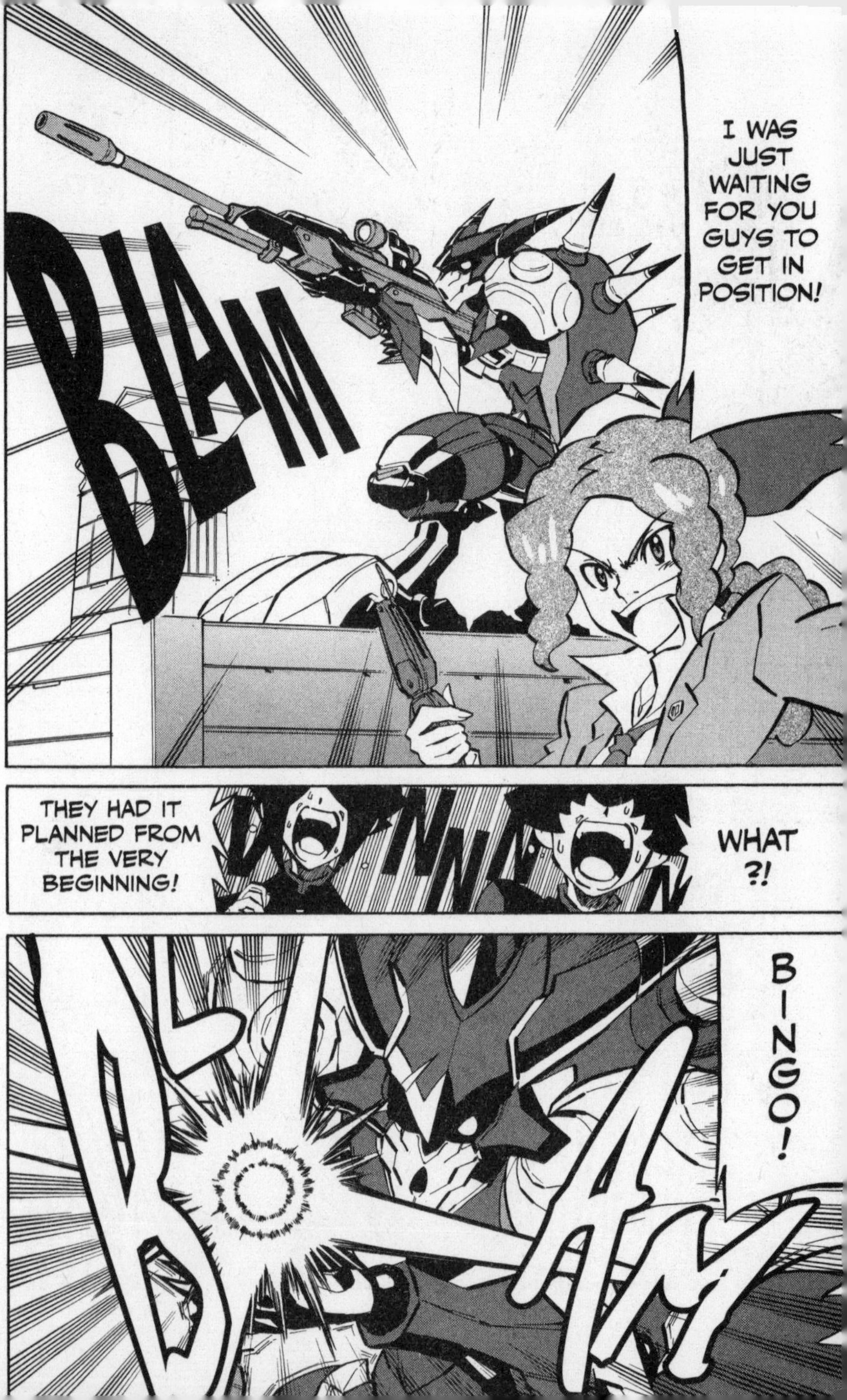
I WAS JUST WAITING FOR YOU GUYS TO GET IN POSITION!
BLAM
WHAT ?!
THEY HAD IT PLANNED FROM THE VERY BEGINNING!
BINGO!
BLAM

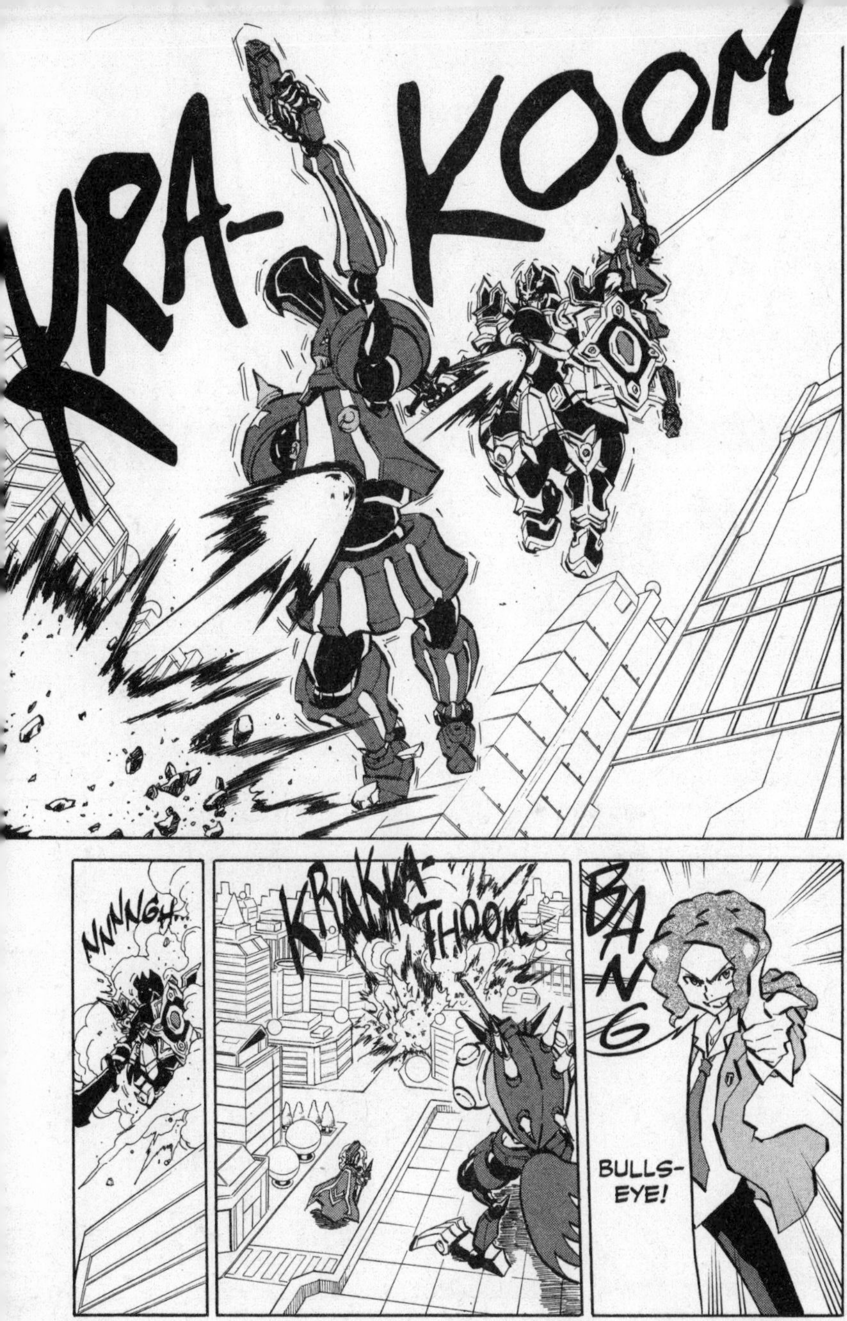
KRA-KOOM
BANG
BULLS-EYE!
KRAKA-THOOM
NNNNGH...

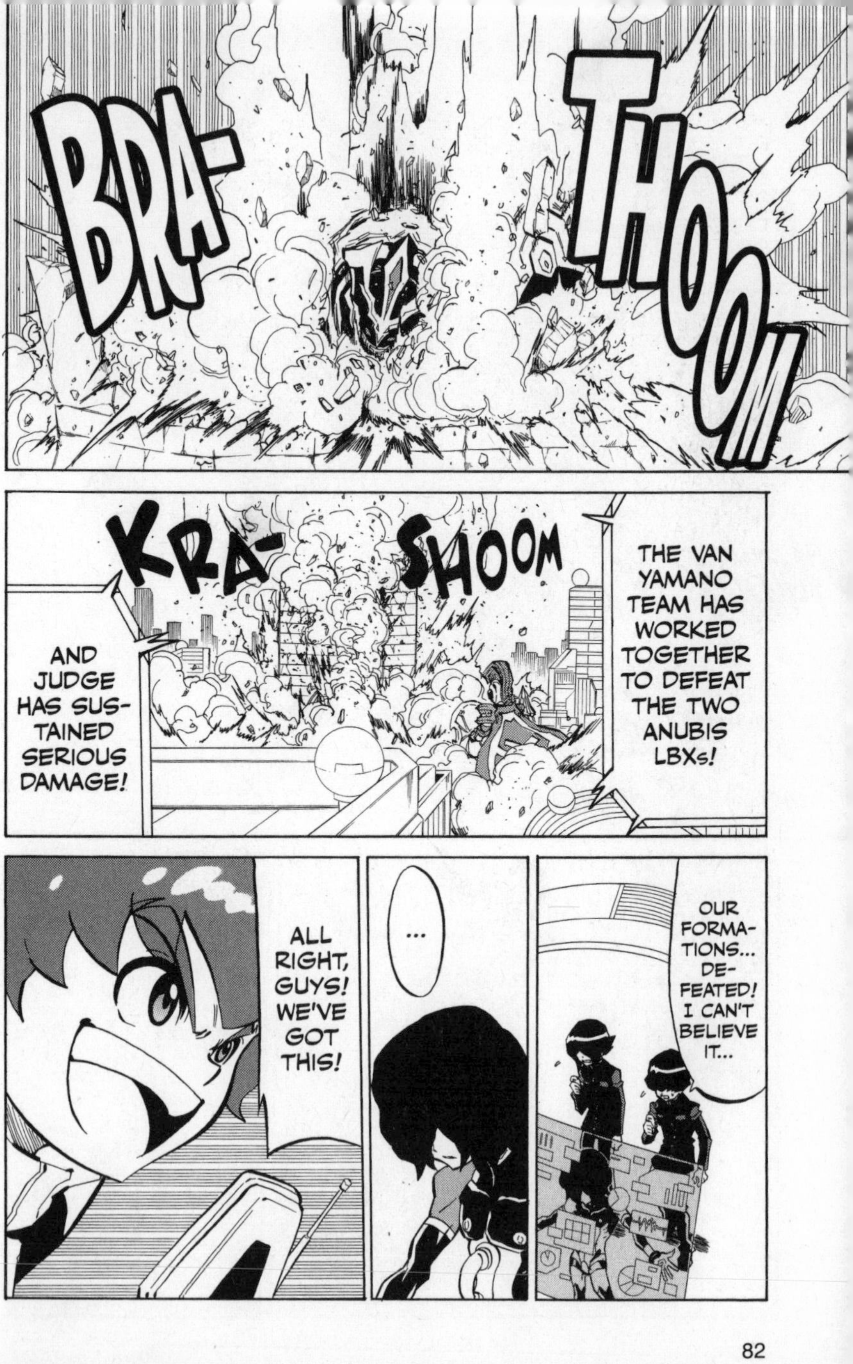
BRA-
THOOOM
KRA-SHOOM
THE VAN YAMANO TEAM HAS WORKED TOGETHER TO DEFEAT THE TWO ANUBIS LBXs!
AND JUDGE HAS SUS-TAINED SERIOUS DAMAGE!
OUR FORMA-TIONS... DE-FEATED! I CAN'T BELIEVE IT...
...
ALL RIGHT, GUYS! WE'VE GOT THIS!

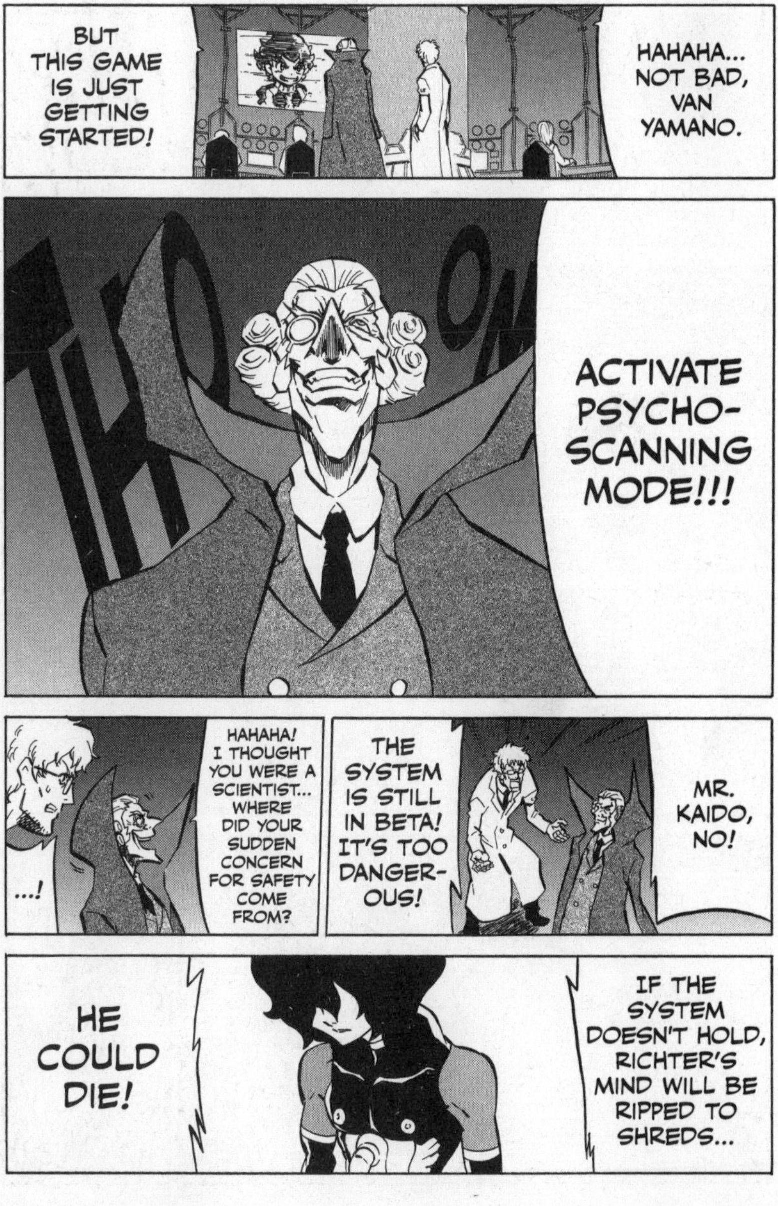
HAHAHA... NOT BAD, VAN YAMANO.
BUT THIS GAME IS JUST GETTING STARTED!
ACTIVATE PSYCHO-SCANNING MODE!!!
MR. KAIDO, NO!
THE SYSTEM IS STILL IN BETA! IT'S TOO DANGER-OUS!
HAHAHA! I THOUGHT YOU WERE A SCIENTIST... WHERE DID YOUR SUDDEN CONCERN FOR SAFETY COME FROM?
...!
IF THE SYSTEM DOESN'T HOLD, RICHTER'S MIND WILL BE RIPPED TO SHREDS...
HE COULD DIE!

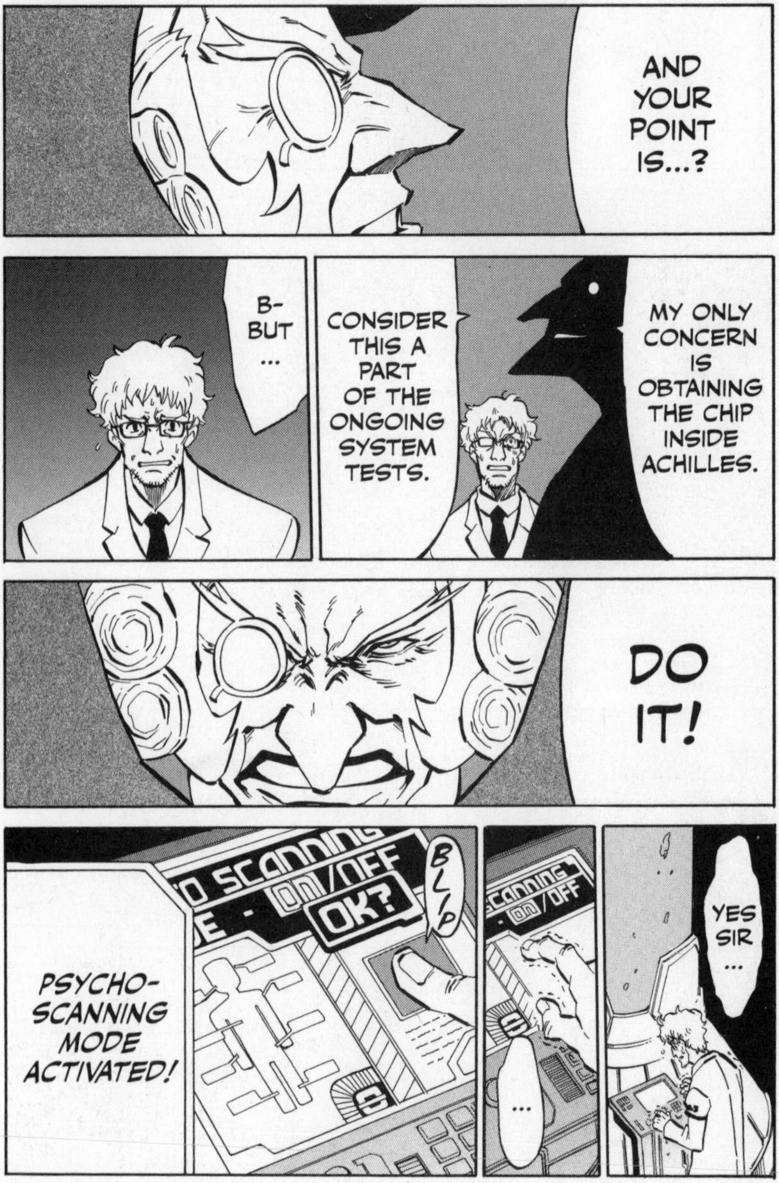
AND YOUR POINT IS...?
MY ONLY CONCERN IS OBTAINING THE CHIP INSIDE ACHILLES.
CONSIDER THIS A PART OF THE ONGOING SYSTEM TESTS.
B-BUT ...
DO IT!
YES SIR ...
SCANNING
ON/OFF
...
BLIP
ON/OFF
OK?
PSYCHO-SCANNING MODE ACTIVATED!

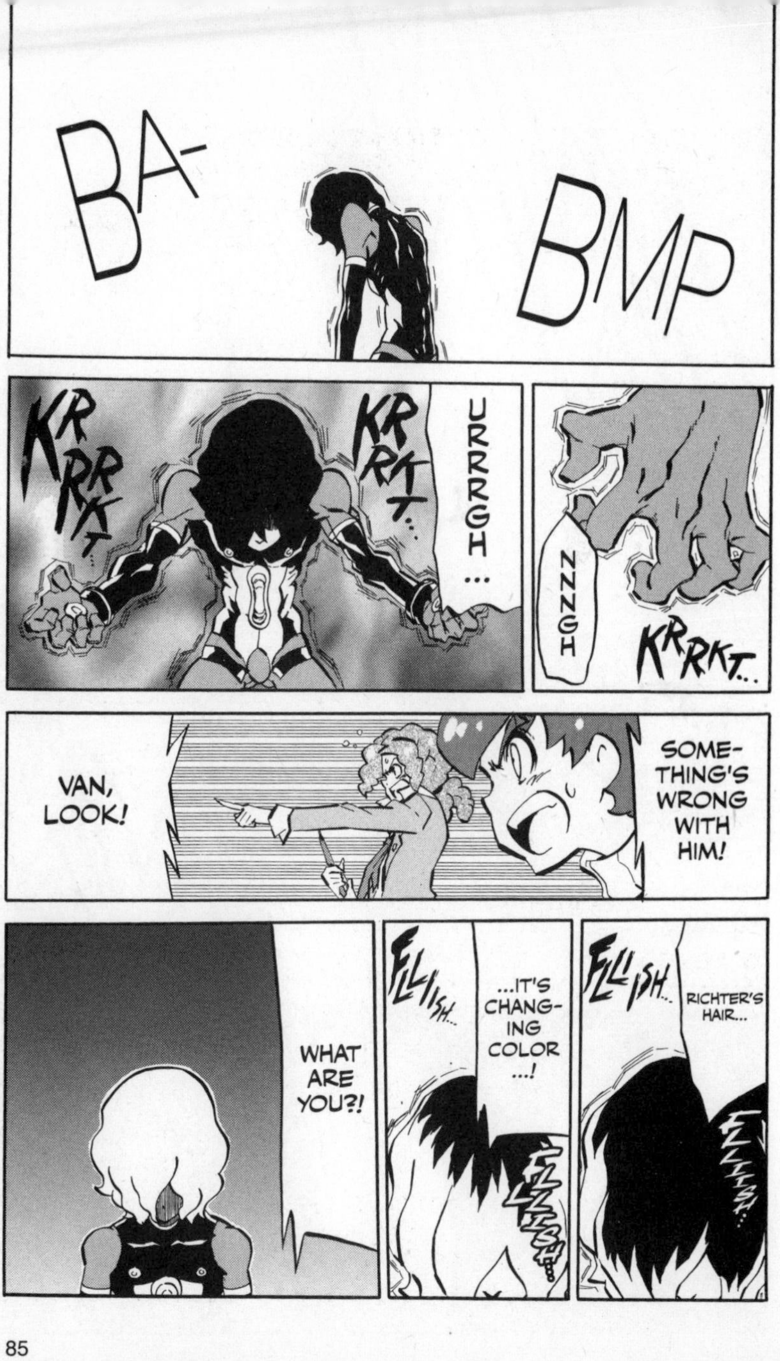
BA-
BMP
NNNGH
KRRKT...
URRRGH...
KRRKT...
KRRRRKT...
SOME-THING'S WRONG WITH HIM!
VAN, LOOK!
RICHTER'S HAIR...
FLLLISH...
FLLLISH...
...IT'S CHANG-ING COLOR...!
FLLISH...
FLLISH...
WHAT ARE YOU?!

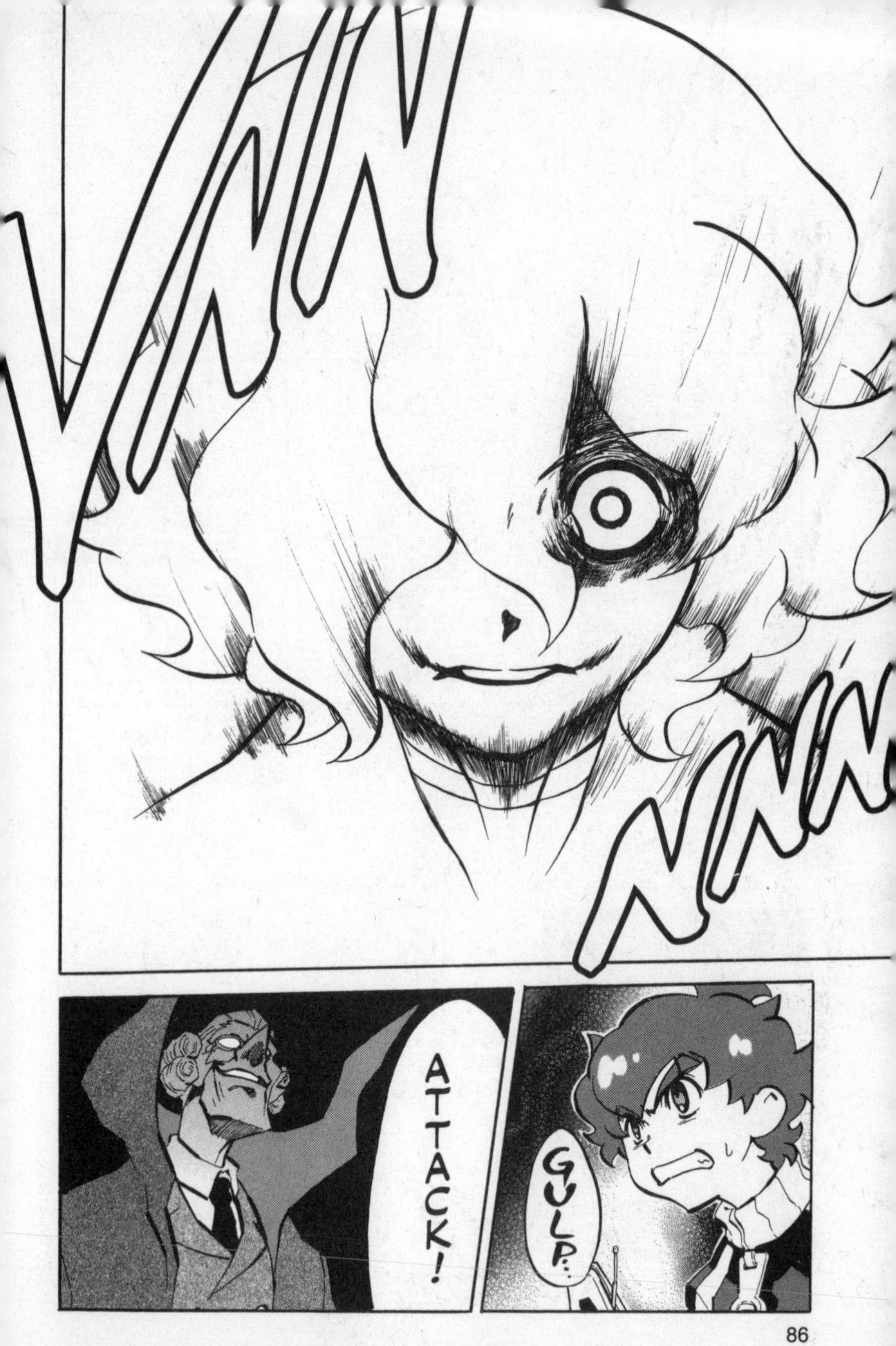
GULP...
ATTACK!

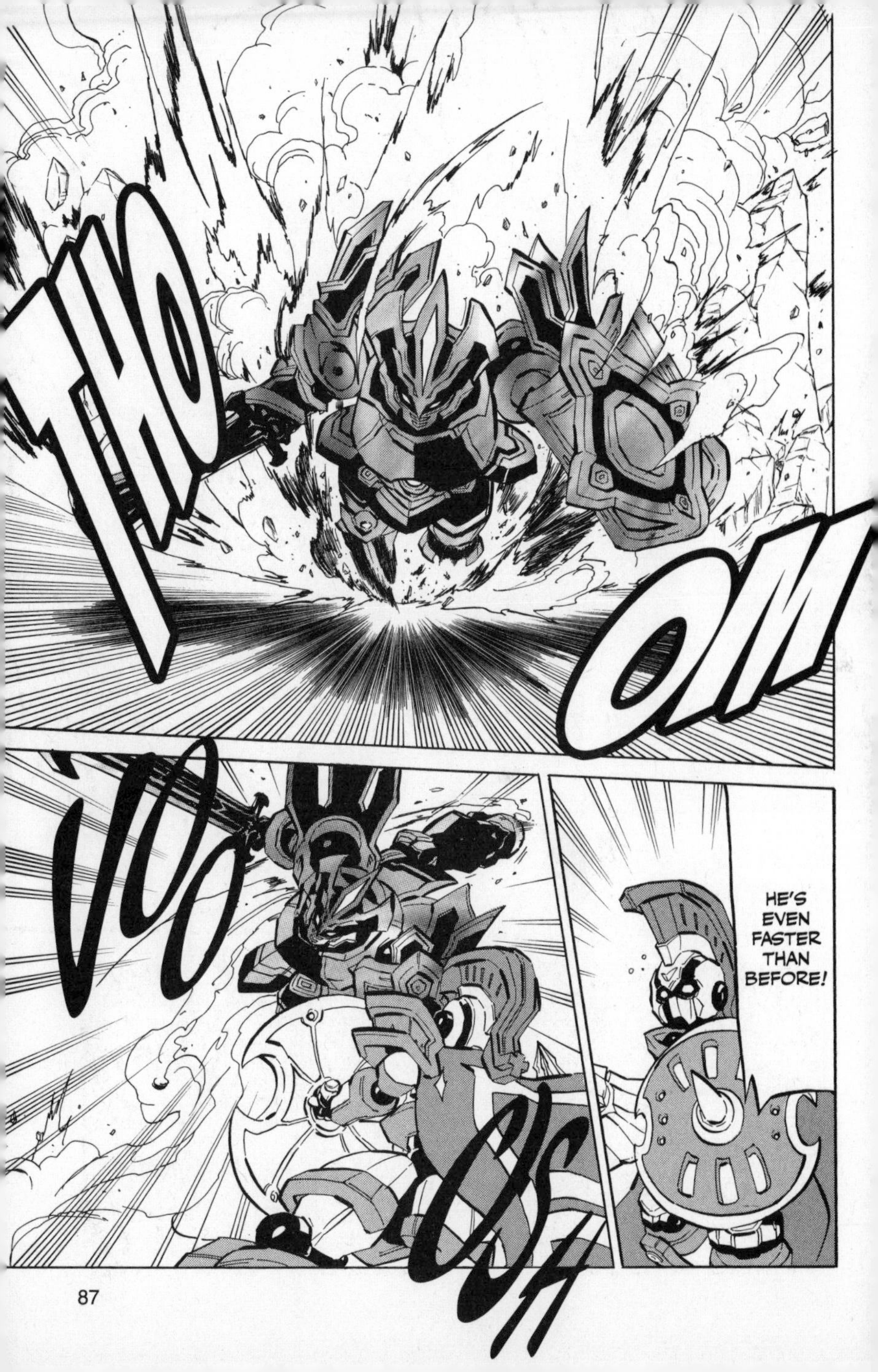
HE'S EVEN FASTER THAN BEFORE!

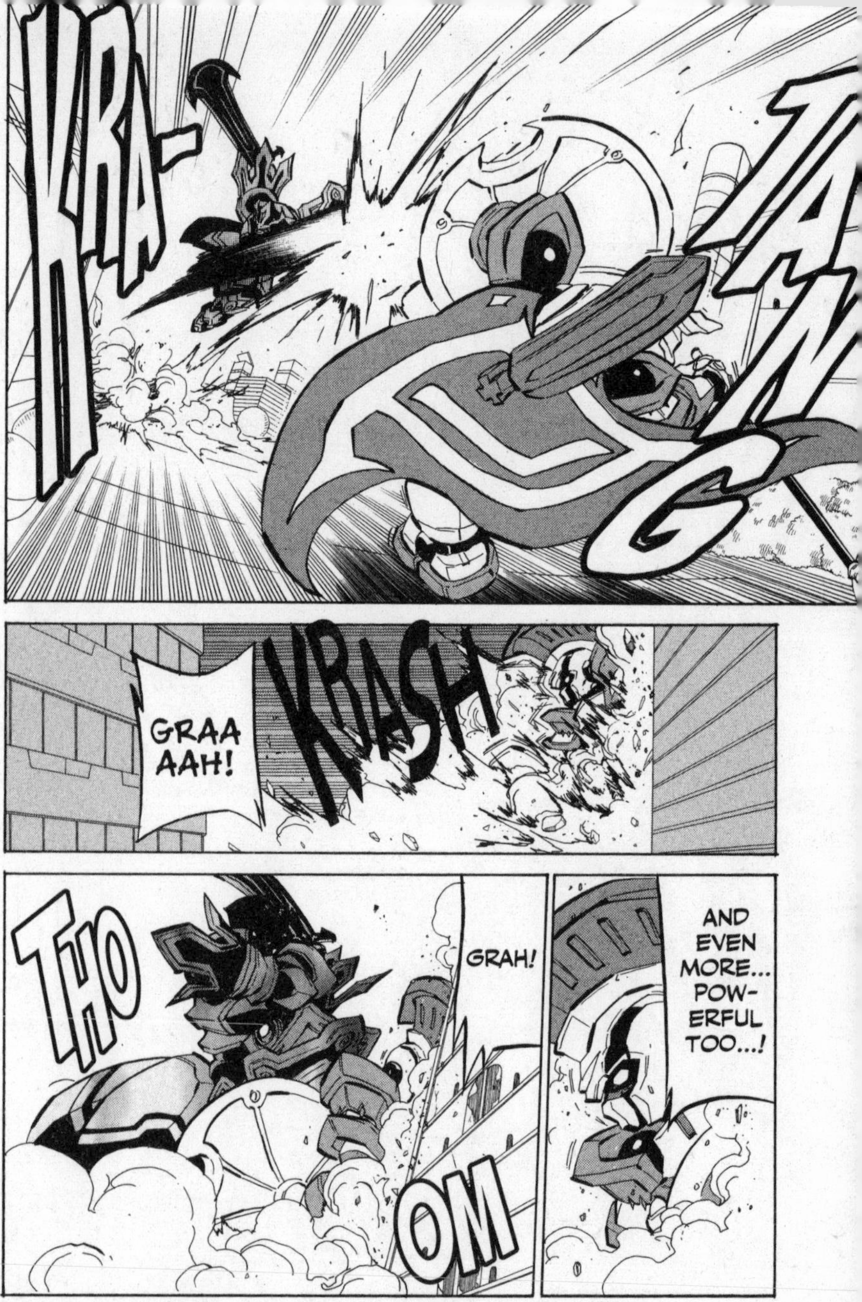
KRA-
TANG
KRASH
GRAA AAH!
AND EVEN MORE... POW-ERFUL TOO...!
GRAH!
THO
OM

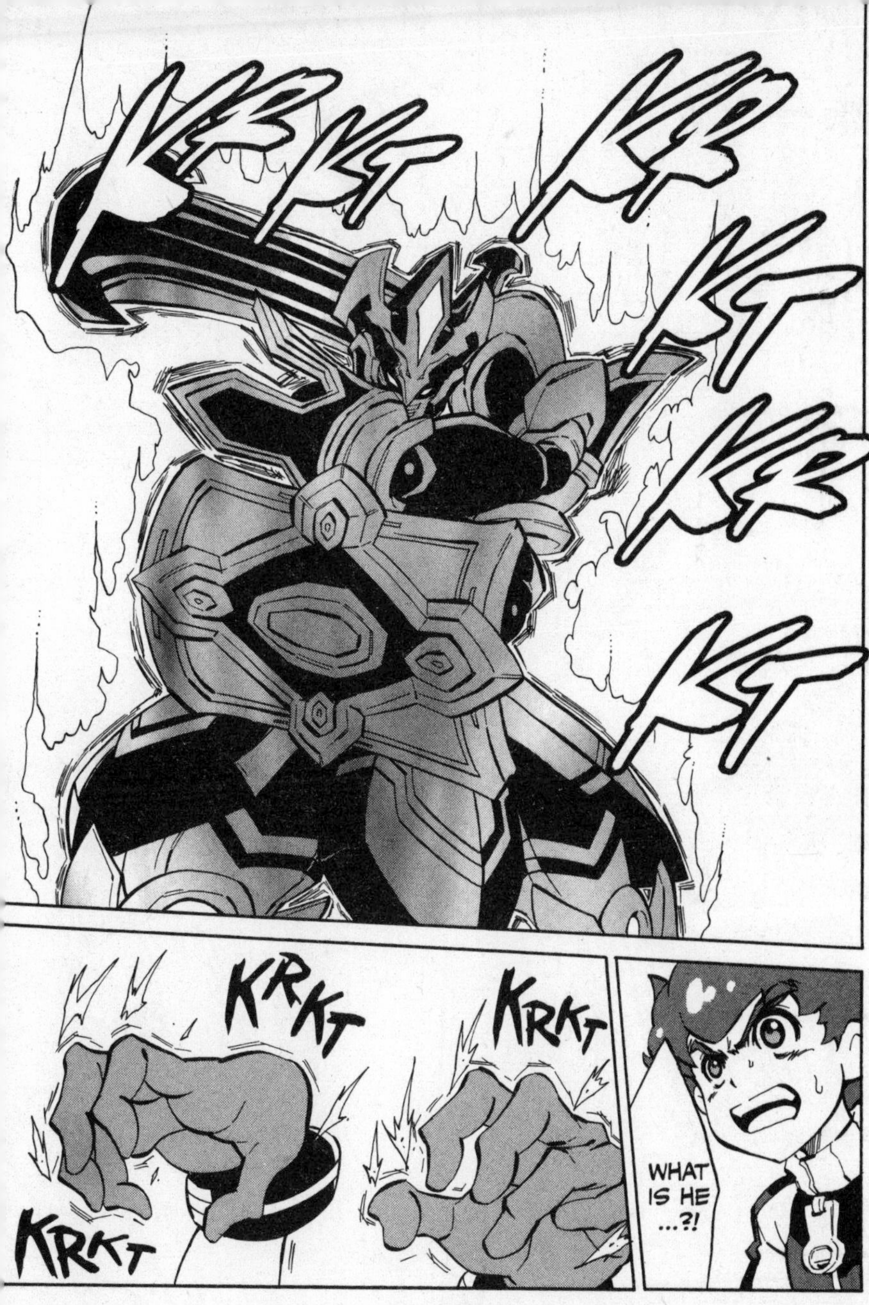
KRKT
KRKT
KRKT
KRKT
KRKT
WHAT IS HE ...?!
KRKT
KRKT
KRKT

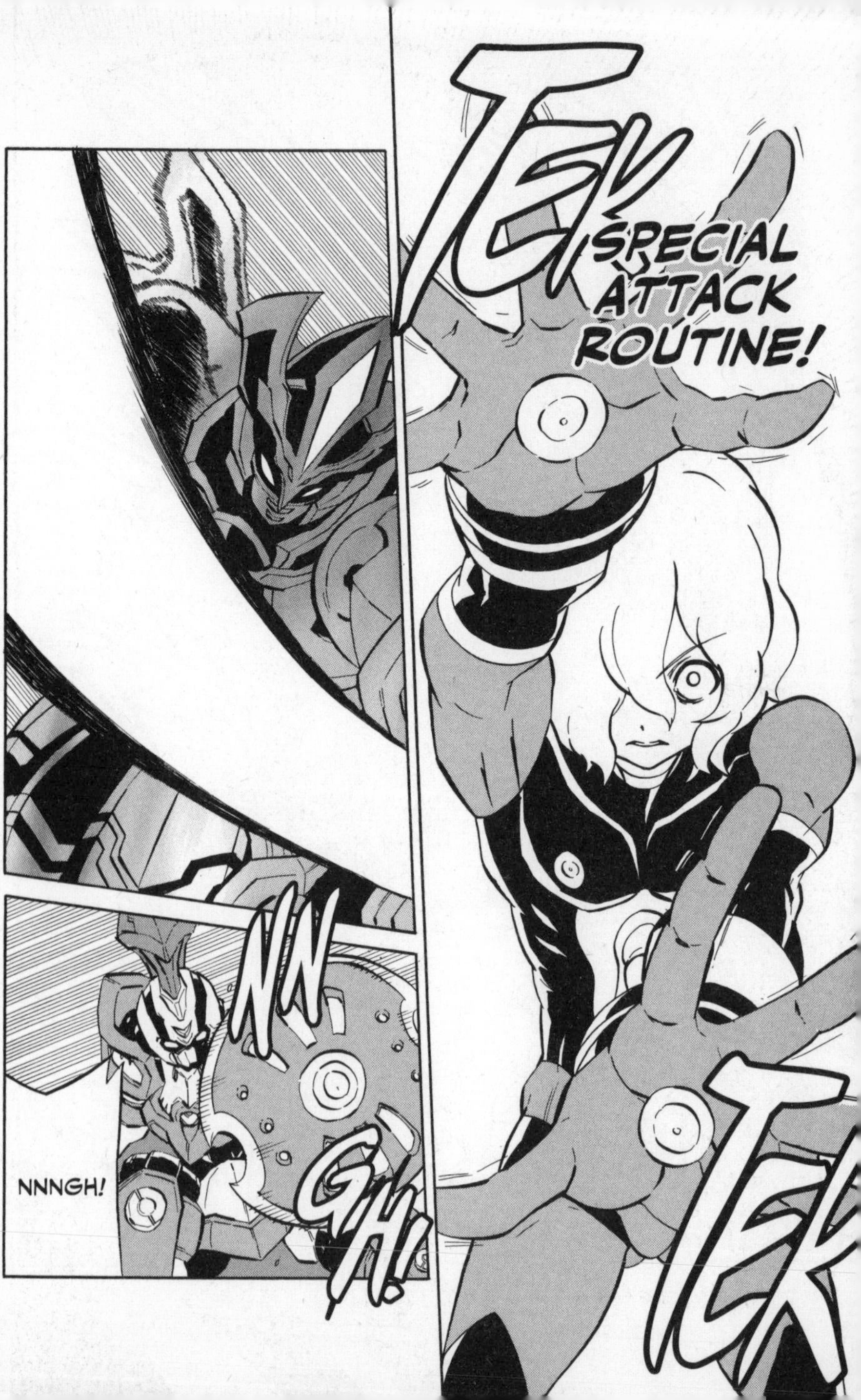
TEK
SPECIAL ATTACK ROUTINE!
TEK
NNGH!
NNNGH!

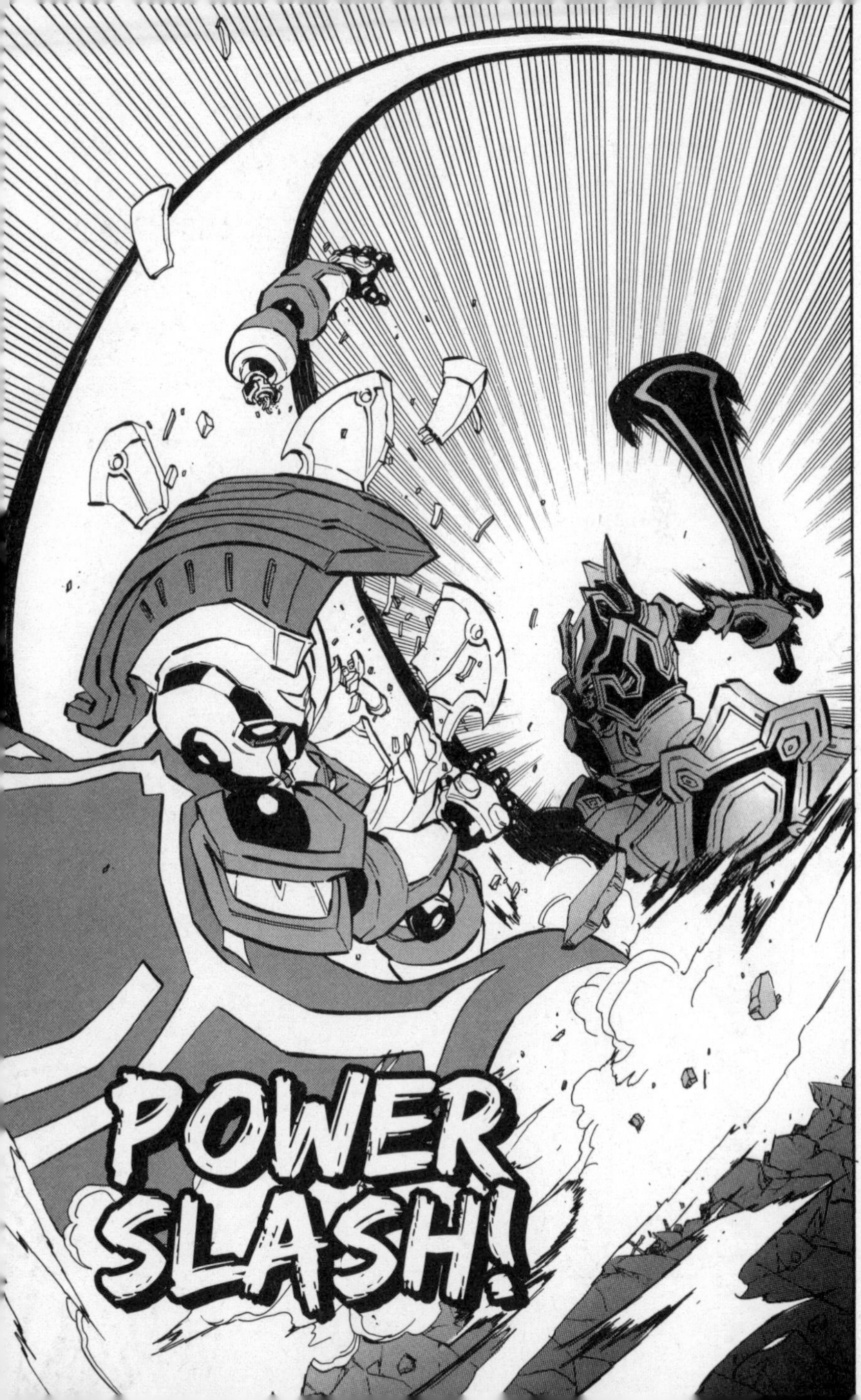
POWER SLASH!

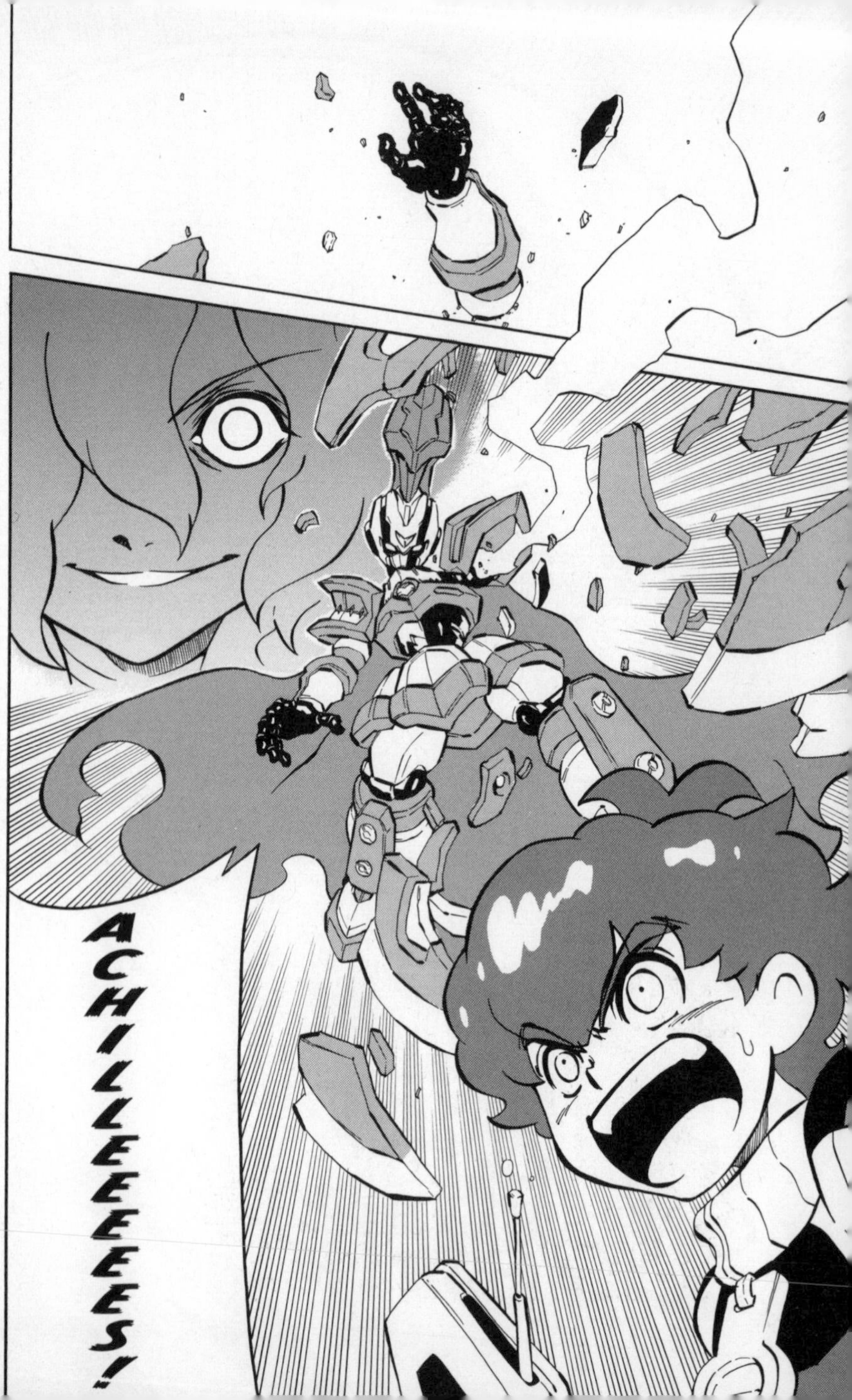
ACHILLEEEEES!

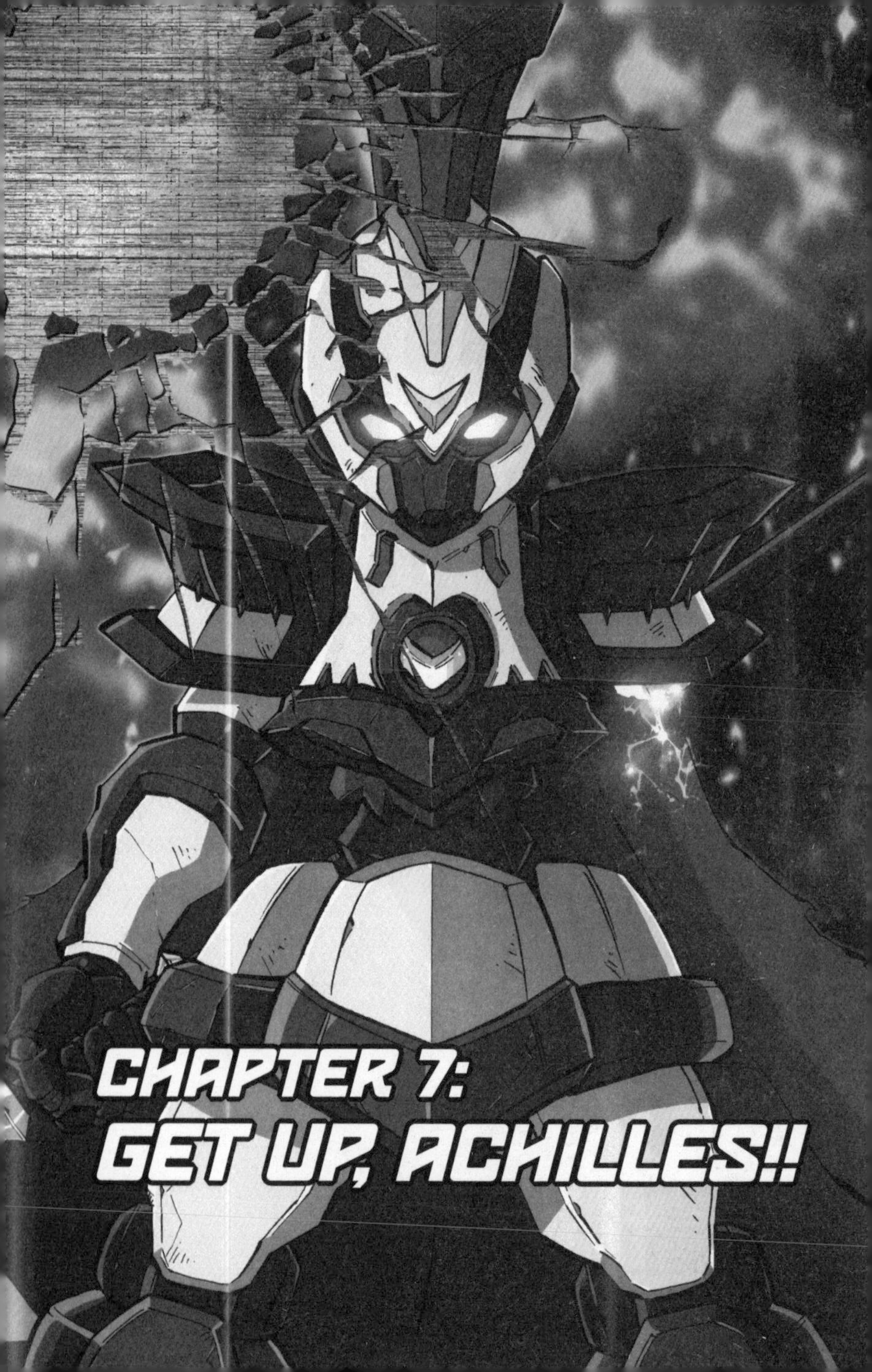
CHAPTER 7:
GET UP, ACHILLES!!

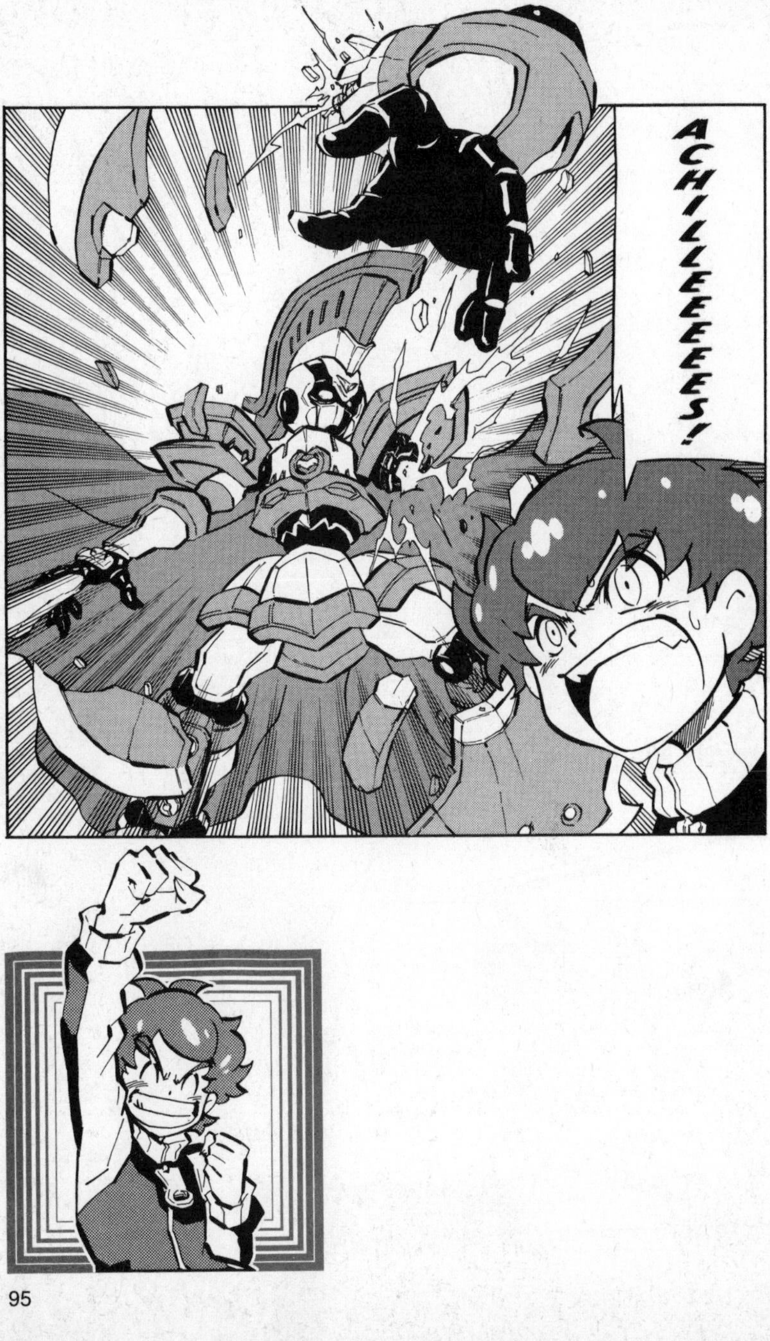
ACHILLEEEEEES!

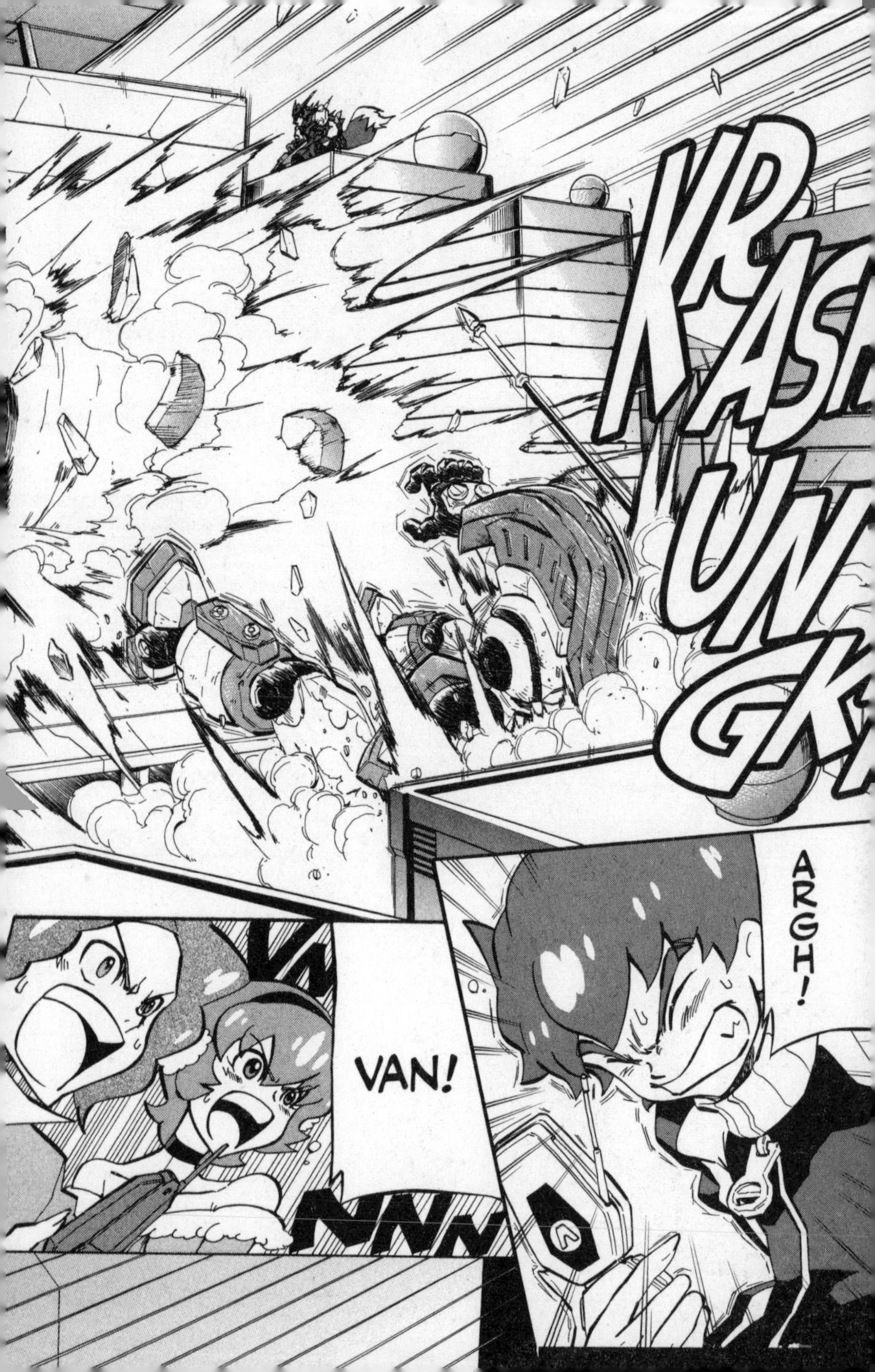
ARGH!
VAN!

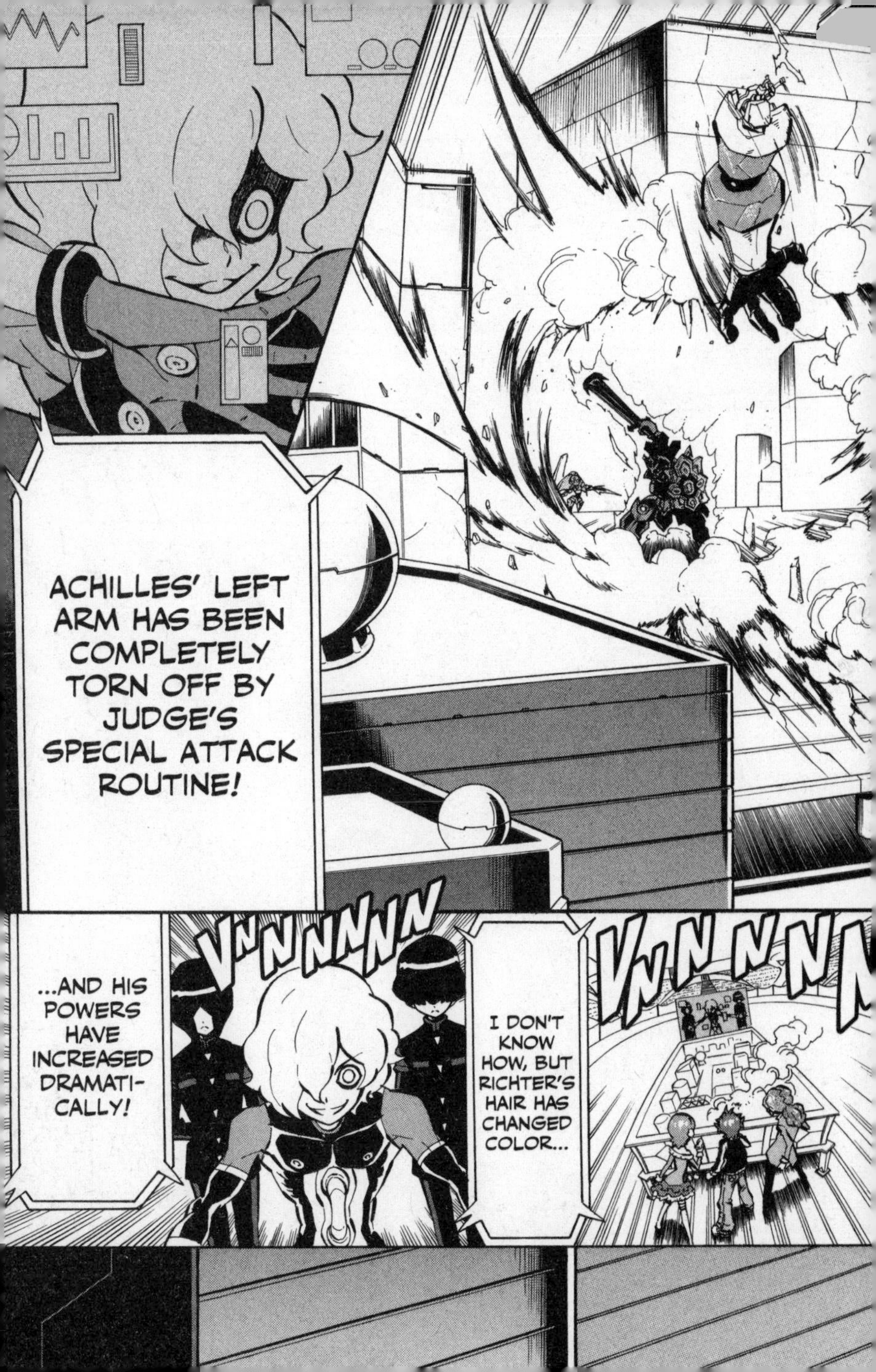
ACHILLES' LEFT ARM HAS BEEN COMPLETELY TORN OFF BY JUDGE'S SPECIAL ATTACK ROUTINE!
VNNNNN
I DON'T KNOW HOW, BUT RICHTER'S HAIR HAS CHANGED COLOR...
VNNNNNN
...AND HIS POWERS HAVE INCREASED DRAMATI-CALLY!

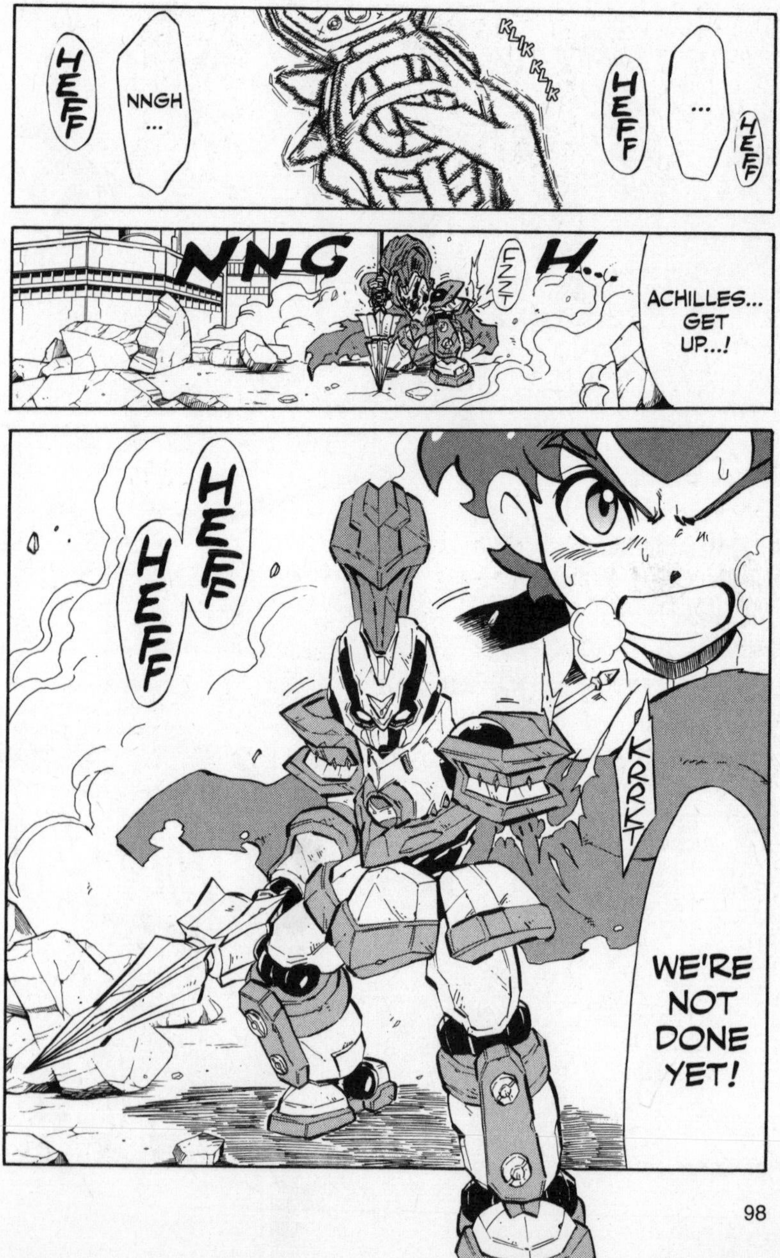
HEFF
...
HEFF
KLIK KLIK
NNGH...
HEFF
ACHILLES... GET UP...!
FZZT
NNGH...
WE'RE NOT DONE YET!
KRRKT
HEFF HEFF

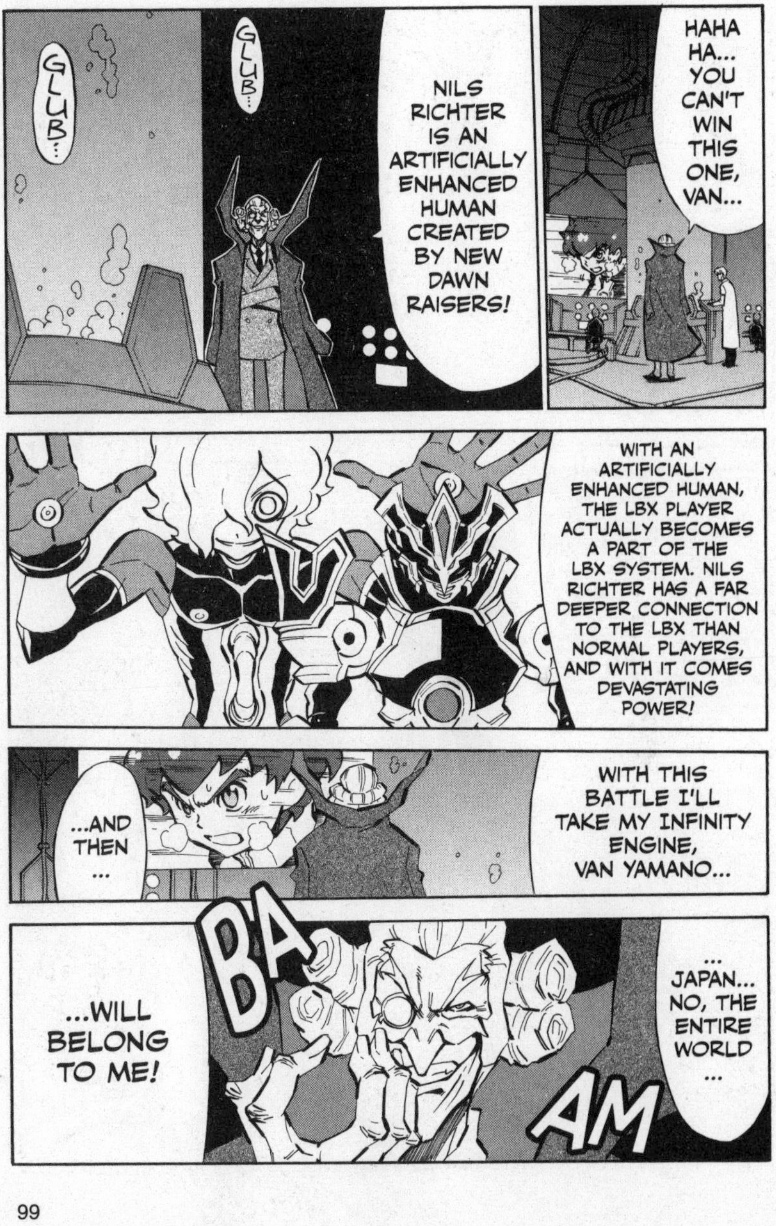
HAHA HA... YOU CAN'T WIN THIS ONE, VAN...
NILS RICHTER IS AN ARTIFICIALLY ENHANCED HUMAN CREATED BY NEW DAWN RAISERS!
GLUB...
GLUB...
WITH AN ARTIFICIALLY ENHANCED HUMAN, THE LBX PLAYER ACTUALLY BECOMES A PART OF THE LBX SYSTEM. NILS RICHTER HAS A FAR DEEPER CONNECTION TO THE LBX THAN NORMAL PLAYERS, AND WITH IT COMES DEVASTATING POWER!
WITH THIS BATTLE I'LL TAKE MY INFINITY ENGINE, VAN YAMANO...
...AND THEN ...
... JAPAN... NO, THE ENTIRE WORLD ...
BA
AM
...WILL BELONG TO ME!

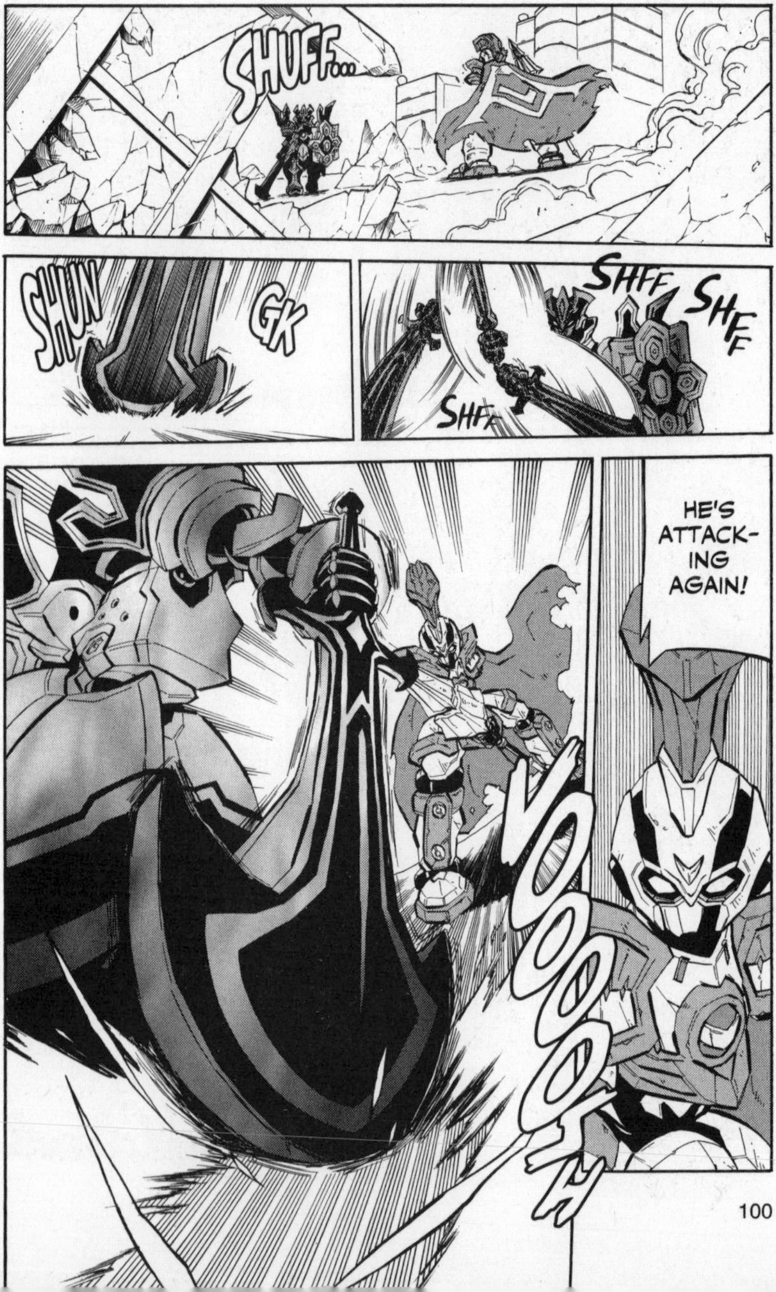
SHUFF...
SHFF
SHFF
SHFF
SHUN
GK
HE'S ATTACK-ING AGAIN!
VOOOOOH

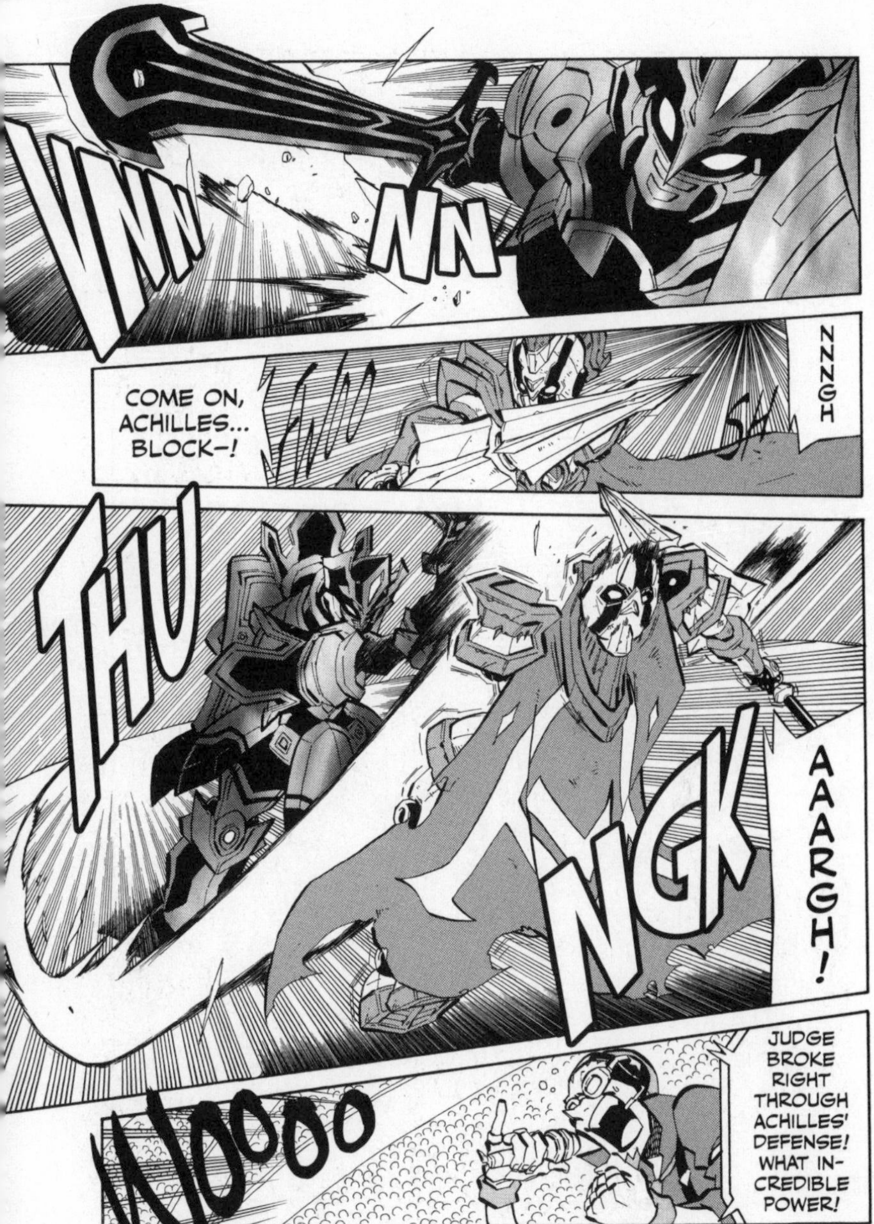
VNN
NN
NNNGH
SH
COME ON, ACHILLES... BLOCK–!
AAAARGH!
THU
NGK
JUDGE BROKE RIGHT THROUGH ACHILLES' DEFENSE! WHAT IN-CREDIBLE POWER!
WOOOO

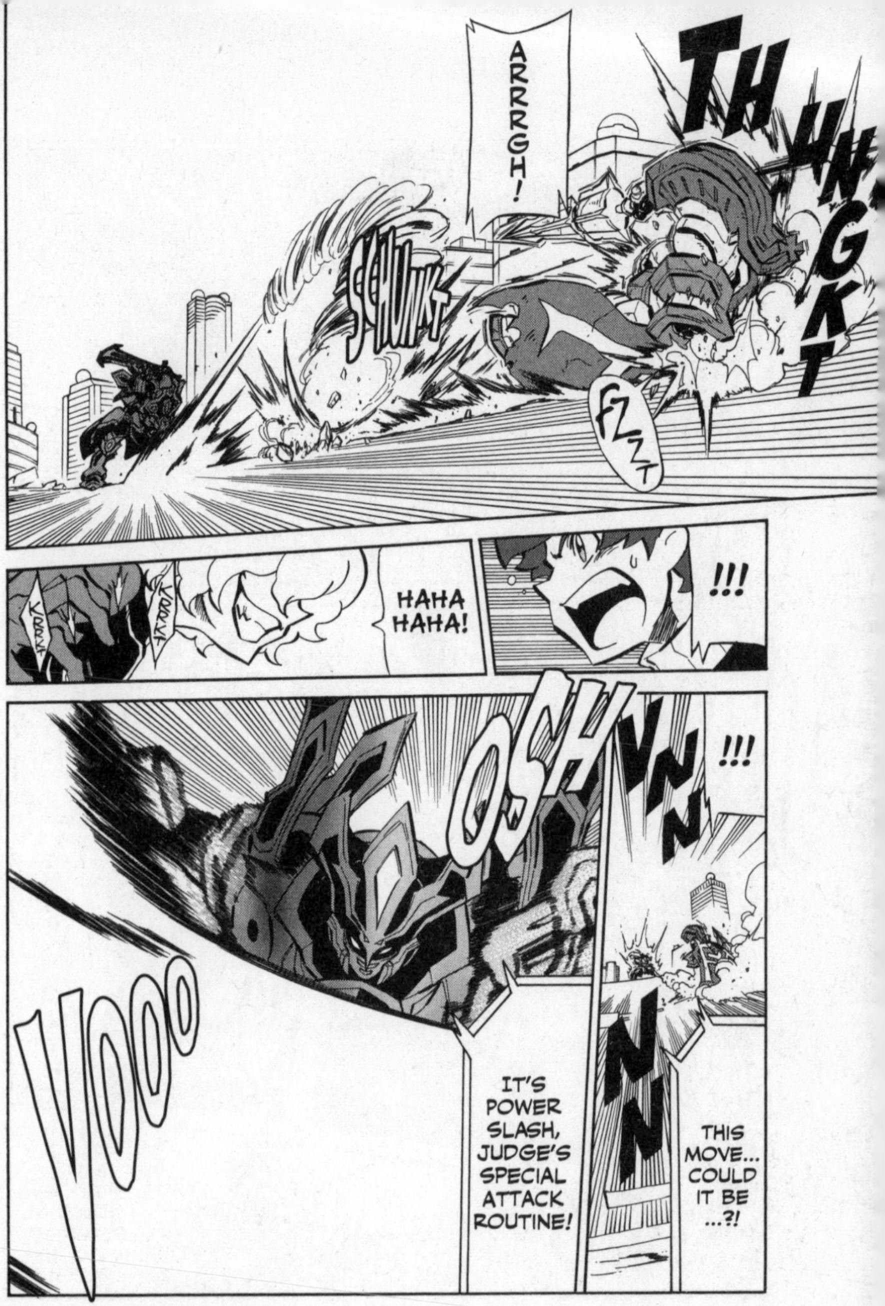
THUNGKT
ARRRGH!
SCHUNKT
FZZT
!!!
HAHA HAHA!
KRRKT
KRRKT
!!!
THIS MOVE... COULD IT BE ...?!
IT'S POWER SLASH, JUDGE'S SPECIAL ATTACK ROUTINE!
VOOO

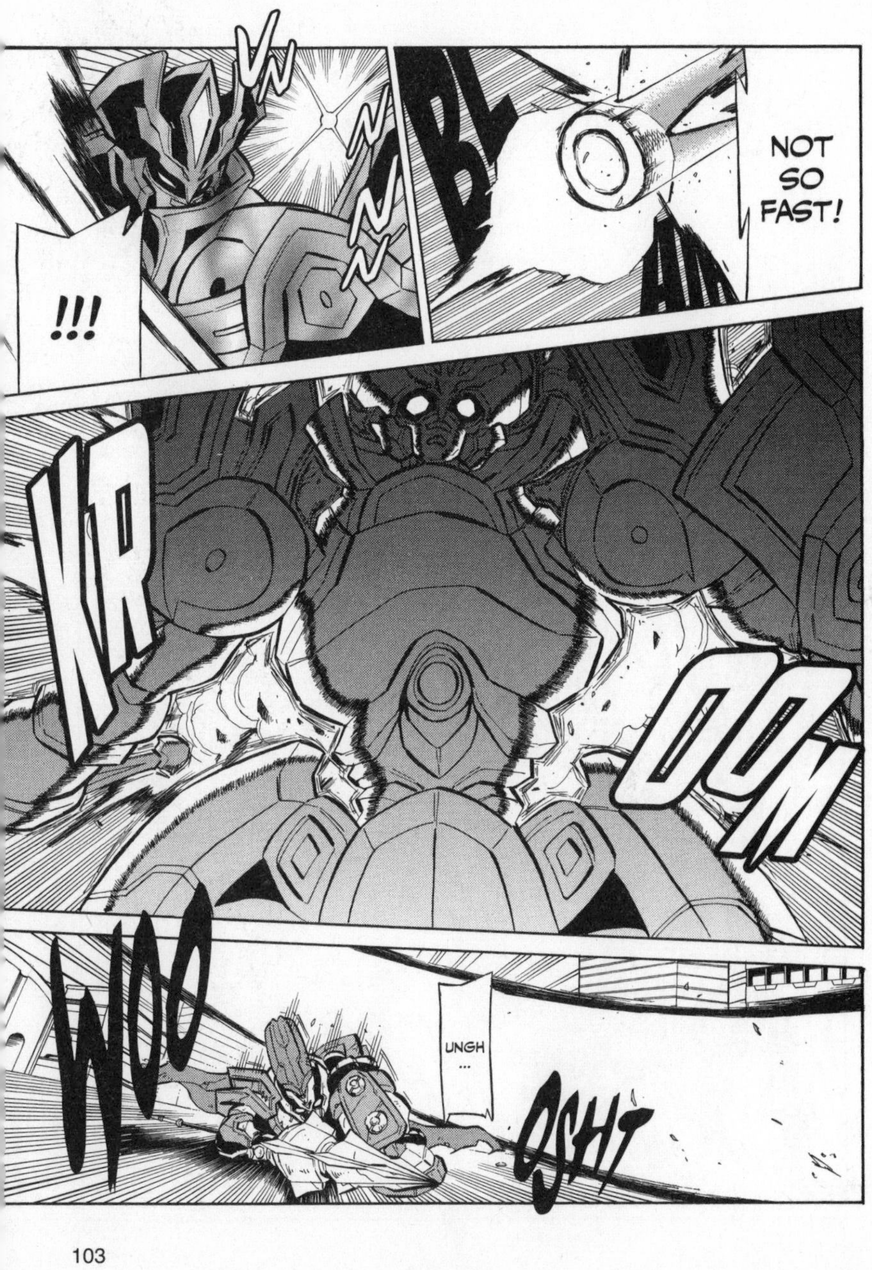
NOT SO FAST!
!!!
UNGH …

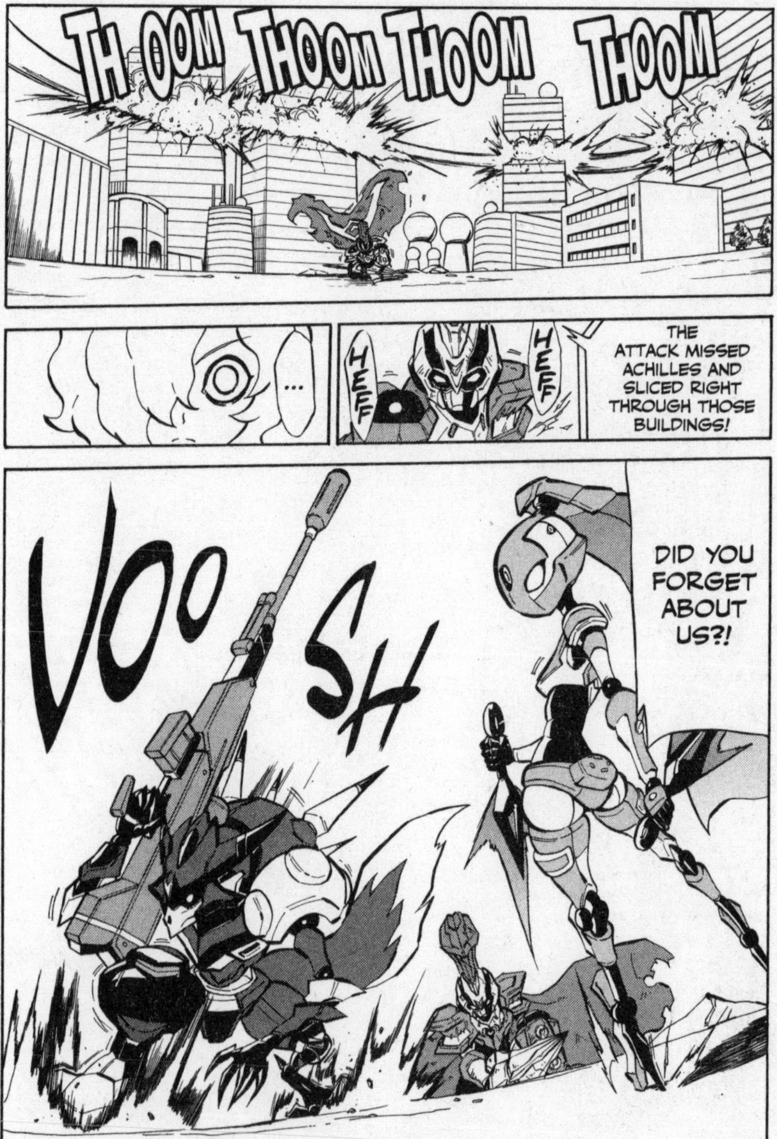
TH OOM THOOM THOOM THOOM
THE ATTACK MISSED ACHILLES AND SLICED RIGHT THROUGH THOSE BUILDINGS!
HEFF
HEFF
...
DID YOU FORGET ABOUT US?!
VOOSH

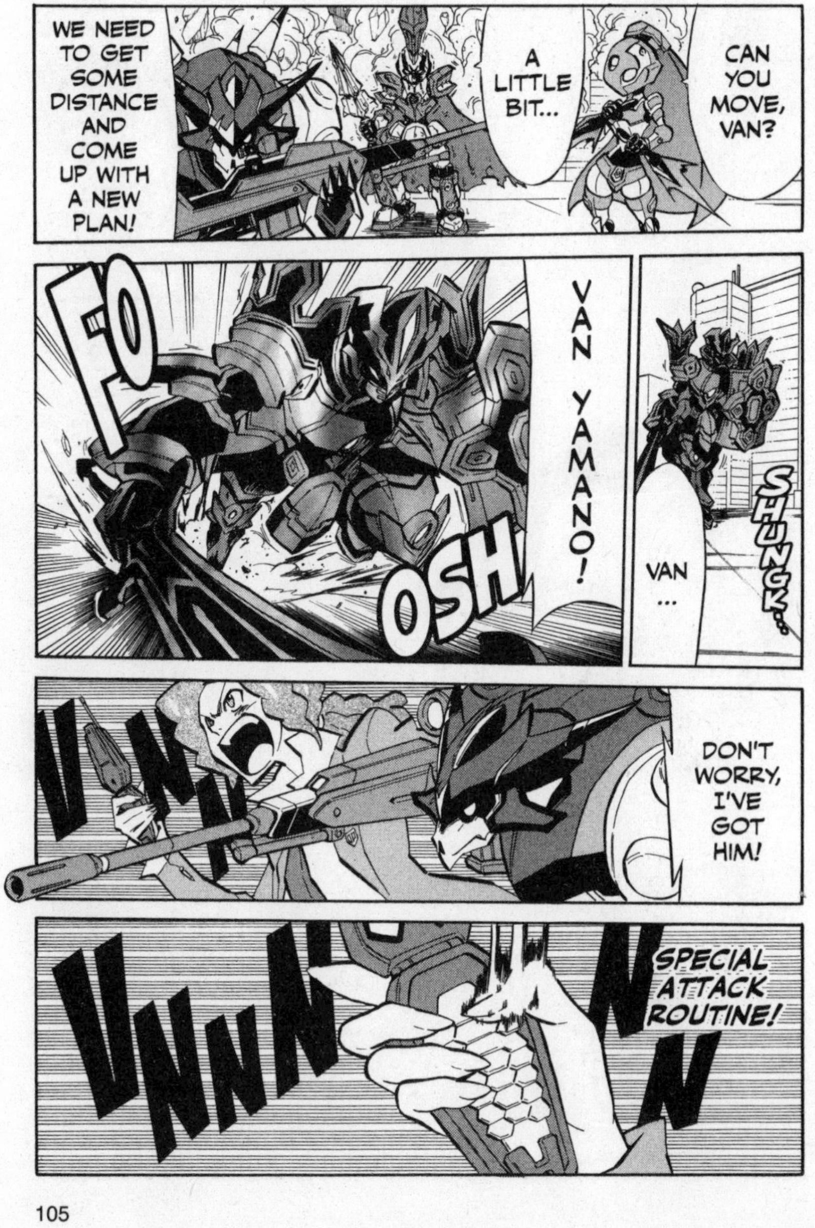
CAN YOU MOVE, VAN?
A LITTLE BIT...
WE NEED TO GET SOME DISTANCE AND COME UP WITH A NEW PLAN!
SHUNGK...
VAN ...
VAN YAMANO!
FOOSH
DON'T WORRY, I'VE GOT HIM!
VNNN
SPECIAL ATTACK ROUTINE!
VNNNNNN

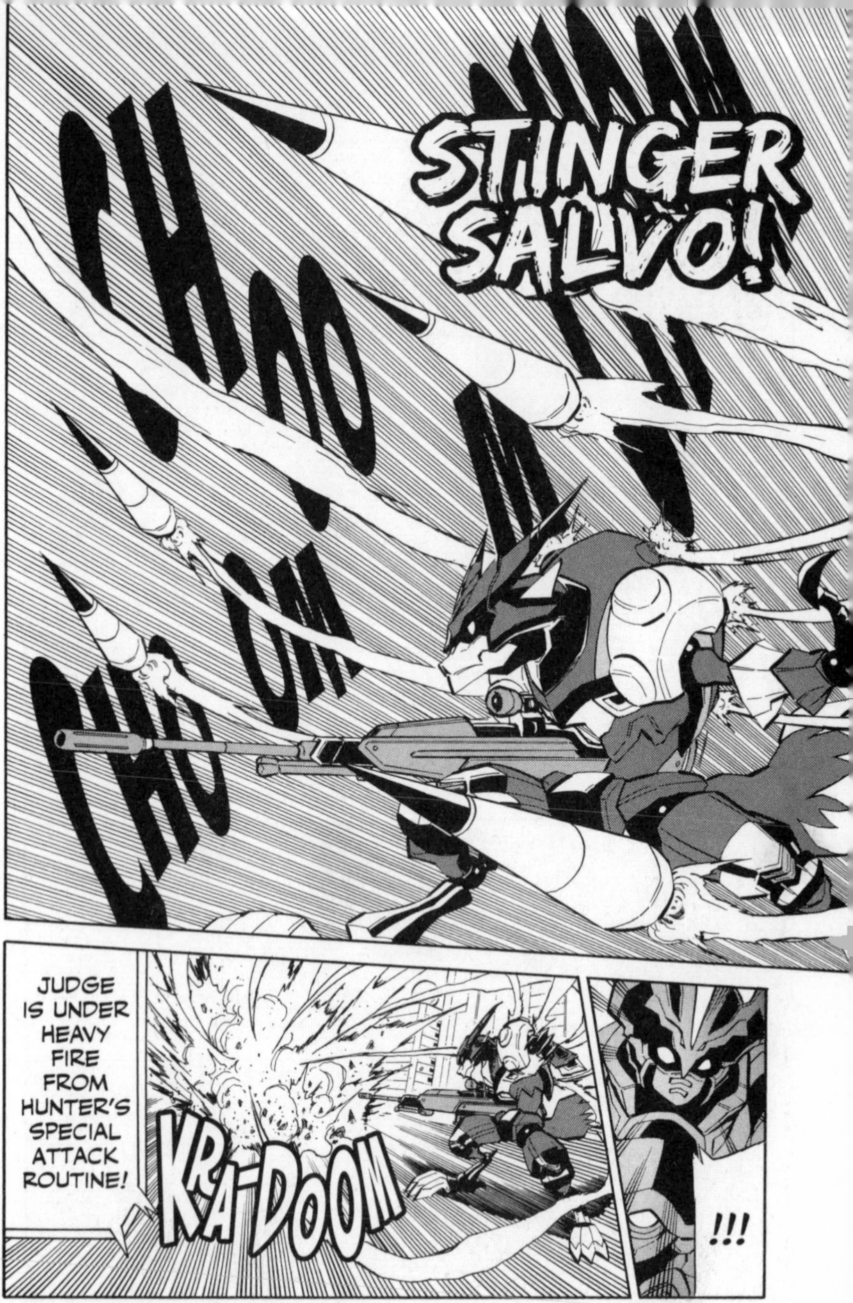
STINGER SALVO!
!!!
JUDGE IS UNDER HEAVY FIRE FROM HUNTER'S SPECIAL ATTACK ROUTINE!
KRA-DOOM

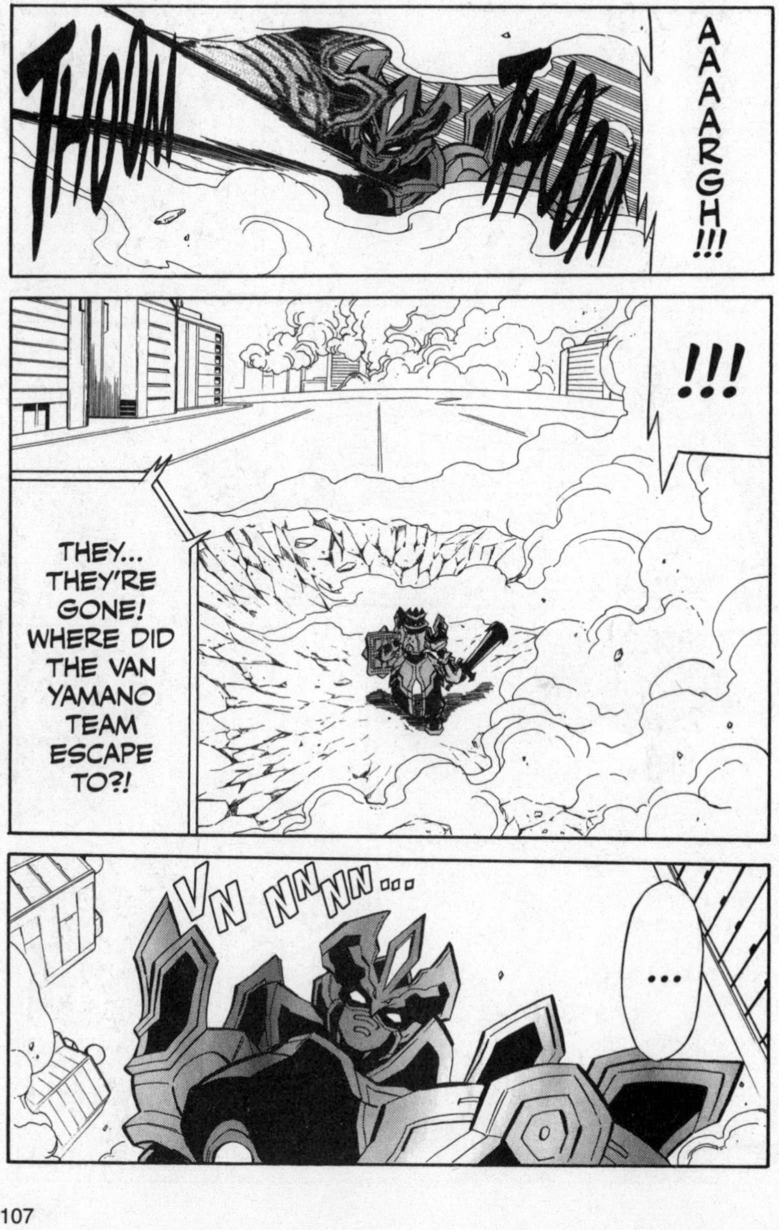
AAAARGH!!!
!!!
THEY... THEY'RE GONE! WHERE DID THE VAN YAMANO TEAM ESCAPE TO?!
...
VN NNNN...

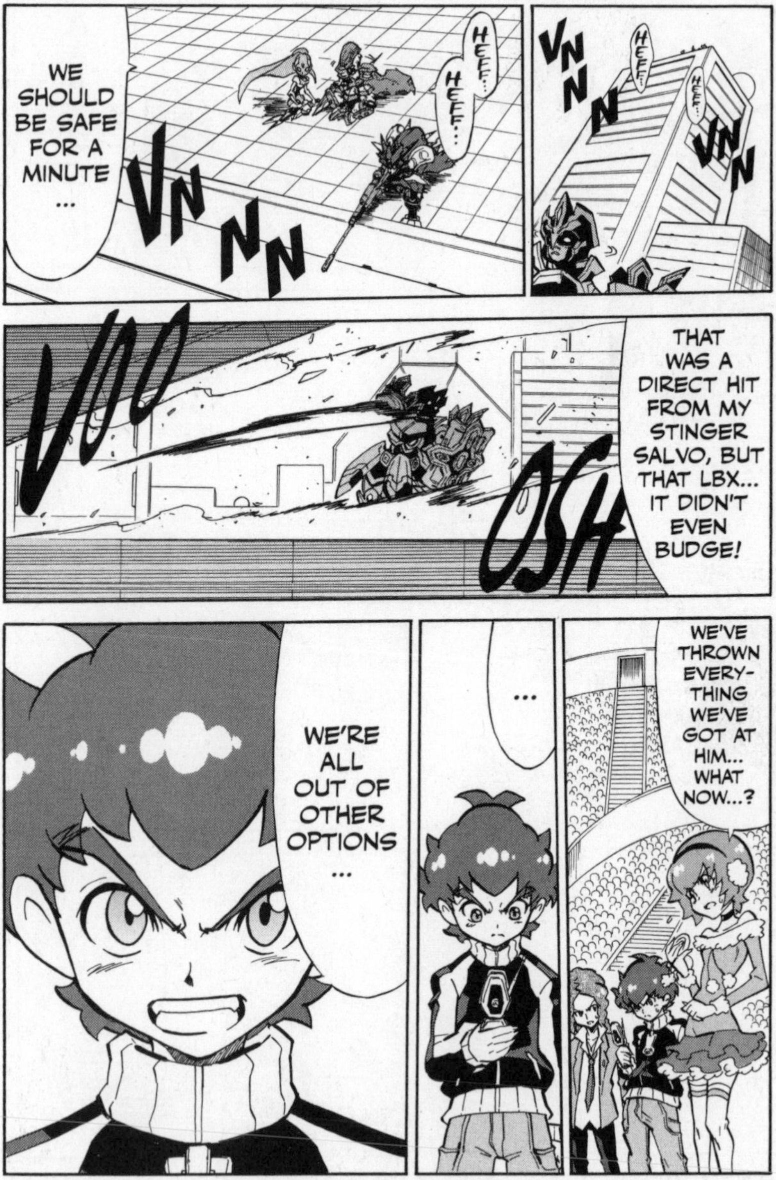
HEFF...
HEFF...
VNNN
VNNN
HEFF...
HEFF...
WE SHOULD BE SAFE FOR A MINUTE ...
VNNN
THAT WAS A DIRECT HIT FROM MY STINGER SALVO, BUT THAT LBX... IT DIDN'T EVEN BUDGE!
VOOOSH
WE'VE THROWN EVERY-THING WE'VE GOT AT HIM... WHAT NOW...?
...
WE'RE ALL OUT OF OTHER OPTIONS ...

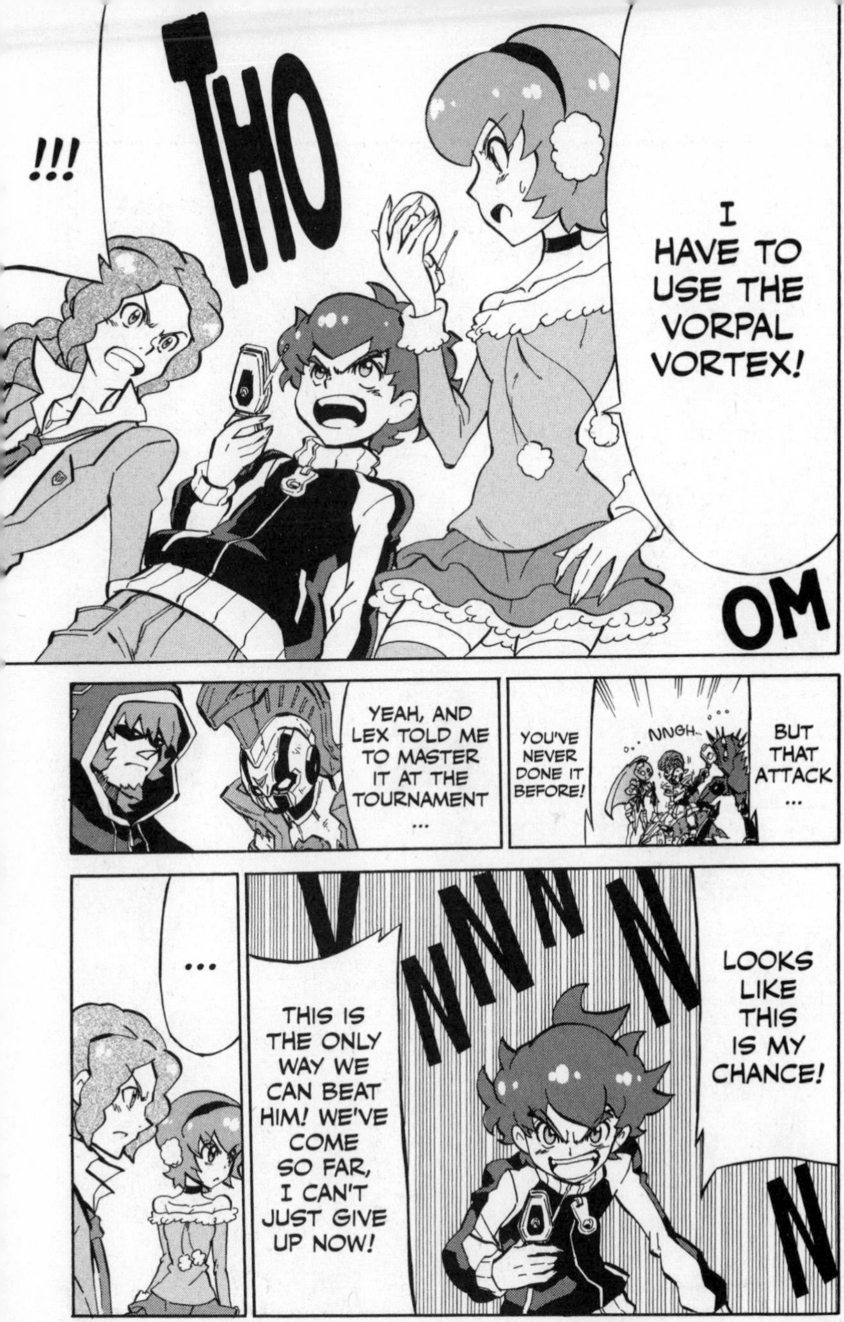
I HAVE TO USE THE VORPAL VORTEX!
THO
!!!
OM
BUT THAT ATTACK ...
NNGH...
YOU'VE NEVER DONE IT BEFORE!
YEAH, AND LEX TOLD ME TO MASTER IT AT THE TOURNAMENT ...
LOOKS LIKE THIS IS MY CHANCE!
VNNNN
N
THIS IS THE ONLY WAY WE CAN BEAT HIM! WE'VE COME SO FAR, I CAN'T JUST GIVE UP NOW!
...

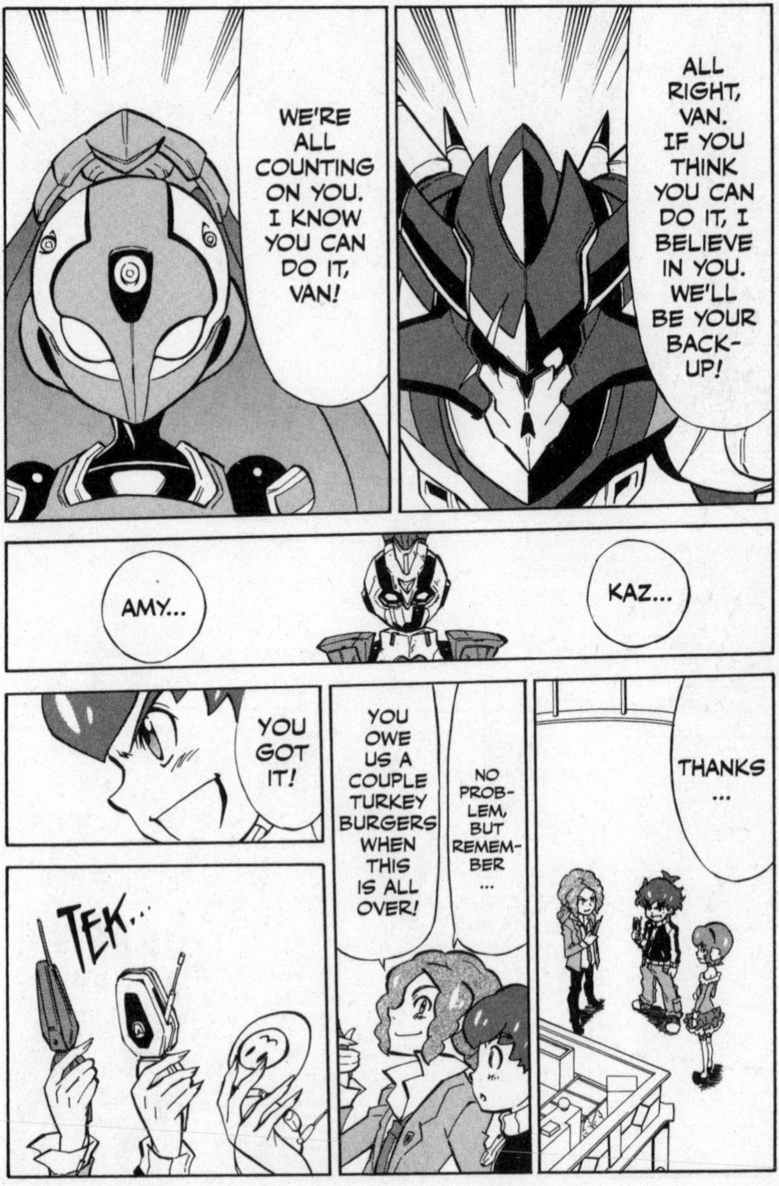
ALL RIGHT, VAN. IF YOU THINK YOU CAN DO IT, I BELIEVE IN YOU. WE'LL BE YOUR BACK-UP!
WE'RE ALL COUNTING ON YOU. I KNOW YOU CAN DO IT, VAN!
KAZ...
AMY...
THANKS ...
NO PROB-LEM, BUT REMEM-BER ...
YOU OWE US A COUPLE TURKEY BURGERS WHEN THIS IS ALL OVER!
YOU GOT IT!
TEK...

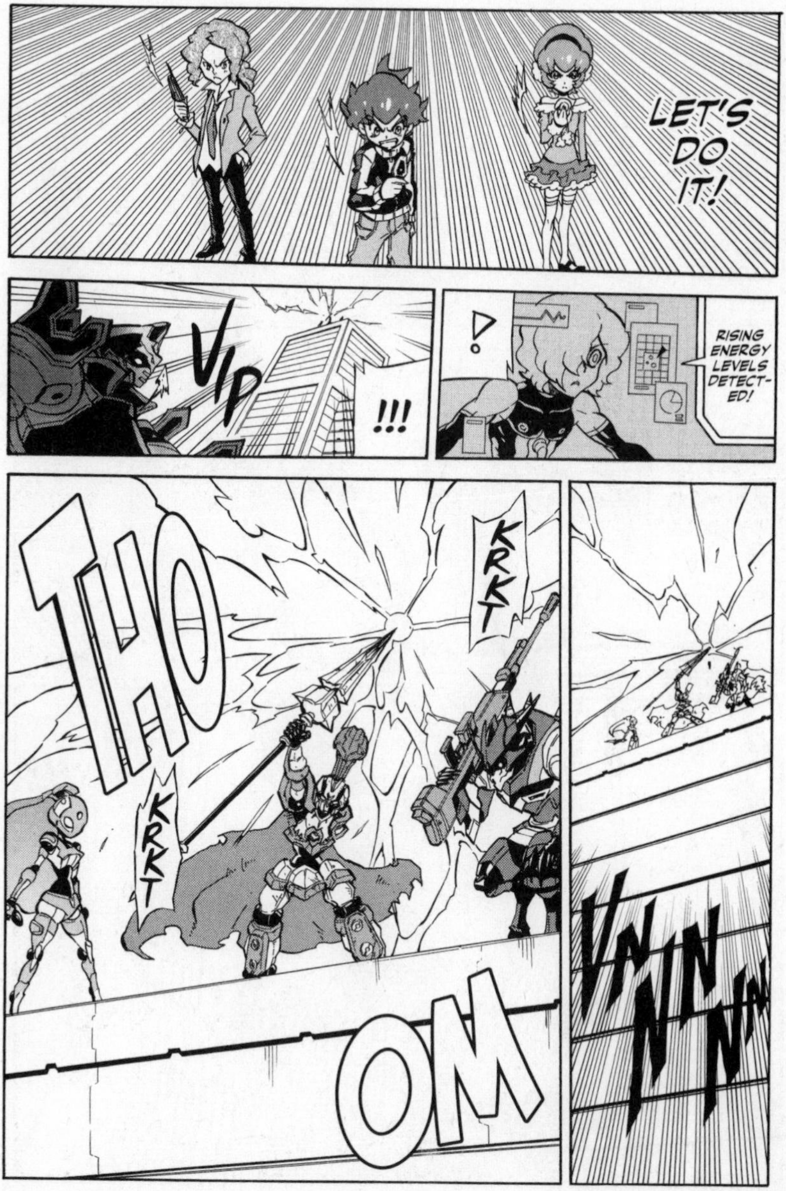
LET'S DO IT!
!
RISING ENERGY LEVELS DETECTED!
VIP
!!!
VNNNNN
THOOM
KRRKT
KRRKT

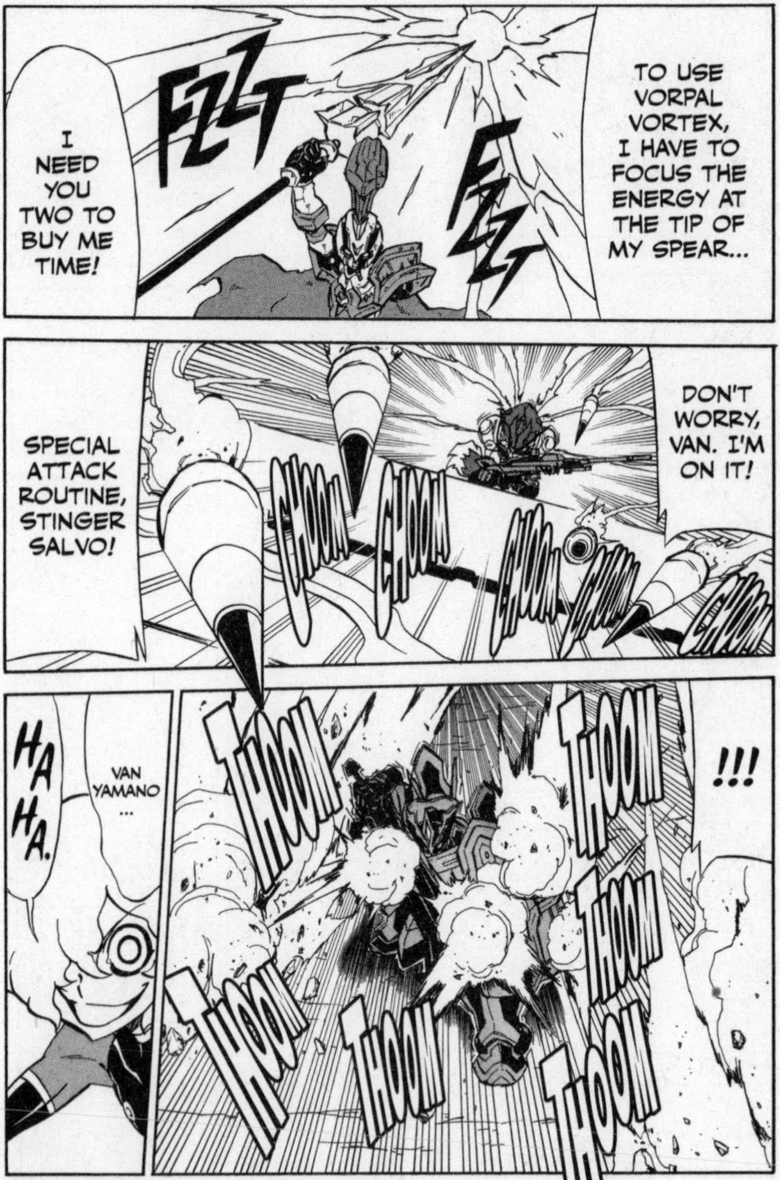
TO USE VORPAL VORTEX, I HAVE TO FOCUS THE ENERGY AT THE TIP OF MY SPEAR...
FZZZT
FZZT
I NEED YOU TWO TO BUY ME TIME!
DON'T WORRY, VAN. I'M ON IT!
CHOOM
CHOOM
CHOOM
CHOOM
SPECIAL ATTACK ROUTINE, STINGER SALVO!
!!!
THOOM
THOOM
THOOM
THOOM
THOOM
THOOM
VAN YAMANO...
HA HA HA.

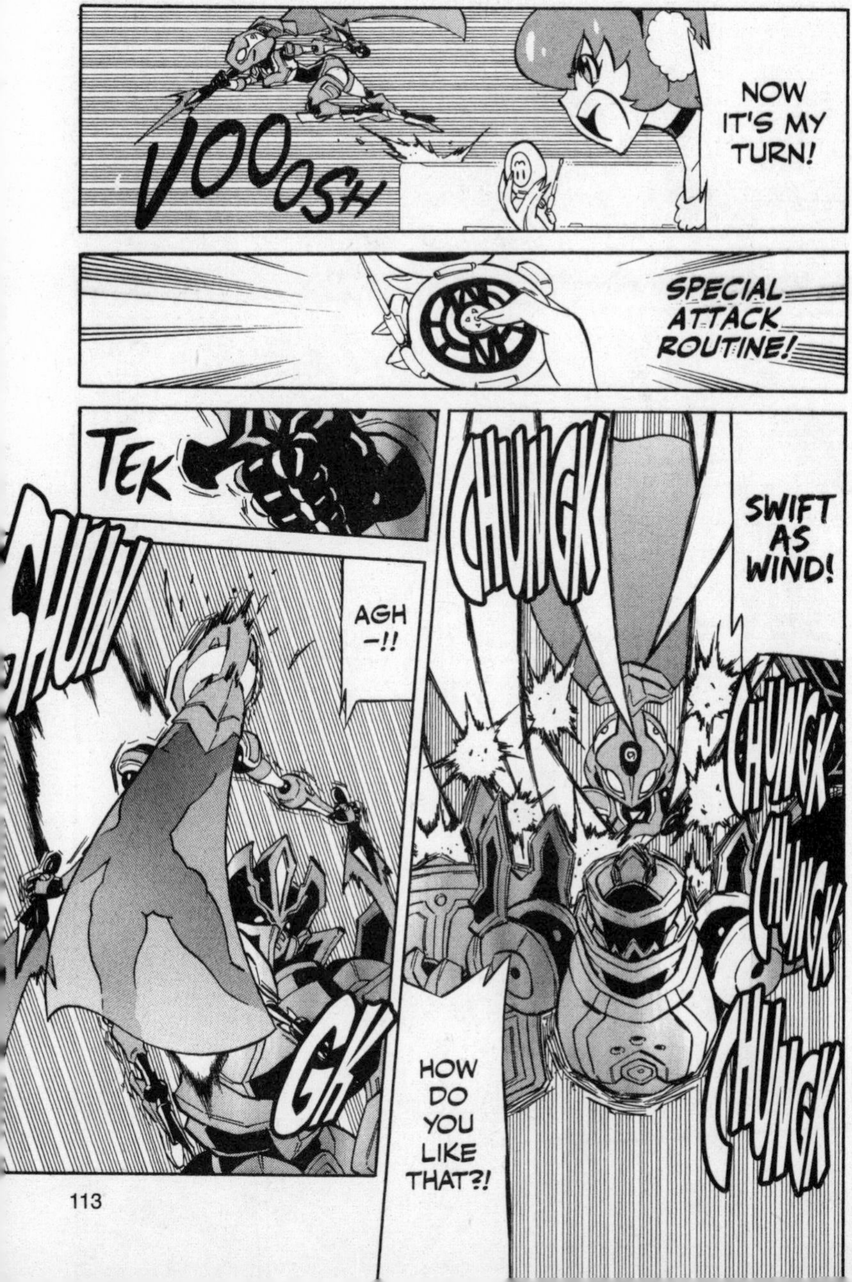
NOW IT'S MY TURN!
VOOOSH
SPECIAL ATTACK ROUTINE!
CHUNCK
SWIFT AS WIND!
CHUNCK
CHUNCK
CHUNCK
HOW DO YOU LIKE THAT?!
TEK
AGH—!!
GK

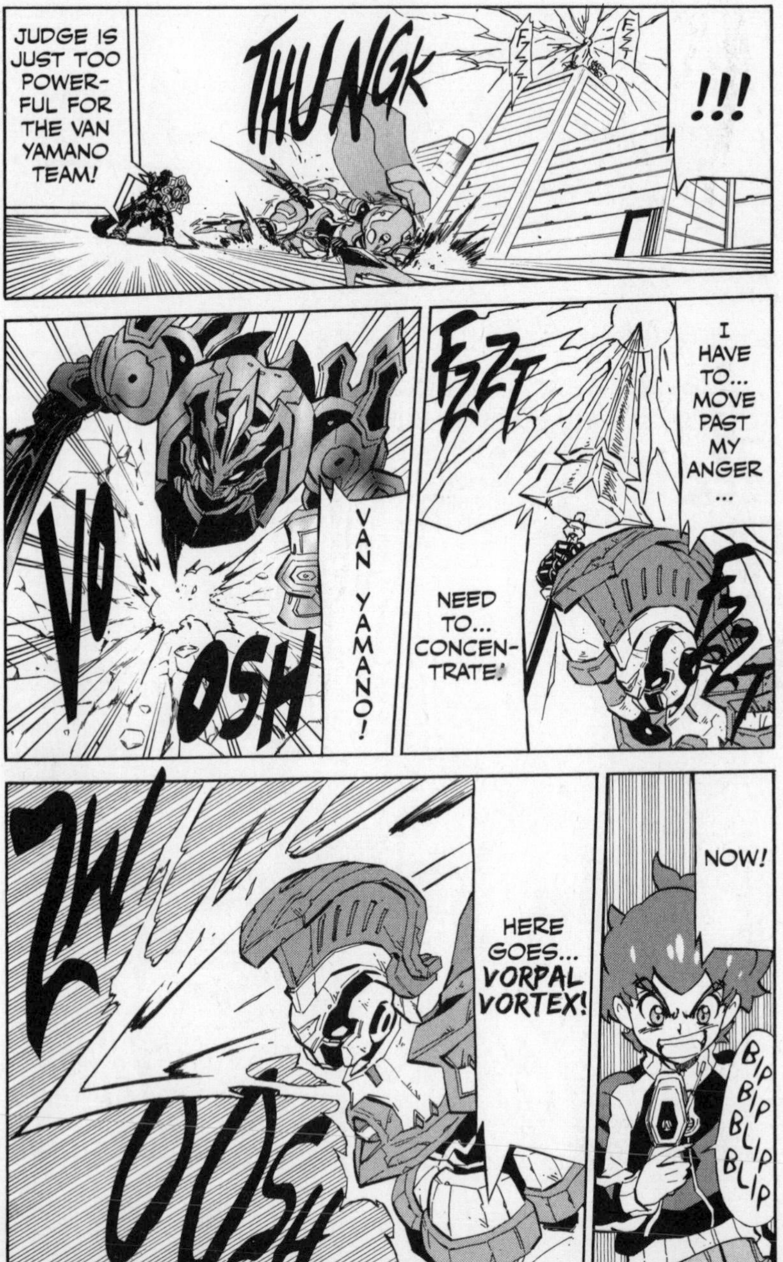
FZZT
FZZT
!!!
THUNGK
JUDGE IS JUST TOO POWER-FUL FOR THE VAN YAMANO TEAM!
I HAVE TO... MOVE PAST MY ANGER ...
FZZT
NEED TO... CONCEN-TRATE!
FZZZT
VAN YAMANO!
VOOSH
NOW!
BIP BIP BLIP BLIP
HERE GOES... VORPAL VORTEX!
ZWOOSH

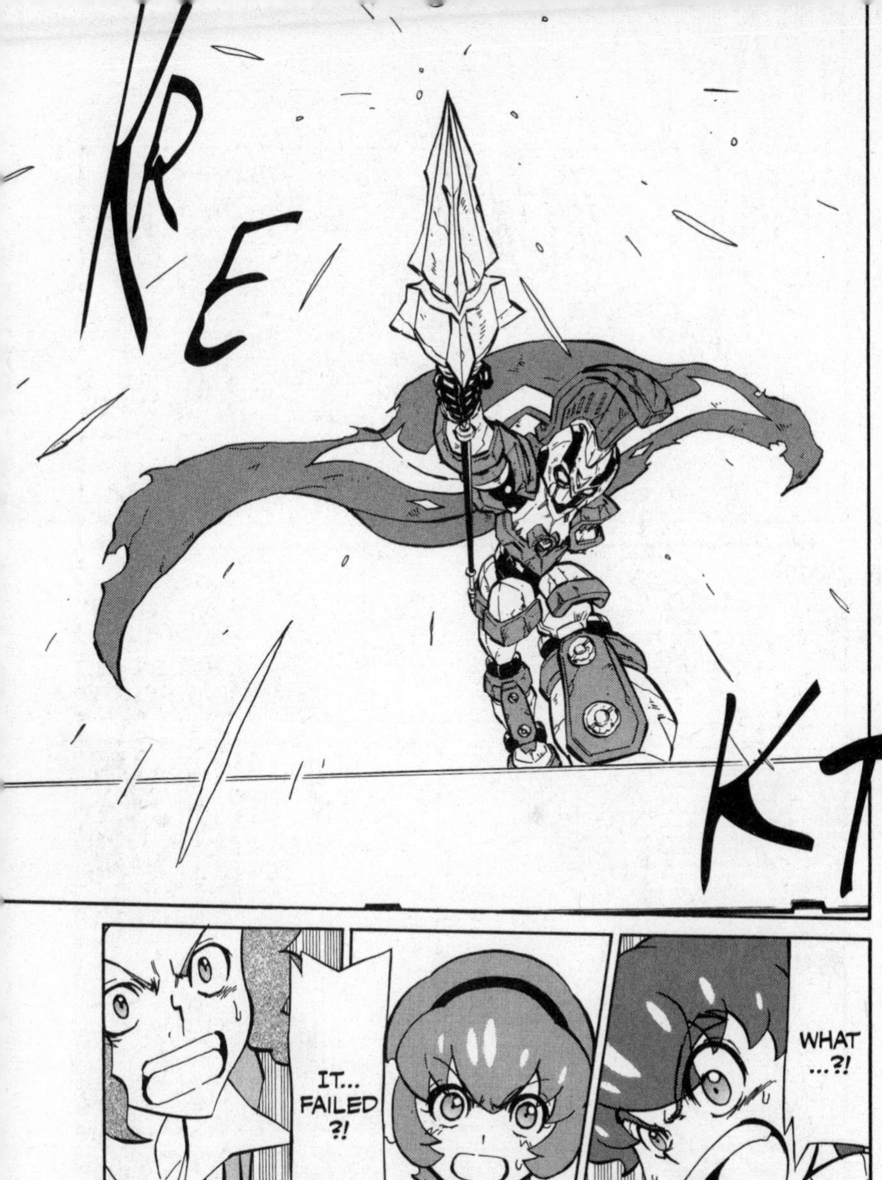
KRE
KT
WHAT ...?!
IT... FAILED ?!

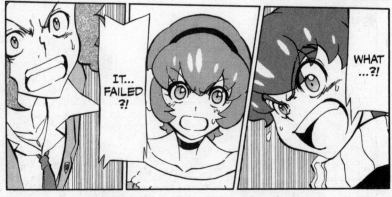

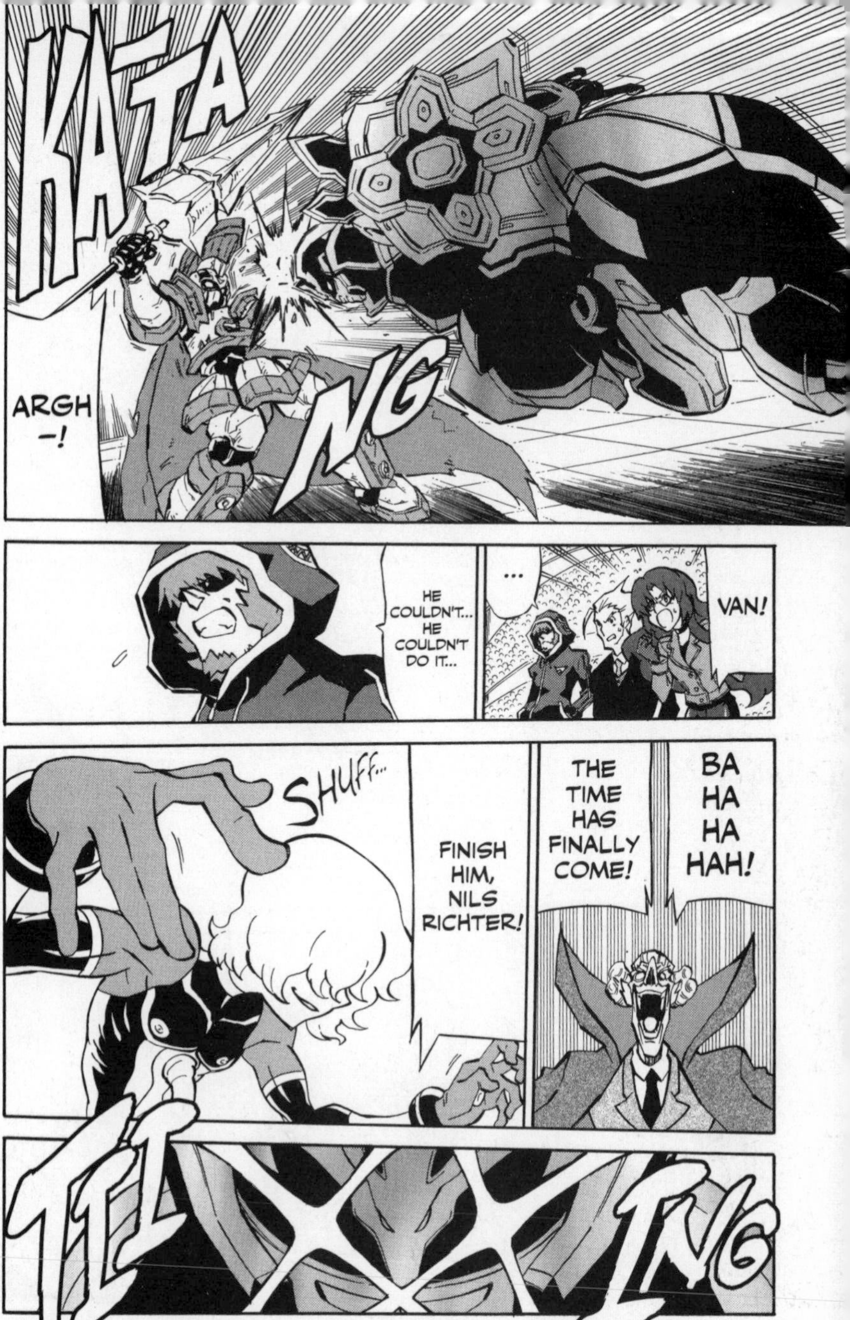
KATA
NG
ARGH—!
VAN!
...
HE COULDN'T... HE COULDN'T DO IT...
BA HA HA HAH!
THE TIME HAS FINALLY COME!
FINISH HIM, NILS RICHTER!
SHUFF...
TIIING

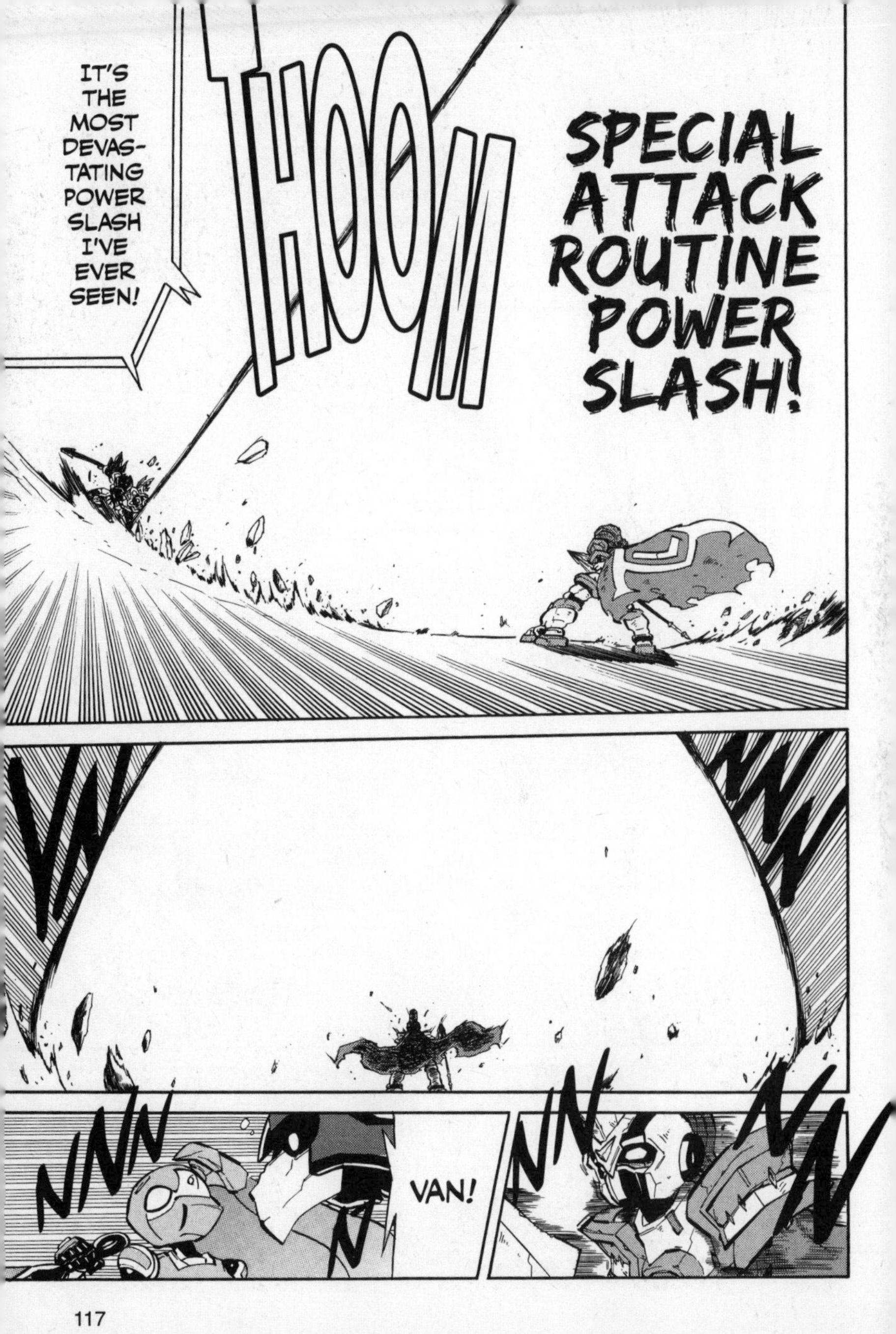
SPECIAL ATTACK ROUTINE POWER SLASH!
THOOM
IT'S THE MOST DEVAS-TATING POWER SLASH I'VE EVER SEEN!
VAN!

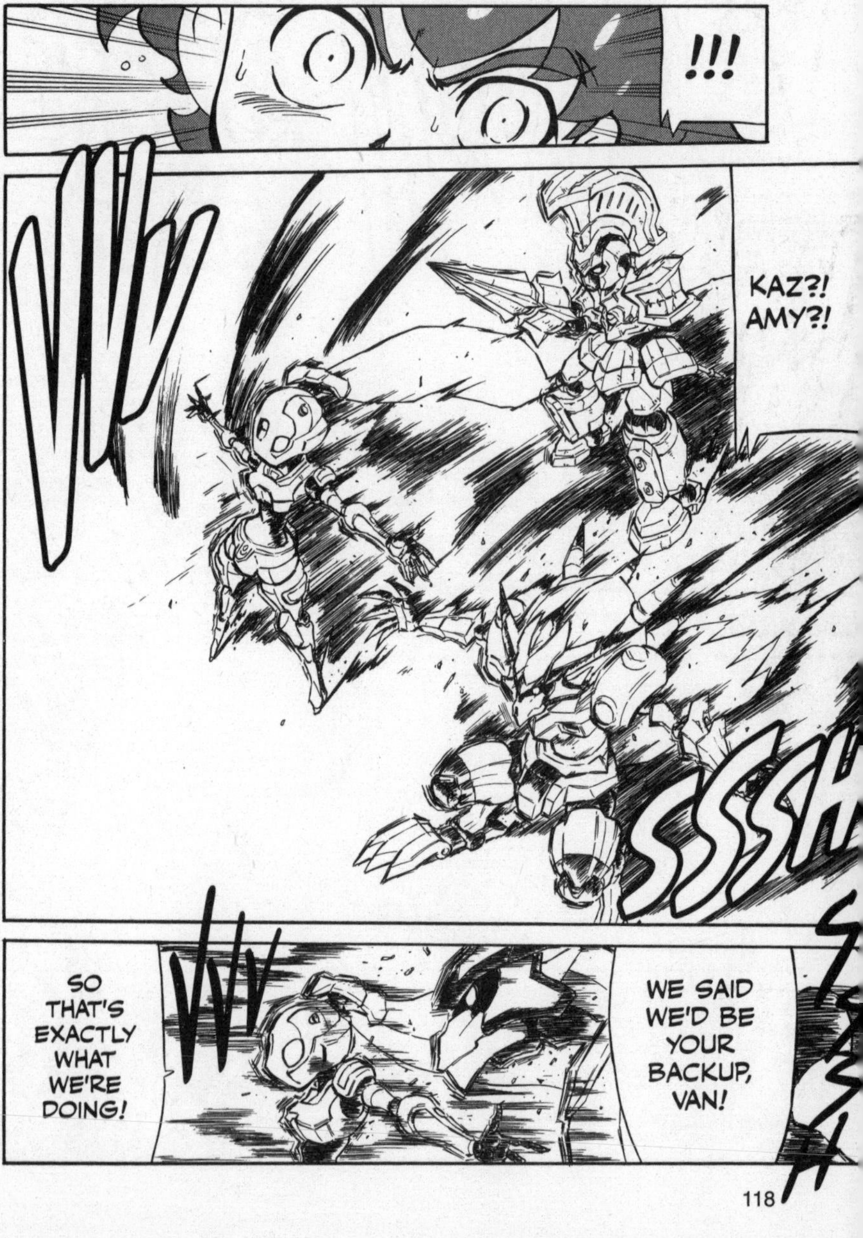
!!!
KAZ?! AMY?!
WE SAID WE'D BE YOUR BACKUP, VAN!
SO THAT'S EXACTLY WHAT WE'RE DOING!

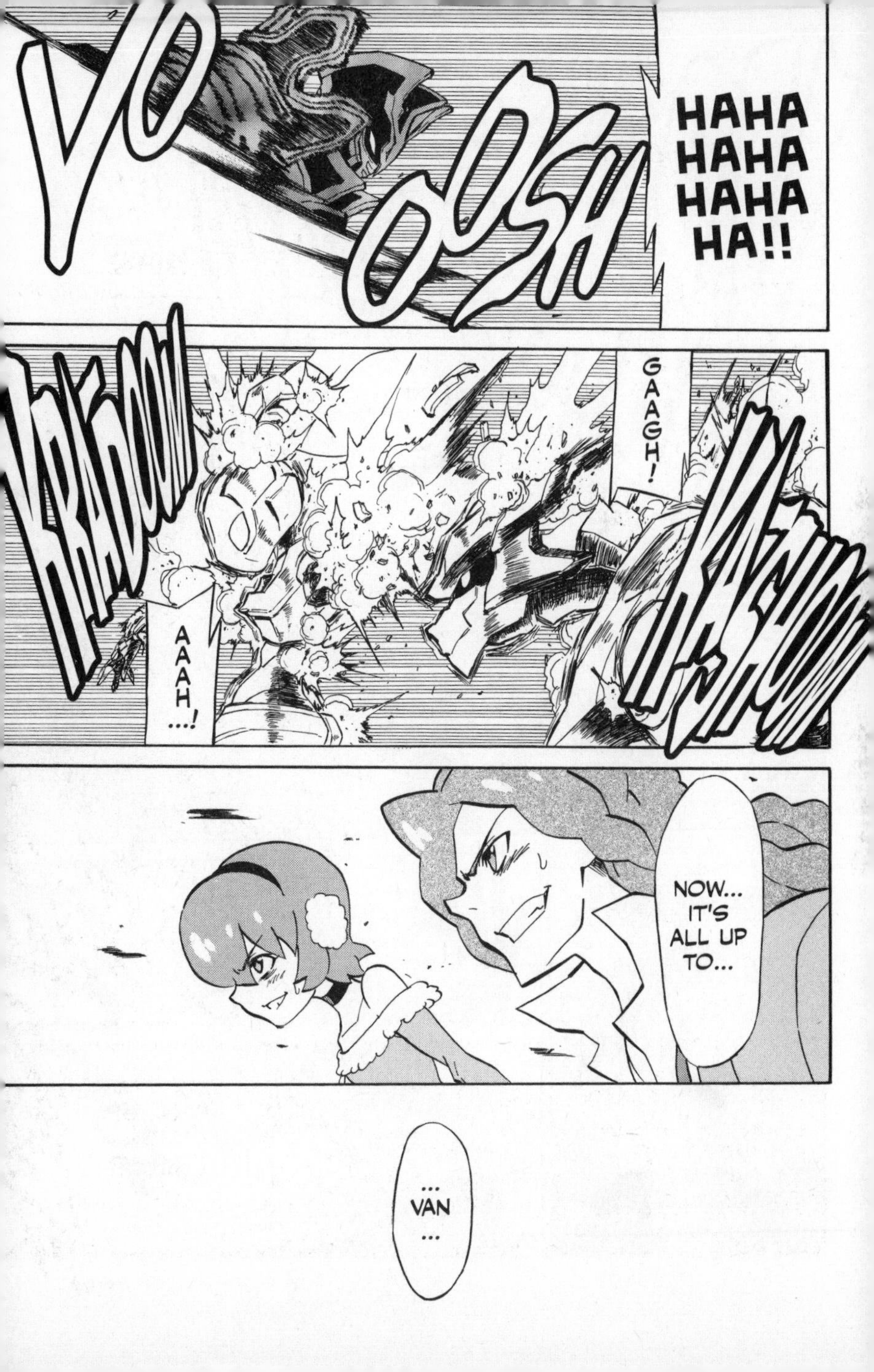
HAHA HAHA HAHA HA!!
VOOSH
GAAGH!
AAAH...!
KRADOOM
NOW... IT'S ALL UP TO...
... VAN ...

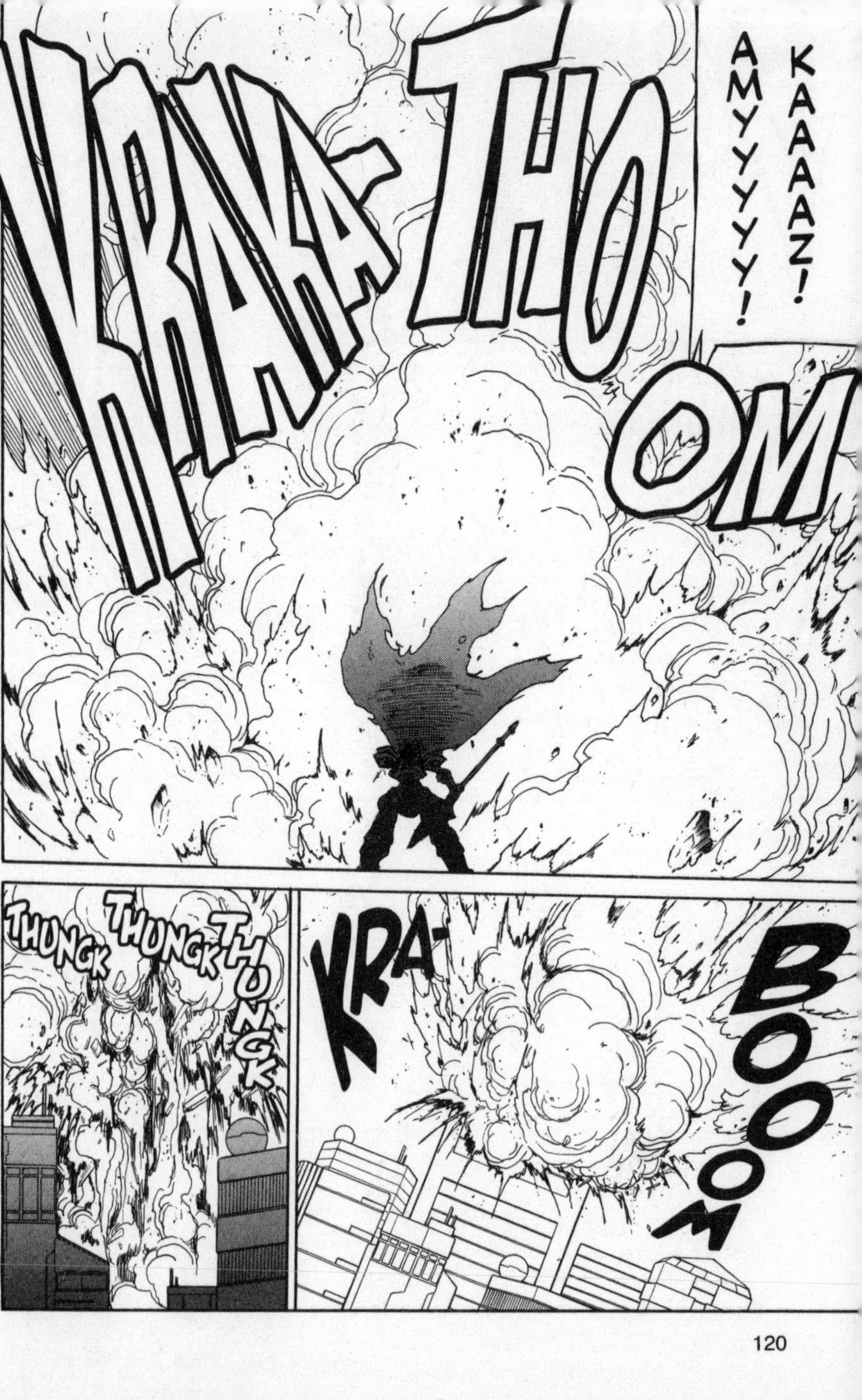
KAAAAAZ!
AMYYYYYY!
KRAKA-THOOM
KRA-BOOOOOM
THUNGK THUNGK THUNGK

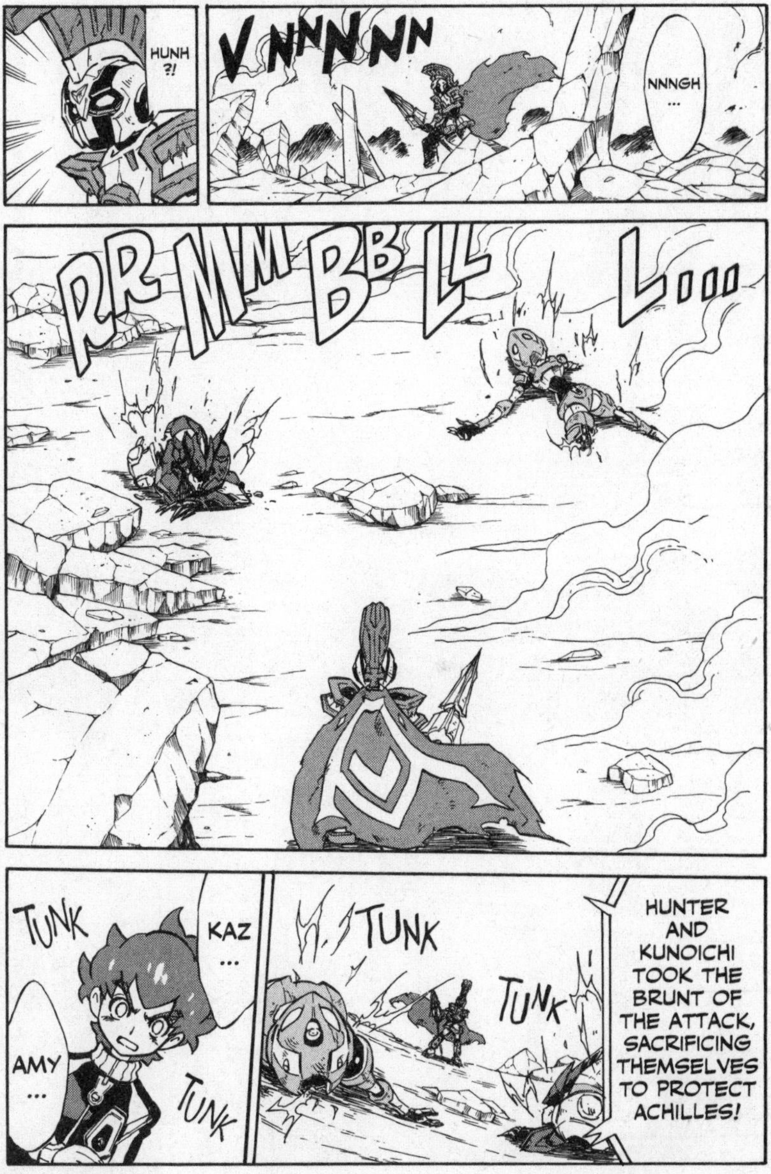
NNNGH ...
VNNNNN
HUNH ?!
RRMMBBLL L...
HUNTER AND KUNOICHI TOOK THE BRUNT OF THE ATTACK, SACRIFICING THEMSELVES TO PROTECT ACHILLES!
TUNK
TUNK
KAZ ...
TUNK
AMY ...
TUNK

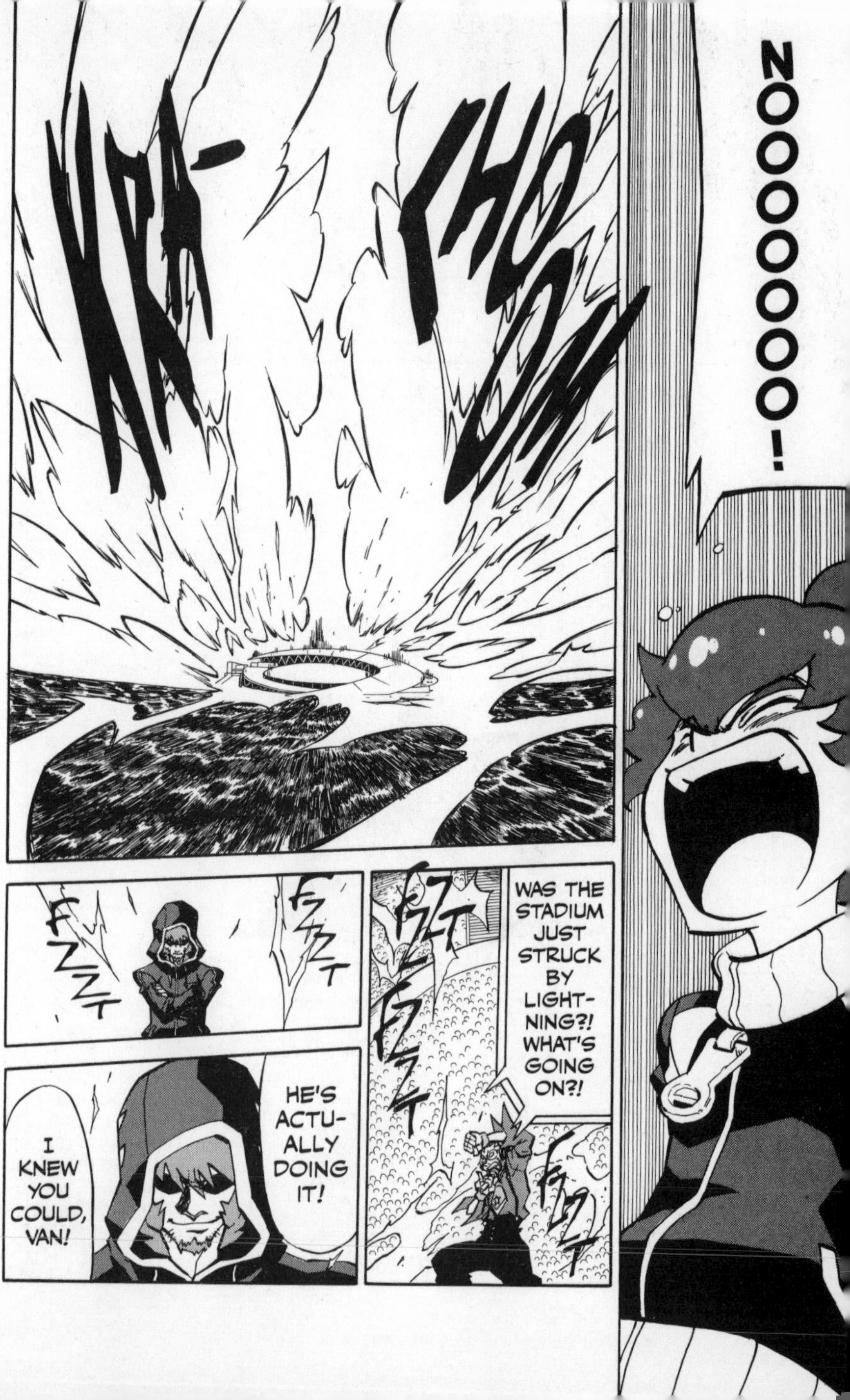
NOOOOOOO!
KRA-CHOOM
FZZT
FZZT
WAS THE STADIUM JUST STRUCK BY LIGHTNING?! WHAT'S GOING ON?!
FZZT
FZZZT
FZZZT
HE'S ACTUALLY DOING IT!
I KNEW YOU COULD, VAN!

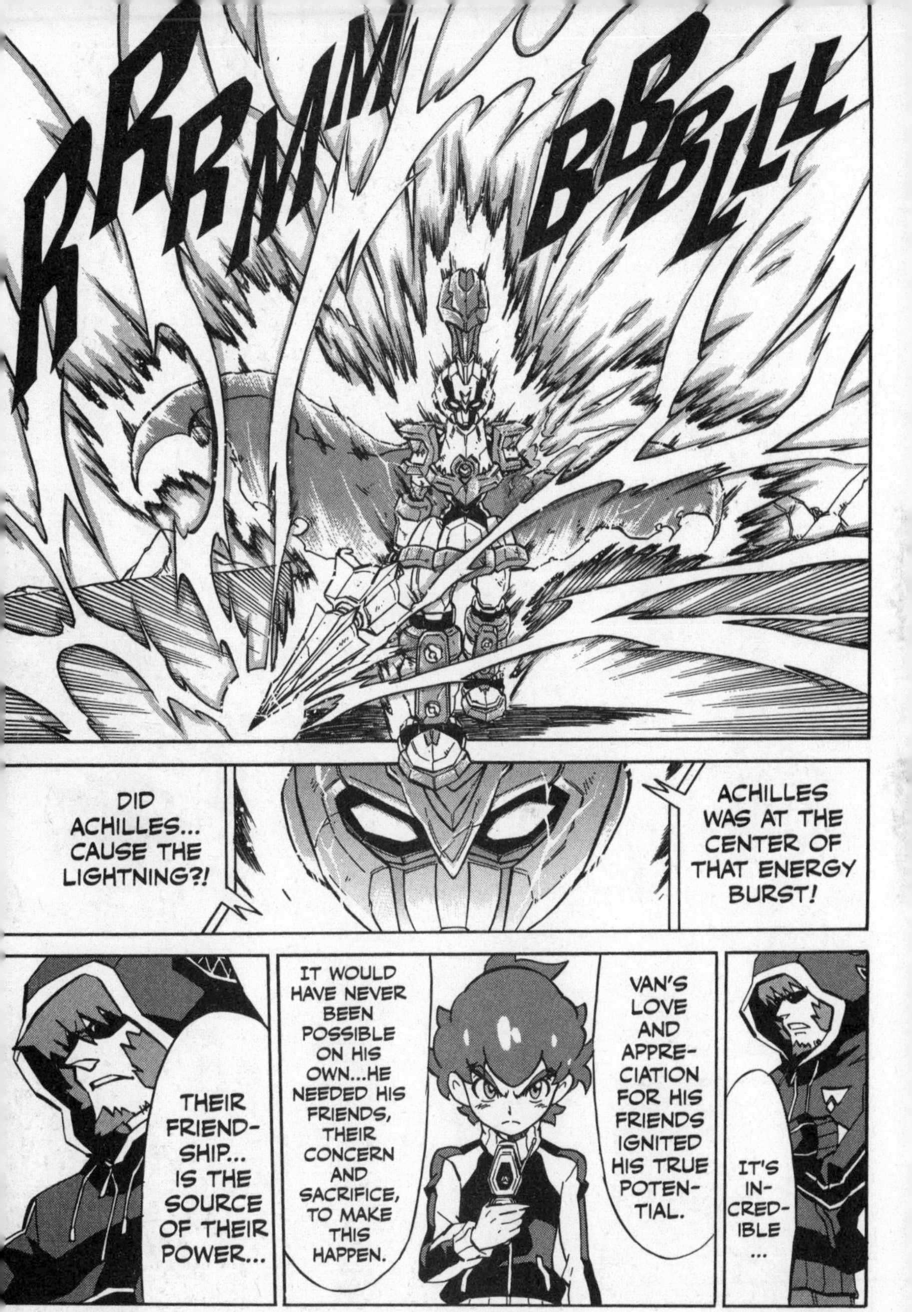
RRRMM
BBBLLL
ACHILLES WAS AT THE CENTER OF THAT ENERGY BURST!
DID ACHILLES... CAUSE THE LIGHTNING?!
IT'S INCREDIBLE...
VAN'S LOVE AND APPRECIATION FOR HIS FRIENDS IGNITED HIS TRUE POTENTIAL.
IT WOULD HAVE NEVER BEEN POSSIBLE ON HIS OWN...HE NEEDED HIS FRIENDS, THEIR CONCERN AND SACRIFICE, TO MAKE THIS HAPPEN.
THEIR FRIENDSHIP... IS THE SOURCE OF THEIR POWER...

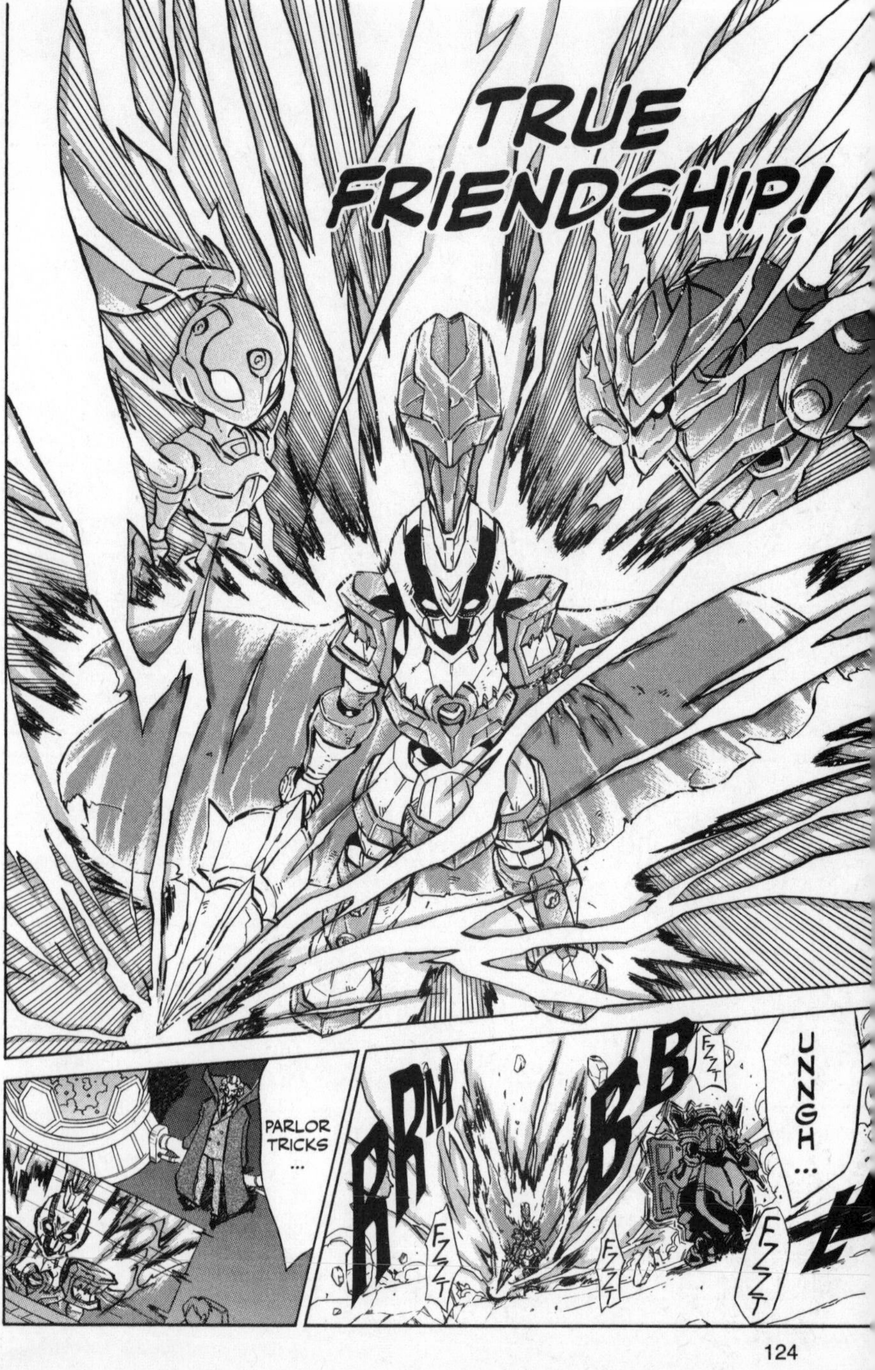
TRUE FRIENDSHIP!
UNNGH...
FZZT
RRM
BB
FZZT
FZZT
FZZT
PARLOR TRICKS...

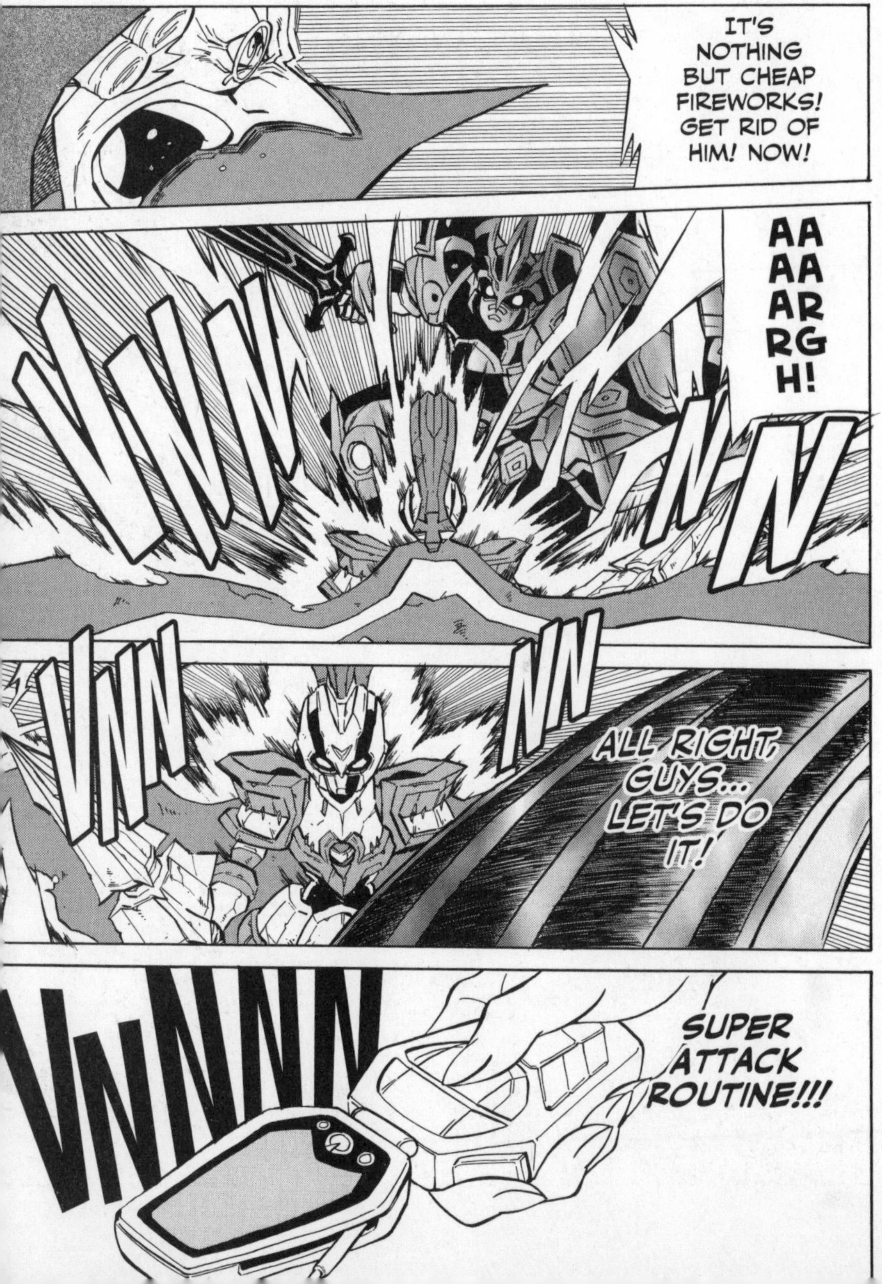
IT'S NOTHING BUT CHEAP FIREWORKS! GET RID OF HIM! NOW!
AAAAARRGH!
ALL RIGHT, GUYS... LET'S DO IT!
NN
VNN
SUPER ATTACK ROUTINE!!!
VNNNNN

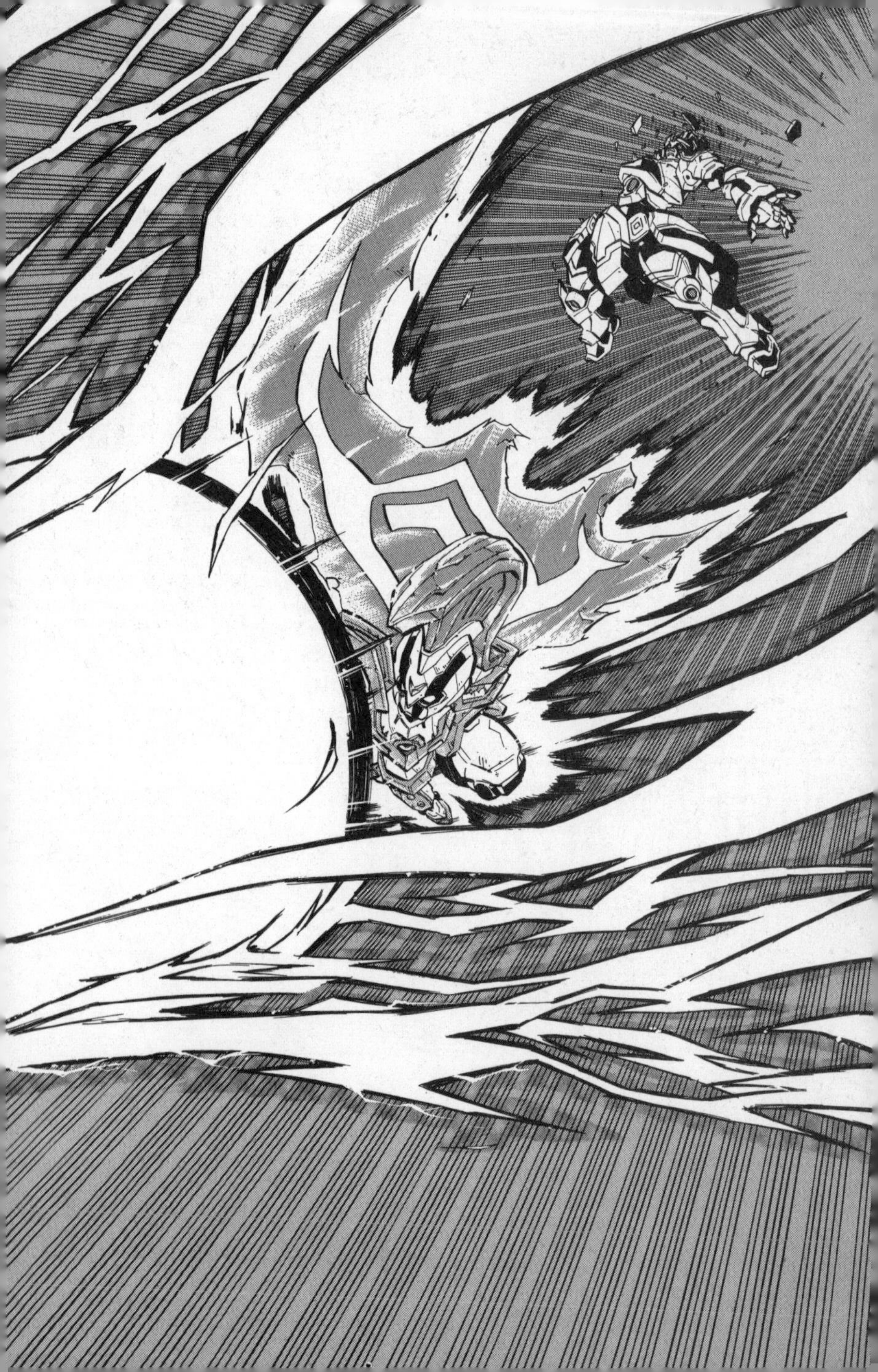

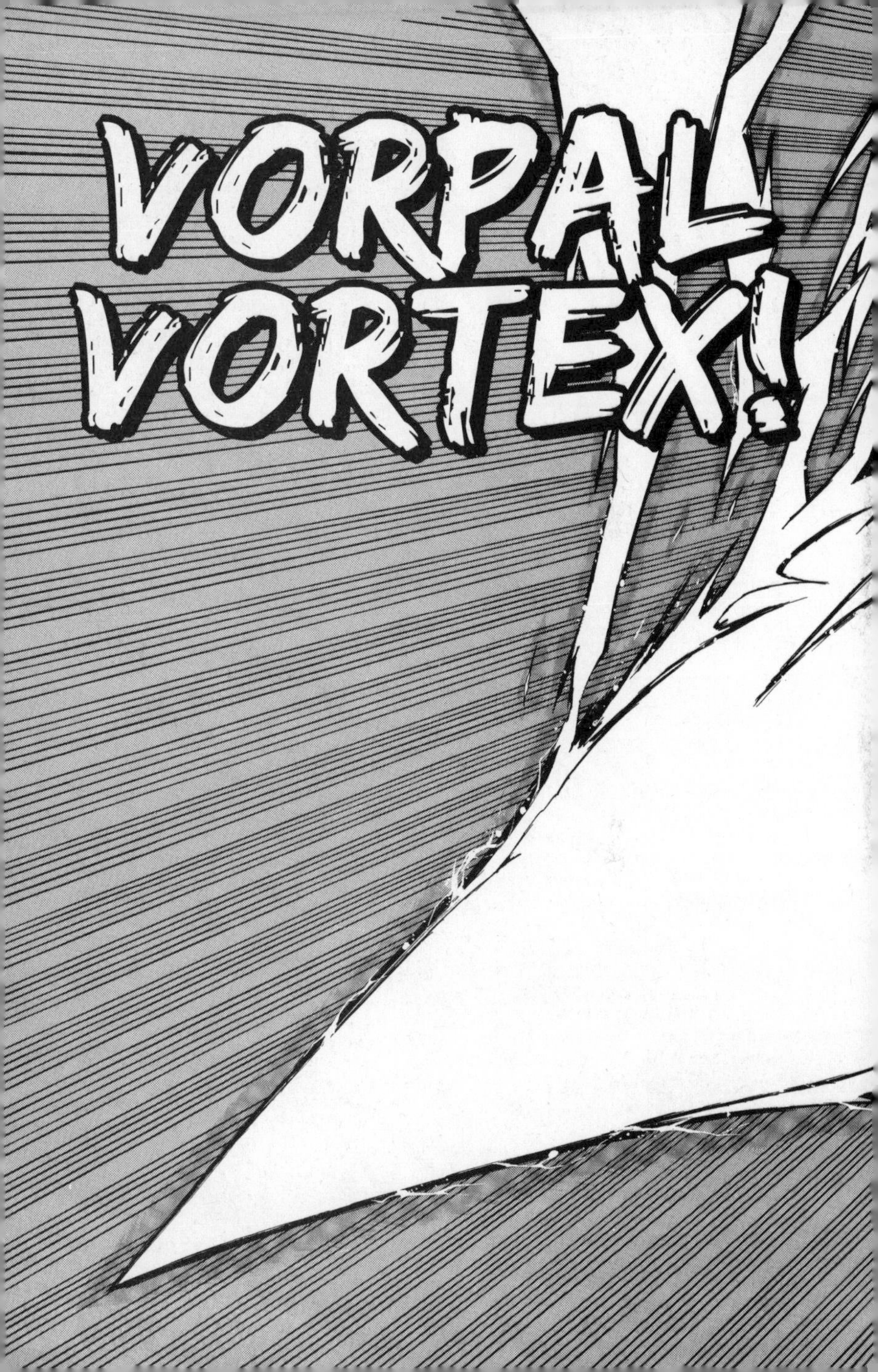
VORPAL VORTEX!

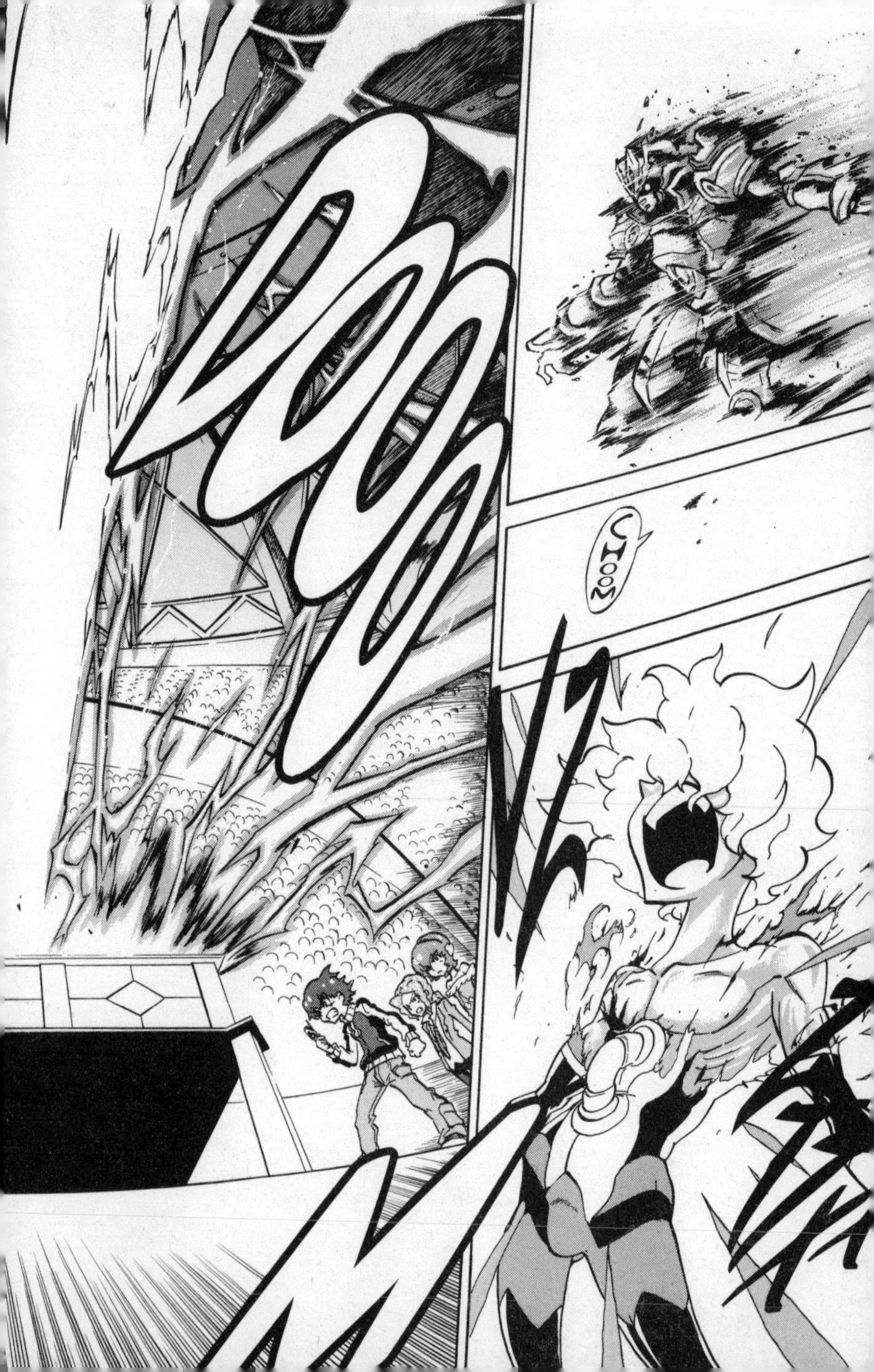
CHOOM

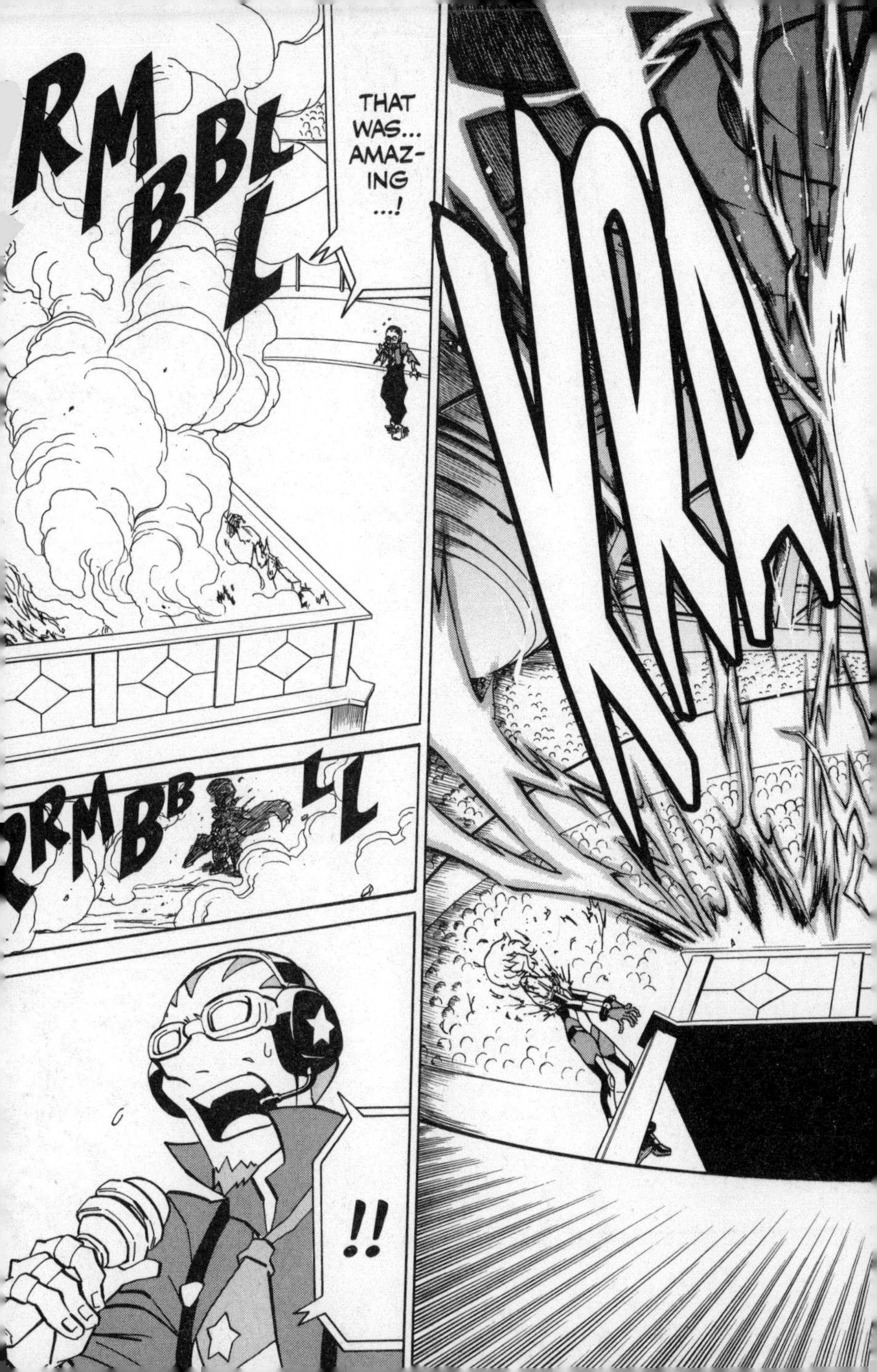
RMBBLL
THAT WAS... AMAZ-ING ...!
RMBBLL
!!

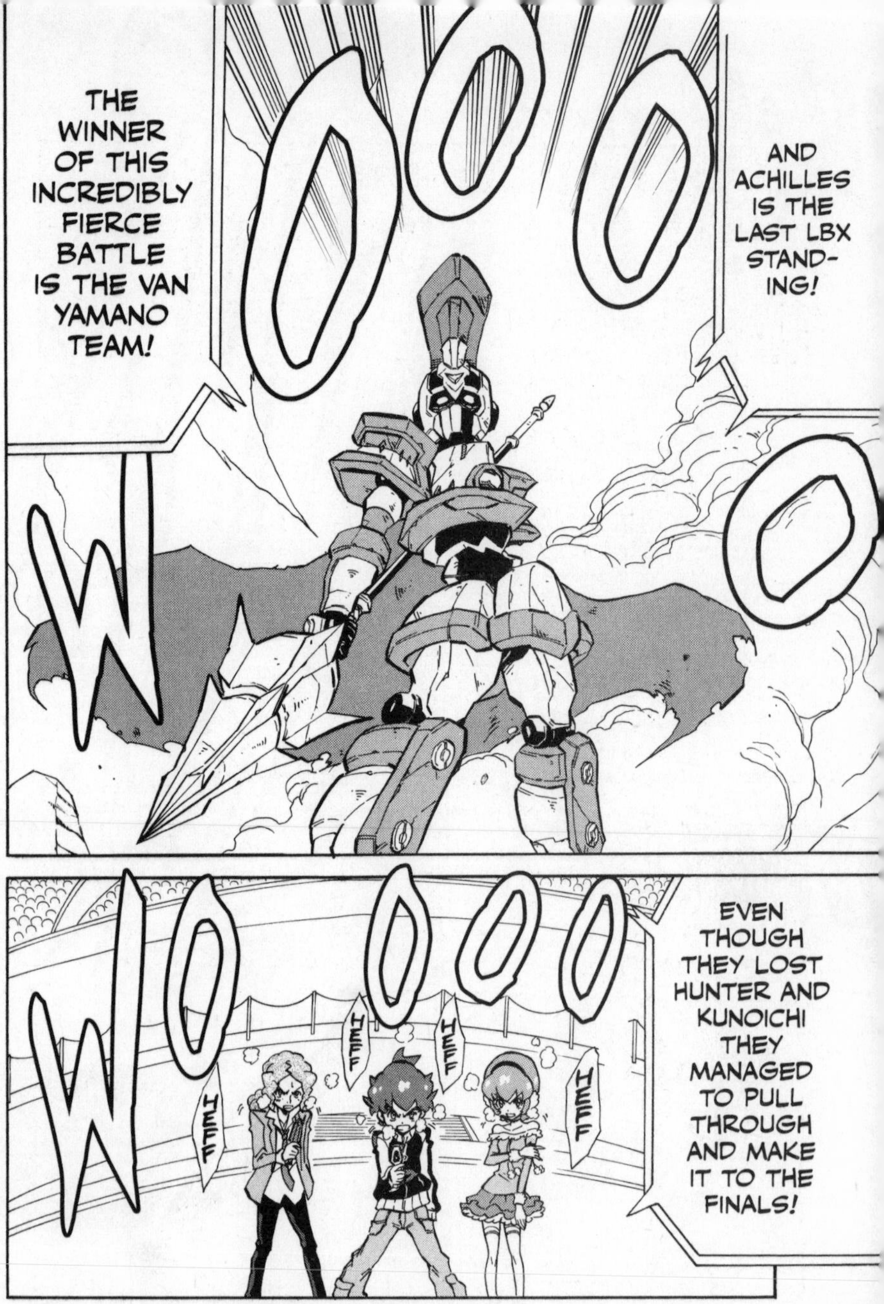
THE WINNER OF THIS INCREDIBLY FIERCE BATTLE IS THE VAN YAMANO TEAM!
AND ACHILLES IS THE LAST LBX STAND-ING!
WOOOOO
EVEN THOUGH THEY LOST HUNTER AND KUNOICHI THEY MANAGED TO PULL THROUGH AND MAKE IT TO THE FINALS!
WOOOO
HEFF
HEFF
HEFF
HEFF

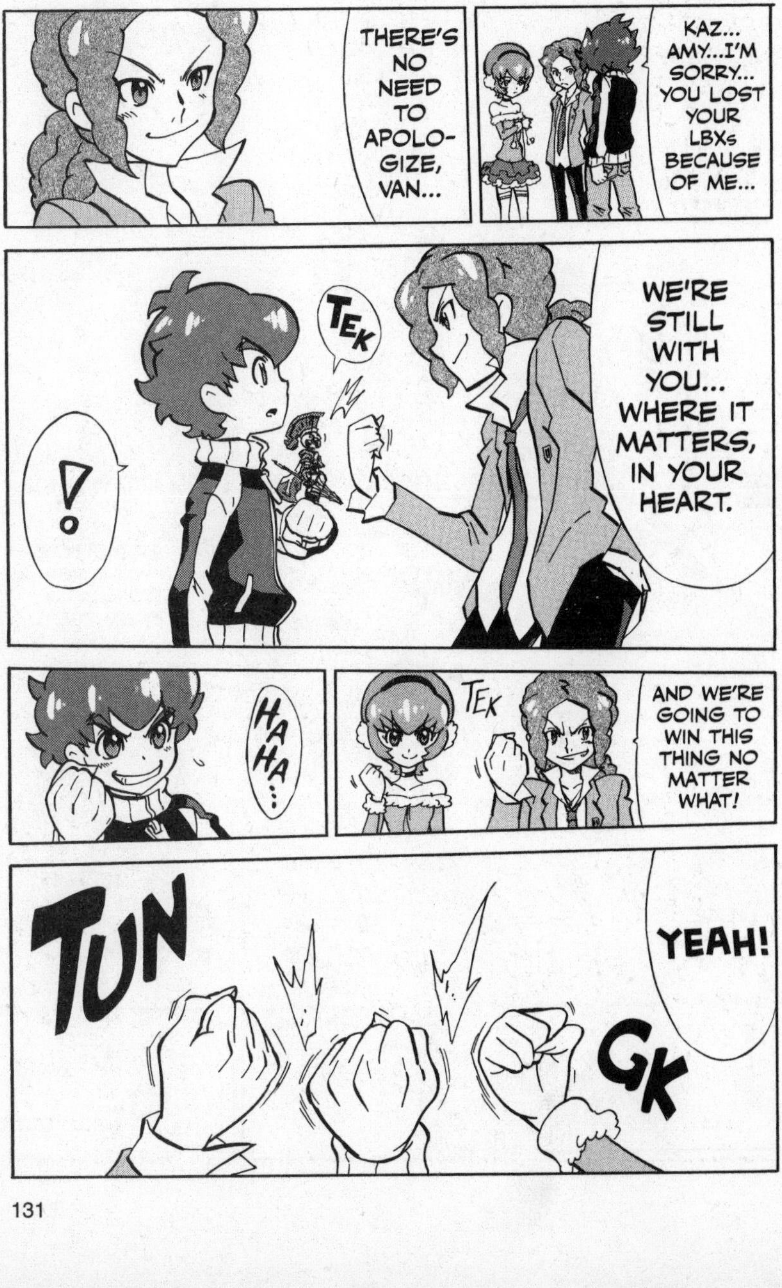
KAZ... AMY...I'M SORRY... YOU LOST YOUR LBXs BECAUSE OF ME...
THERE'S NO NEED TO APOLOGIZE, VAN...
WE'RE STILL WITH YOU... WHERE IT MATTERS, IN YOUR HEART.
TEK
!?
AND WE'RE GOING TO WIN THIS THING NO MATTER WHAT!
TEK
HAHA...
YEAH!
GK
TUN

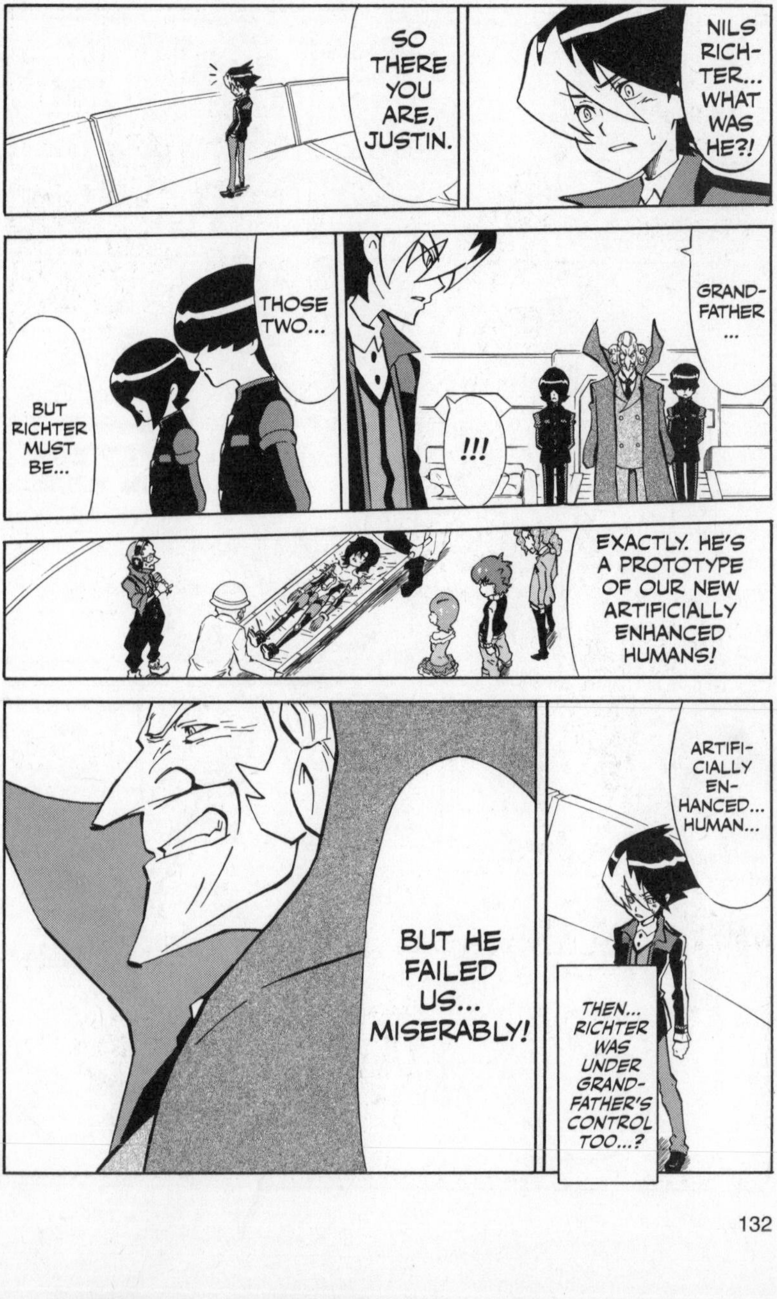
NILS RICH-TER... WHAT WAS HE?!
SO THERE YOU ARE, JUSTIN.
GRAND-FATHER ...
!!!
THOSE TWO...
BUT RICHTER MUST BE...
EXACTLY. HE'S A PROTOTYPE OF OUR NEW ARTIFICIALLY ENHANCED HUMANS!
ARTIFI-CIALLY EN-HANCED... HUMAN...
THEN... RICHTER WAS UNDER GRAND-FATHER'S CONTROL TOO...?
BUT HE FAILED US... MISERABLY!

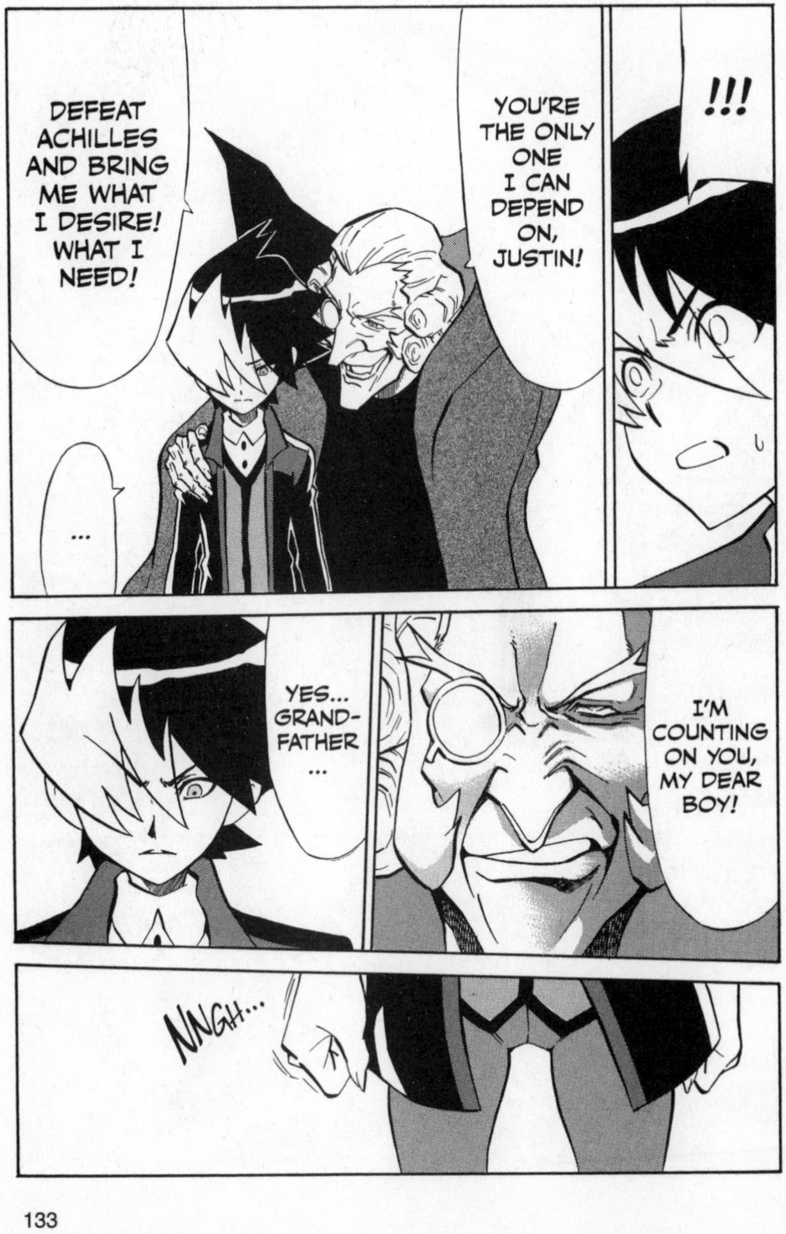
!!!
YOU'RE THE ONLY ONE I CAN DEPEND ON, JUSTIN!
DEFEAT ACHILLES AND BRING ME WHAT I DESIRE! WHAT I NEED!
...
I'M COUNTING ON YOU, MY DEAR BOY!
YES... GRAND-FATHER ...
NNGH...

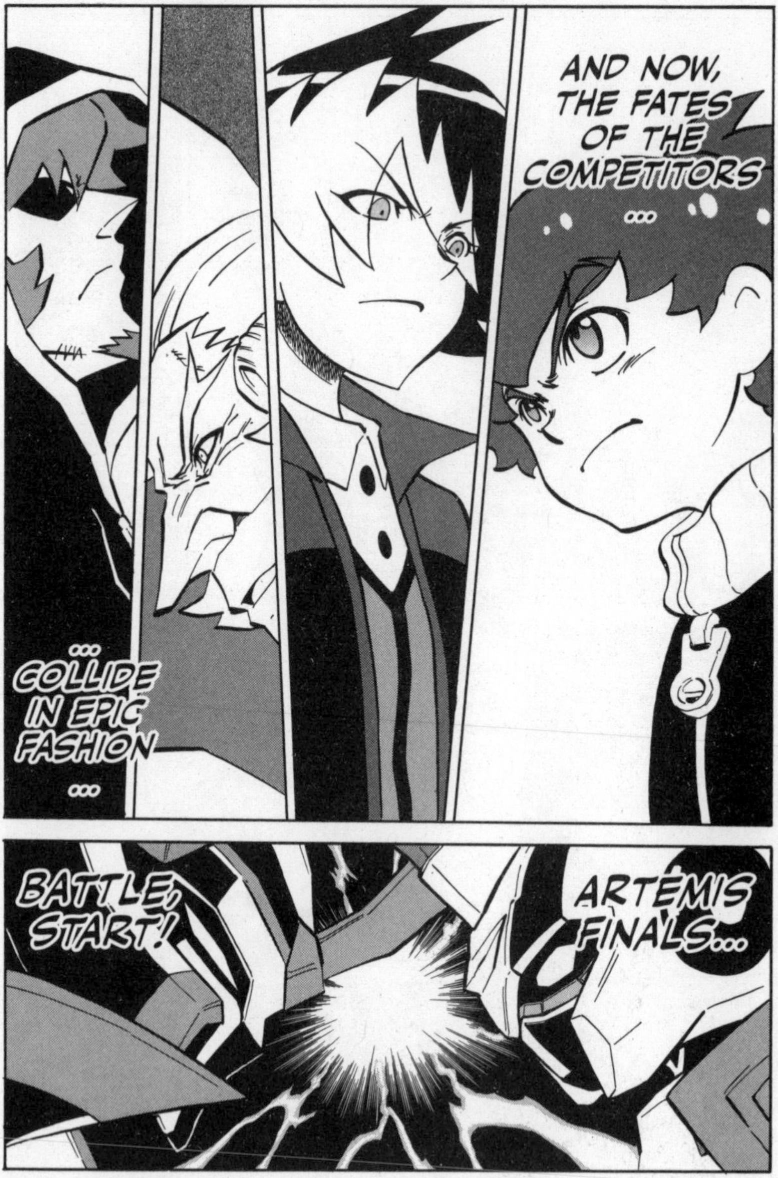
AND NOW, THE FATES OF THE COMPETITORS ...
... COLLIDE IN EPIC FASHION ...
ARTÉMIS FINALS...
BATTLE, START!

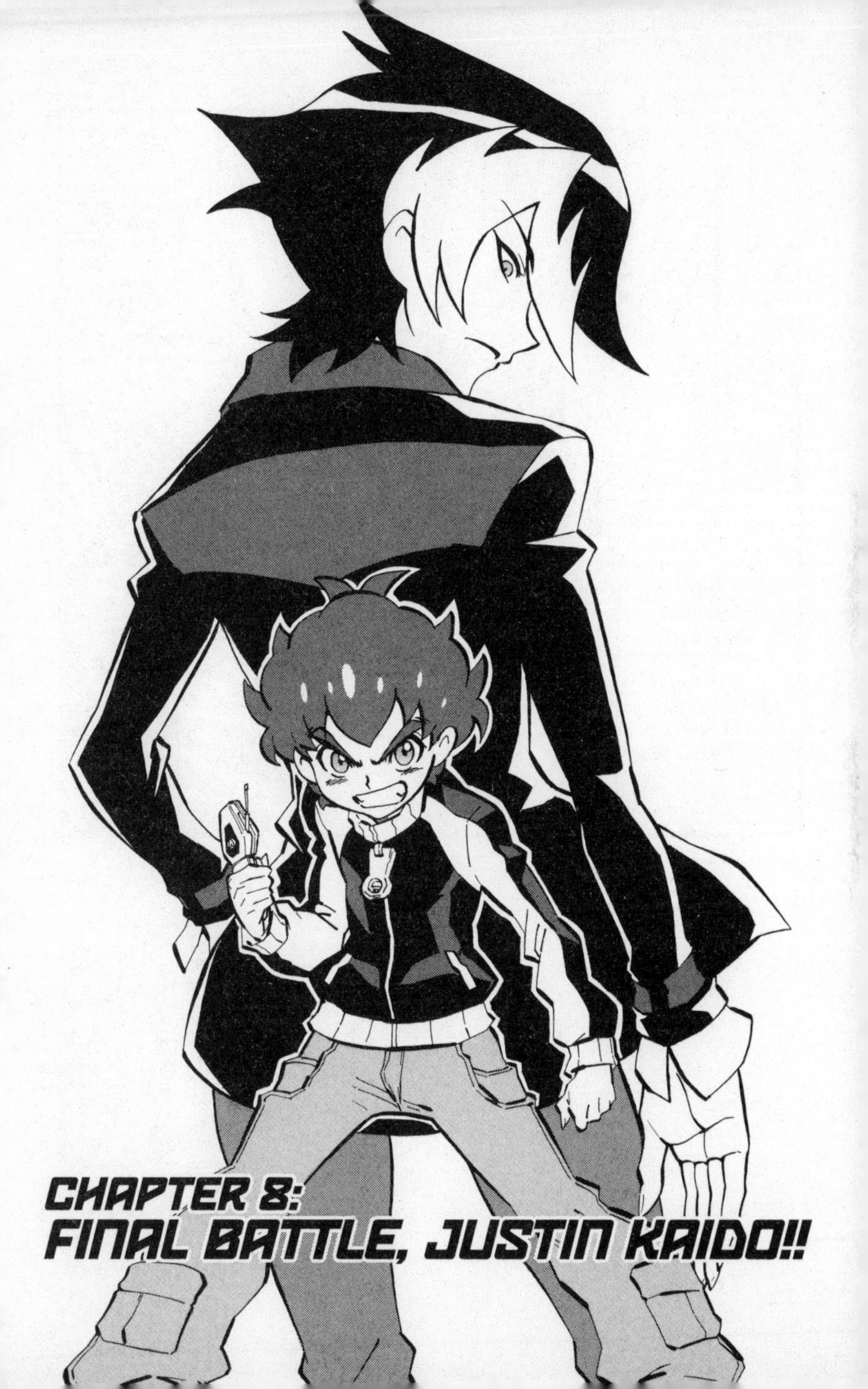
CHAPTER 8:
FINAL BATTLE, JUSTIN KAIDO!!

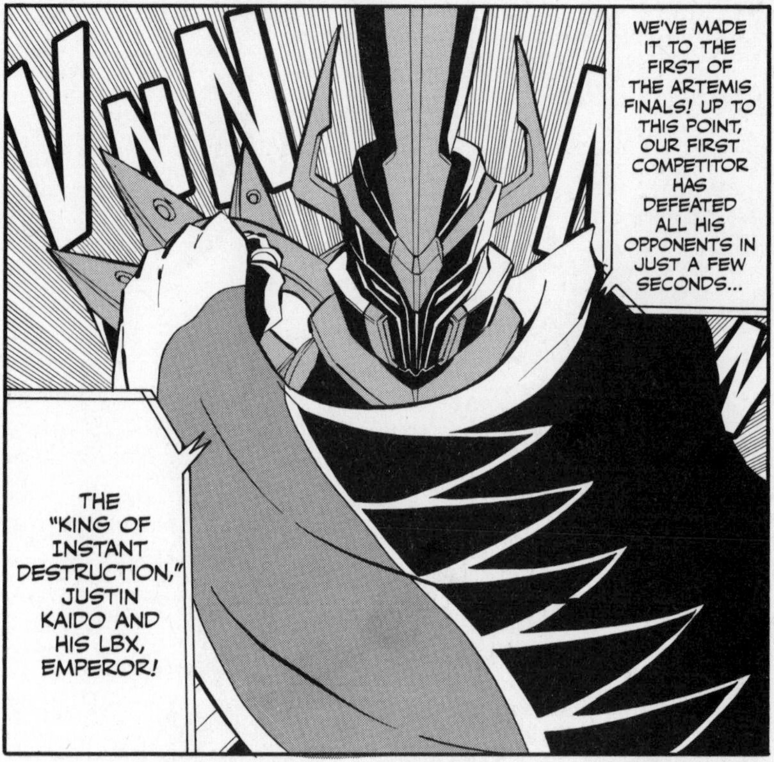
WE'VE MADE IT TO THE FIRST OF THE ARTEMIS FINALS! UP TO THIS POINT, OUR FIRST COMPETITOR HAS DEFEATED ALL HIS OPPONENTS IN JUST A FEW SECONDS...
THE "KING OF INSTANT DESTRUCTION," JUSTIN KAIDO AND HIS LBX, EMPEROR!

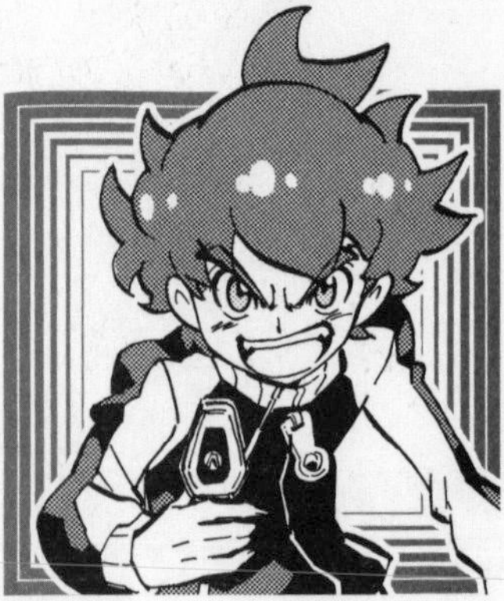

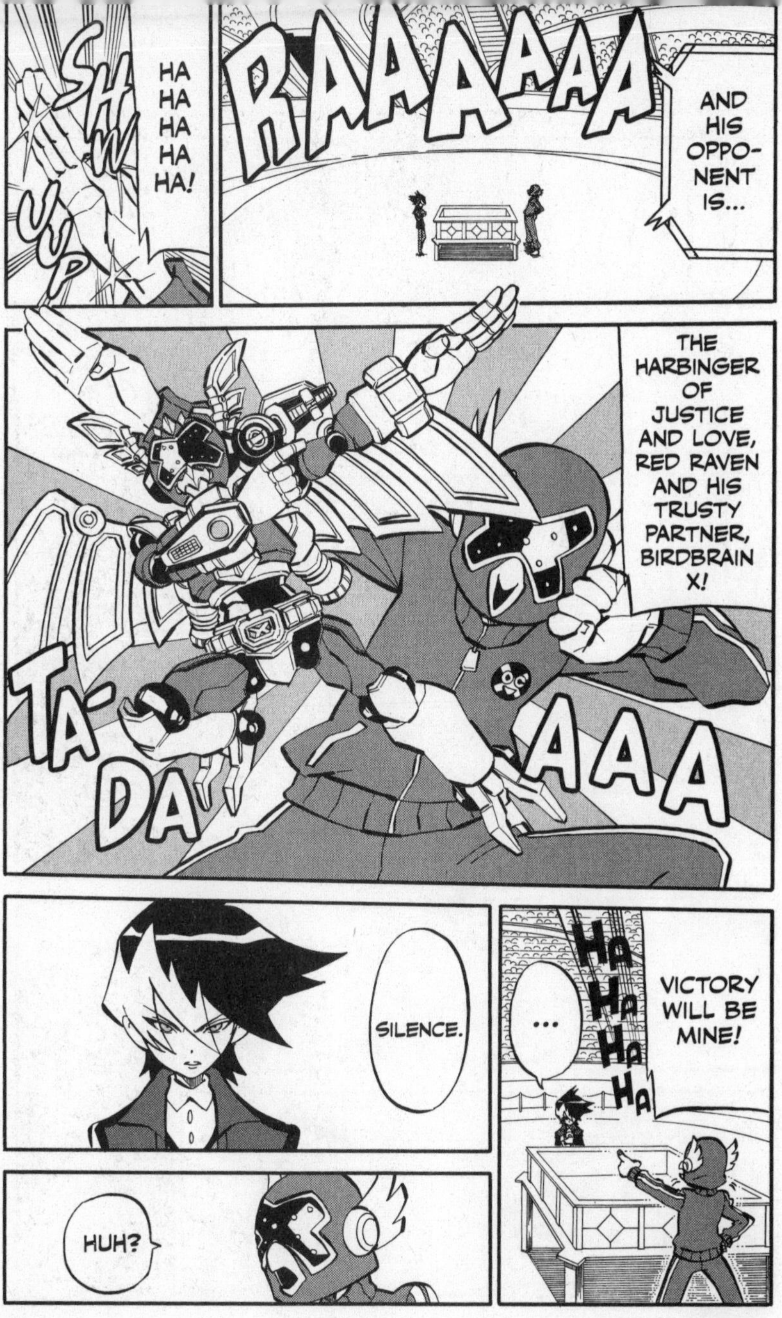
RAAAAAA
AND HIS OPPONENT IS...
HA HA HA HA HA!
SHWUUP
THE HARBINGER OF JUSTICE AND LOVE, RED RAVEN AND HIS TRUSTY PARTNER, BIRDBRAIN X!
TA-DAAAA
VICTORY WILL BE MINE!
HA HA HA HA HA
...
SILENCE.
HUH?

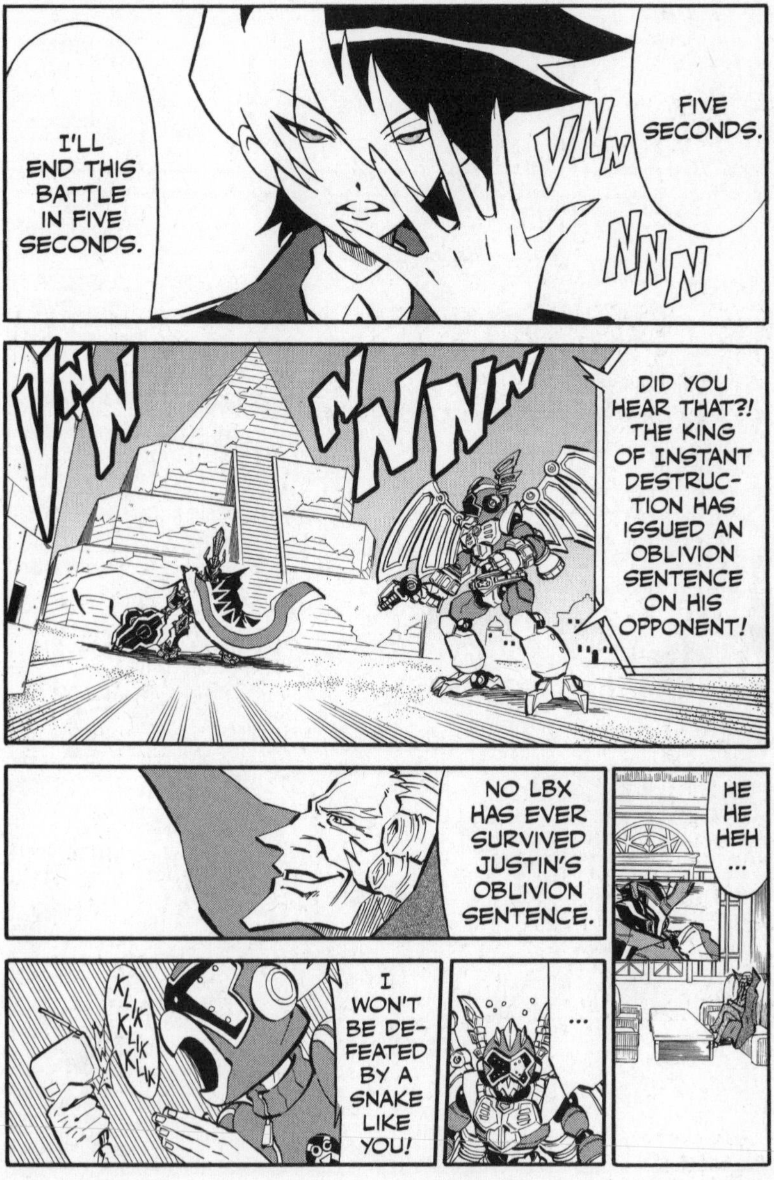
I'LL END THIS BATTLE IN FIVE SECONDS.
VNNN
FIVE SECONDS.
NNN
VNNN
NNNNN
DID YOU HEAR THAT?! THE KING OF INSTANT DESTRUC-TION HAS ISSUED AN OBLIVION SENTENCE ON HIS OPPONENT!
HE HE HEH ...
NO LBX HAS EVER SURVIVED JUSTIN'S OBLIVION SENTENCE.
...
I WON'T BE DE-FEATED BY A SNAKE LIKE YOU!
KLIK KLIK KLIK KLIK

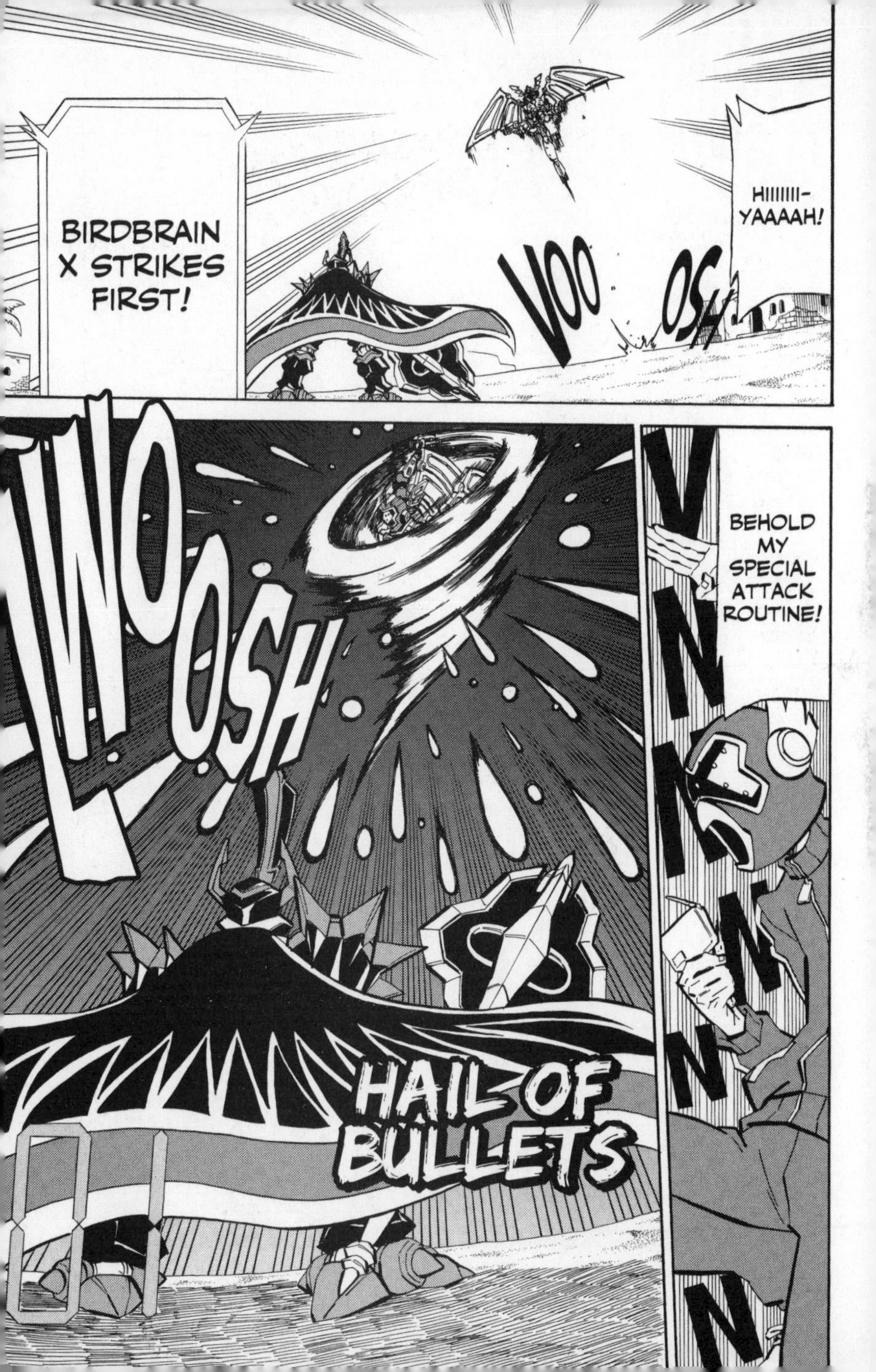
HIIIIIII-
YAAAAH!
VOOOSH
BIRDBRAIN X STRIKES FIRST!
BEHOLD MY SPECIAL ATTACK ROUTINE!
VNNNNNN
WOOOSH
HAIL OF BULLETS

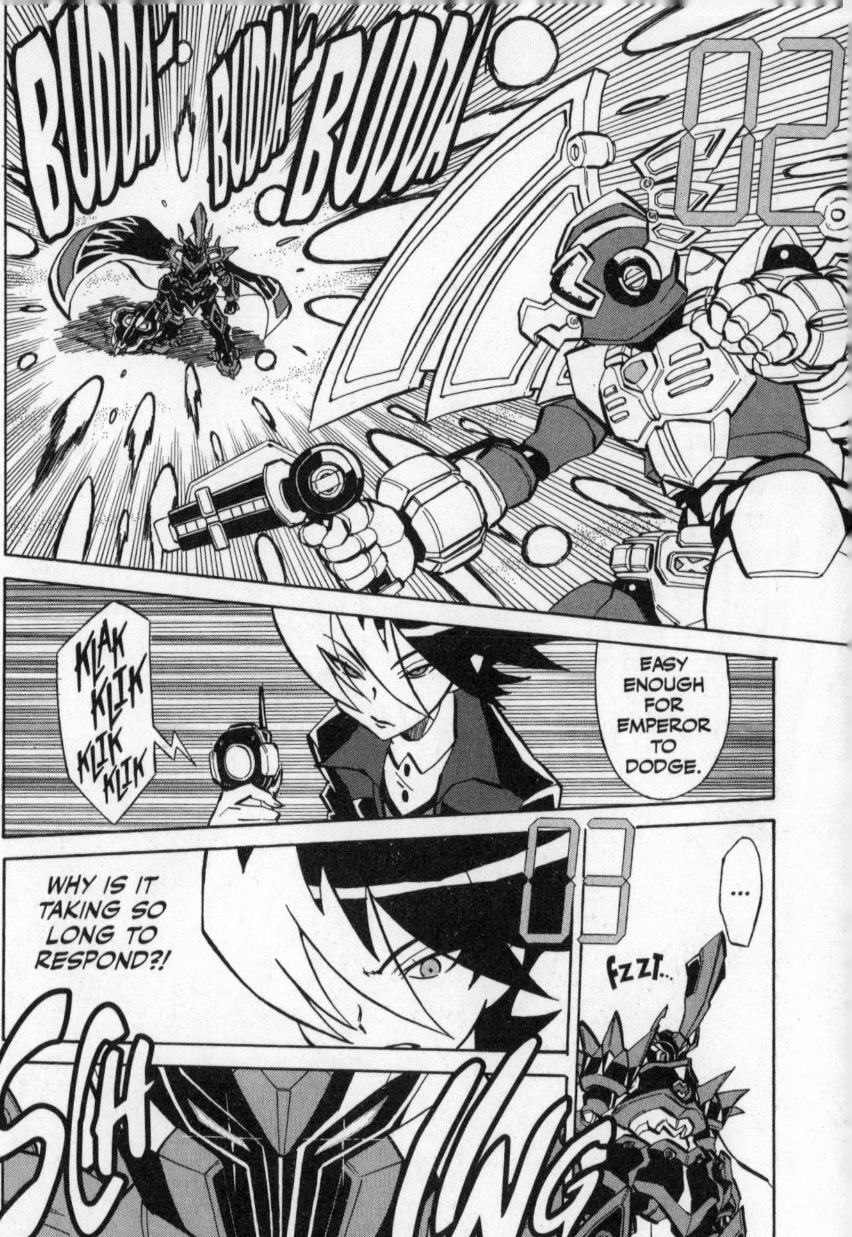
02
BUDDA BUDDA BUDDA
EASY ENOUGH FOR EMPEROR TO DODGE.
KLAK KLIK KLIK KLIK
...
FZZT...
03
WHY IS IT TAKING SO LONG TO RESPOND?!
SCHWING

KA-
BOOM!

JUSTICE ALWAYS PREVAILS!

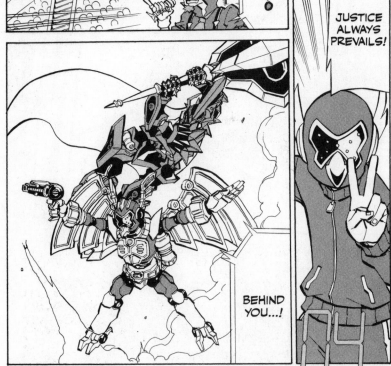

BEHIND YOU...!

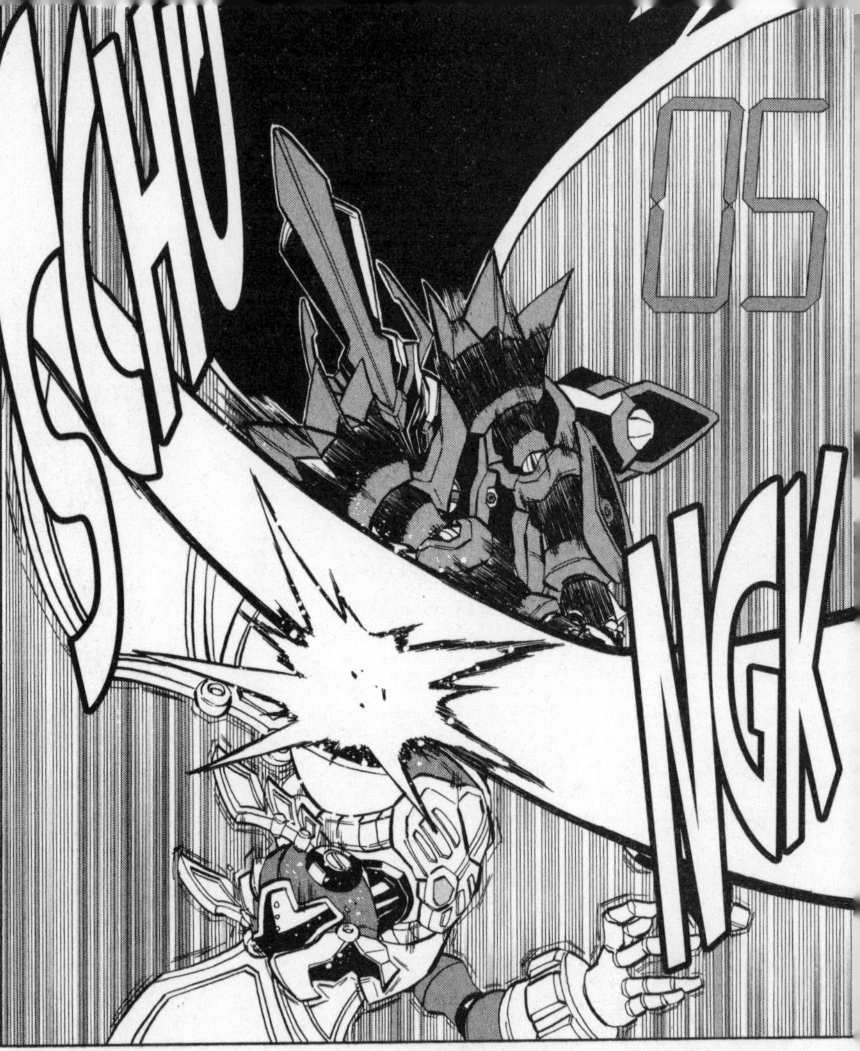
05
SCHU
NGK

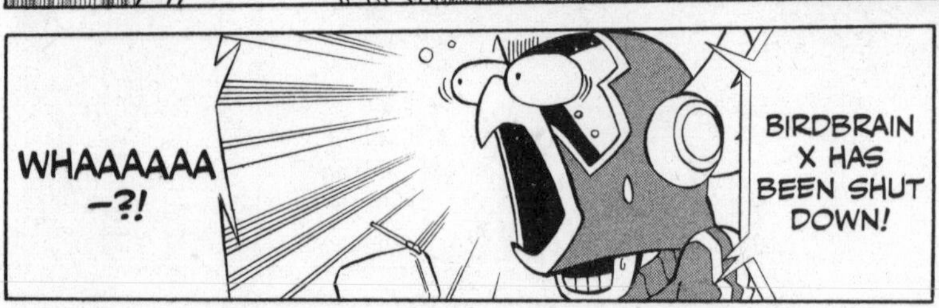
BIRDBRAIN X HAS BEEN SHUT DOWN!
WHAAAAAA—?!

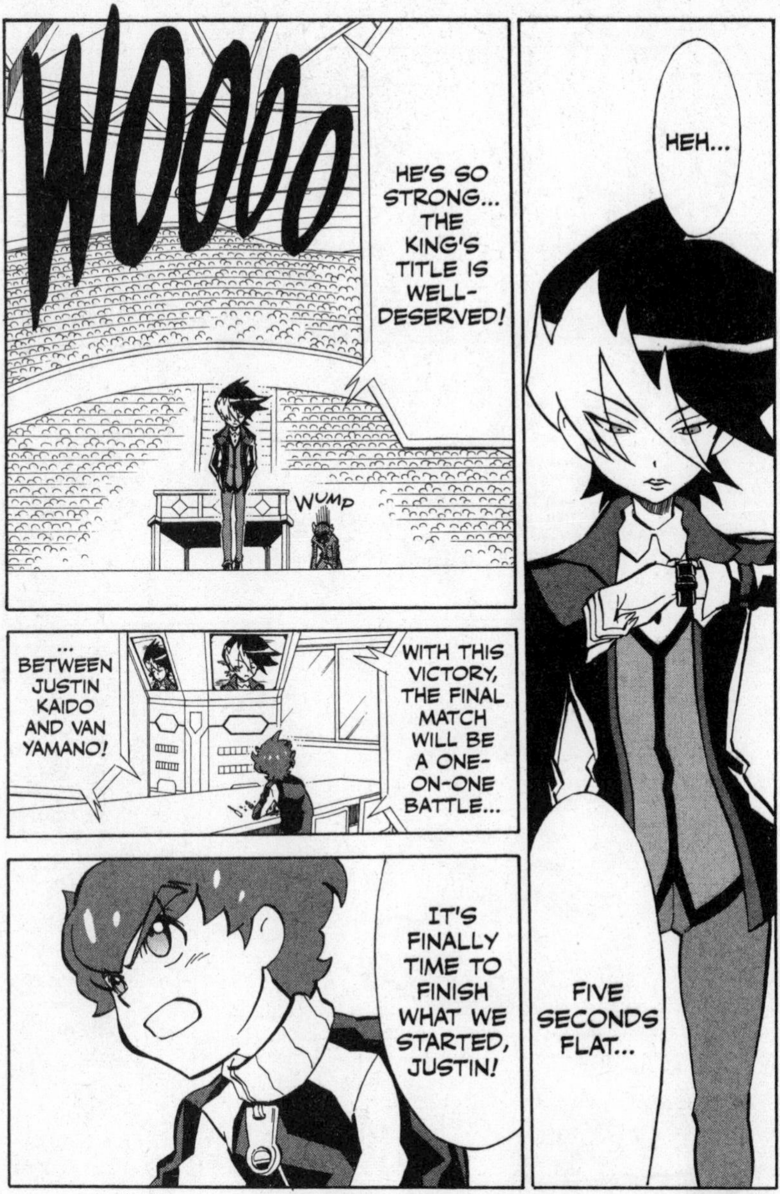
HEH...
FIVE SECONDS FLAT...
WOOOO
HE'S SO STRONG... THE KING'S TITLE IS WELL-DESERVED!
WUMP
WITH THIS VICTORY, THE FINAL MATCH WILL BE A ONE-ON-ONE BATTLE...
...BETWEEN JUSTIN KAIDO AND VAN YAMANO!
IT'S FINALLY TIME TO FINISH WHAT WE STARTED, JUSTIN!

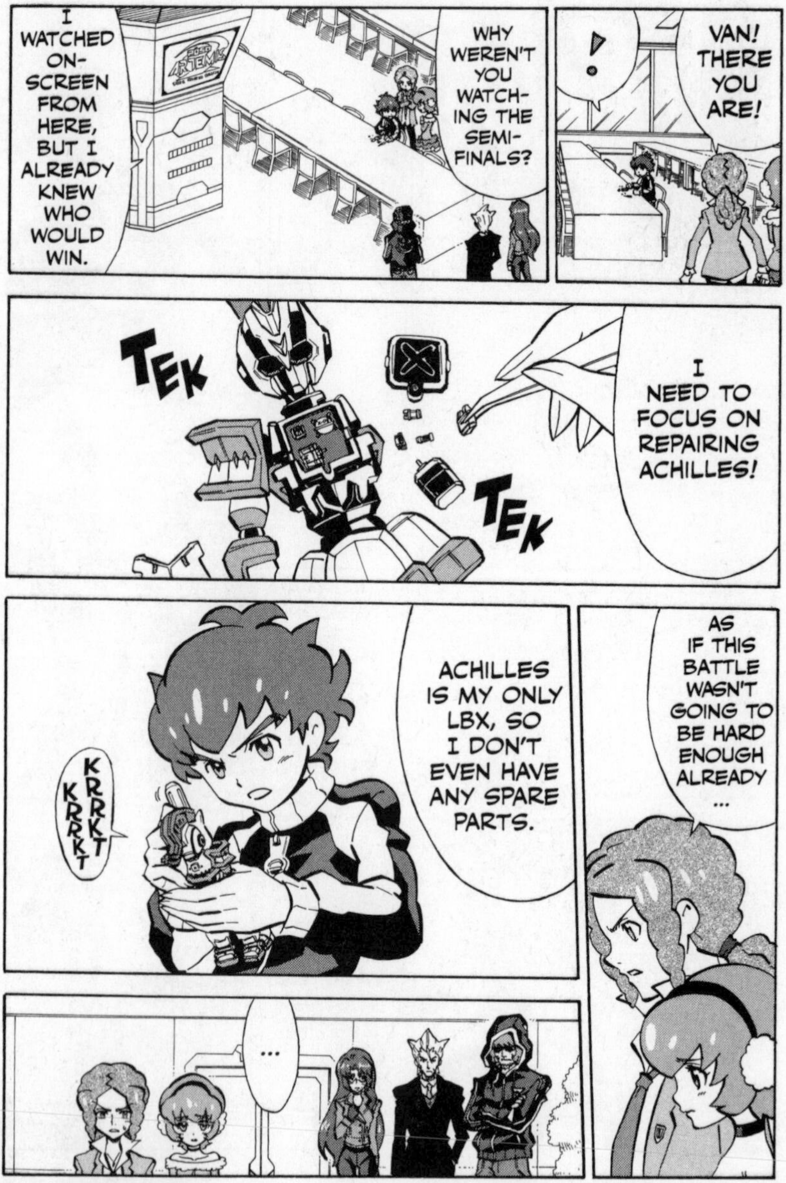
VAN! THERE YOU ARE!
!
WHY WEREN'T YOU WATCHING THE SEMI-FINALS?
I WATCHED ON-SCREEN FROM HERE, BUT I ALREADY KNEW WHO WOULD WIN.
I NEED TO FOCUS ON REPAIRING ACHILLES!
TEK
TEK
AS IF THIS BATTLE WASN'T GOING TO BE HARD ENOUGH ALREADY...
ACHILLES IS MY ONLY LBX, SO I DON'T EVEN HAVE ANY SPARE PARTS.
KRRRKT KRRRKT
...

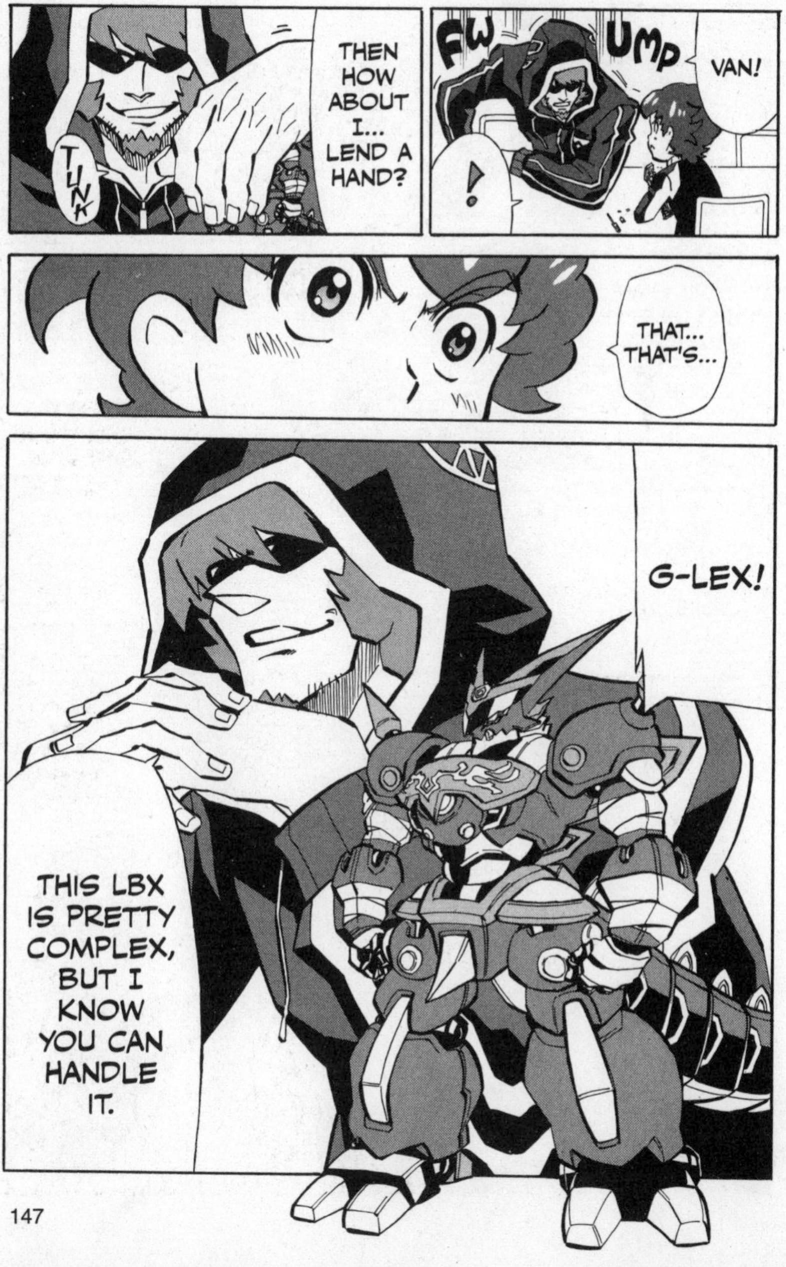
FWUMP
VAN!
!
THEN HOW ABOUT I... LEND A HAND?
TUNK
THAT... THAT'S...
G-LEX!
THIS LBX IS PRETTY COMPLEX, BUT I KNOW YOU CAN HANDLE IT.

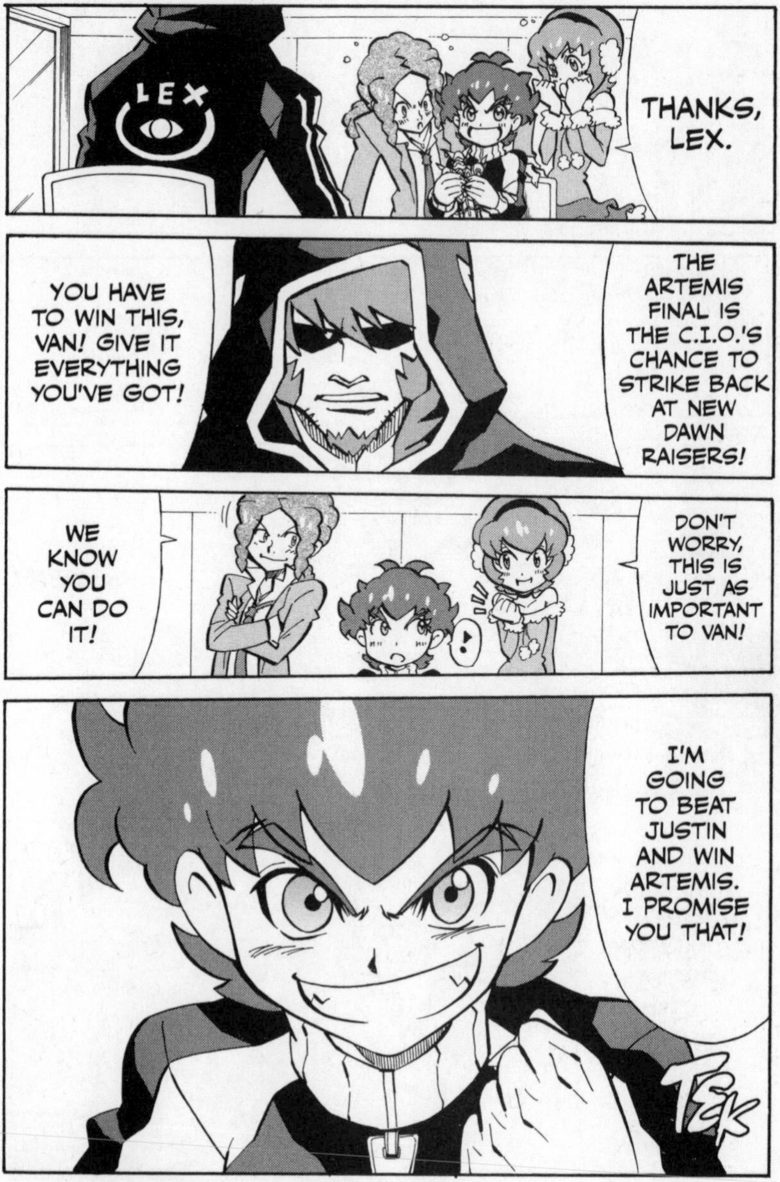
LEX
THANKS, LEX.
THE ARTEMIS FINAL IS THE C.I.O.'S CHANCE TO STRIKE BACK AT NEW DAWN RAISERS!
YOU HAVE TO WIN THIS, VAN! GIVE IT EVERYTHING YOU'VE GOT!
DON'T WORRY, THIS IS JUST AS IMPORTANT TO VAN!
!
WE KNOW YOU CAN DO IT!
I'M GOING TO BEAT JUSTIN AND WIN ARTEMIS. I PROMISE YOU THAT!
TEK

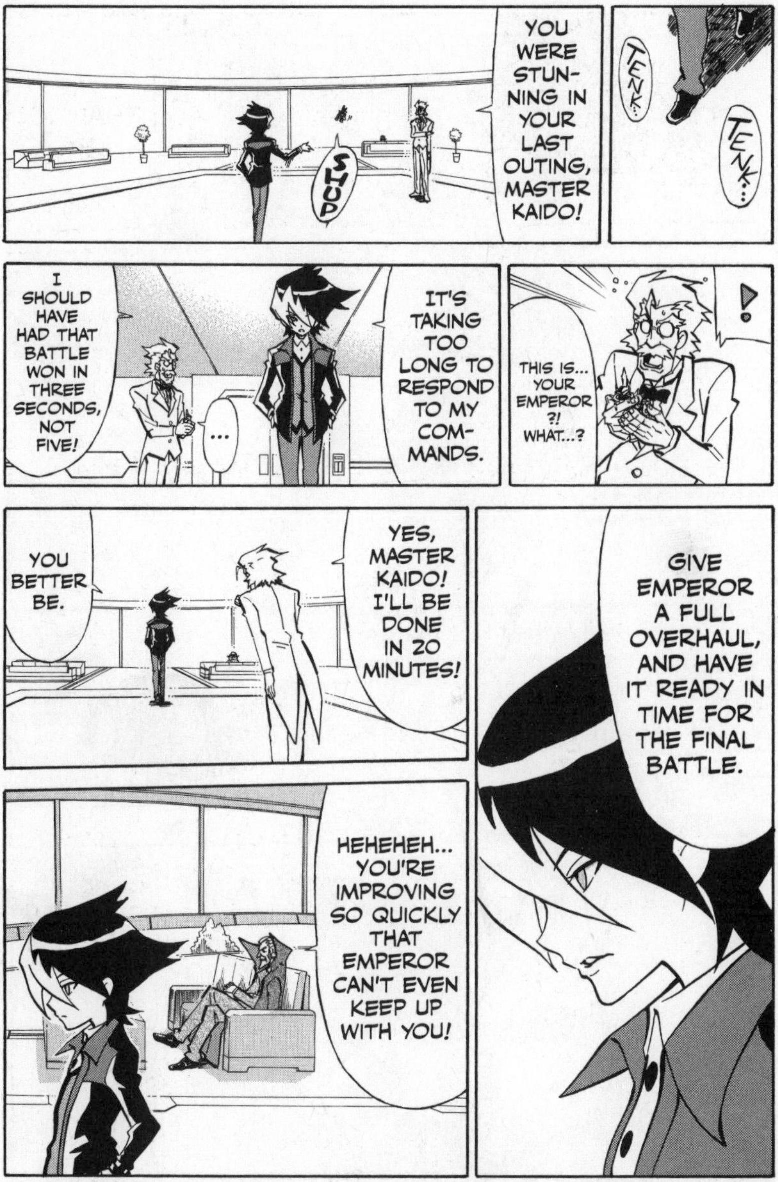
TENK...
TENK...
YOU WERE STUNNING IN YOUR LAST OUTING, MASTER KAIDO!
SHUP
!
THIS IS... YOUR EMPEROR ?! WHAT...?
IT'S TAKING TOO LONG TO RESPOND TO MY COMMANDS.
...
I SHOULD HAVE HAD THAT BATTLE WON IN THREE SECONDS, NOT FIVE!
GIVE EMPEROR A FULL OVERHAUL, AND HAVE IT READY IN TIME FOR THE FINAL BATTLE.
YES, MASTER KAIDO! I'LL BE DONE IN 20 MINUTES!
YOU BETTER BE.
HEHEHEH... YOU'RE IMPROVING SO QUICKLY THAT EMPEROR CAN'T EVEN KEEP UP WITH YOU!

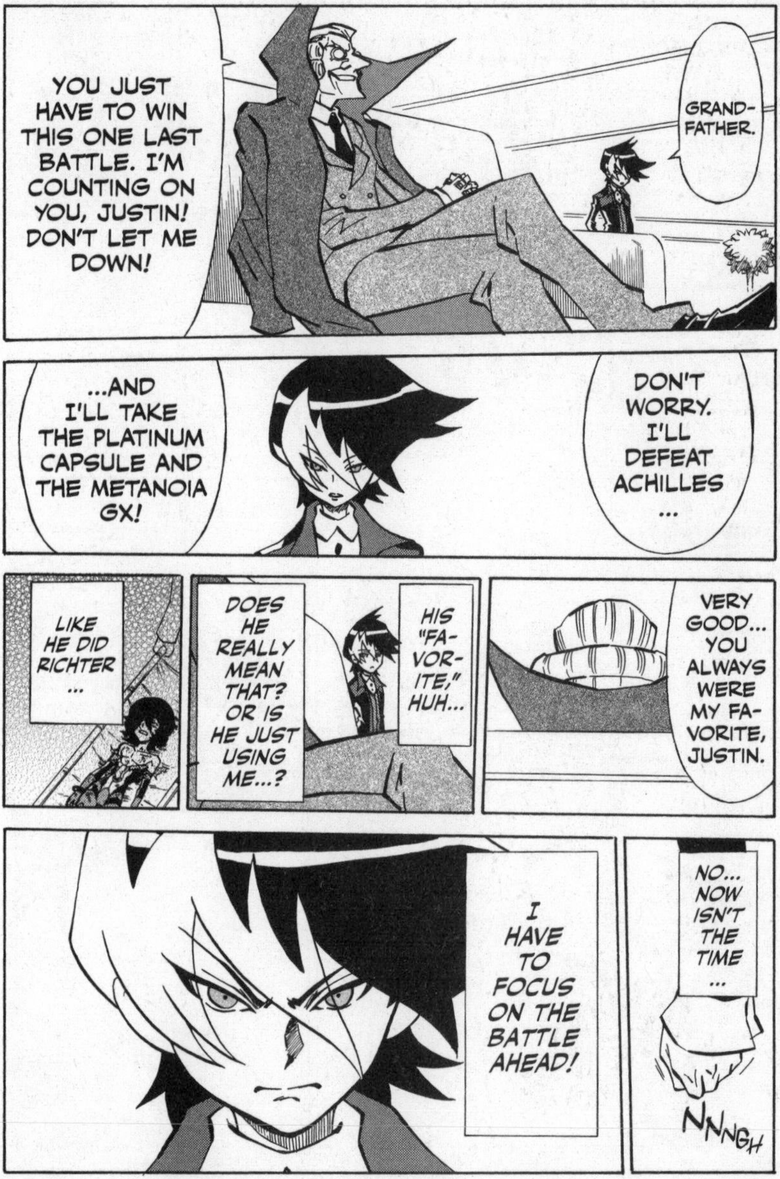

GRAND-FATHER.
YOU JUST HAVE TO WIN THIS ONE LAST BATTLE. I'M COUNTING ON YOU, JUSTIN! DON'T LET ME DOWN!
DON'T WORRY. I'LL DEFEAT ACHILLES ...
...AND I'LL TAKE THE PLATINUM CAPSULE AND THE METANOIA GX!
VERY GOOD... YOU ALWAYS WERE MY FA-VORITE, JUSTIN.
HIS "FA-VOR-ITE," HUH...
DOES HE REALLY MEAN THAT? OR IS HE JUST USING ME...?
LIKE HE DID RICHTER ...
NO... NOW ISN'T THE TIME ...
NNNGH
I HAVE TO FOCUS ON THE BATTLE AHEAD!

WELCOME TO THE ARTEMIS FINALS, WHERE WE'LL DECIDE WHO'S THE BEST LBX PLAYER IN THE WORLD!
WOOOOO
OUR FINALISTS HAVE FOUGHT LONG AND HARD TO MAKE IT TO THE END...
FIRST, THE ROOKIE, VAN YAMANO AND ACHILLES!
WOOOO
GOING INTO THIS BATTLE, ACHILLES HAS BEEN UPGRADED WITH A BRAND-NEW ARM!
AND HIS OPPONENT, THE KING OF INSTANT DESTRUCTION, JUSTIN KAIDO AND DARK EMPEROR MK2!
WOOOO
KAIDO HAS GIVEN HIS LBX A COMPLETE OVERHAUL TO PREPARE FOR THIS BATTLE!
THUNK

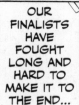

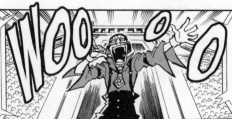

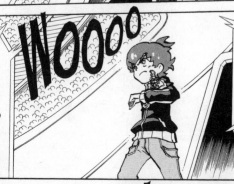

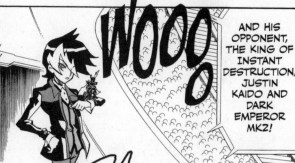

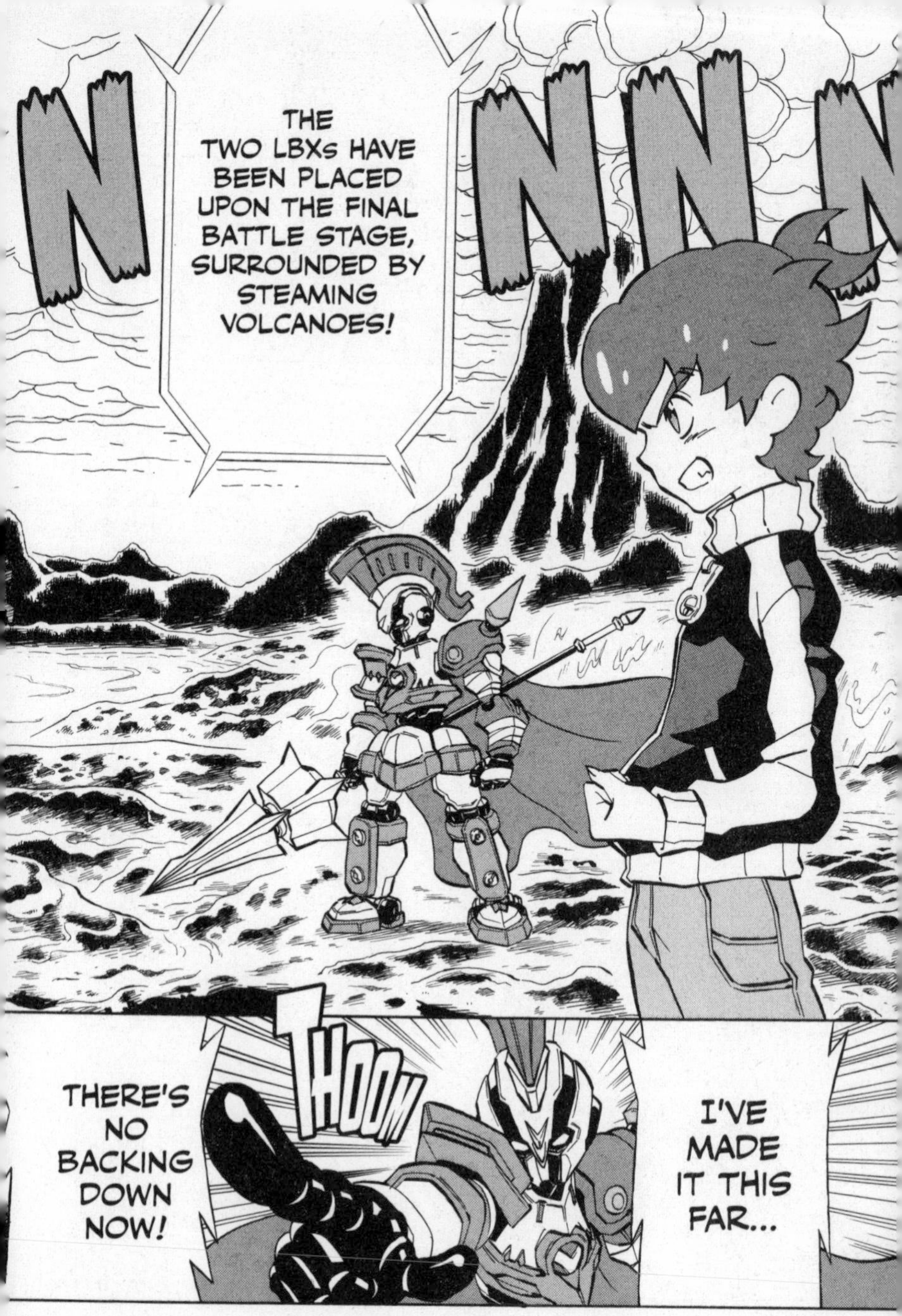
NNNN
THE TWO LBXs HAVE BEEN PLACED UPON THE FINAL BATTLE STAGE, SURROUNDED BY STEAMING VOLCANOES!
I'VE MADE IT THIS FAR...
THOOM
THERE'S NO BACKING DOWN NOW!

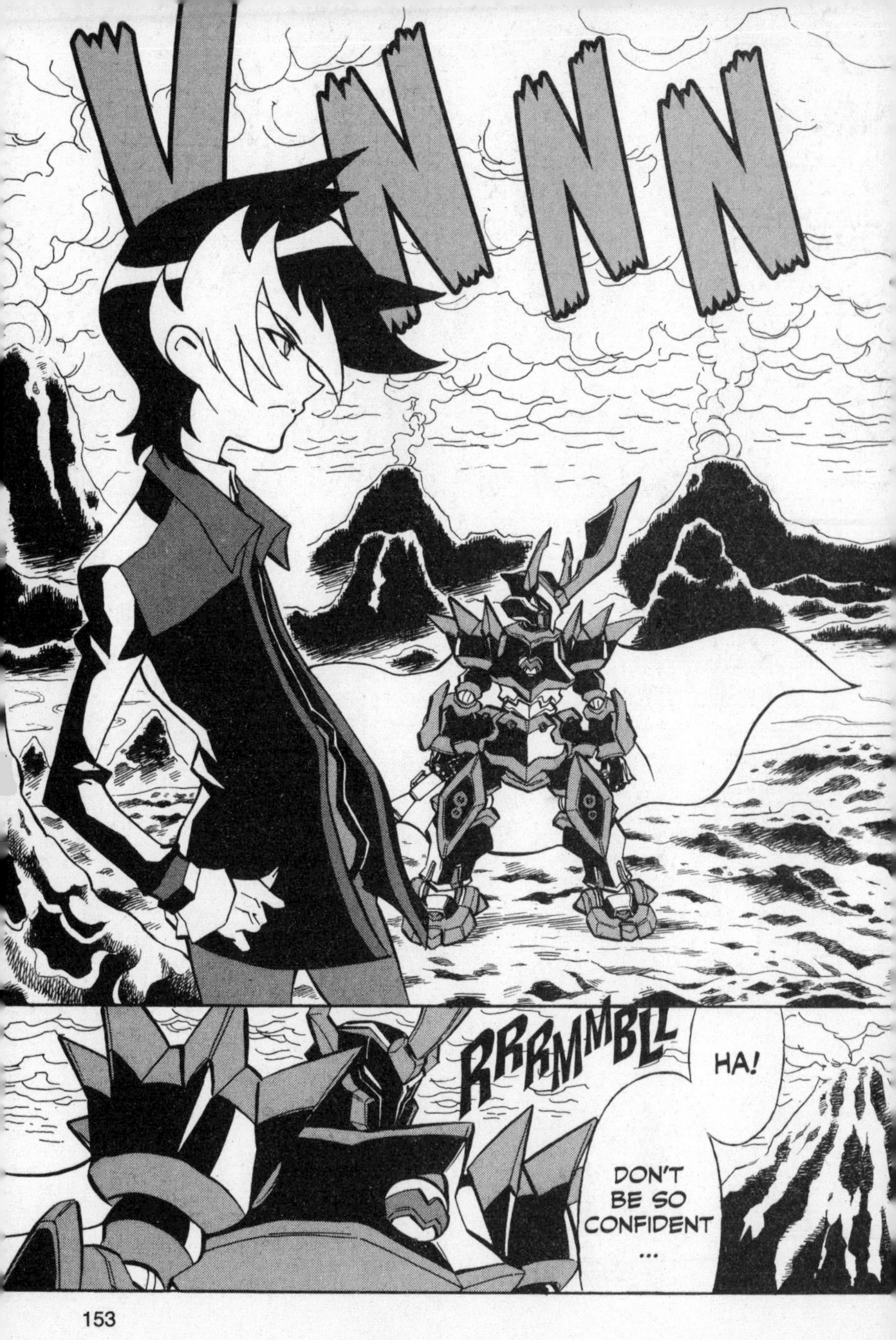
VNNNN
HA!
DON'T BE SO CONFIDENT ...
RRRMMBLL

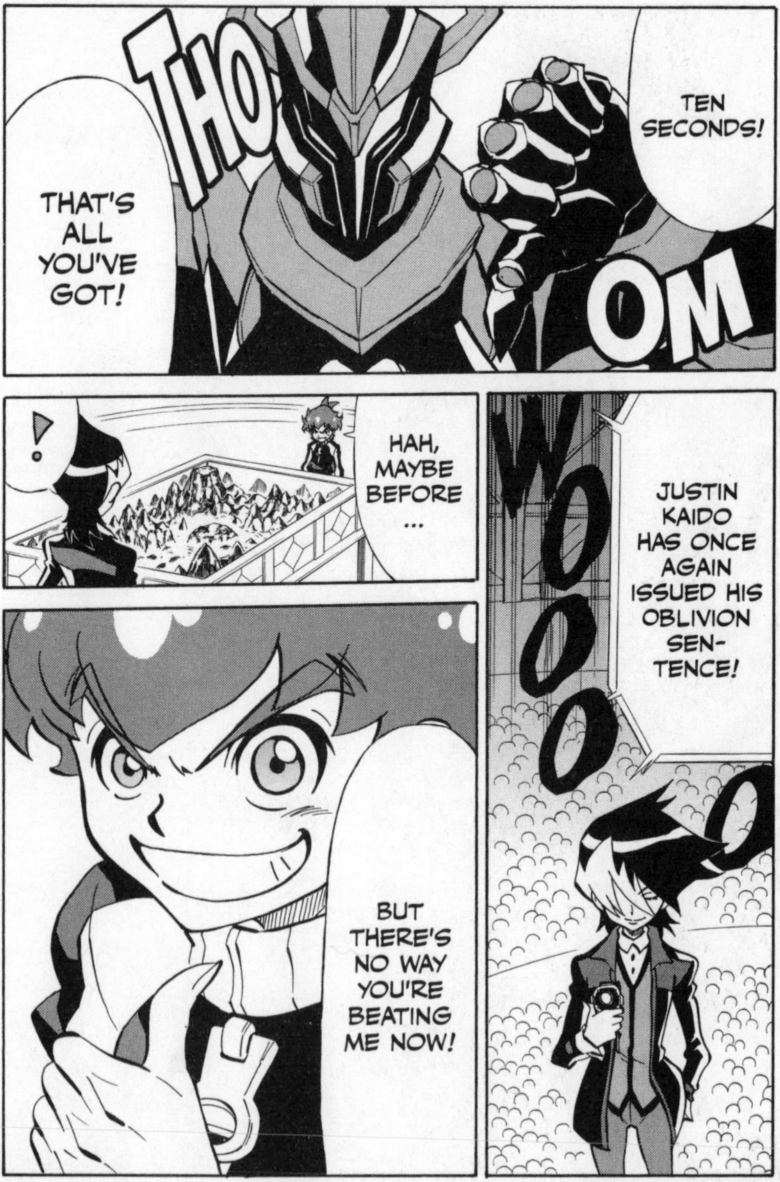
TEN SECONDS!
THO
OM
THAT'S ALL YOU'VE GOT!
JUSTIN KAIDO HAS ONCE AGAIN ISSUED HIS OBLIVION SEN-TENCE!
WOOOOO
HAH, MAYBE BEFORE ...
!
BUT THERE'S NO WAY YOU'RE BEATING ME NOW!

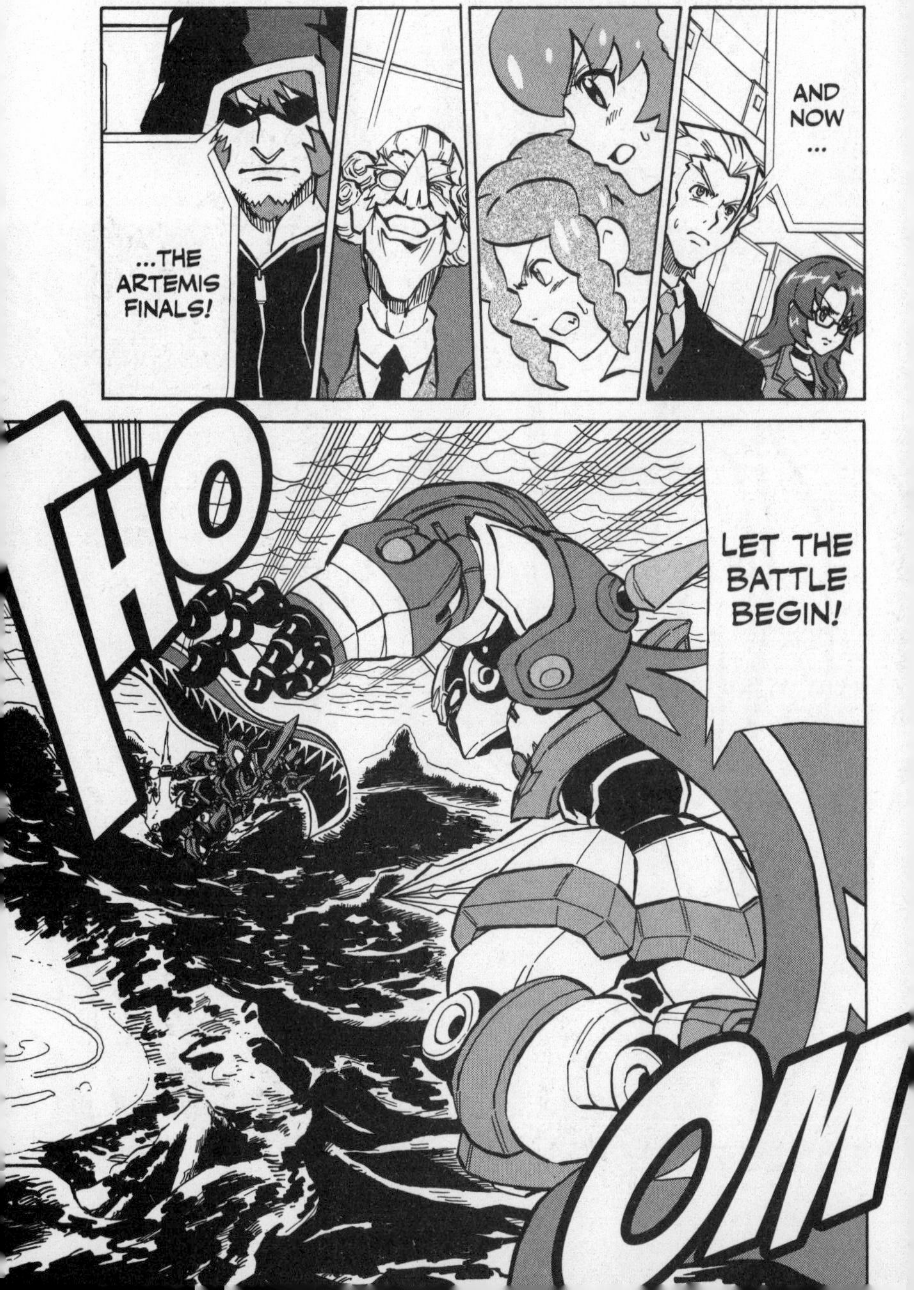
AND NOW ...
...THE ARTEMIS FINALS!
LET THE BATTLE BEGIN!
HO
OM

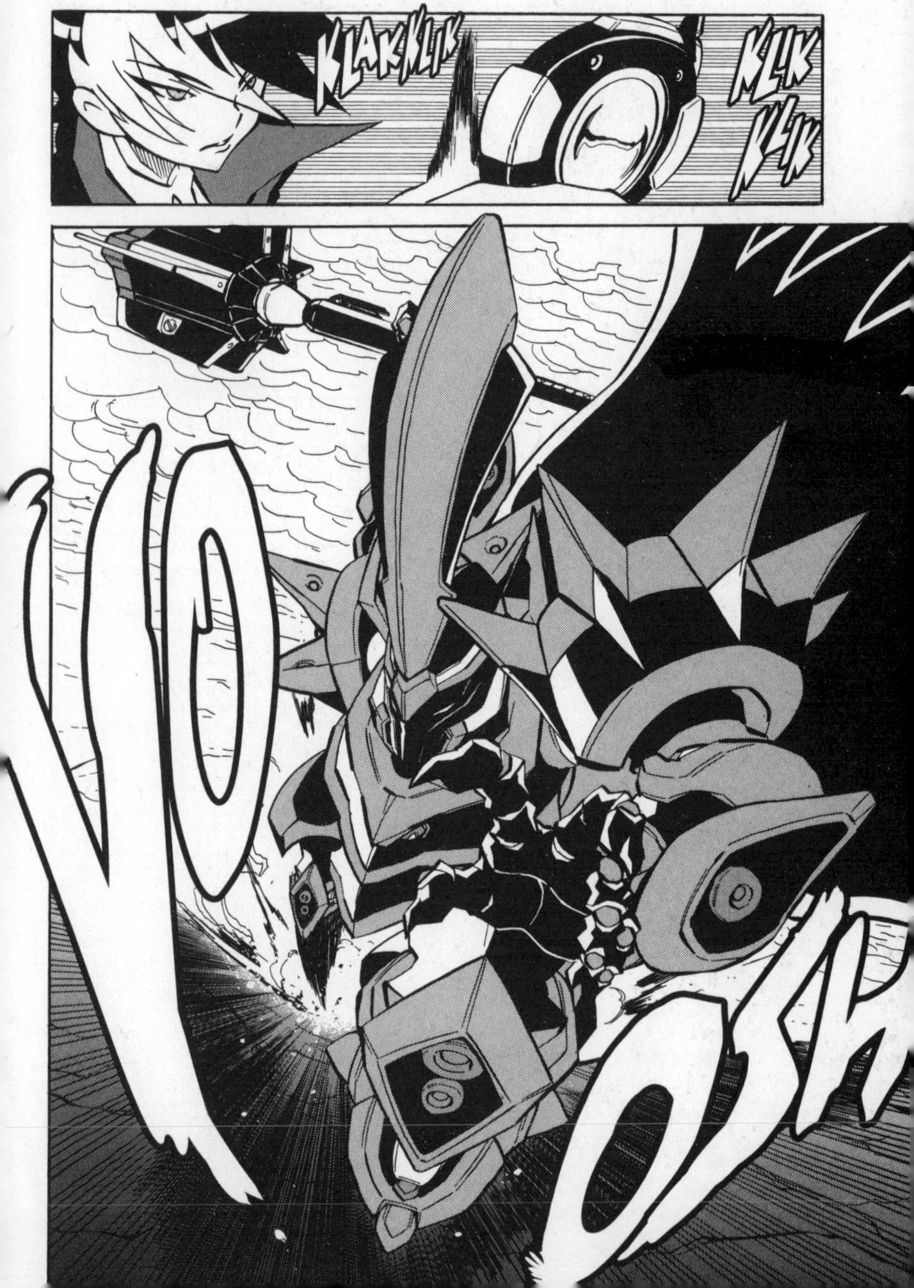
KLIK KLIK
KLAK KLIK
VOOSH

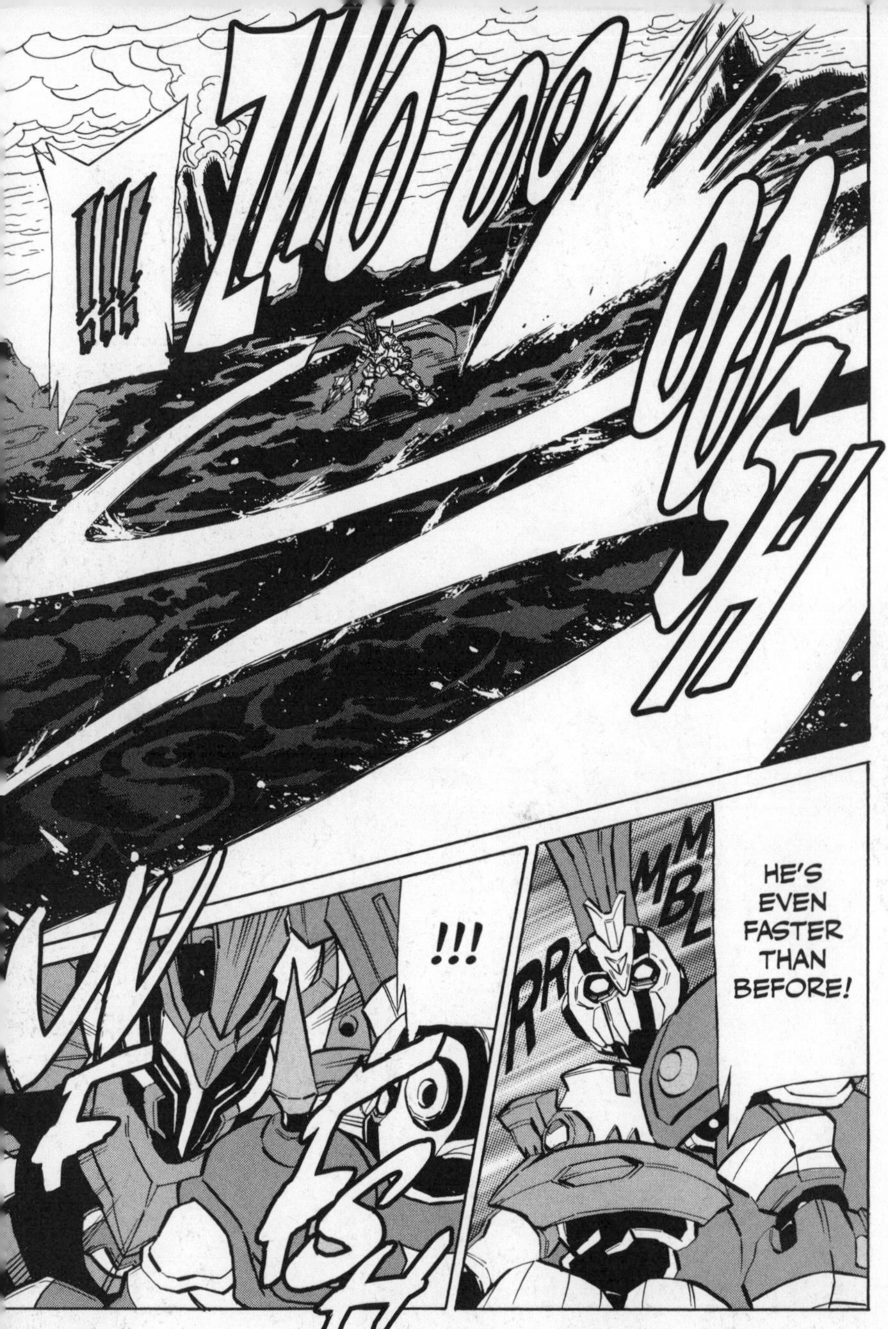
!!!
RRMMBL
HE'S EVEN FASTER THAN BEFORE!
!!!

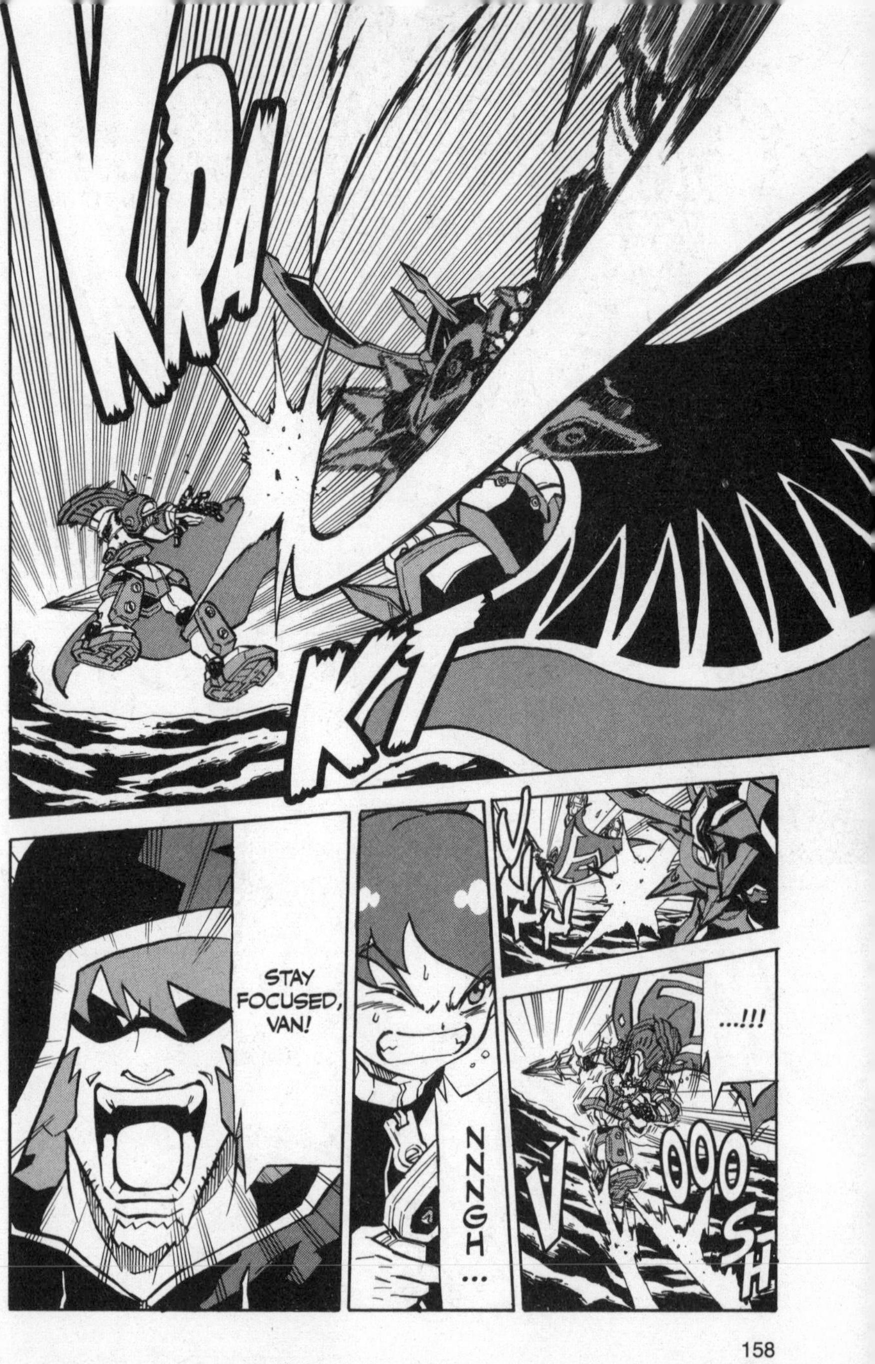
...!!!
VOOOSH
NNNGH...
STAY FOCUSED, VAN!

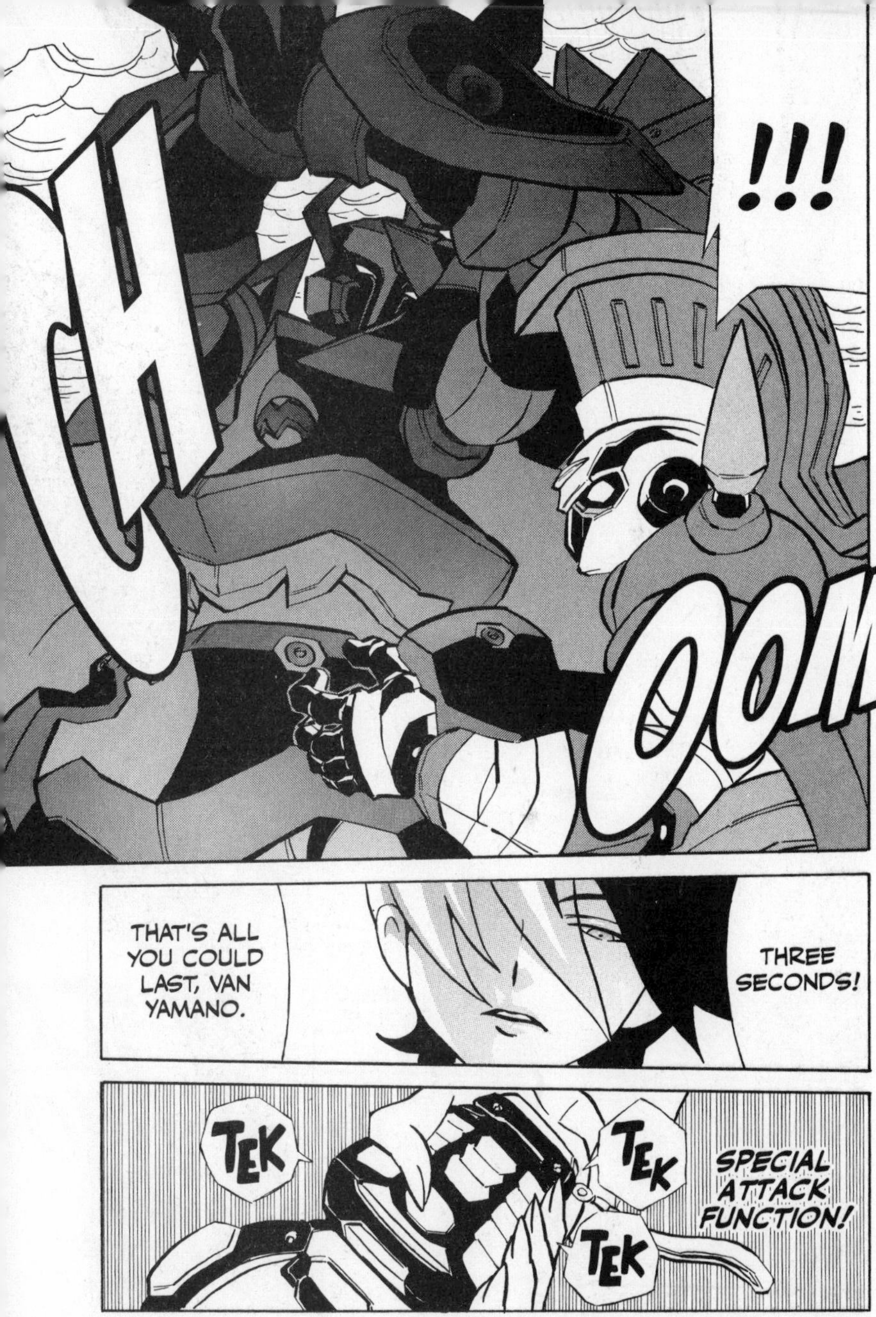
!!!
CH
OOM
THREE SECONDS!
THAT'S ALL YOU COULD LAST, VAN YAMANO.
SPECIAL ATTACK FUNCTION!
TEK
TEK
TEK

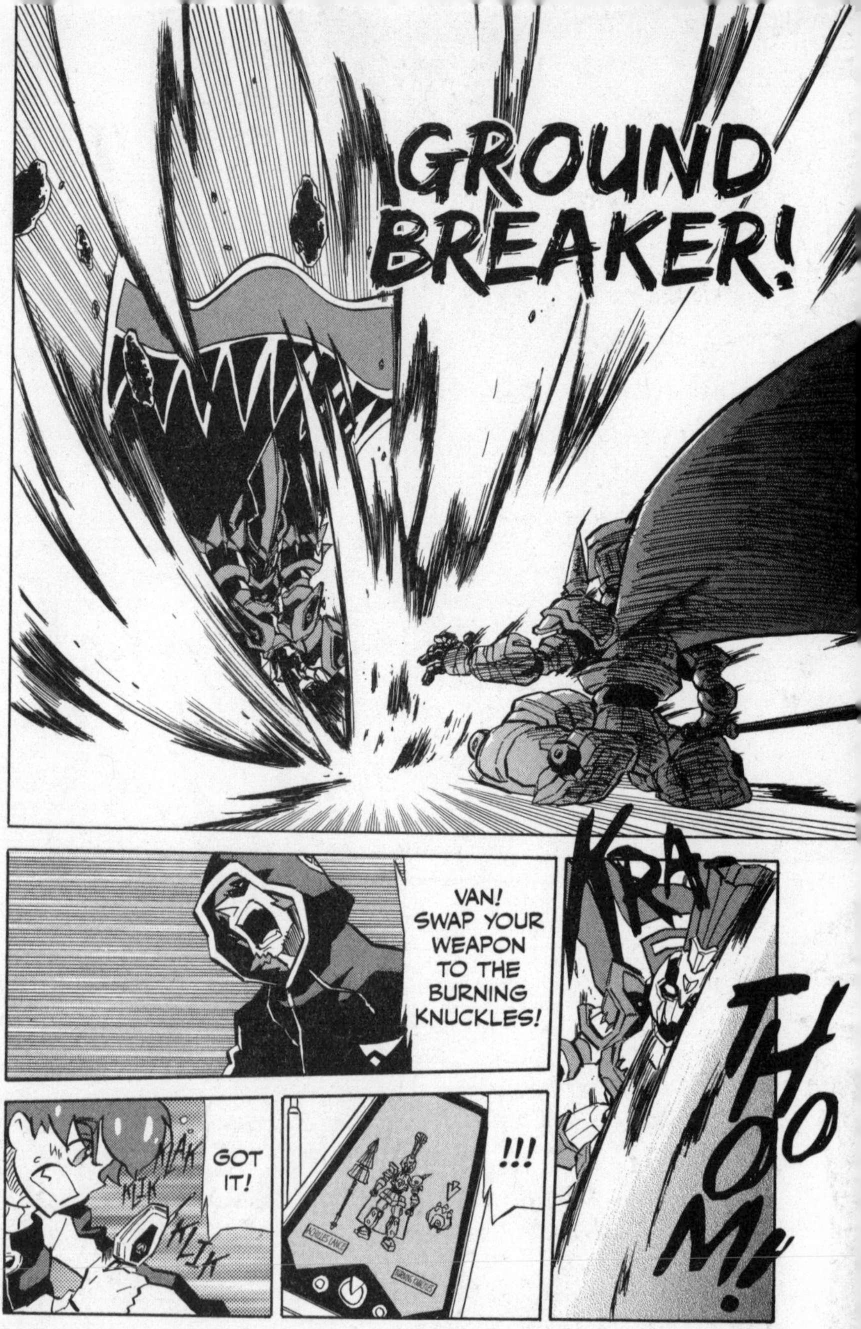
GROUND BREAKER!
KRA
THOOM!
VAN! SWAP YOUR WEAPON TO THE BURNING KNUCKLES!
!!!
GOT IT!
KLAK
KLIK
KLIK

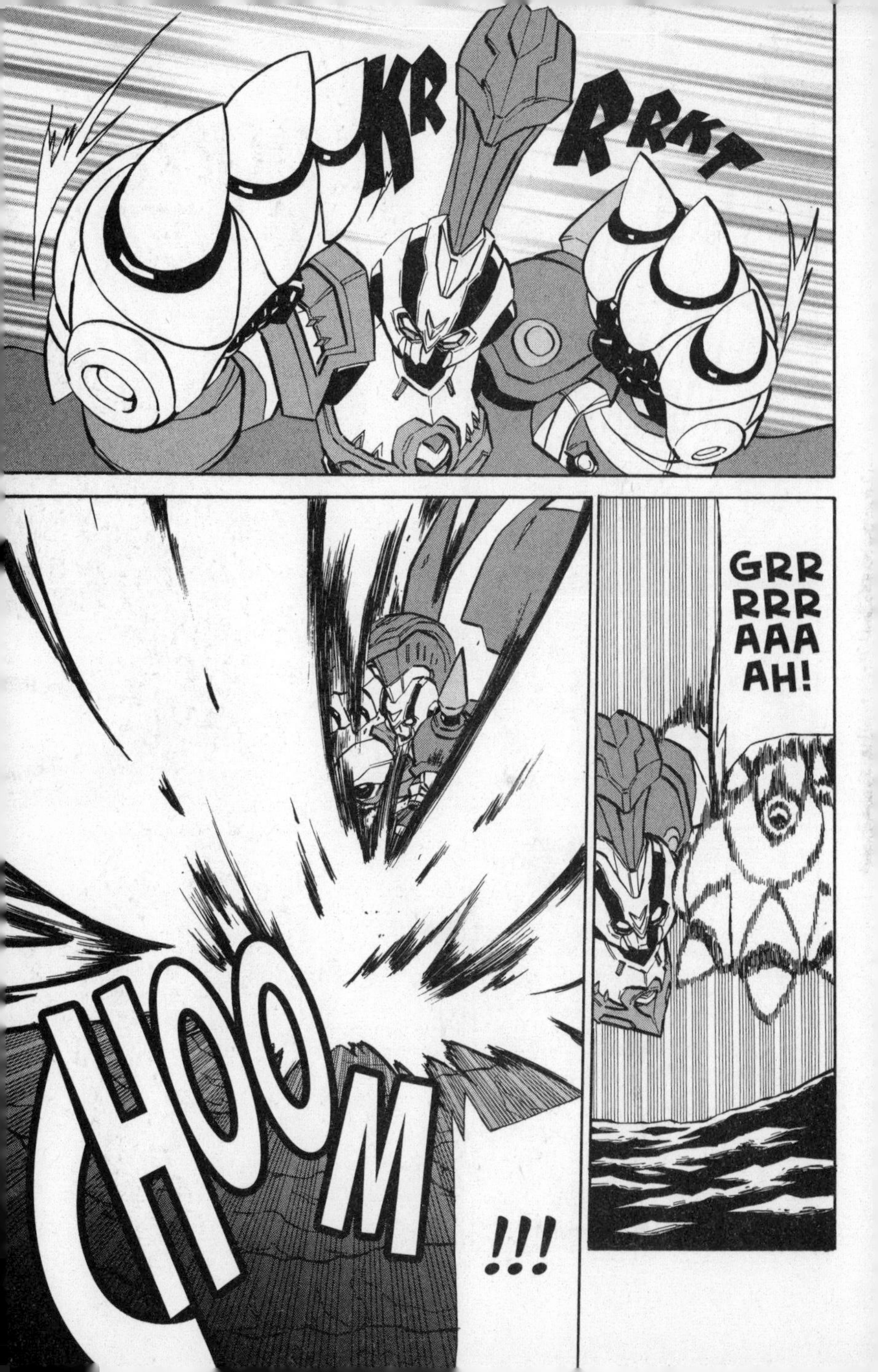
KRRRKT
GRRRRRAAAAH!
CHOOM!!!

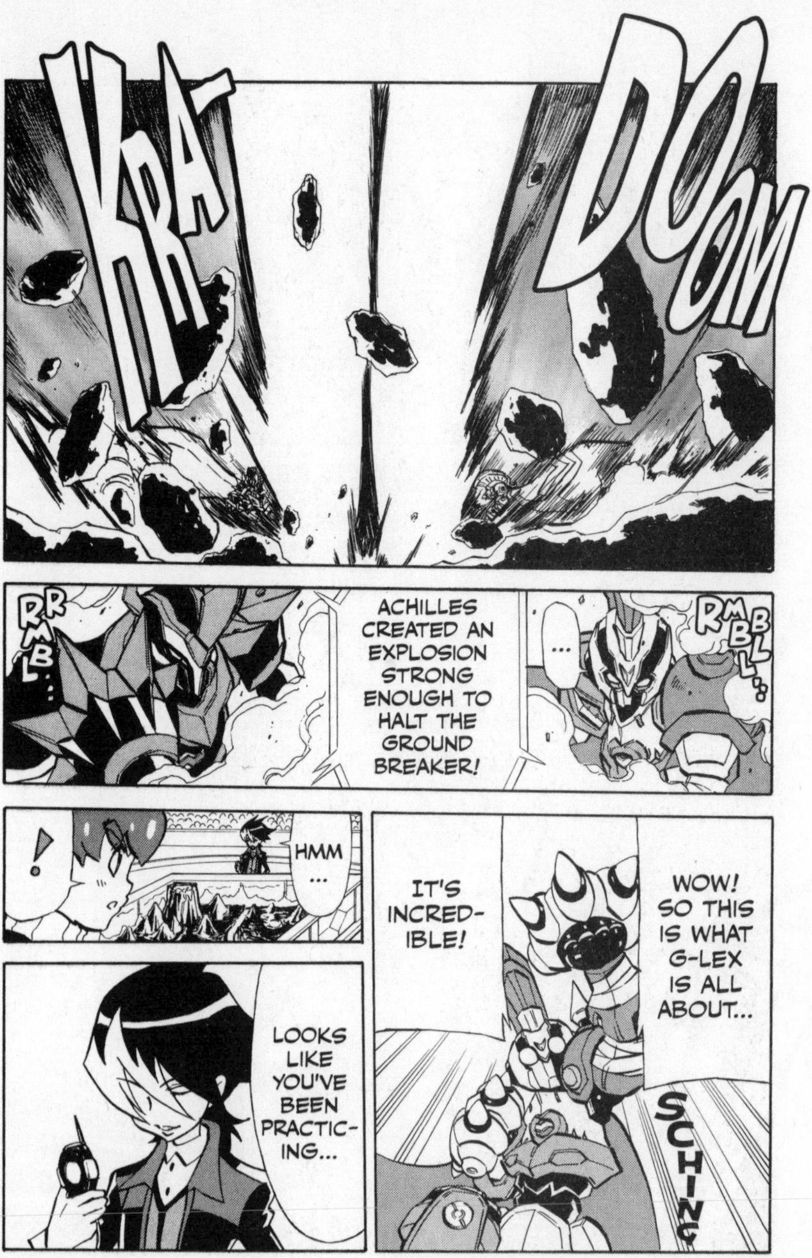
DOOM
KRAT
RMBLBL..
...
ACHILLES CREATED AN EXPLOSION STRONG ENOUGH TO HALT THE GROUND BREAKER!
RRMBL
WOW! SO THIS IS WHAT G-LEX IS ALL ABOUT...
IT'S INCRED-IBLE!
SCHING
HMM ...
!
LOOKS LIKE YOU'VE BEEN PRACTIC-ING...

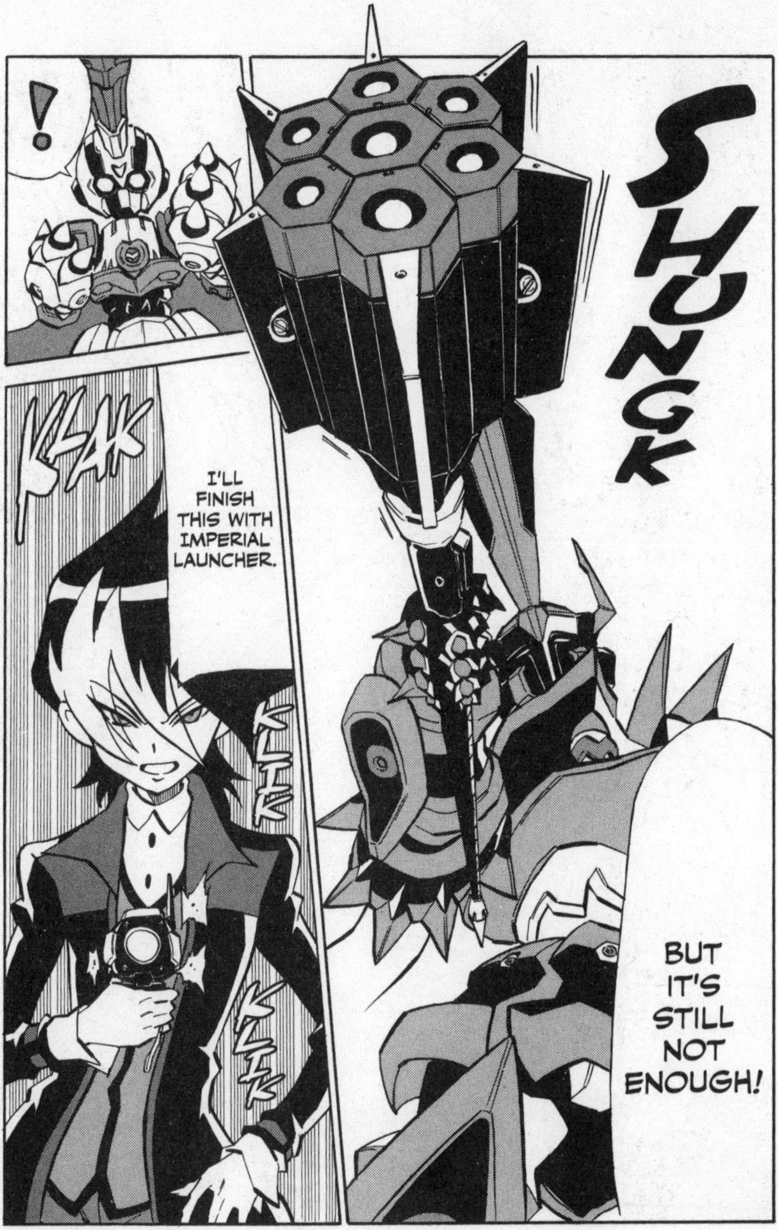
SHUNGK
BUT IT'S STILL NOT ENOUGH!
!
KLAK
I'LL FINISH THIS WITH IMPERIAL LAUNCHER.
KLIK
KLIK

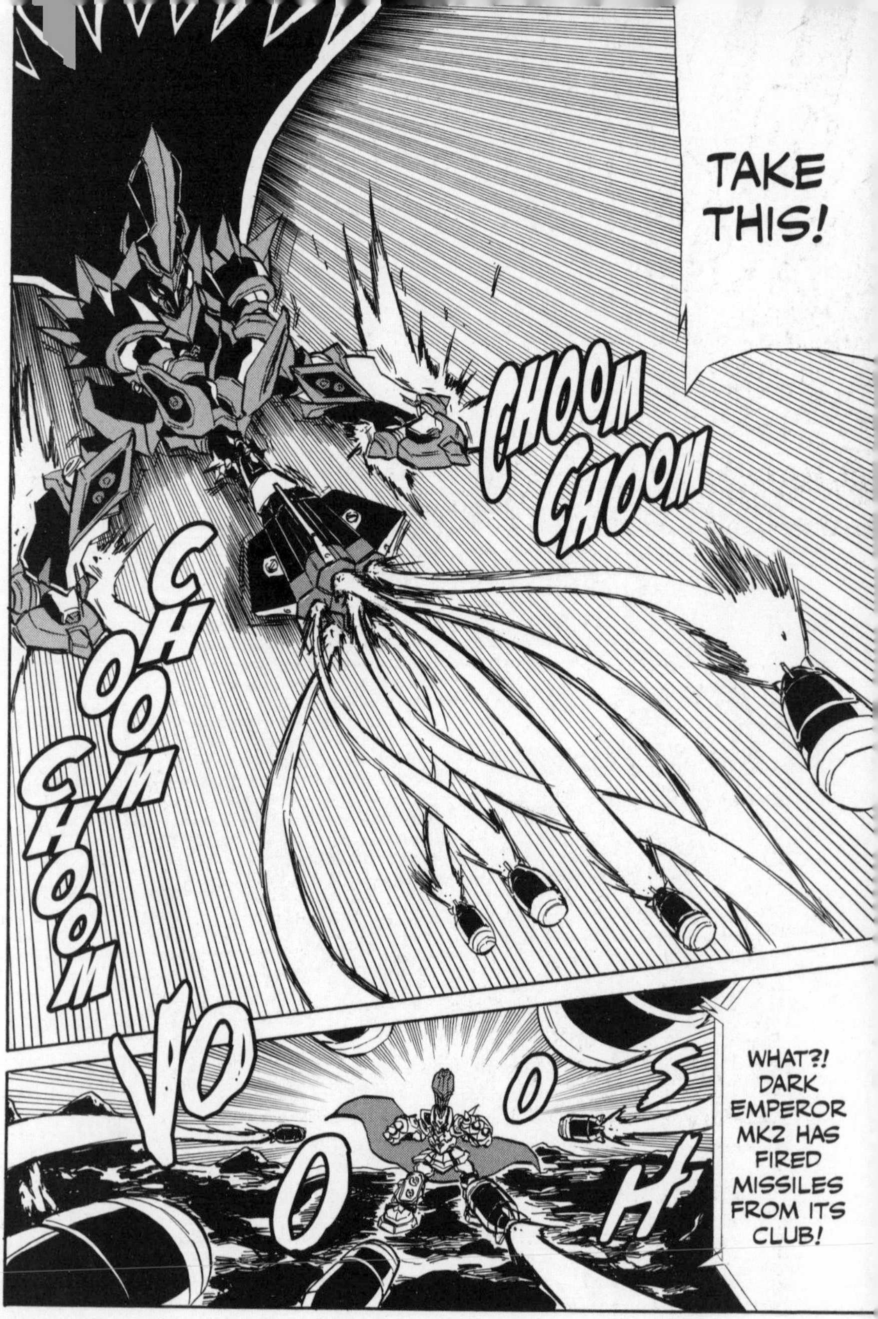
TAKE THIS!
CHOOM CHOOM
CHOOM CHOOM
WHAT?! DARK EMPEROR MK2 HAS FIRED MISSILES FROM ITS CLUB!
VOOOOSH

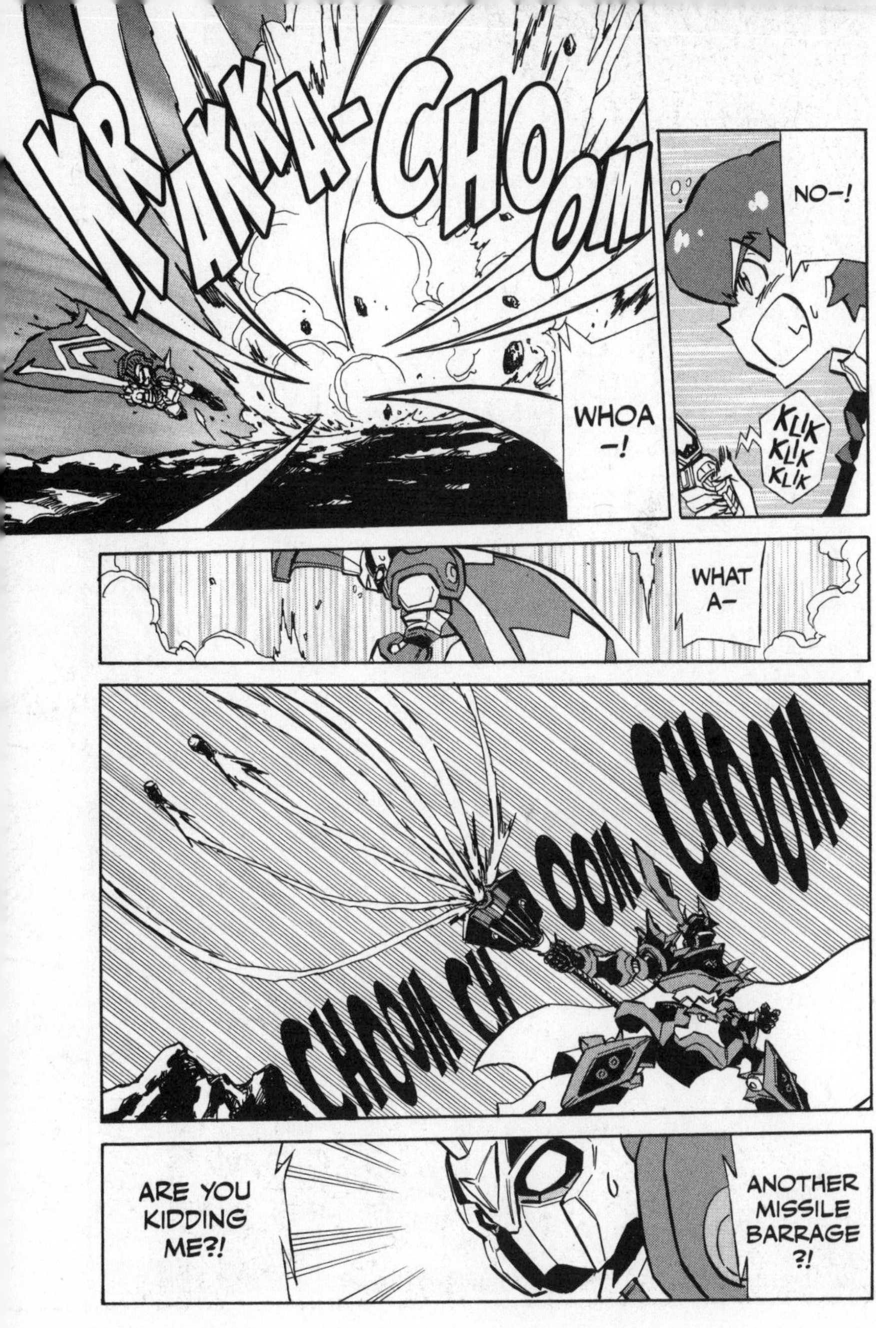
NO—!
KLIK KLIK KLIK
KRAKKA-CHOOM
WHOA—!
WHAT A—
CHOOM CHOOM CHOOM
ANOTHER MISSILE BARRAGE?!
ARE YOU KIDDING ME?!

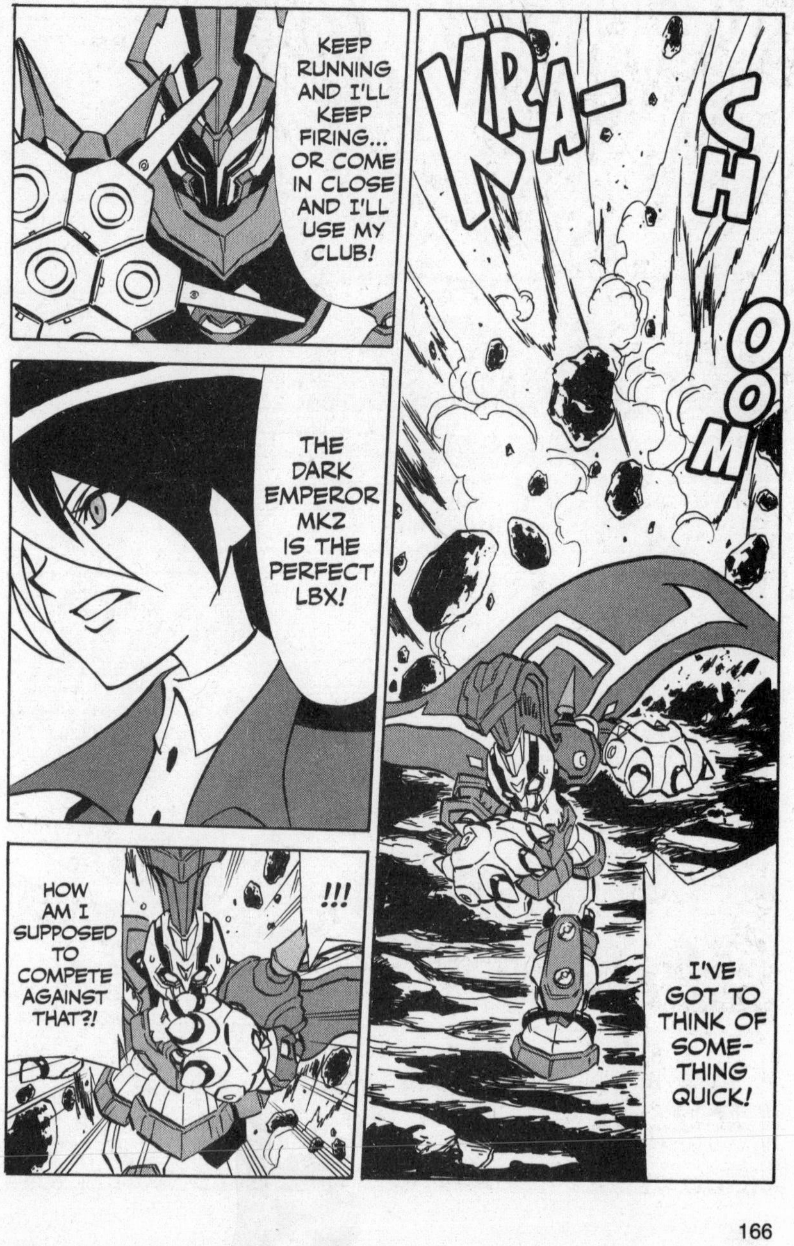
KRA-CHOOOM
I'VE GOT TO THINK OF SOME-THING QUICK!
KEEP RUNNING AND I'LL KEEP FIRING... OR COME IN CLOSE AND I'LL USE MY CLUB!
THE DARK EMPEROR MK2 IS THE PERFECT LBX!
!!!
HOW AM I SUPPOSED TO COMPETE AGAINST THAT?!

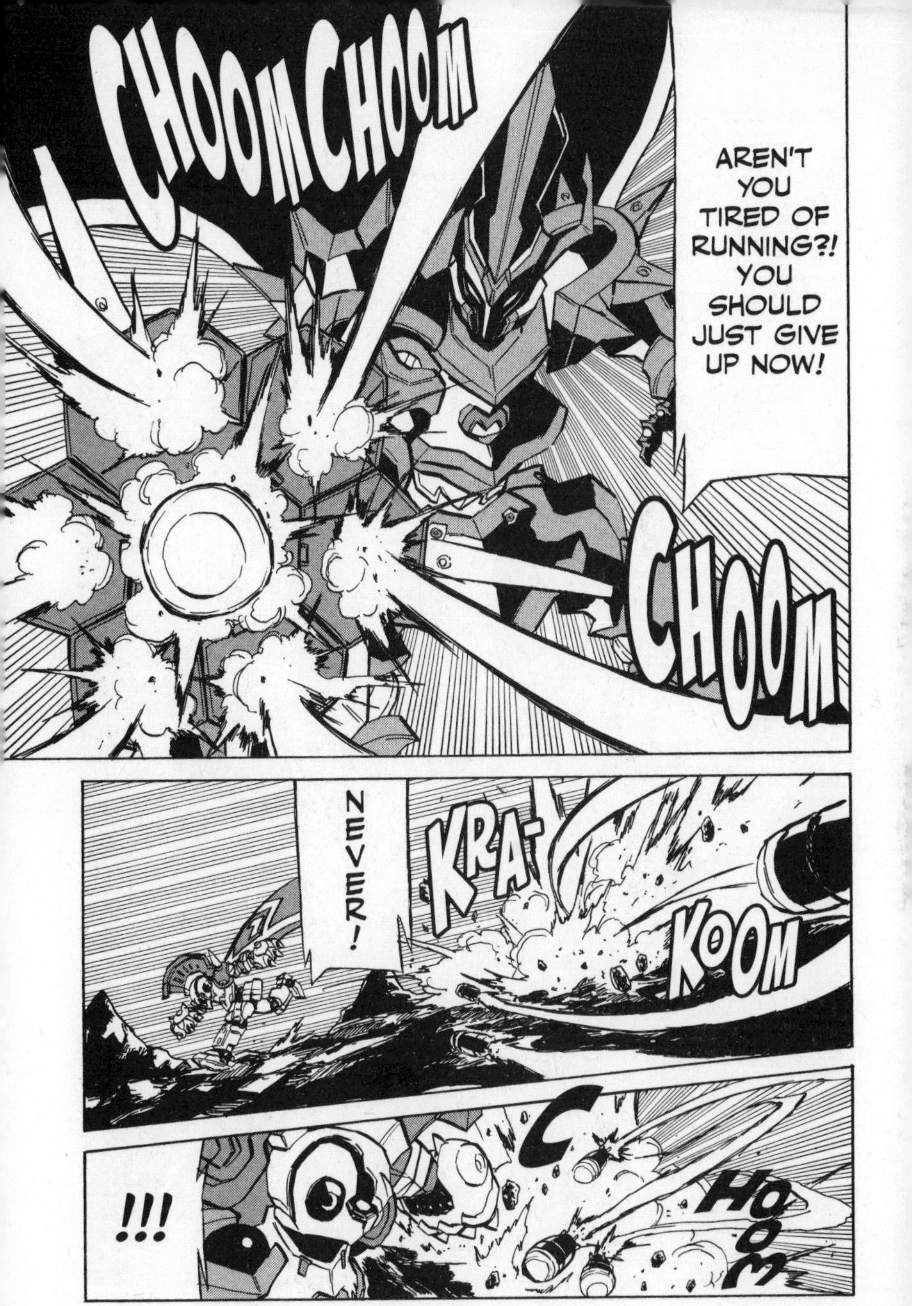
AREN'T YOU TIRED OF RUNNING?! YOU SHOULD JUST GIVE UP NOW!
CHOOM CHOOM
CHOOM
KRA-KOOM
NEVER!
CHOOM
!!!

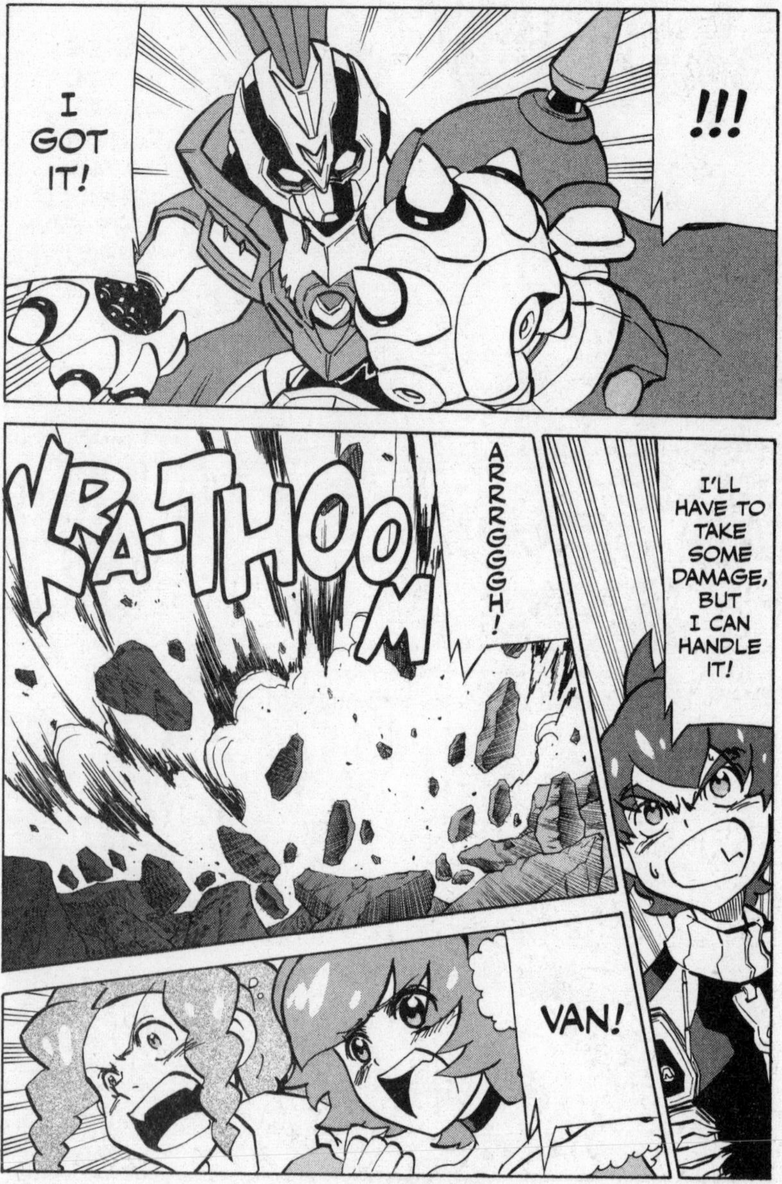
!!!
I GOT IT!
I'LL HAVE TO TAKE SOME DAMAGE, BUT I CAN HANDLE IT!
ARRRGGGH!
KRA-THOOOM
VAN!

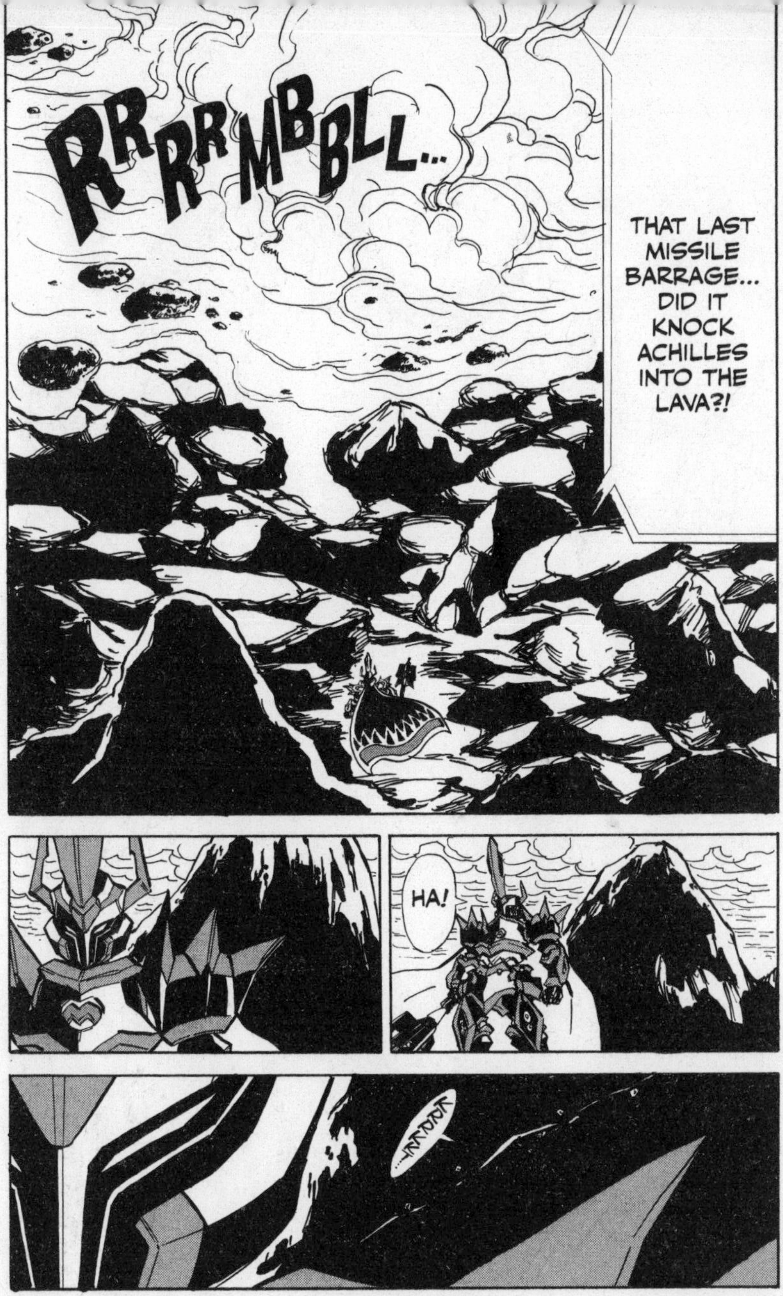
RRRRMBBLL...
THAT LAST MISSILE BARRAGE... DID IT KNOCK ACHILLES INTO THE LAVA?!
HA!
...HRRRRK

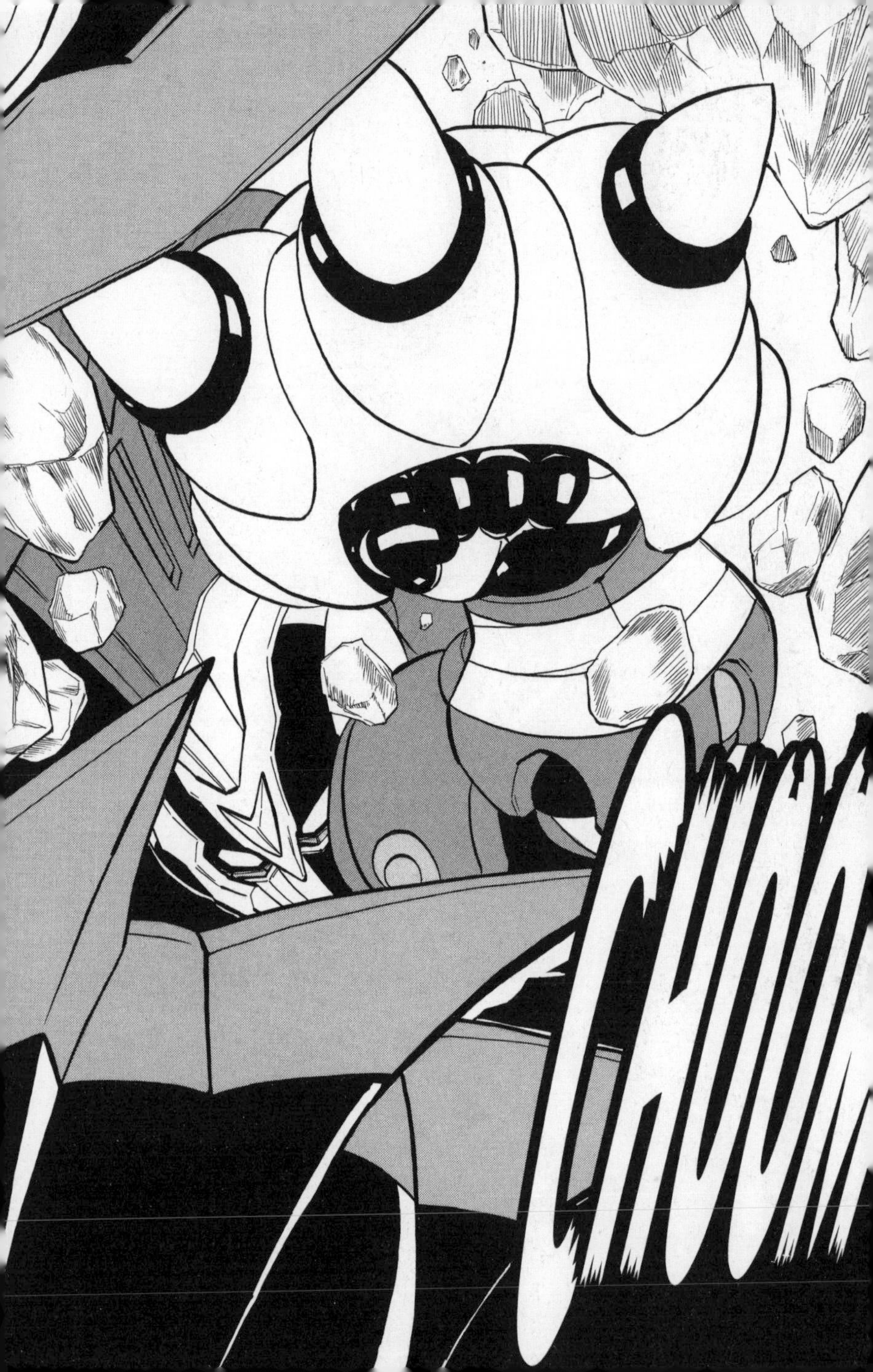
CHOOM

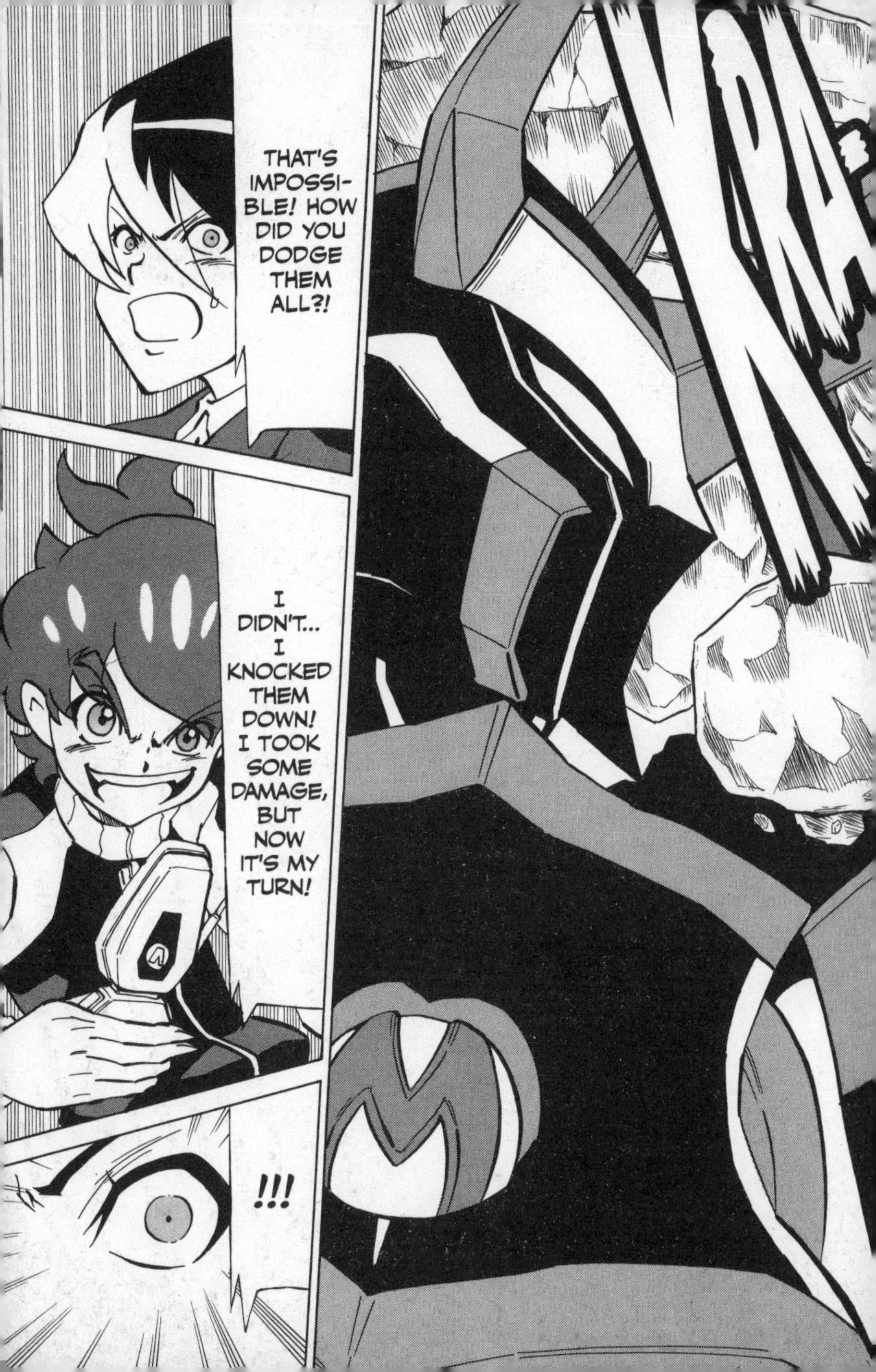
THAT'S IMPOSSI-BLE! HOW DID YOU DODGE THEM ALL?!
I DIDN'T... I KNOCKED THEM DOWN! I TOOK SOME DAMAGE, BUT NOW IT'S MY TURN!
!!!

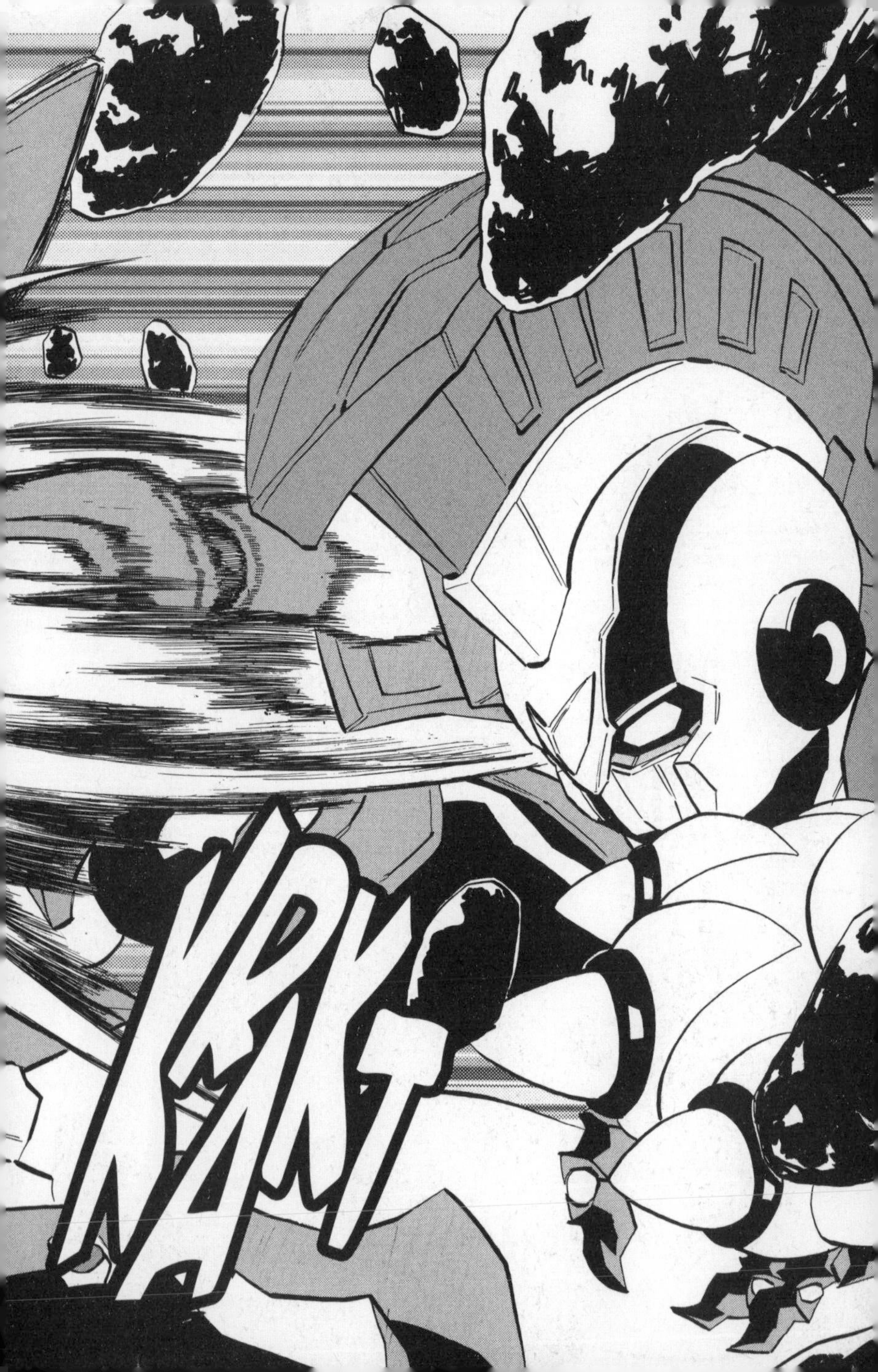
KRAT

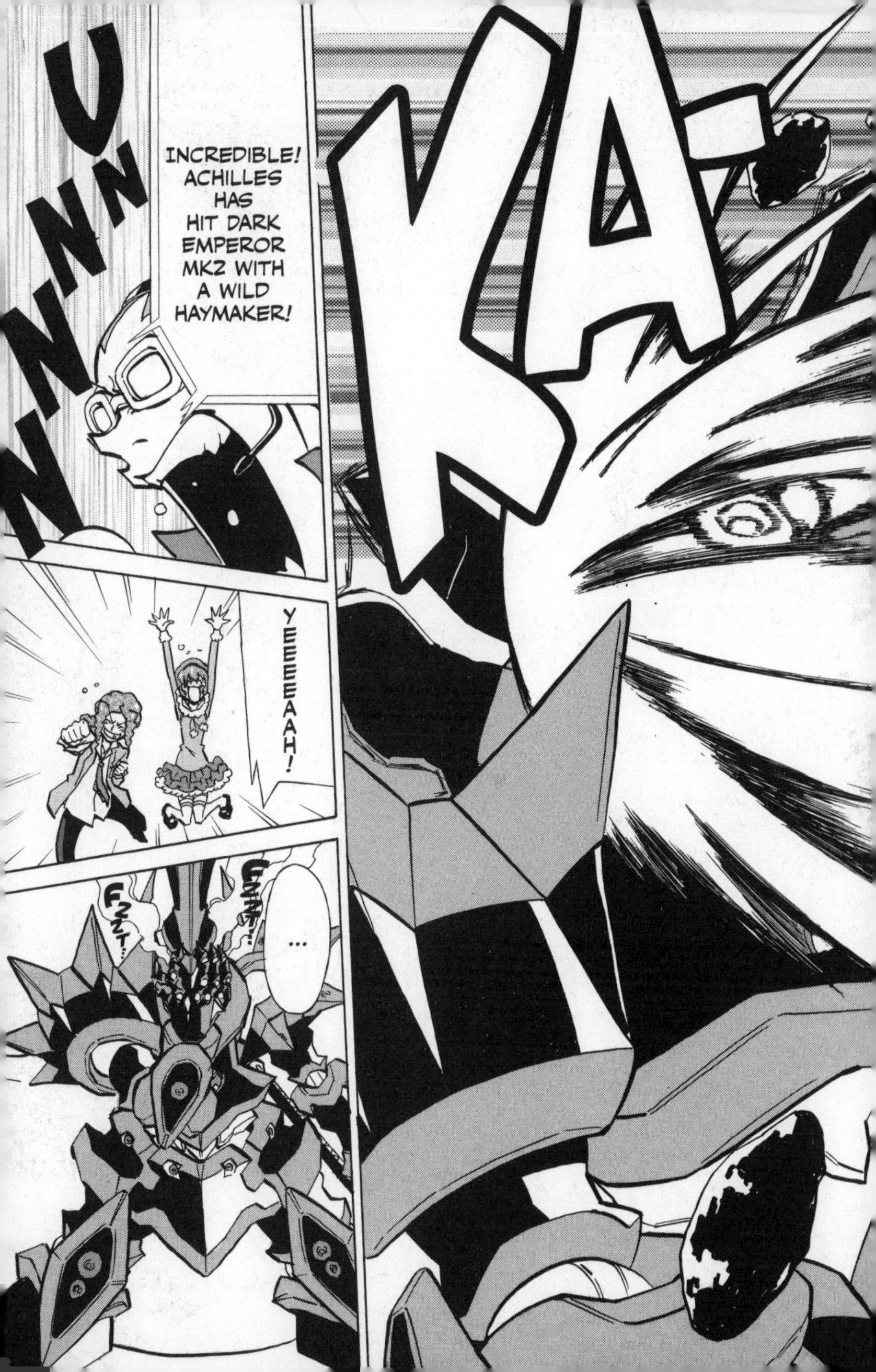
KA-
INCREDIBLE! ACHILLES HAS HIT DARK EMPEROR MK2 WITH A WILD HAYMAKER!
YEEEEAAH!
...
FZZZT...
FZZT...

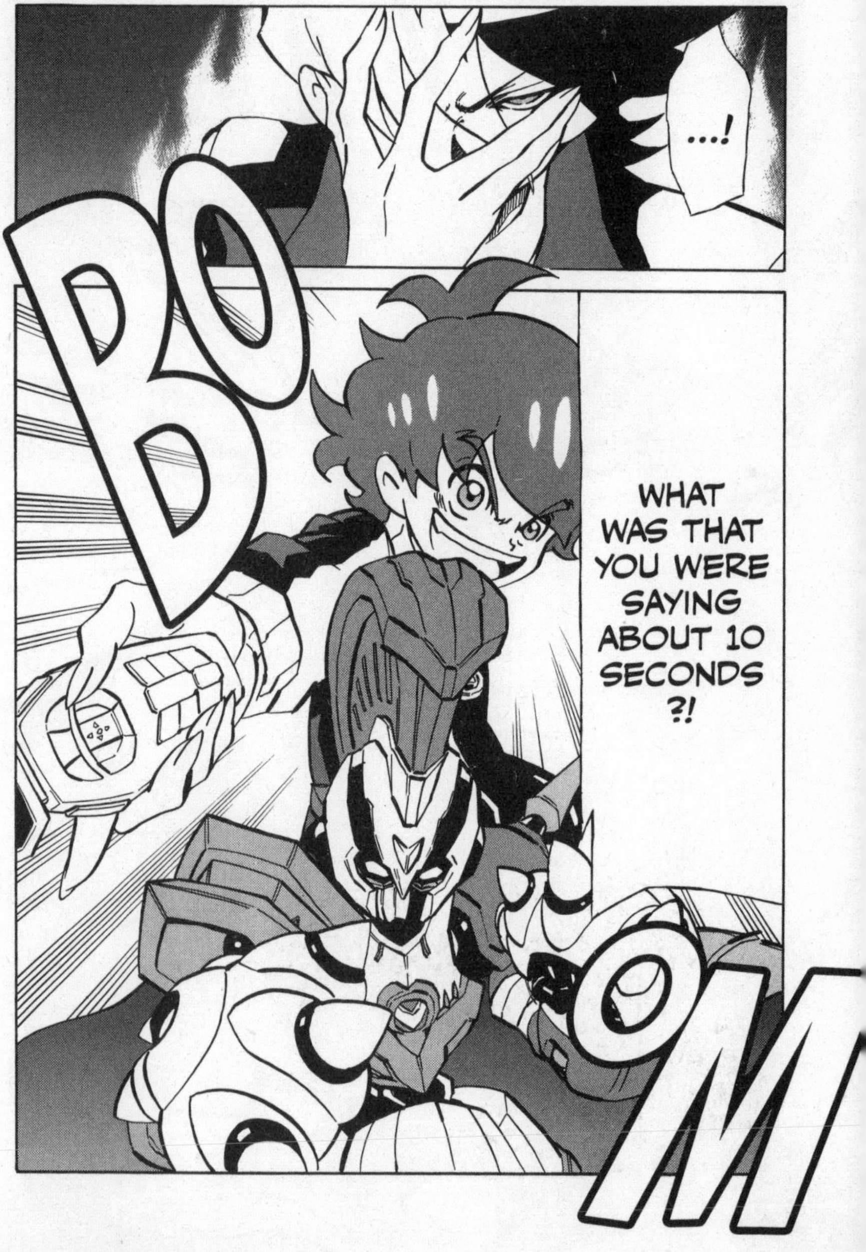
...!
WHAT WAS THAT YOU WERE SAYING ABOUT 10 SECONDS ?!
BOOM

SPECIAL FEATURE

EXTRA BONUS FUNNIES

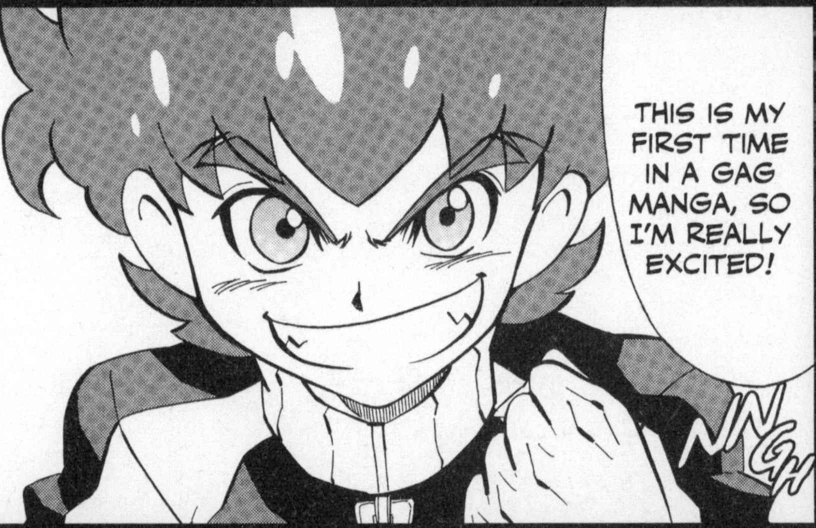
THIS IS MY FIRST TIME IN A GAG MANGA, SO I'M REALLY EXCITED!
NNGH

INCLUDED WITH THIS VOLUME IS A SPECIAL FOUR-PAGE GAG MANGA BY FUJII SENSEI! TAKE A NEW LAUGH-FILLED LOOK AT THESE SERIOUS SCENES!

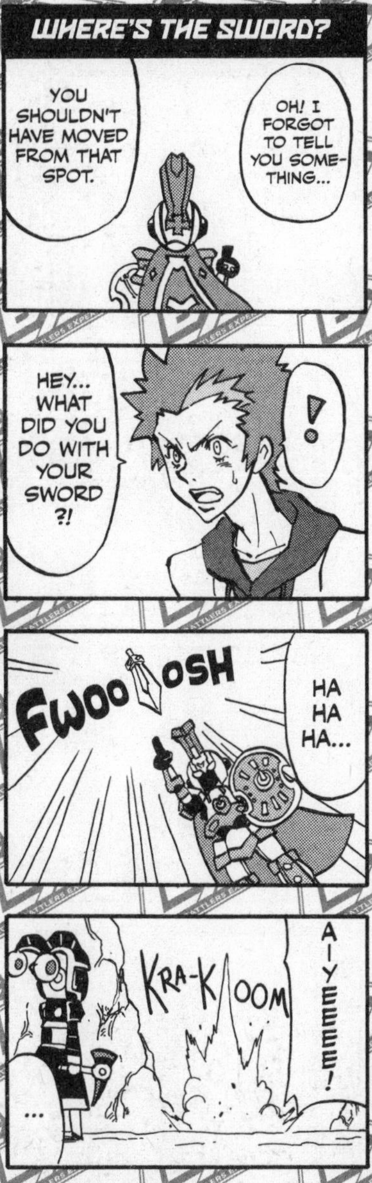
WHERE'S THE SWORD?
OH! I FORGOT TO TELL YOU SOME-THING...
YOU SHOULDN'T HAVE MOVED FROM THAT SPOT.
!
HEY... WHAT DID YOU DO WITH YOUR SWORD ?!
HA HA HA...
FWOOOSH
AIYEEEE!
KRA-KOOM
...

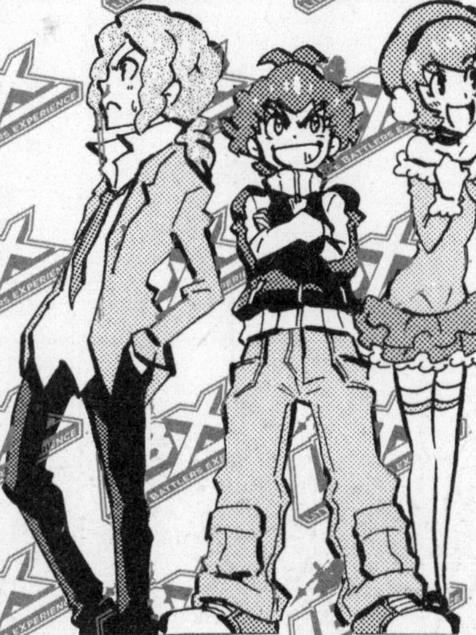

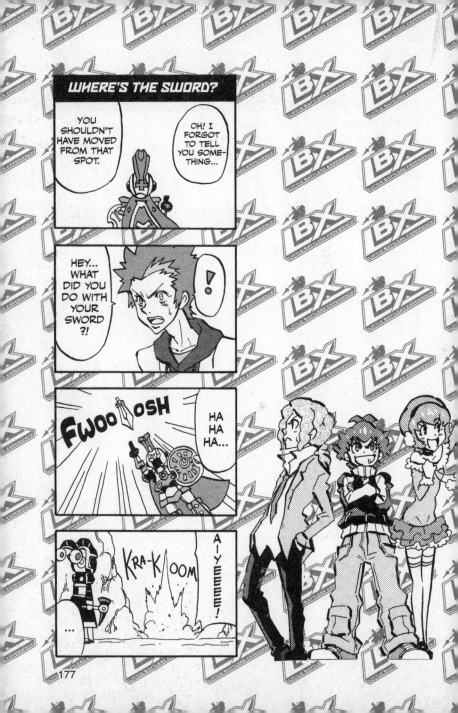

THE BOY SPEAKS OUT

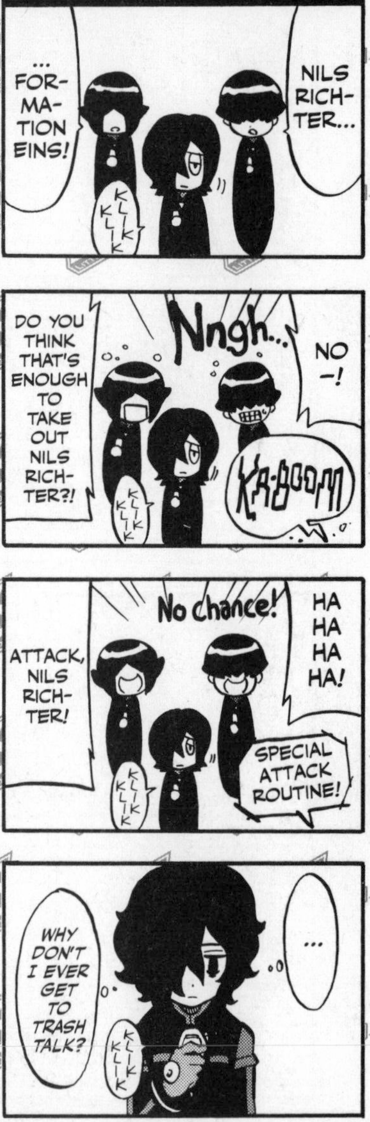
NILS RICHTER...
...FORMATION EINS!
KLIK KLIK
NO—!
Nngh...
DO YOU THINK THAT'S ENOUGH TO TAKE OUT NILS RICHTER?!
KA-BOOM
KLIK KLIK
HA HA HA HA!
No chance!
ATTACK, NILS RICHTER!
SPECIAL ATTACK ROUTINE!
KLIK KLIK
...
WHY DON'T I EVER GET TO TRASH TALK?
KLIK KLIK

VORPAL VORTEX

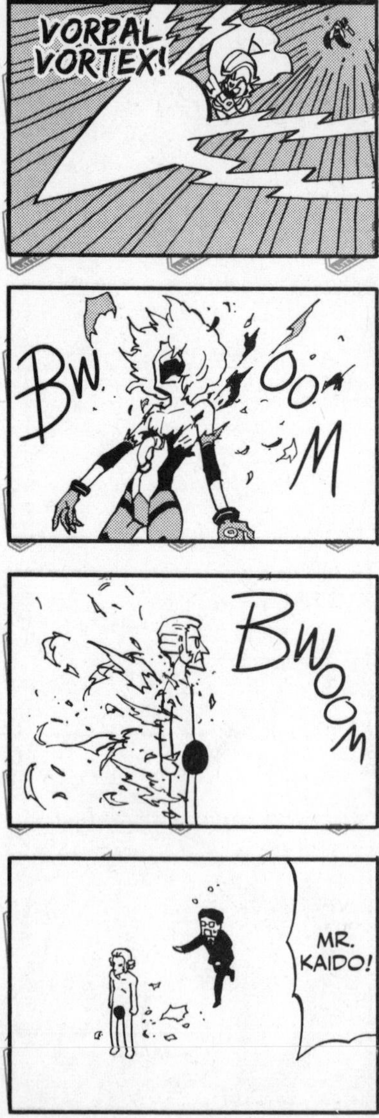
VORPAL VORTEX!
BWOOOM
BWOOOM
MR. KAIDO!

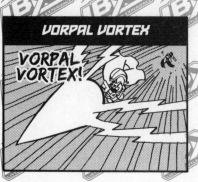

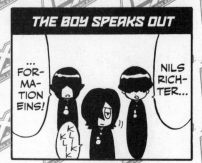

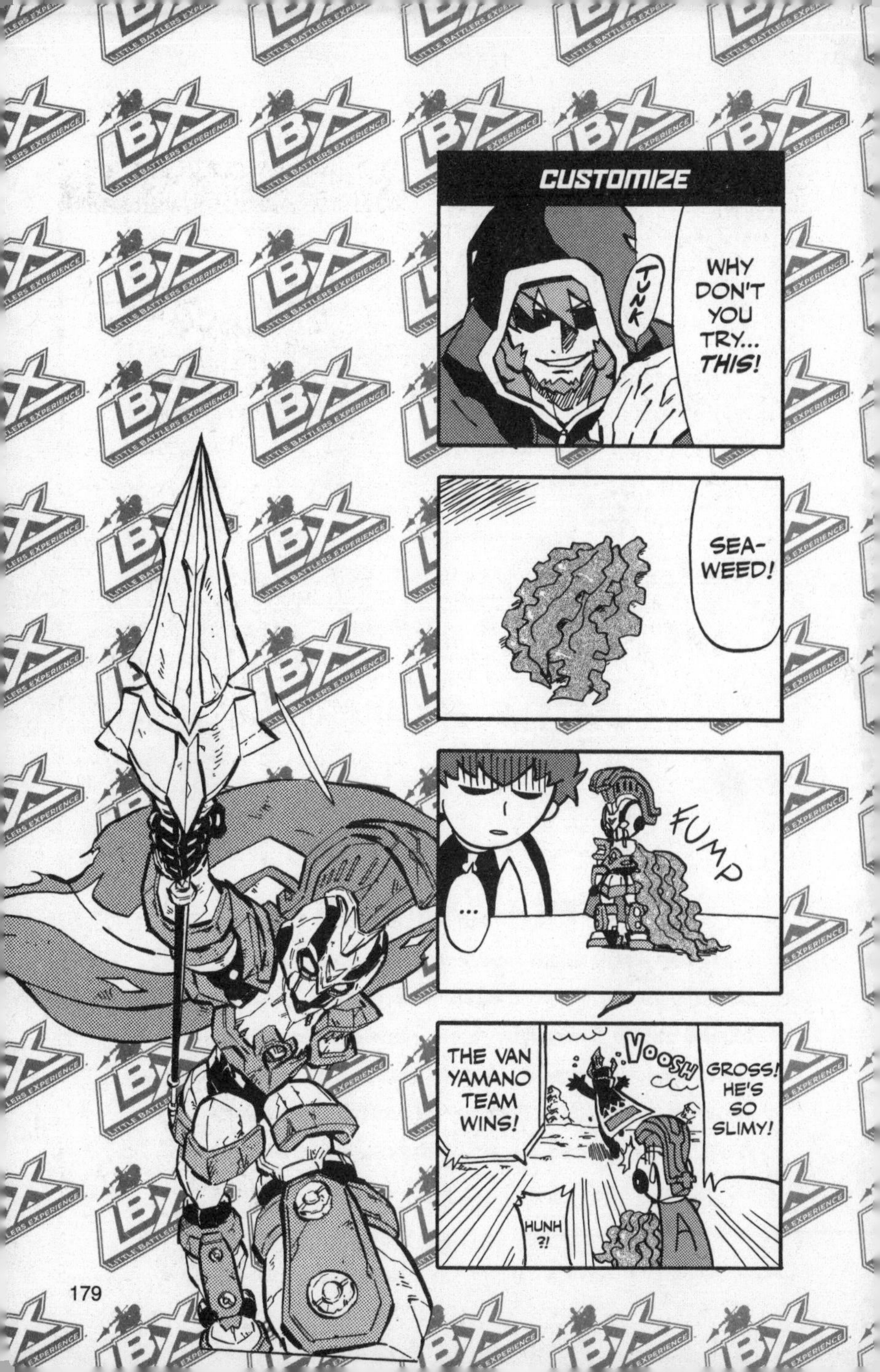
LBX
LITTLE BATTLERS EXPERIENCE
CUSTOMIZE
WHY DON'T YOU TRY... THIS!
JUNK
SEA-WEED!
FUMP
...
GROSS! HE'S SO SLIMY!
VOOSH
THE VAN YAMANO TEAM WINS!
HUNH ?!

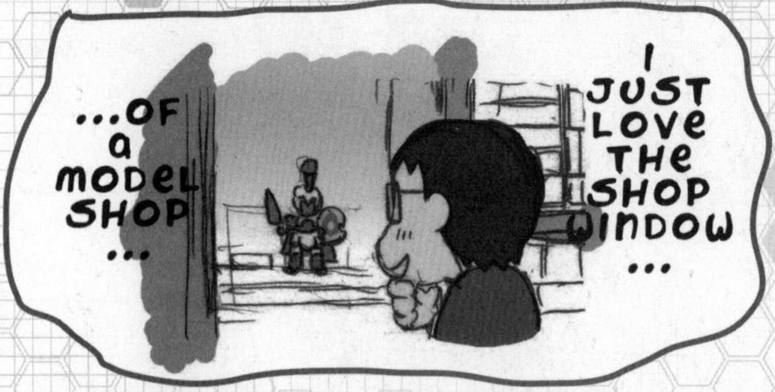
I JUST LOVE THE SHOP WINDOW ...
...OF a MODEL SHOP ...

THE LBX WORLD TOURNAMENT ARTEMIS HAS BEGUN! BUT NUMEROUS FORMIDABLE LBX PLAYERS WILL STAND IN THE WAY OF VAN YAMANO AND ACHILLES!

DON'T LOSE VAN! NOW! BATTLE STAAAART!!!

Hideaki Fujii

Hideaki Fujii was born on December 12, 1977, in Miyazaki Prefecture. He made his debut in 2000 with *Shin Megami Tensei: Devil Children* (*Monthly Comic BomBom*). His signature works include *Battle Spirits: Breakthrough Boy Bashin* and many others. Blood type A.

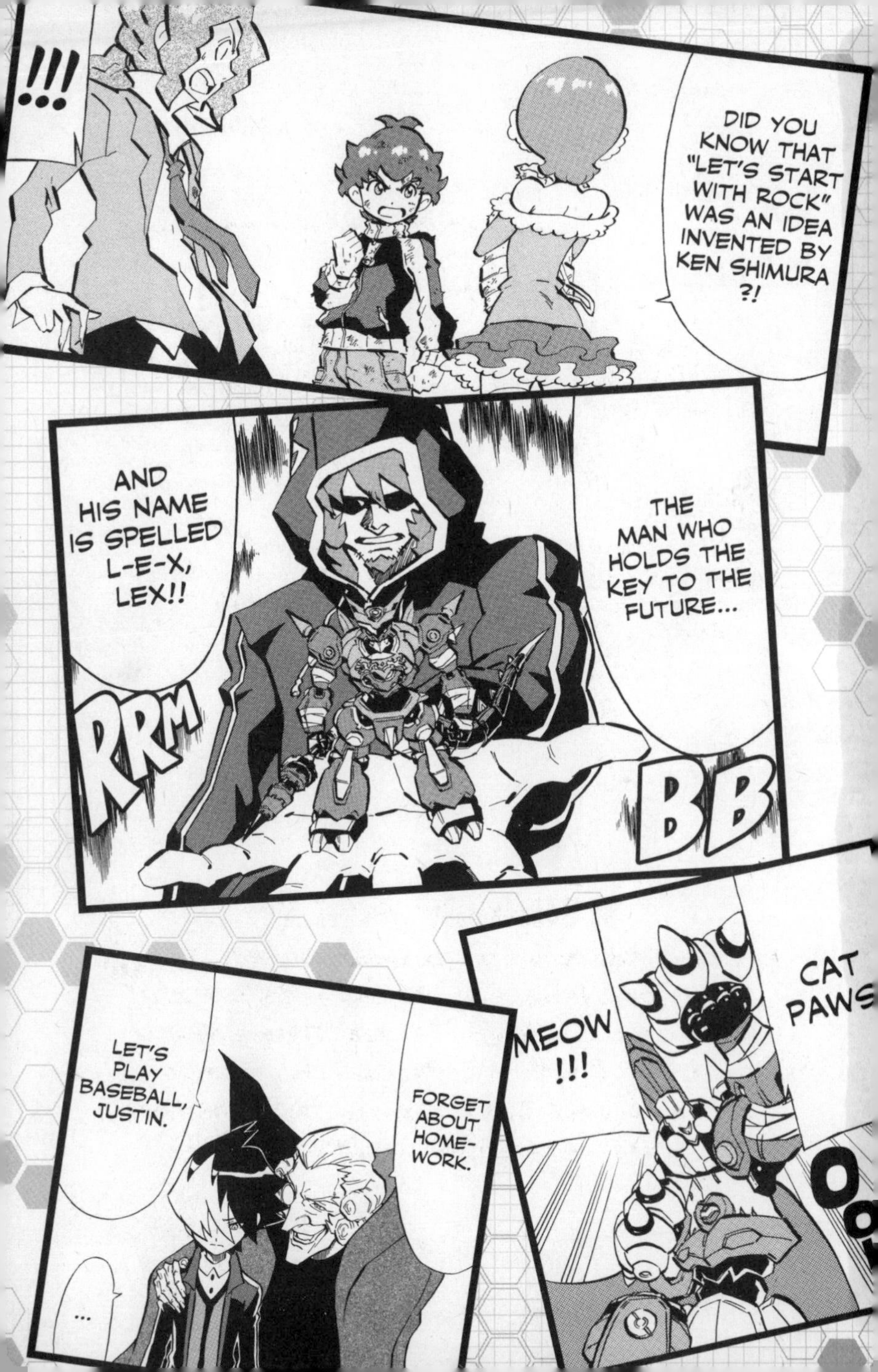
DID YOU KNOW THAT "LET'S START WITH ROCK" WAS AN IDEA INVENTED BY KEN SHIMURA ?!
!!!
THE MAN WHO HOLDS THE KEY TO THE FUTURE...
AND HIS NAME IS SPELLED L-E-X, LEX!!
BB
RRM
CAT PAWS
MEOW !!!
FORGET ABOUT HOME-WORK.
LET'S PLAY BASEBALL, JUSTIN.
...

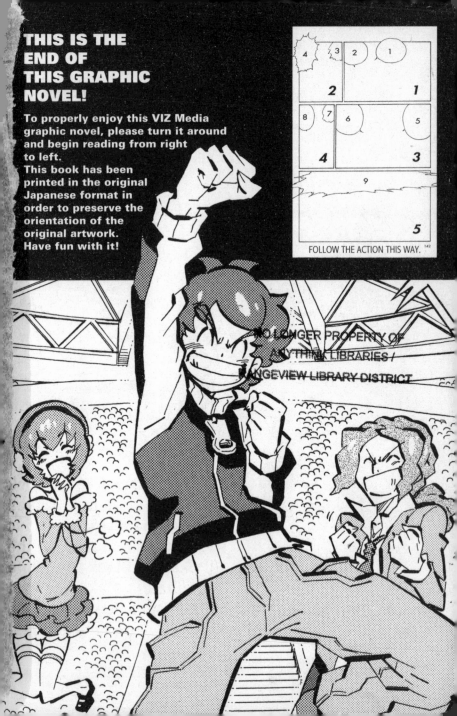

THIS IS THE END OF THIS GRAPHIC NOVEL!

To properly enjoy this VIZ Media graphic novel, please turn it around and begin reading from right to left.
This book has been printed in the original Japanese format in order to preserve the orientation of the original artwork.
Have fun with it!

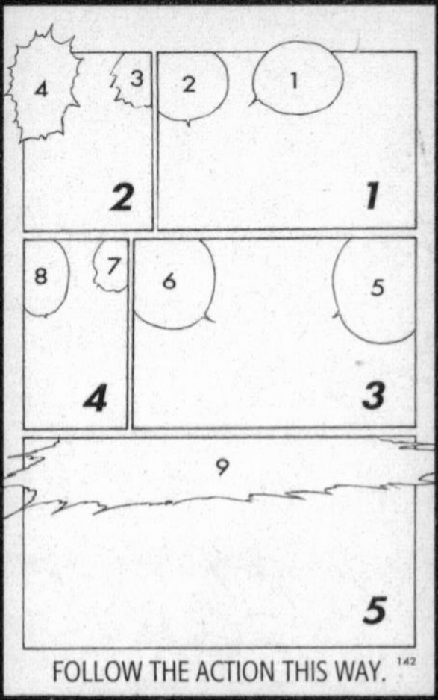
1
2
3
4
5
6
7
8
9
1
2
3
4
5
FOLLOW THE ACTION THIS WAY.

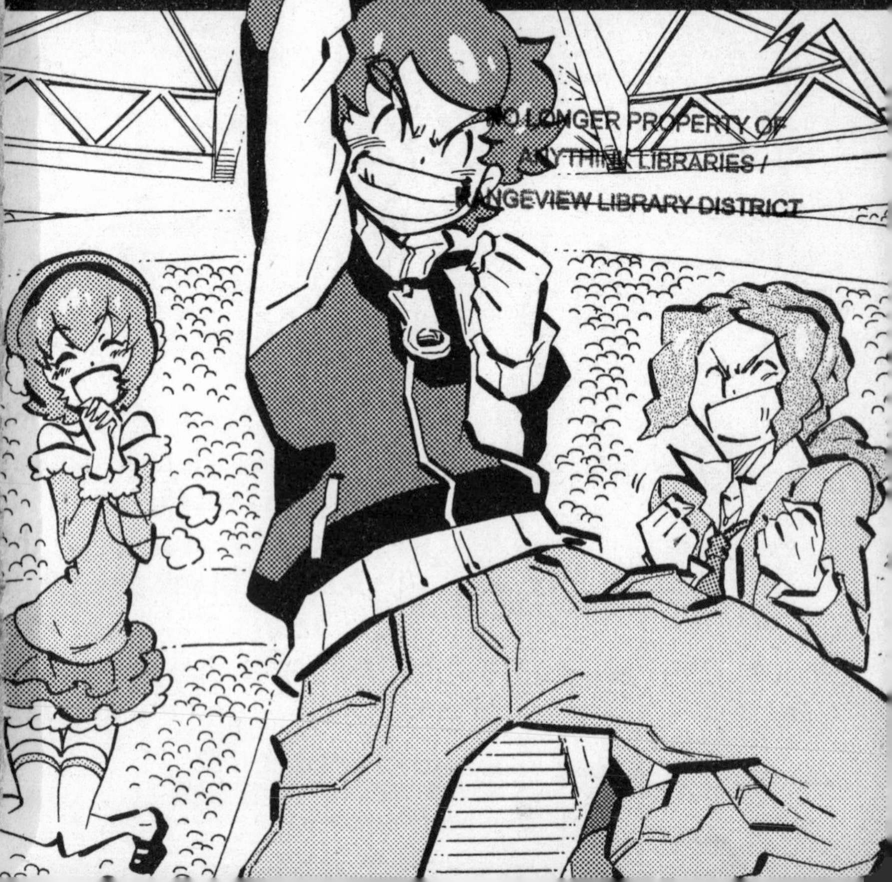